Contents

Introduction	v
Content Advisory	vii
Prologue	1
Chapter 1	9
Chapter 2	18
Chapter 3	21
Chapter 4	25
Chapter 5	30
Chapter 6	34
Chapter 7	42
Chapter 8	47
Chapter 9	58
Chapter 10	63
Chapter 11	67
Chapter 12	73
Chapter 13	79
Chapter 14	86
Chapter 15	96
Chapter 16	107
Chapter 17	116
Chapter 18	121

The Warrior in the Shadows

The Girl with the Gray Eyes
Book 2

L.V. Lane

Chapter 30	191
Chapter 31	195
Chapter 32	212
Chapter 33	218
Chapter 34	226
Chapter 35	230
Chapter 36	236
Chapter 37	244
Chapter 38	253
Chapter 39	258
Chapter 40	265
Chapter 41	270
Chapter 42	274
Chapter 43	281
Chapter 44	286
Chapter 45	291
Chapter 46	296
Chapter 47	304
Chapter 48	309
Chapter 49	313
Chapter 50	317
Chapter 51	321
Chapter 52	327
Chapter 53	331
Chapter 54	338
Chapter 55	343
Chapter 56	352
Chapter 57	358
Chapter 58	362
Chapter 59	368
Chapter 60	373
Chapter 61	378
Chapter 62	385
Chapter 63	388
About the Author	393
Also by L.V. Lane	395

Copyright © 2023 L.V. Lane
All rights reserved.
ISBN: 979-8-3728255-3-6

This is a work of fiction. Names, characters, businesses, places, events, and incidents are either the products of the author's imagination or used in a fictitious manner. Any resemblance to actual persons, living or dead, or actual events is purely coincidental.

All rights reserved. This book or parts thereof may not be reproduced in any form, stored in any retrieval system, or transmitted in any form by any means—electronic, mechanical, photocopy, recording, or otherwise—without prior written permission of the author.

Editing by Steph Tashkoff
Cover by Saintjupit3r

Created with Vellum

Introduction

This is not a romance, although it does have a HEA, but before that, I'm going to introduce you to a man you should run far away from and never want to see again.

Don't believe me?

I knew you wouldn't, but later, when this is all over, I'm going to say I told you so.

Content Advisory

Extremely dark, graphic content, mind-games and manipulation, SA, violence, and gore.

References to past stillborn baby by side character.

Heroes in this series range from sweet to pitch black.

The Warrior in the Shadows

Shadowlanders, and that would really piss him off. So, you must have updated someone. Who did you talk to?"

She blinked a couple of times. "Dan."

"Dan? Just another man in your life? What's Dan's part in this?"

Her brows drew together again with that. "Where is this conversation going? Dan Gilmore. He is an ancient technology expert, a genius really. He's also an omega... I just tried to kill you!"

I raised an eyebrow. "I think you may be overstating your prowess, but yes, I suppose you did contemplate it at least."

"You don't seem very concerned. Why am I the only one shaking?" She stared down at her trembling hands.

I stepped back to give her some space. "I've spent three days being nearly killed. I have several arrow wounds, I've lost a lot of blood, and feel like shit. People trying to kill me is an occupational hazard. That little stunt you pulled barely got a rise." I huffed out a laugh. "It would probably make Bill's day—you accidentally shooting me. He's been sending people to kill me for years. I guess at least I know now that you're not one of them."

"You really think that, don't you? That he wants to kill you."

"I don't think it; I know." I shrugged. "You seem to forget that I'm not squeamish about extracting information when circumstances require it. I have an extensive amount of evidence." And the scars to prove it.

"Why does he want to kill you?"

"That's not a conversation for now. It's time to leave, and your friends will be worrying for your safety, as misplaced as their concern might be, given you were the one about to shoot me," I said dryly.

"I don't know if I can go out there again."

Vulnerability. Hannah had an air of damaged beauty, which for reasons I couldn't quantify, felt integral to who she was rather than being the result of recent events. Some people didn't belong in Shadowland. I'd been brutally honest with her back in Julant when I'd made it clear I considered her a danger to herself and a liability to her team. I'd tasked Garren with keeping her alive during that perilous race to the station. Pity my half-brother had embraced the request so enthusiastically—I still wanted to punch him in the face for that. "Unfortunately, you don't have any choice." I smiled, trying to lighten the mood.

"I'm not giving you a choice, Hannah," I added softly when she didn't move. "You should probably collect anything you need, except the weapon. And if I really must carry you, then I will."

I saw that moment when she realized that I would follow through on the threat. She nodded and drew a deep breath. "I'm ready."

"You don't look ready," I said because she didn't, and she probably never would be. "But I guess that doesn't really matter."

She took a last, longing look around the station before we headed together back out into Shadowland.

Chapter 1

Hannah

I was supremely aware of Tanis' presence as we walked along the corridor. After he'd stood so close, my lungs felt saturated with his essence. My body was tingling with arousal in the way it had been ever since I'd met an alpha, only it was worse around Garren and Tanis. The itch under my skin manifested as a desire to preen and posture before a dominant male, to do anything that might encourage him to *rut*.

I threw a look at him over my shoulder as we neared the door.

Bad idea. Our eyes locked, and the air lodged in my lungs. My stomach performed a slow, sensual dip, and a flood of slick pulsed out.

His nostrils flared, a rumbly growl emanating from his chest before he closed his fingers over the back of my neck and yanked me to him.

Our lips met, and I swear electricity crackled between us at that very first touch. I was on him, trying to climb him, arms entangled around his neck, nails raking flesh, legs wrapping around his body, and he crushed me to him in a way that lit me up. His tongue speared my mouth, and I sucked on it, purring manically, rubbing my crotch against his body, seeking friction of any kind against my sensitive clit.

Deep, mindless urgency ripped through me, his scent smothering me in a way that felt like home. He had saved me during that fateful first Jaru attack and plucked me from danger. I'd been half in love with him ever since, maddened by the way he held himself aloof, and then Garren had come along...

Lips wrenched from mine.

I blinked, dizzy and confused but also desperately horny.

He peeled me off and set me down a pace away, his hands clenching into fists like he was fighting the urge to put his hands on me again.

I wanted his hands. Only the moment of separation allowed some measure of sanity to return. Having been with Garren, I knew if he had been here, he'd be inside me already, and I would be just as mindless in response to him. They were both compelling alphas and dominant men, though different in attitude and ways. Where one was darker and commanding, the other was light and more ready to smile.

I was out of my depth with both of them, *either* of them.

"I'm sorry," I said. Not that I was really sorry. I just needed something to break the stifling impasse before I launched myself at him again.

"I'm not," he said, and, that fast, all the raging lust hit me again.

"What will happen now?" I said, squeezing words past the tightness in my throat.

His lips tugged up slightly on one side. "Now you'll open the door, and we will both continue on to Thale."

"What about Garren?" Heat flooded my cheeks. I felt stupid the moment the words tumbled past my lips.

"Garren will continue with your protection. But, Hannah—" He waited until I lifted my wary gaze. "You may be his for now, but you were always mine."

The Warrior in the Shadows

With those shattering words still ringing in my mind, he palmed the door activation plate, flooding the corridor with sunlight.

∼

I stepped through the door of Station fifty-four and squinted against the glare of the bright sunlight, breathing in air that wasn't saturated in Tanis, and trying to pull myself together.

Being back outside was like waking from a dream and discovering that reality was a nightmare.

The last time I'd stood here, a battle had been taking place, and men, horses, and cries had met in a cacophony of terror. The mood was calm and tired now, the frenzy replaced by orderly sobriety as soldiers moved with purpose on overlapping quests. Bodies littered the ground around the station, and flies thickened the air, excited by the gluttonous bounty. Soon the carrion feeders would arrive to complete the grisly cycle of life. Several fires had been lit, and the smoke drifted sluggishly in the arid air.

I glanced at Tanis, who had watched my silent study of the scene. There was a faint trickle of blood at the side of his throat. My chest rose unsteadily as I realized I'd put it there. I liked seeing my mark on him, wanted to make more, to savage him with my nails and teeth.

He smirked and pressed his fingertips to the scratch before inspecting them. "Staking your claim, Hannah?"

Although I shook my head, my eyes screamed, *yes*.

He gestured toward the tree line. Tearing my gaze from his, I followed his indication to where I could see Adam, the leader of the Rymorian expedition, talking to another man on the far side of the clearing.

"I think you've kept your people waiting long enough," Tanis said.

When I glanced back, I found his expression unreadable. The enigmatic leader had returned. He walked away, leaving me alone at the top of the steep rise that housed the buried power source.

I turned toward the forest. My lips were tingling, and my cheeks were hot. I probably looked thoroughly kissed... and if the wary glances the passing alphas sent my way were any indication, I was throwing off pheromones.

Feeling very much abandoned, I drew a deep breath and went to join Adam.

Spotting me, his face split into a grin. I smiled, too. He greeted me with a hug, the kind, friendly, neutral hug of a man who was a beta and happily married; and how much I needed that simple human connection. "Ah, Hannah, it's so good to see you. Is it done? Operational?"

I nodded. Shared relief blossomed between us. It was done. Despite the odds, it *was* done.

My curious glance took in the man standing at Adam's side, who gave me a nod. He was unknown to me, with short curly hair, dark skin, and a body on the unhealthy side of lean. There was an air about him that made me think him another field scientist.

I looked around. "Where is the rest of the team?"

"Helping with the preparations to leave. Everything got scattered." Adam gestured over his shoulder toward the station. "Did you talk to anyone while you were inside?"

"Only Dan Gilmore briefly. I asked him to erase our communication. I thought it better to check with you first before making an official update. I also left the satellites disabled for sixty hours—it seemed like the right thing to do."

Adam's face softened with those words, and tension left his shoulders. "Yes, a great idea," he said. "We'll be long gone by then."

"If you're not going to say it, I will," the man next to Adam said. "Thank fuck she didn't talk to Bill."

Adam nodded his head at the speaker. "Hannah, meet Jon Sanders. A fellow field scientist," he said, confirming my assessment. "Whose opinions are possibly more extreme than mine."

Jon Sanders? Why was that name so familiar?

"Diplomacy was never my strong point, but after spending two

The Warrior in the Shadows

months locked in a pigpen wondering if every day was my last..." He didn't finish the thought. "All we need is Bill thinking Hannah's waiting at the station and sending a bunch of trigger-happy yahoos in. The station's operational, so he knows someone's here. Better if he's not sure who, and better still he thinks it decided to start itself. We need to leave as fast as possible."

Despite the expressive language and his vocal distrust of Bill, Jon Sanders had an emotive way that I warmed to. Charming in an unorthodox kind of way. Still, I was confused as to where he had come from since, other than my mission, all Rymorians had been recalled.

"What did Dan have to say?" Adam asked before I could broach the subject of Jon being here. "Anything important we should know?"

"Yes. He said there had been talk of a war. That Rymor had declared war on Shadowland. I explained that the Shadowlanders had helped us, and that we wouldn't have reached the station without them."

Adam grunted. "War? Against Shadowland? Good thing we reached the station in time. I doubt he'll get traction for war now the station is operational. I doubt it would have happened either way. Gaia holds tight to their power. They won't backtrack on a millennium of policy without a burning platform."

"Does this change our plans?" Jon asked Adam.

"No," Adam confirmed.

"What plans?" I asked. "Our plans to wait at Thale until the remaining Jaru leave?" Silence greeted my question, and tension entered Adam's posture. "What are you not telling me?"

"The Jaru have already gone," Adam said quietly, "but it's not safe for us in Rymor anymore. Our stay in Thale is indefinite."

"Indefinite?" Perhaps Tanis telling me of our destination should have triggered a warning. Indefinite? What did that even mean? I was still a little woozy from Tanis' kiss and wasn't functioning at my best. I thought I might throw up.

"Here, sit down." Hand on my shoulder, Adam directed me to

the ground, crouching beside me. "Sorry, that came out more abruptly than I intended." His eyes held mine. "Look, there's no easy way to say this, but we can't go back. Not after what happened."

"What's happened? Are we going to make a report? Perhaps they could send a transport?" I didn't want to speak to Bill. Even contemplating it made my stomach churn, yet staying here indefinitely was nothing short of crazy. "Why would we need to stay out here?"

"Reporting won't make any difference," Jon said tiredly. "More likely to fuck shit up beyond all recovery. We weren't held hostage by accident."

"Held hostage by who?" I demanded, looking between Adam and Jon.

"This isn't Hannah's fault, Jon."

"Yeah, I get that," Jon replied. "You said she could be trusted. Now she's talking about running back in and spilling our plans to Bill."

Not so charming, unorthodox or otherwise, I decided.

"She can be trusted. She *is* trusted," Adam said. "Damn it, Jon, you've only just told me what happened with the transport. You know about her relationship with Bill."

Bill—again. It had taken weeks to move past that minefield of a relationship, and now someone new had arrived who probably still thought we were together. Maybe Bill even believed so.

My feelings toward Bill had shifted through many transitions, yet Jon, as a newcomer, knew nothing about that.

What if I *had* spoken to Bill? I'd become convinced that he'd never cared for me as I'd once cared for him. His discord was apparent with the perspective of time and separation.

"Yeah, I know Bill. I wish I didn't," Jon said, his eyes narrowing on me. "Maybe he sent her out here to kill Tanis. Lull us all into trusting her before she finishes his dirty work for him."

I burst out laughing. I probably sounded hysterical. Given what had transpired behind the station's closed doors, Jon's cool, flippant assessment had been a little too close for comfort. "You think I'm here to assassinate Tanis?" I felt my temper rising, and heat engulfed my cheeks. "I admit he does bring out the occasional violent urge, but, so far, I have controlled it. I don't trust Bill any more than you do. I told Dan as much. We should provide an update though, and I was suggesting that option to Adam, who as far as I'm concerned, is still in charge."

Adam rubbed his jaw, and I could see he was poorly stifling a smirk.

Jon didn't even try to hide his crooked grin. "Okay, I admit Tanis does lack some basic social skills, and women wanting to kill him isn't unusual."

I was sure Tay would attest to that, which further charged my temper. The thought of any woman having that level of closeness to him brought out my claws.

"You may be his for now, but you were always mine."

That statement was going to mess with me to no end.

"I'm part of this. I deserve to know what happened. Why are you even out here? I thought all the field scientists had been recalled?"

Jon glanced briefly at Adam.

Adam nodded. "Tell her. She needs to know."

"I was part of the first repair team," Jon said. "The transport that crashed."

Now I remembered that name, from a month ago, back at Julant. It had unleashed Tanis' fury when Adam mentioned that Jon was on the crashed transport.

"I was told you were dead." Ancient technology wasn't an area with many specialists—two less after the crash. Rymor never needed them since maintenance was automated, and faults near unheard of. Ancient technology had relegated itself to a forgotten skill, a historical curiosity. The earthquake changed all that.

The media coverage when the transport left with a repair team was intense. Then nothing had been reported for days until Bill called me to his office and told me the terrible news. It had crashed. The people on board, including the two technical experts, were presumed dead, and the Shadowlanders were now considered hostile.

When I left, the people of Rymor knew nothing about the transport crash nor that the power restrictions were symptomatic of a bigger problem—notably, that they had no protective wall.

"We came down after the halfway point," Jon said. "An explosion. We managed to level out, but the landing was rough, and a flight observer died. Barely had we landed when we came under attack. At the time I thought they were Jaru, but I soon realized something was off. Our captors took us north. We lost another man along the way, a field scientist they beat to death. We traveled for weeks to an old trapper lodge just over the border. There we stayed until Tanis' men rescued us a few days ago."

"The rest of the transport crew survived? They're here?" I asked, horrified by what they had endured.

"Yes, the two technical masters survived, as did the other field scientists onboard. The remaining flight observer was working with them. He died while we were there, killed by one of his own." Jon said. "They had Rymorian technology. At least one PB firearm. They still have it since we didn't find it among those killed... We found Rymorians among them working for an undercover agency. They didn't know a lot other than the primary contact that went by the name of Karry. He wasn't with them at the time. It turns out Karry had orders to locate Adam's group and extract them. If the extraction failed, then his orders were to kill you all."

I shook my head, my denial never forming into words.

Kill us? Someone had been sent to kill us—and kill me?

Adam nodded confirmation, his face solemn. "It's true, Hannah. I wish it were otherwise. Someone in Rymor is behind this. Anyone powerful enough to bring so many people out here with weapons is a threat for reasons far eclipsing our personal safety. We need a lot more information before we can return. I've no idea where we're going to get it. People are trying to kill us, their motivation unclear. For now, better that they know nothing about our location or plans.

The Warrior in the Shadows

With hindsight, I would rather Dan had remained ignorant. I trust Dan, but anyone who can do this—well there's no saying what else they may do, or what they might have access to."

Blood drained from my face. "Oh god. I need to warn Dan."

I went to scramble up, but Adam moved with me, his hand on my arm gentle but insistent.

"It's too late, Hannah," he said softly. "We can't risk more communication."

I wanted to argue, to plead if need be, but Adam's face was set. Tears welled at the back of my eyes, but I blinked them away. What was done was done. Dan was an intelligent man. He wouldn't be reckless, would he? "When will we leave?"

"Soon, I think," Adam replied, releasing my arm. "Tanis is eager to return to Thale."

I nodded. A part of me longed to return home, see my sister and family, and resume my normal life. And yet so much had happened, all these revelations and incidents that had shattered my confidence in a man I'd once been intimately acquainted with. I didn't trust my judgment of what was right. I didn't trust my judgment of people, and I thought Adam's decision not to return might be for the best.

Chapter 2

Hannah

I was still reeling from these revelations when I became aware of someone on my periphery. Turning, I found Garren waiting.

"I'll leave you to catch up," Adam said. On one level, I was aware of Adam and Jon moving off, but I only had eyes for the alpha who stared back at me.

Tall and built, with shoulder-length blond hair and blue eyes, Garren was like the living embodiment of a mythical Viking god created in loving detail and placed within the mortal world. He was fantasy and reality all rolled into one. The strange plate and leather armor, the sword at his left hip, the rough, primal beauty of man and alpha.

His lips tugged up. He took a step forward and hauled me into his arms, and how good it felt to be there.

He stilled abruptly and gave an exaggerated sniff before lifting his head and pinning me with a glare. "Tanis' scent is all over you."

"I... he... we..."

Garren growled, and not in a sexy way, more a lifting-the-hairs-on-the-back-of-your-neck, blood-is-about-to-spill way. I swallowed

The Warrior in the Shadows

hard, wondering what failed cross-wiring in my brain might be responsible for the sudden unmistakable clench to my pussy and the gush of slick.

"We didn't... we only kissed."

His nostrils flared and his eyes narrowed. "I'm going to thump the bastard... Later. I need inside you."

"God, yes please."

Our hands clashed as we both reached for the catch on my suit. What followed was a chaotic jumble of urgent fingers and muttered cursing as my clothes were parted enough for him to slip his hand inside.

"You're very fucking wet, Hannah." His lips pressed to my throat, teeth nipping the skin as his fingers speared deep into my pussy, making it hard to concentrate on his words. "Did you like him kissing you?"

"I... Oh!" His fingertips found the entrance to my slick gland, and he petted the sensitive bundle of nerves without mercy, making me twitch and groan.

"Answer the fucking question," he growled in my ear, "or I'm going to fucking stop!"

"Yes!"

He stopped anyway. "No!" *What the fuck did I just say?*

"Unmated omega. Causing no end of fucking trouble," he muttered as he put me on my hands and knees and came down behind me. A jangle and clank followed, and I waited, quivering with need, before he directed the blunt head of his cock to my pussy entrance and filled me with a savage thrust.

"He's not the one fucking you now, is he?" Garren said, slamming into me slow and deliberate, slapping our flesh together and sending a delicious jolt that sparked nerve-endings to life.

"Not the one plowing this tight, needy omega cunt. I am."

His aggression lit a fire in me, and I loved every rough word, every possessive touch, every deep fuck of his hard cock.

"Not the one ruining this pussy. I am."

He began to power into me, his knot swelling, bringing that tingling anticipation, and no indication that he might withhold that pleasure. Fast, urgent, driving my body relentlessly toward the delirium of release.

"Hope the bastard suffers a hard-on all day. Hope he can't get your sweet fuck-me scent out of his nose. Hope his balls are blue!"

Garren fucked me, but I wasn't thinking only of him. No, I was thinking about Garren *and* Tanis, focusing on that tendril of scent that lingered, of being between them, of taking them both.

His strokes slowed, working the knot in until it lodged perfectly, seeming to swell larger still once it was inside me.

"You may be his for now, but you were always mine."

I came, body turning rigid, heat and pleasure suffusing every pore, as I was lost in deep, glorious contractions over his hard cock and knot. Garren ground his pelvis against mine, and a hot flood bathed the entrance to my womb.

Here, right here, knotted and well fucked, I understood myself.

But as the heady sensations dimmed to a glow and sanity returned, I questioned my actions.

What the fuck was I doing?

What the fuck was I going to do?

Chapter 3

Karry, mercenary field operative

The mighty Jaru camp was reforming as the battle survivors drifted into the area in pitiful, ragtag pockets.

I passed a tribe who were busy setting up their painted tents. We had lost a few tribes, but the Jaru had served their purpose. Being close to so many of them made my skin crawl, but I needed to talk to Ailey, the Shadowlander-Jaru half-breed before I left with that little snitch Marcus.

For the most part, the Jaru ignored me, and only the occasional jeer or insult greeted my passage through their throngs. The battle had instilled in them a brief and unnatural desire not to shed blood. It wouldn't last, but I appreciated the respite so I could speak to Ailey.

I spotted the man in question. Ailey was hard to miss at seven feet and close to three hundred pounds. Thick brown hair fell past his shoulders, and a scraggly excuse for a beard covered his chin. He was an ugly brute with a disposition to match. The Jaru had despised him as a child, subjecting him to vicious and regular abuse. As his Shadowland heritage kicked in, that had shifted toward wary respect that had risen to fanatical adoration over recent years. Ailey had a skill for killing Shadowlanders, and that was all it took for him to be revered.

I would have described him as a complete psycho, but compared to Bill, not so much. How Bill had established the initial arrangement, I would never know. Now Ailey was just another cog in the Bremmer war machine.

My operation had gone poorly—a complete fuck-up to be blunt. Bremmer wouldn't let me back into Rymor without some halfway decent news. I should be cutting my losses and finding a place out here, but my stubborn streak had never learned to quit.

"You've got a nerve." Ailey scowled down at me as I neared. I'd brought three Rymorian men with me, but if Ailey decided to get nasty, we were fucked.

I raised my hand. "Yeah, I hear you. It's a mess. You've done no better, though, have you? And you weren't ready, even though you've been sitting on your ass for the last month. We were hounding Tanis' men the whole way. Must've hit his group a dozen times or more before he reached that station."

"You don't hit very hard."

I shrugged. "If he were easy to kill, we wouldn't still be out here."

Ailey grimaced. "Had another problem at the old trapper lodge."

"Problem?" I was instantly alert.

"The prisoners—they got out."

I swore long and creatively. Finally, after a few minutes of silent fuming, I got my temper under control enough to ask for the details. "What happened?"

"We were attacked."

"Another group of Jaru?"

"No, Thale men."

"What the fuck?" Thale was Tanis' home fortress, *his* men.

Ailey's eyes had turned vacant, and he radiated an edgy stillness that made me think he was about to go on a rampage.

"Bill has got your daughter," I reminded him. "You need to focus,

The Warrior in the Shadows

Ailey. Focus on sorting this shit out." Staring Ailey down was like staring down a mad dog. Any sign of weakness on my part, and I was dead.

He shook his head and seemed to rouse from wherever the fuck he'd been—probably imagining himself crushing Bill's skull between his bare hands. "He's dead if he touches her. He knows that."

I gave him a flat look. It would be nice to deal with someone who wasn't a lunatic. "Much as I'd love to see you rip Bill limb from limb, it's not going to happen. Now, how many got away?"

"Most of the Jaru were slaughtered. I haven't been back to check."

"Squealers? Did they take any of my men?" Thale soldiers getting their hands on Rymorians pretending to be Jaru would not end well.

Ailey shrugged. "Yeah, probably. You tower dwellers don't know how to keep your mouths shut."

"The Shadowlanders don't step over the border without a good reason. Someone got suspicious, and that means we should be worried."

"Too much shit going on to worry about a few squealers."

I scratched at the rough stubble on my chin. "I need to get back. Marcus needs to be places—assuming I don't kill the little prick first for all his whining. You need to get ready, too. We've come too far to stop now."

"Gonna kill him when this is done." Ailey's lips lifted in a cruel sneer.

"You gotta stay alive to do that," I said. I let out a slow, frustrated breath. "I'll see you on the other side. If all goes well, you may get to see your daughter again, and if you don't—well, it probably means you're already dead."

With that, I turned and left the ramshackle Jaru camp. My deal with Bill had gone from bad to worse. When you were at rock bottom, you made desperate choices. The twenty years in prison I'd evaded by working for Bill didn't look so bad anymore.

Hopefully, I'd feel better once I'd beaten a sense of urgency into Marcus.

If not, I'd beat the fucker some more.

Chapter 4

Rymor

William (Bill) Bremmer, Chancellor of Rymor

I hated gala dinners, all those fake smiles worn by fake people whose only interest in me was the potential influence I could provide. Business moguls seeking my advice on this or that, charities seeking funding, and political worms seeking to expand power. Everyone had an agenda; everyone wanted something.

I made my way through the crowd making polite conversation and doing my best to avoid any commitments. Of course, the imminent war and yet another terrorist attack—this one thwarted by the police—occupied everyone's mind, which added to my vexation. Usually, I loved my job and the power it afforded. During gala dinners, I did not.

The setting was exquisite; the grand ballroom of the Millennial Center in the harbor city of Tranquility was both vast and spectacular. The high-domed room was a re-creation of a bygone era that had been lovingly crafted using the original tools, building techniques, and materials. It had been listed as a site of historical importance, even though it was a mere five hundred years old, simply because of the effort required to build it. Crafted from a combination of glass and wrought iron, the views of both sea and city were stunning in every direction.

My mother funded the event at an exorbitant cost that made a negligible impact on my father's wealth. It made her happy, so I couldn't see any harm in it other than my obligatory attendance. There was no genuine affection behind my inclusion. It was the simple fact that my presence raised the price of the tickets—it was for charity, after all.

"William, darling!"

Only my mother called me William. "Mother." I kissed her proffered cheek. "You look lovely." She wore a full-length ball gown of pale-blue silk. Her hair, more white than blonde, was styled in an elegant chignon. Diamonds dripped from her ears, neck, and wrists. She had graceful aging down to an art. It was only under the surface that the cracks became apparent.

"I'm so glad you came. When can you visit again? You must see the new landscaping in the south garden. Absolutely stunning!"

We talked about inconsequential matters: the charities, her gardens, and those fat dogs she kept. At times, I wanted to shake her and demand to know why she remained in that hell with my father—why she still lived in the family home so tainted with bad memories.

I wondered how she would react if I told her I despised her for what she allowed to be done, almost as much as I despised my father for doing it.

"I've been busy, Mother. Between the power problems and that most recent declaration of war on Shadowland, time has been scarce. I know how important my attendance is to you, but I won't be able to stay long."

"Oh, what a shame. Don't you have people to take care of the little details?"

Only my mother would refer to Rymor's single most significant disaster as 'little details'. Of course, the upper echelons of society were not impacted by the power restrictions the way the masses were, and the triviality of war barely scratched their perfect world.

I suppressed my irritation and plastered on an indulgent smile. "Not always, Mother."

Noticing two of my security team heading discreetly toward me, I questioned my decision to turn my communicator off.

Excusing myself, I turned to see what they wanted.

"Sir, Station fifty-four is operational."

Operational? No, I hadn't misheard. It took considerable effort not to react. *Who the fuck has started the station?* "You're certain?" A foolish question. Theo wouldn't have sent someone to interrupt me without reason. Whatever Theo's schemes, he remained faultless in his work.

"Yes, sir."

"I'll come at once," I said before returning my attention to my mother. "Sorry, I need to leave."

Her face fell. Fury seethed inside me for the news, but I derived satisfaction in upsetting her finely orchestrated plans.

In a moment of clarity, I realized my treatment of Margaret bore striking similarities to my father's treatment of my mother.

Strangely, that association, and the realization that I was, in fact, not so different from my father, didn't trouble me as I felt it should. I would never marry Margaret, nor did I desire to father children with her, but my need to control had taken a more extreme turn of late —*ever since Hannah left.*

While my relationship with Hannah was the subject of much media interest, Margaret had been a private liaison that the world knew nothing about, save for a few colleagues who might have guessed. I enjoyed compartmentalizing my life. On one side, Hannah, the beautiful technical master that the press had touted as my future wife, and on the other side, the darker world where Margaret and I played.

But now Hannah was gone, and Margaret couldn't hope to fill

that void. Not that I'd seen Margaret recently. It must have been weeks, maybe as much as a month. Even at work, our paths hadn't crossed. The war, and Rochelle Stevens, the daughter of councilman Carl Stevens, provided a distraction and a credible replacement for Hannah.

I'd cast an angel into hell by sending Hannah into Shadowland. The sweet, addictive omega I'd corrupted and fucked. She would be out of the way by now if Karry had done his job. Her reported death was the excuse for war. Any whisper of her survival would be disastrous.

But if Hannah hadn't started the station, then who?

"Will I see you this weekend?" My mother's eyes searched mine and brought me back to the present, making me aware that I'd stood motionless for too long.

I had once found her gentleness an enviable quality against the backdrop of my father's authoritarian ways. Now I recognized it for the flaw that it was. "Unfortunately not."

"When then?" Her neediness increased my loathing of her. She suddenly looked old and haggard; the great beauty she had been as a younger woman was long gone, leaving a pitiful shell behind.

"I don't know," I said. "I'll be in touch when I can."

I turned and walked away, following my escorts through the crowd and out to where a transport waited to take me back to Serenity.

As I eased into the seat, an unexpected face greeted me from the viewer. "Where's Theo?" I demanded as the transport took smoothly to the sky.

The man on the communication viewer was flustered. "We can't locate him, sir." Nielsen stood in on the few occasions Theo took leave, but that was always with prior notice. "He's not at home, and his personal communicator is off." If it were anyone else, I might presume them to be socializing, but the thought of my machine-like personal assistant having fun was laughable. Theo didn't make

The Warrior in the Shadows

mistakes or oversights—except *that* one—and he certainly wouldn't miss a critical communication for frivolous reasons.

My frustration at Theo's absence battled against my deeper concern that his disappearance was somehow related to the station news. "How long ago did the station become operational?"

"Several hours ago, sir."

"Who brought it back to operation?"

"We don't know, sir."

"I'll be arriving shortly. I expect some answers by the time I do." I snapped the viewer off. The station couldn't be restarted without human intervention at the source, which meant one of three people had reached the station and repaired it. Two experts were my prisoners, and one should have been dead—or my prisoner.

Who started the station?

I needed an update from Karry, my man inside Shadowland, but I'd given him strict instructions not to bother returning without completing his task. Since dramatic events must have unfolded, no help would be forthcoming there.

What the fuck has happened?

There were too many potential scenarios, none of which helped my main agenda: war, the entire premise of which was based around the lack of power and the lack of experts to fix it. I had fabricated evidence to support the notion that they were dead—it would be detrimental to my plans for anything contrary to be revealed.

Those plans were in a precarious position. Layered over this quagmire was a deep unease surrounding Theo's sudden and unexpected disappearance.

Chapter 5

Nate, illegally created being

Theo and I made our way covertly into Dan's apartment to wait for him. Today would be the first time the three of us had been in the same place together.

My life had changed dramatically in the weeks since I left Dan's summer home. My simple beginnings were far behind me. This vibrant and, at times challenging, new life had been an exciting ride, though rarely in a good way.

I wasn't human, at least not in the usual sense. I was an organic being, as was Theo, created from the smallest cells upwards, and the result of Dan's quest to create Artificial Intelligence taking an unexpected turn.

From the moment I'd achieved physical consciousness and opened my eyes, my life had been filled with a sense of latent danger, which had begun three years earlier with Bill secretly sending teams into Shadowland.

While I didn't believe a divine spirit guided my path, as Dan did, nor in other unquantifiable concepts such as fate, I did believe in the

The Warrior in the Shadows

random design of the universe—randomness that had led to me being alive in the here and now.

"I often wonder why Dan didn't create himself another body," Theo pondered aloud from where he lounged on Dan's couch.

A degenerative muscle disease had left Dan bound to a personal mover, which had likely saved his life. Had he been physically able to make the trip to the station, Dan would have been missing, too.

He was now the last remaining ancient technology expert in Rymor.

"Maybe he was worried it would draw attention to us," I said, wondering where Theo was going with his line of thinking.

"If he did create a new body, it would raise some important questions," Theo continued as if I hadn't spoken. "I mean, is it possible to create a body without creating a mind to go with it? If you can't, then would you be killing someone when you replaced their brain with Dan's?"

"That's a little macabre," I said, smirking. Theo had lived a stoic life while out in the world. In private, he was less orthodox, as I'd discovered when we first met two weeks ago. I still found it hard to believe he had been working as Bill's personal assistant to spy on the chancellor's corrupt ways.

Theo grinned back and sipped contentedly on a Berry Blast. He enjoyed fruit juice, it seemed. While our personalities were different in many ways, there were strong similarities in our looks, with only a slight variation in our height, build, and the shade of our auburn hair. We could easily have been brothers.

Which made me wonder where Dan had gotten the base DNA from…

"He's here," I said.

We stood, and our expectant faces turned toward the door as it opened.

Dan's thinning crop of white hair was ruffled, and his frail frame appeared leaner. Seeing us, his eyes widened, narrowed, and widened again so rapidly that Theo and I burst out laughing.

"What in the blazes are you two doing here? Are you trying to get yourselves arrested?"

"It's okay, Dan," I said. "I can wipe our presence off monitoring. No one knows we're here. It seemed the safest way to speak to you since you're being watched in public."

I grimaced. I could have handled that better.

Dan drew a deep breath. "Damned if I care. It's so good to see you both."

There were tears in Dan's eyes as we shared a hug. "You're a pair of goons, look at you." We both grinned back. "And pleased with yourselves. Nate, what's all this about wiping yourself off monitoring, and how did you figure that out?"

"Nate tested his data-wiping skills on the CIA headquarters," Theo said, chuckling.

"Are you crazy?" Dan said thickly.

"Probably," I said. "I needed answers and that was the only way to get them."

Dan's eyebrows shot up. "And entering the CIA headquarters was the only way? What have I unleashed onto the world?"

"I got my answers." Only not the ones I'd wanted, and no one was the wiser. It all started with that fateful trip to the picturesque town of Azure and my first trip outside Dan's home. The most exciting day of my short life... until I saw Ella Duvaul taken. Then, shortly later, I'd found out that she was gone, terminated, her life snuffed out. Still trapped in Shadowland, Hannah didn't yet know about her sister's terrible fate.

Theo's sensitive eyes found mine like he could sense the darkening of my thoughts, and he placed a hand on my shoulder. He'd told me many times that it wasn't my fault—I still felt I had failed.

Theo turned to Dan with a smile. "Do you feel safer now?"

Dan huffed. "I suppose so. Actually, no. What else have you been up to since you left? What else should I be concerned about?"

"Why don't we tell Dan about our plans?" Theo said, winking for my benefit, further lightening the mood.

The Warrior in the Shadows

"That sounds ominous. What do you two have planned?" Dan asked.

"We're going to visit Bill's house. The one near the Shadowland border," I said.

"Visit it? Do you mean break-in?"

"Yes, he does." Theo walked back to retrieve his fruit drink.

"Are you crazy?"

"We should all get comfortable," Theo said, flopping back on the couch. "This may take some explaining. Nate, I think it's time to tell Dan about your *special* skills."

Dan rolled his eyes. "Special skills? What's all this about?"

I grinned. "You remember when we were at your house, and you mentioned that one of the cybernetic implants was a little experimental..."

Chapter 6

Shadowland

Hannah

The week after we left the station was incident free, and the people with me now were much different to those with whom I'd left Rymor several months ago.

The first change to our number had been with Luke's death on that infamous forest path. It had been the first time I experienced a Jaru attack and the day I met Tanis. When I closed my eyes at night, I could still see the terror on Luke's face as he collapsed to the forest floor. If not for the arrival of Tanis and his party, we would all have died that day.

Then, while we waited at Julant, while Adam's life hung in the balance, Marcus, who had so openly disliked me, had fled during the night. I hadn't been sorry to see him go. The next day, Adam had regained consciousness, and Red, who had been sent to investigate the transport crash, had joined us.

Finally, a week ago, at the edges of the station, saw the addition to

The Warrior in the Shadows

our number of the transport crash survivors. We were eleven in total now, a rag-tag group bearing the mental and physical scars sustained during our time beyond the wall.

Our increased numbers comforted me, along with the presence of six sections of soldiers from Thale, and a further ten sections from two other fortresses. It made for an ungainly procession, but after the furious pace that had taken us to the station, I found our current progress pleasantly slow.

Garren rode beside me. Directly in front of me rode Adam and Red. Following us were the two technical masters and the rest of the Rymorians. Garren's section surrounded us, and other sections rode ahead and behind. Supply wagons were distributed throughout the column so that tents, food, and other essentials were always close at hand. When we stopped for breaks or to make camp, the group was so vast that all we could do was condense into a shorter, thicker column.

Throughout the day, messages would be sent along the line. When evening came, and we made camp, the leaders would ride ahead to meet with Tanis. The cohesive nature of such a large and unwieldy group surprised me, as did the way they worked autonomously while still under that central control. It seemed improbable that one man could govern a country as extensive as Shadowland without the assistance of technology: this vast sprawling country that included five great fortresses, many cities, and everything in between.

Yet somehow Tanis did.

The quieter aspects of the journey had afforded me plenty of thinking time. The future remained uncertain, and my thoughts often shifted through a myriad of emotions as I unpicked what had happened. Jubilation that the station was working. Despair that I was heading farther away from home. And a cold sickly sensation that my sister didn't even know where I was because Bill had forbidden it.

It wasn't only about me. My fellow Rymorians were similarly stuck, every one of them with friends and family back home.

Home. Rymor was still my home, and this was still simply a wild adventure, although one yet to be done with me. I was here for the foreseeable future, and so I may as well embrace it in all its savage glory because once it was over, I'd have no reason to visit again. Instead, I would return to my empty spiritless life, never to experience that soul-shattering carnality I did when Garren was inside me.

I was torn straight down the middle. No matter how this played out, I would lose something precious. And wasn't that sad?

I worried, too, about myself, about Dan, and about Ella. I hoped she'd worked out my message and spoken to Dan; that Dan had let her know I was safe. Only there were risks in all this. Learning that the transport survivors had been kept prisoners over the Jaru border left a deep and pervasive sense of unease. Ella openly distrusted Bill at best and hated him at worst. She was tenacious. What might she do?

I wish I could've spoken to Dan for longer. It felt like we'd barely started when we stopped again, and never covered anything in between. Flustered by the possibility of monitoring intercepting my communication, I'd barely let him speak. Whether that was paranoid or prudent, only time would tell.

The imprisonment of the missing transport team by Rymorians disguised as Jaru was mind-blowing. I kept thinking of ways they might have been mistaken. Only I knew the two technical experts personally. Joshua and Daren were intelligent, stable men, neither of them subject to flights of fancy, and they were unwavering in their account of events.

At the center of the controversy was Bill, the man I thought I had known, who I thought I had loved, who taught me not to be ashamed of my sensuality. We had been intimate many times—he had been inside me, brought me to climax.

Tanis hated him. Everyone had issues with him. It had just taken me a while to wake up to the truth.

Mixed with this disillusionment with my former partner was the profound loss I felt in not being able to speak to Ella, someone I

The Warrior in the Shadows

regarded as my best friend as well as my sister. The last arguments between us remained the saddest part of our enduring separation.

The call to rest dragged me out of my ruminations. The vast column of riders began to bunch, spilling into the surrounding forest to either side of the track. "This has to be the slowest journey ever," Garren muttered. "I'll be glad when we reach the Great Northern Road so we can pick up the pace a bit."

"I thought you liked the slower journey?" I asked, smiling. I nudged my horse in beside Red's, and its head swung down to crop at some of the creeping plants. The lands had become greener as we traveled farther from the station and was uncomfortably humid some days.

I caught Garren's watchful gaze. He still thought me incompetent on a horse, which was insulting given I hadn't fallen out of the saddle since the day of the Jaru attack.

Only, knowing he was watching me, I didn't look what I was doing. My foot tangled in the stirrup, and I landed on my ass in the dirt.

Someone chuckled—Edward, I thought.

"Here!" Red hauled me back to my feet. "That horse is at least three hands too big for you. Little wonder you struggle."

Garren growled. Red immediately took his hands from me and stepped back.

My heart pounded in my chest. For the most part, Garren was an even-tempered alpha, but I'd noticed ever since we'd left the station that he took exception to anyone touching me for whatever reason.

"Is she riding her own horse?"

That cool, clipped tone and the light tendril of scent wafting over me sent a sweet clench deep in my pussy and a telling trickle of slick. Every tiny hair on my body rose to attention, even as my temper flared.

My body might be intrigued by the alpha, but his personality left much to be desired. "Why is he asking you if I'm riding my own horse?"

The last time I'd spoken to Tanis, I'd been pointing a gun at him. *And then we kissed.*

"You may be his for now, but you were always mine."

"Quiet," Garren grunted. Closing a big hand over the back of my neck, he hauled me against him, pressing my face against his chest. The combination of the scent hit, the dominance of the move, and the calming feel of his fingers against my skin when I'd been craving them all morning momentarily robbed me of thought. "She's riding her own horse. The pace is slow, and she's managing well enough."

I tried to jerk away. Garren purred, and I instantly softened, which also pissed me off. His methods of subjugation when I had something to say were all kinds of wrong.

I glared over my shoulder at Tanis. He wasn't smiling, but I still got the impression he was amused, whether at Garren's handling of me or my vexation with the way it was done I wasn't sure.

Was he also thinking about our kiss, about the way he'd claimed me with his words?

"I hope you're being careful with her."

"The fuck?!" Garren said. "Don't fucking go there."

"I'll go where the fuck I want," Tanis continued, voice calm and clear. "You won't like the consequences if you trigger her heat. She's an omega new to cock. The risks are high. Are you knotting her?"

"None of your fucking business," Garren growled.

"You're knotting her," Tanis said flatly. "We can't sit around for a week while she goes into heat. Don't knot her, it will trigger her."

"You're such an asshole!"

"And you are thinking with your dick."

"And you're not?"

My eyes bounced between them. Garren's hand tightened slightly where he clasped me to him, which, coupled with his aggression and the fact that he and Tanis were openly discussing my heat and knotting me, was making me all kinds of needy, definitely arching, *presenting.*

Tanis' laughter was dry and humorless, and I instantly stilled. "If

The Warrior in the Shadows

I was thinking with my dick you'd be lying in a pool of your own blood, and I'd be balls deep in her cunt."

Bomb dropped, he stalked off.

Garren growled and tossed me over his shoulder before stalking off with me in the opposite direction.

I was aroused and angry at myself for being aroused, so I kicked and thrashed about. "Put me down, you brute!"

He put me down, more of a drop to the forest floor, where he stared down at me. Scrambling to my feet, I stomped up to him and poked him in the chest. "Why did you do that? Why did you shut me down?" I thought about telling him to keep his dick to himself, but there was no point in adding 'delusional' to my problems. He'd just take it out, and we both knew I would fold at the sight of him.

His nostrils flared. "Because when two dominant alphas are talking, omegas instinctively know not to interfere. Only you don't have a fucking clue."

That stung, like I was defective or something. "How could I know when I'd never been around an alpha before?" Never mind two. "And that's just insulting that omegas should be quiet. Why should I be quiet?"

"You don't get it do you?"

I threw up my hands. "No, so why don't you fucking tell me?!"

Fisting my collar, he took me down, crowding over me, making every synapse in my body fizzle with arousal. I was acting provocatively, baiting him when he was already aroused from his verbal sparring with Tanis. It was reckless on my part, yet he didn't frighten me, and pushing him was the highest order of thrill.

"You're unmated," he bit out. "Your scent is all over me and all over every other fucking male. You should be mated. You're not. That means you have no ties to me, no bond, and all your instincts are driving you to challenge."

"Challenge what?"

"Not what, who," he bit out, his big hand closing over the front of my throat, making me feel controlled and aroused all at once. "Me,

Tanis, and any other male your omega side deems worthy." His hand lowered, catching the opening of my suit and tugging with deliberate slowness as if daring me to object. "You know what you're doing right now, and what you were doing before, preening before Tanis, acting reckless, because you want what will happen." He thrust my bra out of the way, and his warm hand, calloused from sword use, enclosed my naked breast. And squeezed. "You want attention from an alpha, his eyes on you, his interest." His hand continued on, parting my suit before freeing his belt buckle and shucking his pants down past his hip. His cock bobbed free, the scent hitting me. "And his cock."

Denial hung on my lips as I dragged my gaze from his beautiful thick cock and met his eyes, seeing all the fierce emotion there, rocked by it because he seemed playful, and lacking in seriousness most of the time... all of the time, actually, except now.

"He said you shouldn't knot me," I said. My body trembled with need, slick leaking from my pussy and dripping onto the forest floor, yet I had to know. "That I might go into heat."

"I shouldn't," he agreed.

"Then why do you?" I asked quietly.

With a snarl of frustration, he lined up and thrust deep, making us both gasp. I clung to him, pussy quaking as he held still while buried intimately, reveling in how perfect it felt, how nothing mattered when he was inside me like this.

"Because you fucking beg me to," he said, his voice a soft purr beside my ear. "Because I'm only fucking human." He dragged his hips back before slamming home, bringing that delicious surge of hot, achy pleasure-pain. "And my instincts are clamoring, demanding that I give *my* omega what she fucking wants and needs." He began to power into me, amplifying every sensation. "Because it feels fucking good when I do."

I knew he would knot me even before I felt the swelling, heady pleasure as the thick bulge slipped in and out of my pussy. And when he finally thrust deep for the last time, when I was full, perfectly full,

The Warrior in the Shadows

stuffed to capacity with cock and knot, I came harder than I had ever done before.

Yet the pleasure was about more than him being inside me, a cock filling me how I needed it. It was about his words, their earnestness, and how they instilled a sense of connection that went beyond the physical.

He rolled, taking me over him, planting his hand over my ass, and pressing me a little deeper, reigniting all the nerves to a heightened awareness of how he filled me up.

"You're clever, Hannah, not in the way Tanis is, but in your own way. I'm not. So, if I can understand what is happening here, I'm certain you can too. It's not even the physical need that drives me anymore, but what I feel here." He tapped his chest. "I crave the submission you give me when I knot you. I want to imprint myself upon you more than I want my next fucking breath."

I buried my nose against his chest, wishing we were undressed so I could get the richness of his scent and feel the warmth of his skin against mine. His words shook me. *My* omega, he'd called me his. Was this bonding? Did I want to bond? Could I bear the thought of not bonding and letting him go?

I couldn't find words to respond, nor could I even coherently grapple with this revelation in the privacy of my mind.

"It's a battle every time I'm inside you," he said, voice soft and raw, "between giving you what you want and keeping you safe."

Chapter 7

Hannah

We returned to the camp where the rest of the Rymorian contingent were tending to horses or taking a rest. Garren muttered something about needing to talk to Tanis, remounted, and rode ahead.

"Here." Red passed me a food pack in an overly careful way, like he was afraid to accidentally touch me.

"Sorry about earlier," I said, although why I felt the need to apologize for Garren's territorial display eluded me. I sat down between him and Edward as they made some space for me.

"Don't mind it," he said, waving a dismissive hand and smirking. "I've been traveling in Shadowland for a long time. I know how alphas are with omegas. I should have known better."

My mind tried to process that, but it was messy in there. My pussy was still throbbing softly where Garren had knotted me. I came from a place where being civilized was the norm and male displays of ownership were unheard of. Yet I'd craved precisely this, hot sex with a demanding rough male. I couldn't have it both ways, didn't want it

The Warrior in the Shadows

really, yet I was still caught with a foot in both worlds and I was still subject to the effects of a lifetime of conditioning.

I wanted to ask Red how he felt about it, when he had stopped being shocked, or whether he was still shocked but had learned to ignore it. My cheeks heated as I made a show of examining the dry crackers, while inside, I considered what kind of lover Red might be, whether his experiences in Shadowland had changed him.

He might be a beta, but he was big, handsome, and supremely fit in a way I'd always been drawn to. He had a gentle, easy-going manner—everyone liked him.

I shouldn't be thinking about getting hot and sweaty with Red, because, really, I had enough going on in my mind with Garren and Tanis. Yet all I could see was Red, a playful smirk on his lips as he coaxed me to pleasure with those large, capable hands, of him trying to maintain his decorum but then failing and taking me roughly, knowing I craved it. He'd been working in Shadowland for years and had seen the ways of alphas and omegas. In this wilder place even betas must experience pleasure differently from the sterile Rymorian norm. Maybe he had indulged in said pleasure, had lovers, and taken those ways back to Rymor where he would, at first, shock and then delight his partners.

I needed to think about something else, which brought my focus back to the dry nut cracker in my hand. "Thanks, but I've not reached starvation levels yet so I might give it a miss."

Red chuckled, a pleasant sound made more so because I'd been the one to provoke it.

"Travel rations are an acquired taste," he said. "I always try to visit a city during a rotation; they have fantastic food, but it's incredibly unhealthy."

"I've never been to a Shadowland city," Edward said wistfully.

I'd never seen a city. But Julant had given me a taste of Shadowland, and I was curious now. I kept staring at my cracker, but I was thinking about Red in a city, of him stopping in a tavern for food and beer, of a pretty serving woman winking at him as she delivered his order, of him telling his companion he'd be back shortly, before following the pretty woman into a passage out the back, of seeking hands and urgent kisses, of her begging him to lift her skirts and fill her with his cock.

"But since I'm going straight to a fortress, I can't complain," Edward continued, snapping me back to the present with a jolt.

Edward indicated his cracker. "And I'm with Hannah about this. I'd rather gnaw on my own arm than eat a travel cracker."

I laughed. Amused but also relieved by the distraction.

What was wrong with me? All I could think about was sex.

Jon joined us and began regaling the group with a story.

"So, you were in that station with Tanis for ages," Edward said to me. "What were you talking about for so long?"

I eyed Edward, wondering where his question had sprung from. Today was the first time I'd seen Tanis since the station. I'd almost confessed the gun incident to Garren on a couple of occasions, but dropping an off-hand comment about nearly shooting his brother seemed awkward, and the moment had never felt right.

"I don't remember," I lied. How did he know we'd been in there a long time together. He hadn't been near the station when I came out. The first people I'd seen were Adam and Jon. Had they been discussing me? Were my feelings toward Tanis transparent?

Smothering my guilty thoughts, I stared at the leathery meat and hard, nutty cracker and tried to summon enthusiasm. Hot food was available in the evening. Maybe I would wait?

A surreptitious glance confirmed Edward was expectantly waiting for an answer. Determined to ignore him, I picked up the cracker and bit down.

"Really?" Edward said. "So, you don't recall threatening to kill Tanis if he didn't leave you there? Because that's what Jon said happened. I guess he could've made it up."

Edward gave Jon an innocent, questioning look while I choked on the cracker. Just as I became convinced I might die choking on it, Edward thumped my back, and I managed to swallow down the dry

The Warrior in the Shadows

hunk of rock-like cracker. I made a mental note that eating travel crackers was a health hazard.

I glared at Edward before realizing I had the group's undivided attention.

"I didn't threaten to kill him." I glanced at Jon to find him smirking. "I just kind of pointed it... I was already holding it when he came in."

That Tanis had told Jon what had happened mortified me. Jon sitting there with a mile-wide grin that didn't help, and the avid interest of the group completed my embarrassment.

"Why is this the first I've heard about this?" Red said, sounding disgruntled.

"I cannot imagine why Tanis felt the need to mention it. He didn't seem concerned at the time," I said.

"I told him straight that I thought Bill had sent you out here to kill him. You being such an unlikely assassin—makes you a perfect recruit for Bill." Jon said bluntly. "Afterward, Tanis told me you pointed a PB at him with the safety off. His words were 'that woman couldn't put down a rabid rat.'"

My eyebrows rose. I could hear Tanis saying those words in his clipped, derogatory tone, like my not shooting him was a personal failing.

Edward snickered.

"Harsh," Red said, laughing.

I laughed, too. Pointing a gun at Tanis had been crazy. I'd been carrying around the unconscious weight of self-reproach for far too long, and it felt good to laugh about it.

"Does Garren know?"

Jon grinned. "He's disappointed you didn't follow through."

I groaned.

I hadn't expected Tanis to tell anyone. It was almost like he was proud of it.

Garren's return interrupted the laughter. I'd only half-acknowledged that another rider accompanied him when Edward sprang to his feet. Collective heads turned.

Marcus?

As he got down from the saddle, slow and clumsy, I cataloged injuries that could only have come through violence.

"What happened?" Adam asked.

Marcus swayed where he stood. The blood on his clothing was old, but it told a story. His right eye was purple and swollen shut, and his right arm hugged his stomach.

I'd never liked Marcus. He'd been rude to me from the first day we met, yet I would not wish this suffering on anyone.

"A lot of stuff," Marcus said, his voice rough and unrecognizable. "A lot of bad stuff."

Adam placed a gentle hand on Marcus' shoulder. "Here, sit down until we get the call to move out." He turned to Garren. "Where was he found?"

"With a small group of Jaru—maybe a dozen." Garren replied, his gaze shifting from Adam to Jon. Something passed in that look that further tickled my unease.

Miraculously, and against all the odds, Marcus was back.

Chapter 8

Rymor

Nate

We left Dan's apartment, knowing it might be a long time before we saw each other again. Determined to find out more about Bill, Theo and I both agreed that drastic steps were needed.

"Have you bypassed it yet?"

Theo, I discovered, didn't do espionage well when someone else was in charge. It was the dead of night, and we were attempting to break into the grounds of William Bremmer's house.

I frowned at Theo.

Theo grinned back, his teeth flashing white in the poor illumination.

"It's not easy to do this. A mistake could be fatal."

Theo's smile dropped, and his eyes widened.

I smirked.

"That wasn't funny," he muttered.

"No?" I thought Coco would have found it funny. Coco, who said I was a cyborg with the IQ of a door scanner. Who blushed bright red when I pretended we were a couple in front of the coffee shop waitperson. Then she had laughed when she realized it was only a game. I often spent downtime thinking about how her whole face lit up and her eyes shone when she laughed, and how it made me feel warm, a little breathless, weightless, and full of joy. "It's done now."

The high-security gate swung open with a gentle *whirr*.

Theo exhaled a puff.

I could spend all day thinking about Coco and never be bored, but that was for later, and right now the magnitude of what we were about to do settled in. This was Bill's house, and we were about to break in.

Beyond the still-opening gate lay a broad stone driveway. At its end, an imposing house rose out of the surrounding landscaped gardens in smooth lines of windowed walls.

"You're sure he doesn't have any human security?" Theo asked. "The political elite often prefer the personal touch, and Bill is paranoid."

"No, it's safe. The surveillance is automated. State-of-the-art kind of automated, which makes it easier for me. You know Bill better than me. Does he strike you as someone who trusts his home to a real person who can fall asleep?"

"No, I suppose not."

"See, no alarms or SWAT team. I've diverted all the drone monitoring. Trust me, I've spent a lot of time planning this."

We followed the curving drive toward the house. A transport landing bay was just visible in the moonlight to the right. On the plans, the rear entrance appeared superior for ease of access, as the door was close to the central network hub.

The rushing sound of waves breaking increased as we rounded the side. The rugged southern coastline bordered the rear of the property, and as it appeared before us, we came to a collective stop.

The Warrior in the Shadows

"So, that's the sea," Theo said. "I never thought it would be so infinite."

The landscaping was minimal on this side of the building, with expansive, sweeping lawns ending at a low outcropping that gave way to a beach. Beyond was the sea, stretching out in all its vastness, with gentle waves that peaked and glistened in the light of the moons. The air was sharp and salty, and the breeze was warm against my skin.

My life experiences were limited. Theo, despite being out in the world, had lived an uneventful life through necessity. There had been no opportunity for either of us to visit the sea.

As we turned away from the sea and continued on to the house, a faint droning sounded.

"Is that a—" Theo glanced over his shoulder. "I thought you said he had no personal security?"

"I, ah, did." I also looked back as the unmistakable sound of a transport drew closer. "Maybe we should run?" I started running —*fuck*—we both hit a sprint.

There was nowhere to hide!

Out of options, we dived for the ground as we reached the house —at least it provided partial cover.

"Who is it?" Theo hissed.

"I don't know." I hissed back.

"You're supposed to know everything!"

I forced myself to stop panicking long enough to check the relevant systems. The flight was automated and controlled by AI. "It's an unscheduled flyover," I said.

We pressed flat to the ground as the drone passed over our heads.

"I have 'encouraged' their system to report an all clear," I said, relieved when the sound of the drone faded away.

"*Trust me,*" Theo muttered, sarcasm dripping from his tone. He rolled his eyes at me as he dusted himself off and stood. "Anything else going to surprise us?"

"Possibly," I admitted, rising to my feet and grinning, because defeating systems was fun.

Theo shook his head. "You're enjoying this way too much."

He was right. I was. The security proved easy to bypass, and the rear access door slid open. Inside, the decor was elegant, with simple lines, light colors, and wide spaces that spoke of taste and wealth.

"I thought Dan's place was impressive," Theo said, moving deeper into the room to stare out the windowed wall. "Feels wrong, doesn't it?"

I nodded. "Let's see what we can find."

The electronics layout guided me, energy pulsing around me as systems detected and forgot me with immeasurable speed. The hum of wireless communication drew me along a corridor and down a wide staircase.

Theo followed.

I paused at a section of the wall that appeared outwardly indistinguishable. From behind it came an avalanche of electronic communication.

"What are we doing here? Does he have a home office?" Theo whispered beside me.

"Just... wait." I pressed my fingers against the wall, sensing an intense buzz of virtual information. "Ah." I found the release. The wall to my right *clicked* and began moving.

Theo jumped back. "Okay, wow!"

The shifting wall revealed a dull metal door.

I shared a glance with Theo.

"Yeah, open it. If we're about to be electrocuted or get locked in behind a trap door, may as well get it over with."

It opened... to reveal an empty room.

"Not what I expected," Theo said, staring around the featureless space.

"You can't see it yet, but it's all here." At my command, the plain white wall to the right transitioned into a viewer. A chair emerged from the floor and slid smoothly into the center of the room. "I'll take the seat as it looks like it houses the controls. You may want to grab a chair from another room, we could be here for a while."

The Warrior in the Shadows

"Fine, I'll grab a chair."

The passage of his footsteps faded away.

"Let's see what you have for me," I said as I sat back in the chair. I was in Bill's home, violating his private space. The immorality of my action battled against my underlying belief that Bill was amoral and that the truth needed to be uncovered.

My venture into the CIA had been exhilarating and then shattering.

Would today be as difficult?

I rested my palm on the plate, and the wall viewer before me came to life.

First, I wanted to find any reference to the security flyover. I uncovered several additional security measures. Had I known about them before, I wouldn't have been so blasé about breaking in. The security flyover was run by a private company and was triggered randomly. With a bit of manipulation, the algorithm was slightly less random, and I temporarily disabled the rest of the security measures.

Satisfied that a SWAT team wasn't about to descend on us, I returned to the reason for our visit—Bill's private information archives—and began shifting through his data.

The viewer stopped on an image of Theo in his apartment. It was dated ten days ago, right before he fled.

"I guess he was watching me then."

My attention swung to where Theo stood in the doorway. "Sorry, I must have subconsciously thought about you."

"Hmm, be careful what you think about." Theo placed a bright blue beanbag next to my more impressive seat.

"Bill owns a beanbag?" I raised my eyebrows.

"Of course not. I printed it. You know I love anything retro-style. We'll be here for a while, and I want to be comfortable." He flopped down with a *whoosh* and sipped on an equally bright bottled fruit drink that he must have also printed. "He's got a professional grade printer with an instant chill feature—ice cold Berry Blast for the win."

Not only had he used the printer without checking, but he also hadn't brought me a drink! "And you couldn't find any other seat that would do? I hope he has a professional grade destructor to go with his professional grade printer and chill feature, or you'll be carrying the beanbag out with you."

"Does he?"

I thought about letting him sweat out the prospect of carrying the beanbag home. "Yes, he does." I turned back to the viewer, now filled with images of Theo at various locations.

"He *really* likes to watch," Theo said, the beanbag creaking as he moved.

"It begins with your first interview, tapers off after a couple of years, and then picks up again here. A date about two months ago flashed up on the viewer. I wonder what prompted the new level of scrutiny?"

"He, ah, discovered something I tried to hide from him."

"What?! Are you nuts? And you stayed working for him after?"

"It was a communication from a field scientist. Geoff Redfern was traveling with Shadowlanders after Bill 'unofficially' declared them our enemy. I should have deleted it. I thought he'd forgotten about it—he hadn't." Theo gave a pointed look at the viewer. "So, what else is there? Records of Dan or Ella? What about Hannah?"

"Hannah, Dan, and a whole lot more. There's a tagging system and a suite of algorithms trawling the global monitoring data for anomalies. Why don't we start with the most recent tags and work back?"

"As good a starting point as any," Theo agreed, his expression somber. "Coming here was the right decision, wasn't it? I mean I knew it would be, but—" He gestured at the image of a prominent and married senate member in a compromising position with a woman who definitely wasn't his wife. "Seeing it life-size in front of your face really drives it home."

"Do you want me to do this?" I always thought Theo odd for entrenching himself in Bill's world of politics, but perhaps now I

The Warrior in the Shadows

understood. It was ugly but necessary. He'd done what he'd done because he could, and because no one else could. But he'd paid his dues, over and over, gathering parts of a puzzle we had yet to understand.

Theo's lips thinned. "No, I'm definitely in. Let's get on with this. The quicker we start, the quicker it'll be done."

And so began the process of unraveling the information I'd found.

⁓

I sat with my legs hanging over the outcropping and stared at the ocean, Theo at my side. We were still at William Bremmer's home on the southern reaches of Rymor.

The sea was so blue and so beautiful that it hurt my eyes. Gentle waves crashed against the beach a little distance away, the sound interrupted by the occasional *craw* of the seabirds that came and went in the breeze.

Too many thoughts swirled around my head to process—the information we'd uncovered was dark and confronting. I felt soiled by it like I might never wash it off. The more I discovered, the more I knew I must continue.

"I need to go out into Shadowland," Theo said. "You know that, Nate?"

I nodded, staring sightlessly at the water. We were both unique, human in some ways and not in others. I wished there had been more time to know Theo before fate drove us apart again.

"We both knew this was coming to a head. I'm ready for whatever's next, and I know you are, too... Dan knows too much, and all of it puts him at risk. He'll need your skills to keep him safe, and Coco Tanis, too. We're all in this together now. The lines are drawn, and the sides are clear."

I snatched my gaze from the water at the mention of Coco.

"I know that you care about her," Theo said. "Every time one of us mentions her it's written all over your face. Those images were hard for me, but harder for you."

I sighed and turned away again. "I hardly know her." Coco was John Tanis' mother and had been a friend of Dan's for many years. I met her when she visited Dan, and they discussed their mutual concerns regarding Bill in detail. Mere weeks had passed since she'd accompanied me on that fateful trip to Azure—it remained one of my fondest life memories, at least until a certain point.

"*I like you, Coco,*" I'd said without thinking, feeling a strange, giddy sensation unfurling in the center of my chest. Only I meant something more, and I'd read enough to know that *like* shouldn't turn to *love* that fast, that it took time, familiarity, and reciprocation before it could fully form.

Only it had formed for me in the space of a single day, my mind cataloging our every interaction, from her touching my hand and realizing I was organic to our exploration of the town and that aborted visit to the coffee shop. Then afterward, the seriousness of our conversation with Dan on what to do next.

She was a measured woman, intelligent, beautiful, and so incredibly strong. I thought many people might come to fancy themselves in love with her.

So here we were, and Coco had become one of many unwitting stars in Bill's personal peep show. I didn't know why Bill felt the urge to watch so comprehensively or, having observed and discovered whatever he needed to know, chose to keep that information at hand.

Did he sit down there often, watching and re-watching his favorite parts?

"And that makes a difference?" Theo asked earnestly.

I exhaled with a huff. "No," I admitted before noticing Theo's rueful smirk.

My humor didn't last, though.

Seeing the intimacy between Coco and the field scientist, Jon Sanders, had been uncomfortable. More than uncomfortable, if I was honest. I knew they had been friends, but not exactly how close.

The Warrior in the Shadows

Coco had talked about Jon Sanders with affection and genuine concern, given he had been on the crashed transport. While I'd not lingered on that particular scene beyond understanding it was recorded, it incensed me that Bill saw it and kept it.

Bill had surveillance in her apartment and workplace and knew Jon had warned Coco about his concerns. Her conversations with Dan were recorded by the public monitoring system and carried no details beyond seeing the two of them together. There were no recordings from Dan's summer home, which was a small positive note.

Then there was the rest of it. Hannah had been the subject of frequent and comprehensive watching. So too, Margaret Pascal, which had been a sordid journey.

Then there was Bill's man, Karry, and all the other people Bill had sent into Shadowland, and his progress in establishing a base at the abandoned fortress at Talin. Unfortunately, there were gaps in the information. If the parts I found worried me, the missing parts worried me more.

Karry had visited this house several times, yet, unusually for Bill, none of what had transpired had been recorded. Bill had chosen to delete or switch those recordings off.

Bill had been collecting information for a long time, ten years in fact, and the list of revelations was long.

Nowhere was safe, not for Dan nor Coco, yet these dangers paled beside Theo's determination that he must go to Shadowland.

"Either of us could go into Shadowland. You could look after Dan and Coco. Scott Harding is a bit of a scary prospect, but nothing like Shadowland." Scott Harding was the head of Global Operations, which included the Global Monitoring and Shadowland Field Operations, aka home of the field scientists. Scott was openly critical of Bill for recalling the field scientists from Shadowland. They hadn't been allowed back since the infamous transport crash. Scott had argued that their presence in Shadowland was critical, now more than ever. Bill had disagreed. If we wanted to form alliances within Rymor, which we definitely did, Scott was a good place to start.

Theo grinned. "We both know I don't have your finesse with the systems. It's okay, Nate. We both have our part to play."

"I won't let you down," I said, a lump in my throat, humbled and grateful to have known Theo, even for such a short time.

"I know you won't. I won't let you down either."

We left it there and sat in silence, both knowing we would be going soon and that we may not see each other again for a long time.

There was a possibility we might not see each other again, period.

"What will you do out there?" I glanced at Theo, but my generated brother's face was closed off.

"Find John Tanis," he said.

That first tag in Bill's collection played on my mind and doubtless would continue to do so. It was a conversation between Bill and John Tanis, and the only recording of the two men together. Bill's records showed that they next met in Shadowland, and after that, only one of them was destined to return to Rymor.

I had come to know over the duration of watching those recordings that Bill, as a person, was fundamentally wrong. But that first recording—a conversation between Bill and John Tanis—explained the depth of their former friendship and possibly what had driven them apart.

It had left me overwhelmed.

Had John Tanis driven Bill off this self-destructive cliff?

Had Bill already been on that path?

"Is he really the right choice?" I asked.

Right and wrong had gotten blurred by that conversation between the two men. Bill was no longer so unequivocally bad, nor was John Tanis unequivocally good or blameless. Even in their younger years, the strength of those two personalities had been apparent. What had ten years done to those dominant minds?

I knew, precisely, in Bill's case, but John Tanis had been off the radar for all of that time.

The Warrior in the Shadows

"More like the lesser of two evils," Theo supplied with a humorless smile. "Let's face it, you don't take out someone as powerful as Bill Bremmer, unless you can find an equal and opposite force... I know you wanted to believe that John Tanis was something better, that he'd turn out to be a hero, even, but that recording has torn that theory apart. He's not part of Moiety, though, and I'm convinced he had nothing to do with that terrorist attack ten years ago. Even a cursory review suggests evidence was fabricated. It is what it is. Life is rarely clean cut when regarding right or wrong... You heard what Jon Sanders said in that recording, John Tanis hates Bill, and that's enough for me. Anything else is a complication."

Theo was right. We had no alternative anyway.

"Do you think that he'll help?"

"I've no idea," Theo said at length. "Unfortunately, I have no idea."

Chapter 9

Bill

I had experienced a number of frustrating days since the infamous station restart. While the return of power from Station fifty-four was ultimately good for Rymor, it wasn't conducive to my plans for war. I didn't want the news made public, not yet anyway. Once I got approval through the upper house, and the forces had left, it wouldn't matter much. Until then, any murmurs of restored power would only raise questions about the validity of war.

I was a man adept at the art of juggling diverse concerns, yet even by my standards, there were a few too many balls in the air.

The levels of blackmail I'd called upon to manage those flying balls had become an unwieldy and complex monster. The information was contained for now, except for Global Operations. Scott Harding, who directed said division, was now my personal nemesis, second only to John Tanis himself. It didn't help that the bastard was squeaky clean.

Scott wanted the field scientists back on active duty. All his points were valid, and he'd been vocal in citing corruption when his requests had been blocked. Since it was correct that corruption was at work, his complaints were justified.

"What do you have for me?" I addressed the man sitting opposite me in my State Tower office, aware I'd been lost in my thoughts for some time. Seeing Damien Moore's nervous, wide-eyed regard, I schooled my expression and forced my frustrations away.

Damien Moore came to my attention several years ago. An investigative archaeologist who had been researching the origins of Rymor —specifically, how the colonists got here. My initial interest had been a simple desire to support any cause that would ruffle Gaia's feathers. Later, it shifted into a deeper fascination.

"I do have some excellent news!"

The ever-present forest stretched to my left, and the unremarkable Damien fidgeted in the chair on the other side of my desk. Damien wasn't a man blessed with a natural social presence. Our conversations were bumbling escapades where I was forced to drag every stilted word from his mouth.

"And what is this news?" I asked bluntly. The station situation had put me in a foul mood. Then there was Theo's disappearance. His replacement, Nielsen, was doing an average job. When Theo eventually surfaced, it would be a toss-up between interrogating him and setting him to immediate work fixing Nielsen's mess.

"Yes, I believe that I may have found it."

"It?" I sat a little straighter. I'd anticipated a lot of historical jargon. Damien's idea of good news usually consisted of finding another potential clue. "Not a clue, but actually *it*?"

Damien's fingers fidgeted over the middle-age spread thickening his waistline. "We would need to verify its location—now that we have one."

"And this location is?" If he didn't give me a straight answer immediately, someone would need to prise my fingers from around his throat, which be unfortunate for everyone.

"It's—" Damien paused, his nervous eyes blinking slowly as if reading my nefarious thoughts. "We uncovered records that indicate it was buried in the collapsed crater left by an extinct volcano in the heart of the Jaru plains. It was placed there after the colony was established..." I zoned out. "...a stable rock location to house it. The energy source was placed into stasis in case the colonists needed to leave. Over time, I believe it was simply forgotten. It's immense and impractical for use other than the interstellar transport of vast numbers of people."

Damien had achieved what had once seemed impossible. He had located the colony founders' ship, the vessel that had brought the first Rymorians to the planet they named Serenity all those years ago.

The very existence of Rymor was a much-ignored controversy. The scientific community and Gaia remained firmly encamped in their well-established and disparate views. The scientists, for their part, had accumulated an extensive body of evidence suggesting Rymorians, along with a wide collection of plant and animal life, were not native to the planet at all. It was, therefore, reasonable to assume the abundant, fertile land we now possessed had once belonged to someone else, someone who had doubtless been reluctant to give it up. Perhaps Gaia was a faction born of that guilty past—a dark past that had driven this misplaced determination to protect the very people they had previously abused. Yes, this would screw with Gaia's belief that a divinity placed us here. I smiled.

Damien smiled—it held a nervous edge.

"How many people can it hold?" I asked.

"Ten thousand according to the record, including sufficient storage space for supplies needed both during the journey and after. There were other sister ships, but I can find no record of those being stored. It's probable they returned to their home world shortly after colonization."

I nodded thoughtfully. If I timed it right, this would piss off Gaia and provide a nice distraction. Gaia, full of fervent power mongers, guarded access to Shadowland. Clearly, we had once had greater intimacy with the world at large, given we had the likes of Station fifty-four out there, so far from the wall. It was time to ease

The Warrior in the Shadows

their stranglehold on Shadowland. "What about the master switch?"

Damien's brows shot up, and he blinked several times. "The Armageddon switch? But that's a myth."

"Yes, and so was the ship," I said. "Since we've now located the ship, it's not unreasonable to assume it contains the switch—as it's alleged to."

"B-but," Damien stammered, "the only reference that ties the two together, is the master switch arriving with the ship. If the colony was unsuccessful, they could return the planet to its natural, technology free state before leaving. There is nothing to suggest they might leave it on the ship. Rather, I'd expect them to keep it somewhere much safer, possibly even destroy it once the colony was established."

I formed a steeple with my fingers. "I'll want verification of the ship's existence as soon as possible."

"Verification?" Damien echoed. His face flushed, and his fingers restless against the material stretched across his ample waistline.

"Yes," I replied. "I'll need the site checked and proof that the interstellar ship is there... It is there, isn't it, Damien?"

"I... yes, of course," Damien stuttered. "I presumed we would need approval. Gaia will want to be involved."

"Gaia will want to shut this down," I said heatedly. "And I've no intention of letting a bunch of heretics block such a momentous discovery. I'll have a team mobilized. You'll want to go with them I assume?"

Damien's jaw hung slack in a way that made his already unappealing features even more so.

"Good," I continued, taking Damien's lack of response for acquiescence. "My office will contact you for the details. Expect someone to be in touch soon."

Damien finally roused himself from his stupor enough to realize that he was being dismissed. Still in a state of numb compliance, he rose unsteadily from his seat and made his way out of the room.

My smile was pure satisfaction. Perhaps it was time to send a few more people beyond the wall. Talin, the abandoned Shadowland fortress, was useful as a stepping-stone for entry into indigenous lands. Situated to the far northeast of Shadowland, it was close to both Rymor and the Jaru Plains, and already home to numerous personnel and supplies that could expedite Damien's research trip.

I would establish an autonomous government body to handle the founder ship investigation, and let Damien take the credit. I wanted evidence of the ship promptly. While Gaia was busy grappling with the discovery, I could progress my plans for war.

Chapter 10

Peter Paxman, Global Monitoring Duty Manager

Global Monitoring, a subsidiary of the wider Global Operations, had changed dramatically over the last few months. After the excitement of the power failure and subsequent restoration, the facility was back in business again.

The power was back, along with the satellites, barriers, and the sea-shifters. Unfortunately, outside Global Monitoring and a few high-profile individuals, most of Rymor remained ignorant of this fact.

I wasn't comfortable with keeping secrets, nor did I understand why. Half of the team had been asked to sign a non-disclosure agreement. The rest had been placed on permanent leave and told not to return until further notice.

No such luck for me. I was still on the job.

On top of the crazy events in Shadowland and the station, there had been another bombing, with Moiety claiming responsibility for the death of nearly eighty people at a transportation hub. After decades of relative peace, they had been steadily increasing the frequency and severity of the attacks.

The world was going to hell, and Monitoring had a front-row seat.

Forcing my focus back to my work, I pushed a few wispy strands of graying hair from my forehead and surveyed the pictures before me at maximum magnification. The image was grainy, but even so, I knew I was looking at bodies...lots of bodies littering the grounds around the station, interspersed by blackened mounds, which I suspected might be burnt bodies.

This post-carnage scene told a vivid story. That this had happened immediately before the power restoration was also worthy of note.

"Not quite an Almoret, but the most notable battle we've seen in years." Tom sat to my left. He'd been browsing and cataloging the information for days and was all but sleeping here.

"It's not a great location for a battle," I mused. The grounds around the station were steep due to the underlying dome that housed the buried power source.

"Can you imagine what it must have been like?" Tom gushed.

It wasn't the first time Tom had made such an exclamation. He was new to the job and still displayed that annoying level of enthusiasm that I'd lost years ago.

I'd missed my fishing holiday, and at this rate, I'd never be going fishing again.

"When do you think they'll make it public?" Tom asked. His fingers glided over the interactive desk surface as he pinched and tapped to select the data.

"I've no idea." I continued tagging items from my feed. "It's not something we should discuss."

The whole subject made me uneasy. Tom, for the most part, appeared oblivious to the underlying malaise. We were about to go to war with Shadowland, and the news was rife with speculation. The hottest conspiracy was based on a theory that the Shadowlanders allegedly possessed Rymorian weapons.

The Warrior in the Shadows

"I can't see why not." Tom glanced over. "It's a reasonable question. They have to let everyone know about it eventually."

Yes, eventually, I thought. If Tom hadn't guessed that this room and our conversations were being monitored, I wasn't enlightening him. All I was interested in was keeping my head down, doing as I was told, and not questioning a damn thing.

Tom returned his attention to his work. "What about who did this? These people are lying dead all over the place—are we allowed to discuss that?"

"We can definitely discuss that, only I've been studying it for days, and I've still got no idea why or exactly who. That region is empty other than the station and holds no value or significance. Shadowlanders or Jaru, against themselves or each other, neither holds more merit. Perhaps more important is the question of why it happened right before the power restore... It can't have started on its own—at least one of our people reached the station. Perhaps they're still there?" I left it hanging. "All we can do is document what we find. Minds greater than ours are working on this. We just need to do our part."

"I know." Tom turned back once more to his work. "I guess I don't understand why we're still going to war."

I sighed. "We've still got people out there, Tom, you know that. We have to find them."

"Yeah, I know, but war, I mean that's serious, like more serious than Almoret serious."

"I know, Tom, I know. It'll all come out in the end. It has to. As I said before, we should keep our heads down. Do our bit."

"I wish they'd tell us more about why we're doing this," Tom said. "It would help if we knew what we're looking for, what's important and what's not. I'm an analyst, it's my job to look for patterns. Helps if I have something to aim for. I feel like a well-trained monkey. I wanna get involved with the good stuff, you know?"

"They'll tell us when they're ready. We know more than most."

"More than most is still jack shit," Tom muttered.

I chuckled. Tom flashed a grin. "Yeah, well, you better keep working on learning all you can about jack shit."

Chapter 11

Shadowland

Tanis

"How are you doing?" I asked Jon Sanders, who sat opposite me in the tent, a field scientist whose experience spanned several decades. He had been a friend to my mother for most of that time, and an integral part of our lives. Although he wasn't my biological father, he had willingly filled that role.

He had accompanied my mother, Coco Tanis, on her fateful trip beyond the wall more than thirty years ago when she met my father, Javid. And he'd accompanied me on a different fateful trip outside, which had led to my exile.

Jon had been part of every event that mattered in my life, and would thankfully be part of many more.

"Yeah, I'm good enough," Jon replied. His time in captivity had left him lean, with skin stretched over bone. "You know me. Not one for worrying about the shit I can't control."

I barked out a laugh.

The tent flap was pushed aside, and Tay entered. A member of my personal wolf guard, she was tall, certainly taller than the average Rymorian man, and wore her long dark hair in a single braid. Her hand rested on the hilt of her ever-present sword. "Han wants to speak to you," she said brusquely—she was still pissed about the fish incident and Julant.

I nodded, and she exited.

"I'll leave you to it then," Jon said. He grimaced as he stood and stretched his shoulders out. "What I wouldn't give for a medical scanner."

I watched him leave with a smile, which faded too soon because I had suspicions about why Han wanted to see me. I drank long and deep from my beer before leaning back into my chair and wishing today wasn't the day I needed to start rationing the beer. Supplies were running low, and I wasn't looking forward to them running out.

Five minutes later, Han arrived.

"You need to have another word with him," Han said in his usual measured way. Only the tic thumping in his jaw said all was not well. Han and his younger brother, Danel, were big, stolid section leaders, utterly dry, and eminently calm.

"I put him in your section for a reason," I said. If the unflappable Han couldn't cope with my younger half-brother, Agregor, I would end up dealing with him myself. Enough was going on with Marcus' return. No one trusted him as far as they could throw him, but short of torturing him, which was definitely on the table, it was a case of wait and see.

Then there was Garren and Hannah.

What I didn't need was a young alpha testing his boundaries. At fourteen, Agregor was already almost as tall as Garren with an attitude. He'd spent much of his life at odds with our father and caused no end of trouble at their home fortress, Luka. He couldn't report to

The Warrior in the Shadows

Garren without one of them spilling blood, so I'd put him with Han on a trial basis since leaving the station. Han had been unusually tense ever since.

"I'm going to kill him," Han elaborated with unexpected heat, raking his fingers through his thick thatch of blond hair.

"Better you than me."

Han rolled his eyes.

"What did he do?"

"Fighting. The other man will be out of commission for a week."

I tried not to be impressed, but Agregor *was* only fourteen. "Fine. Send him in."

Han left with a speed that had me reaching for my beer again, only to find it was empty.

"Tay!"

The tent flap opened, but it was a scowling Agregor and not Tay who entered.

Did Han have him waiting outside?

"You wanted to see me?" he mumbled in my general direction.

"I did," I said, noting the color on his cheeks as I rose and rounded my desk.

I let the silence stretch between us until he began to fidget. He wasn't far short of me in height, but unlike Garren, who favored our father, Agregor took his mother's looks with a dominant, hooked nose, hazel eyes, and mid-brown hair. He would be big even for an alpha when he stopped growing, and already showed significant muscle bulk.

I'd had my fill of my father's wayward offspring over the years. Perhaps it was for the best that Agregor was close, where I could keep his insubordination in check before it became a problem.

"It was only a scuffle."

"Han said he won't be fit for duty for a week."

If Agregor had shown any humility or genuine regret, I would have kept this to a discussion, but that cocky grin was far too reminiscent of Garren at his worst. I didn't have the patience to repeat those painful years over again. Garren still tested my patience, even now. Danel's prediction that Garren's relationship with Hannah was a novelty that would wear off was way off the fucking mark. Garren had knotted her despite the risks and was probably still knotting her despite me calling him on it.

I didn't realize I'd punched Agregor in the face until he staggered back.

"What was that for?"

I punched him again, and the last word came out with a squeak.

He now appeared marginally contrite, but a residual glower remained.

"Your father doesn't want you. I recommend you take this opportunity to make a place for yourself in Han's section. Your last chance if you don't want to end up like your older brothers."

"Are you threatening to kill me?"

I smiled. It didn't reach my eyes.

"Logan doesn't follow you," Agregor said, "and he's doing alright."

Logan was between Garren and Agregor in age and had left our father years ago to join a religious sect. I believed Logan to be clinically insane, but he didn't interfere with me, and the mutual avoidance suited us both.

"Logan isn't a thug, and I'm more than happy for him to follow his own path."

"Now I'm a thug?" Agregor demanded.

I punched him a third time—I held nothing back. He landed on his ass with a thud, pinching his bleeding nose.

"Fuck! What the fuck? Seriously!" He continued to mutter and grunt as he got to his feet, scowling at me the whole time.

"Cut the damn language."

"Now I can't swear?" Agregor's voice rose an octave.

"No."

"You swear all the time, and so does Garren."

The Warrior in the Shadows

"I don't need to explain myself to you, and Garren knows when to show respect."

"Garren's a dick. He could beat you if he tried."

The sneer was back. A heartbeat later, I'd fisted Agregor's collar and dragged him so close we were nose to nose.

"Don't tempt me, Agregor. Our father wouldn't mourn your loss any more than he did your other brothers. Garren knows how to lead, but he's not a leader." I gave Agregor a vigorous shake. "I knew more about combat and fighting at eighteen than Garren ever will. I knew more about tactical warfare at eighteen than Garren ever will. That is why Garren follows me, and that is why you will show Han some respect, or our next conversation will be significantly more painful."

He tried to jerk free, but I fisted his throat and took him down to the floor where I pressed my blade against his cheek.

His eyes widened and he froze.

"Don't delude yourself into thinking this will end well for you. It won't. Understood?"

"I... um... yes," he stammered.

I pulled the blade away and dragged my wide-eyed brother to his feet. "Get back to your post and try not to kill anyone or piss off Han for the remainder of the journey."

"I have to defend myself," Agregor said, but there was wary respect. "Everyone knows who my father is—that I'm your half-brother—they always want to make a name by putting me down."

"You could have just said as much," I said. "And there are many ways to disable a man and make him look like a fool without breaking him."

Agregor fidgeted. "Will you teach me?" He rubbed the back of his hand under his nose, which was pink and puffy. "To do that trick you did?" He gestured toward the floor.

I raised an eyebrow. "You want me to teach you to fight so you can use it against me later? That's not how this works."

"I won't," Agregor said, words tumbling out. "I want to be here.

I've wanted it for ages. I—you know—that's how Garren acts, and I thought it was an alpha thing."

That wasn't where I expected this to go... "It's definitely not an alpha thing. Do you see Danel or Han acting like that?"

"Well, no, I guess not."

"Good. Don't copy Garren, he's an asshole and I think about stabbing him most days. I could be persuaded to train you assuming I hear no more complaints from Han."

"You won't!"

I shook my head, failing to hold back my smile this time. "We'll see. I'll send for you in the evenings when I have time. Don't assume it will be every day."

Agregor's broad grin was a marked difference from the scowl that he had brought in with him.

The tent flap burst open, and Garren stormed in. "We need to discuss that tower dweller prick, Marcus," he said without preamble. Seeing our younger brother in the tent, Garren gave him a hard cuff across the back of the head.

"What the actual fuck!" Agregor glared at Garren.

"Heard you're causing trouble again," Garren said, eyeballing Agregor's puffy nose and bloody collar. He grinned. "I see Tanis has been working on your attitude."

"Back to your post, Agregor," I said lest they set about one another in my tent and undo the small progress made. "And remember what I said."

Agregor nodded and, giving Garren the one-finger salute, stalked out of the tent.

"What's gotten into him?" Garren asked, staring after our younger brother.

"Nothing," I said, my amusement at Agregor fading. "Better bring the others here—and find out what beer stocks are left. I've a feeling I'm going to need them tonight."

Chapter 12

Hannah

We reached the Great Northern Road the day after Marcus' dramatic return, and the pace picked up. At the end of the third day, and with the turn toward evening, the great column began to bunch, and we made camp. Garren was called ahead to speak with Tanis, leaving me with Adam and the team. Fires were lit to cook from, and our two tents were erected.

It was my turn to care for the horses. As I was almost finished, and as had happened every evening since his return, Marcus sought me out. I wished I could muster enthusiasm in seeing the missing Rymorian, but we'd never been on friendly terms. For reasons that eluded me, he seemed determined to change that now.

"Your riding has really improved," he said, helping me with the last saddle, whether I wanted him to or not.

All he'd done for the first four weeks of our trip was grunt or scowl at me. I wanted to believe his terrible experience had transformed him for the better, that there was a silver lining to the dark cloud he'd endured, but my sense of charity was in short supply, and his sudden over-enthusiasm to help me only freaked me out.

"Thanks, Marcus. What about you? Feeling better?"

Our words were mundane and awkward. I'd tried to recall a single instance of him speaking to me directly before he ran out on us. After days of deliberation, I was still coming up blank.

"I feel much better, thanks, Hannah," he said, following me as I joined the others where they gathered in front of our tents.

I sat down.

Marcus sat beside me.

I fought back a childish urge to move somewhere else.

Having finished his duties, Red greeted me with an easy smile and Marcus with a nod. I wished tonight's chores had taken longer. Anything would be better than sitting here and suffering this stilted conversation.

"I heard you were redirected to join us?" Marcus asked Red. "How long have you been out here?"

"I've lost track—it must be six months." Red shrugged. "At least. We were at the end of a three-month rotation when we were sent to the transport crash."

"I've no idea what the date is or even the day of the week," I said. Spring was heading into summer, and the air was warm and humid. "I miss my family." I spent so much time worrying about this or that, but the moment I stopped the mechanics of surviving, that loss came crashing back.

"Yeah, I know," Red said. "I try not to think about what my family thinks about me, because whatever it is, it's not good. I try not to think about what next, either. I'm not sure I want to call Rymor home anymore."

"Do you have a large family?" I blurted before I could censor myself. I'd found myself drawn toward Red over the last few days—thinking about him in ways I probably shouldn't, given I was so enthusiastically intimate with Garren.

Something was wrong with me, a burning recklessness invading

The Warrior in the Shadows

me. Sex with Garren had gotten steadily wilder, with an almost compulsive, desperate edge. He knotted more often than he didn't, and I begged, pleaded, and did anything I thought might work in my favor on those occasions when he refused. Tanis' determination that we should be careful only drove me further on. I still wanted Tanis, but now I also wanted Red, the steady beta who had an easy smile and a measured attitude no matter what was happening. I'd caught his eyes several times when we'd had no reason to look at one another. Maybe he was merely curious about the omega, Bill's former partner, or the only woman close at hand.

"My parents, and a younger sister who's at college. I've not lived at home for a while, but I see them off rotation whenever I can. You?"

There was a loaded element to that question, and his eyes searched mine. Was he asking about Bill? "Just an older sister, who warned me not to get involved with Bill. Really wish I'd listened to her—hindsight and all that. My parents passed away when I was a kid. I adore my two nephews. They would have been so upset when I didn't turn up for my birthday."

Red frowned.

"I wasn't allowed to tell anyone where I was going."

"What? Why not?"

I shrugged. "Bill said only he and his personal assistant could know."

"Sounds like bullshit. Is that even legal?"

"Probably not," I admitted, not wanting to acknowledge how stupid I'd been, over and over, where Bill was concerned.

I trusted Red, I realized, in a deep, with-my-life kind of way.

I also thought I trusted Bill, my inner voice cautioned.

Only, had I? From that very first evening, I'd understood Rymor's chancellor had fundamental flaws. At the time, I'd been much enamored with his risk-taking and unorthodox ways, his boldness and charisma. And the sex... I was very much enamored with the sex. Only it had all been a façade, and even the sex had often struck a discordant note. I had been too naïve to know better.

I was still naïve, but at least he'd broken me of one kind of gullibility.

Marcus remained quiet while we talked, and I glanced across to find him lost in thought.

"What do you think is happening in Rymor now the power is back?" I turned to Red.

"No idea. We're on the wrong side of enemy lines, except these people aren't the enemy. I still can't believe Rymor intended to launch a war. It's about as fu-messed up as it gets."

"Please don't censor yourself on my part. I've met Jon Sanders."

Red chuckled as Edward joined us.

"Where is Jon?" Edward asked as he sprawled back against the floor, propped himself on his elbows, and stretched his legs before him.

"He went to speak to Tanis," I said. "Garren took Jon and Adam with him."

"I expect they have plenty to talk about now a bunch of homeless Rymorians are about to turn up at Thale. Everyone knows we're not allowed inside," Edward said. "I'm not expecting a jolly welcome."

"What do you mean not allowed—"

"What about the war?" Marcus cut me off. "I heard there's still going to be a war."

"Where did you hear that?" Red asked, turning a troubled gaze toward Marcus. "The station's operational now, and the barriers are in place. Rymor has no reason to go to war."

"Shadowlanders are going to attack Rymor," Marcus muttered half to himself. "We all know they can't be trusted."

My eyes shifted between Marcus, red-faced and angry, Red's frown, and Edward's slack-jawed surprise.

"I admit, I'm not completely at ease among Shadowlanders," Red said. "Their culture and ways are different from ours. This is your first time out here, so don't judge them too harshly, nor by your own experiences at the hands of the Jaru. I'm still learning, and I've been doing this for years. The reason we're going to Thale worries me

The Warrior in the Shadows

more than the Shadowlanders do. As for war; that makes no sense, and doubly so now the wall is in place. Troubles out here are extreme. They have more than they can comfortably handle with all the Jaru attacks. Even so, they are not a credible threat to Rymor, with or without the wall."

"Well, the Shadowlanders get my vote," Edward leaned up. "Although that crazy bastard in charge scares the shit out of me at times. I can still remember him popping you, Red, back at Julant after you'd withheld info." He slapped one hand down onto the other and smirked. "You were raised to hero status after surviving that punch."

I laughed.

Red chuckled and shook his head. "Not one of my favorite moments, Edward. Thank fuck he pulled the punch."

Daren, one of the two technical masters, interrupted the conversation when he arrived with food. We ate around quiet conversation. All the while, I was thinking about Marcus' words, that there might still be war, and Edward's determination that we were unwelcome at Thale.

"I'm turning in," Daren said, yawning the moment he finished eating.

As he made his way to the tent, Marcus stared after him.

The polite façade Marcus had presented since returning had revealed a few cracks tonight. No one else appeared concerned. Red had brushed the matter off. Neither he nor Edward, now talking about their favorite music, had given Marcus' visceral words credence.

Neither should I.

Yet I did.

Not necessarily the comments about war, but something else about his outburst bothered me. We had never gotten on, and maybe I was struggling to let go of the past. These exhausting times left me unwilling to expend energy making friends with someone I actively didn't like.

"I'm turning in." Marcus stood abruptly, focused so intently upon the tent that he walked as if under a trance.

I watched him leave. I was worn out from the hard riding and the strain of being polite. The sun had faded, and soon everyone would take their rest. I wanted Garren to return, not even for the distraction of intimacy, but because I needed to talk to someone about Marcus.

I should probably have talked to Adam, but I was reluctant to and couldn't even say why.

Edward turned in.

Red went to check the horses for the last time.

Garren didn't return, and neither did Adam. It seemed the matter would have to wait until the morning, and, resigned, I decided to turn in, too.

Chapter 13

Tanis

With the turn toward evening, a couple of lamps had been lit, bringing dull illumination to my tent. From the comfort of my chair, I savored one of the last bottles of beer. At times I missed ready electricity.

At times I missed considerably more.

"Do you want me to send them in now?" Tay asked.

I took a drink of my beer and tried to summon enthusiasm for the discussion to come.

"You've been drinking too liberally of that foul beer you love so much. Perhaps you need a better distraction from all these tower dweller troubles?" Tay said, face perfectly straight.

"No, you had better send them in," I replied with a smile. I'd first met Tay not long after my exile; she had been part of my personal guard since I took control of Thale. I'd been sleeping with her off and on ever since. On any other day, I might have been inclined to make them wait, but I wasn't convinced Garren's burgeoning temper would tolerate any delay.

She smirked and left the tent with the words, "Perhaps later, then, John Tanis."

Only I thought it was unlikely to be later, given all the distractions and my growing obsession with a particular omega.

I didn't want a mate, even assuming I could have one. Breeding was an important part of the equation, and thanks to my exile, I was trapped out here, sterile. If Garren's antics drove her into heat, I thought that I might actually kill him.

My past had set my opinion of women. I didn't hate them, but I didn't trust them either. First, my mother's manipulation, then Ava, the woman who inadvertently became responsible for my exile, had seen to that. My relationship with Tay was convenient, nothing more, and that was the way I preferred things.

I was going around in circles, trying to convince myself that I wouldn't kill Garren, a brother I'd grown to more than merely tolerate, over an omega I barely knew. But I wanted her, and if she went into heat and Garren was still fucking her, there would be blood on the floor.

Heaving a deep breath, I took another drink of beer. I wasn't reckless. I was a leader, and had been pragmatic in my rise to power, and in holding it ever since I'd come to terms with the fact that Shadowland was my forever home. I couldn't offer offspring to an omega, so I'd never sought one beyond mind-blowing sex. I'd rutted a few through their heat, those who were already mated, if their relationships were that way inclined. It was understood an omega had needs, most especially when in heat, but even at other times. There was no fear of entanglement if they were mated. Usually, her alpha would approach me if his omega showed interest.

I enjoyed it. Hell, Danel and Han had fathered half the damn empire. Omegas went weak-kneed and broody when those two entered a settlement.

But I never fucked unmated omegas. I steered well clear because to claim one would be to damn her to a childless life, or to have to

The Warrior in the Shadows

accept another alpha into her nest during heat and know with certainty that it was his child growing in her womb.

I wasn't convinced I could share my omega, no matter what she needed. I'd suffered too many vivid dreams about gutting Garren to trust myself. Maybe if he'd met an omega elsewhere and then returned fully mated and bonded, I could have shared like that as an outsider to their bond during heat, and at other times when they wished.

But not Hannah. She was mine or no one's.

My brooding was interrupted by the arrival of Garren, Adam, Jon, and Javid. A lively discussion ensued about the ongoing Jaru attacks dogging our return.

"Despite warnings not to drift from the column, we lost two men earlier today," Garren said.

"I lost a dozen horses last night when a night guard fell asleep," Javid muttered. "If the idiot hadn't been killed, I'd have run him through myself."

"They didn't scatter back to their lands as I hoped," I said. "Their warlord is now reforming his camp according to scouts."

"I've reissued warnings," Garren said. He glanced over his shoulder as the tent flap opened and Kein, my best scout, entered. "But I'm more concerned about that tower dweller prick Marcus."

"He concerns me, too," Adam said. "But what can we do?" Adam was the only person inside the tent still inclined to give Marcus the benefit of the doubt. Jon appeared to favor Garren's assessment, and I wasn't far behind.

"Kill him." Javid provided his personal assessment with all his usual aplomb. It elicited a soft chuckle from Garren and left no doubt about which side of the kill or don't kill fence he sat on.

Javid had remained with his own men for most of the trip, which I was grateful for. While I appreciated that my father's presence at the station had been critical to the battle's success, I could only spend so much time in his company before the strain started to show. As a child, I'd assumed Jon Sanders was my father. At some point, it dawned on me that I looked nothing like him.

It was only years later, when I changed, that I realized my father was a Shadowlander, and when questioned, my mother confessed.

I met Javid five years ago when I went to war with him. My mother had never mentioned my father by name, or that he was a fortress leader. Jon had stepped in with that revelation when he feared I might kill him. The subsequent peace agreement with Javid had an edgy aspect. That my father was under my command was a tenuous affair. He suffered no qualms about challenging decisions he disagreed with.

I'd slugged my father more than once during the early days of our truce. Wrong in Rymor. Normal out here. Those explosive encounters had instilled begrudging respect from Javid toward me, his eldest son. I believed that nothing less would have worked.

It was a little fucked-up, I reflected, but fucked-up had been working so far.

"I agree with Garren, Marcus is a threat," I said. "We just don't know what form that threat will take. But it's your decision, Adam." I wasn't sure why I was leaving control of this with him. My gut told me to end Marcus, but while circumstances might have been exceptional, this was still a Rymor matter.

Then there were the other concerns under frequent discussion. My gut also told me that Bill wouldn't let slide an opportunity for war. The station might be operational, but while Adam and his team remained in Shadowland, and were therefore missing, they might also be used as the spark. None of them wanted to return, which I understood and supported. Personal relationships aside, if Bill wanted them dead and/or out the way, keeping them alive was likely of strategic importance.

The drama surrounding Marcus was simplistic compared to whatever the fuck Bill was up to—kill him or keep him—yet despite days of discussion, neither option had gained more weight.

I'd spoke to Marcus when he first returned, but he'd been

The Warrior in the Shadows

severely beaten at the time, and I'd gotten nothing useful out of the exchange. I'd told Garren to take him back to his people. Perhaps it was time for another more in-depth conversation?

"He's been broken," Kein said with uncanny clarity, smoothing fingers down the side of his long drooping mustache.

I sighed. "Yes, I fear you're right." There was the unequivocal truth that my gut was warning me about.

I watched Adam's brows pinch together. He was an experienced field scientist, stable and tough enough to hold his own out here. But he was also a good man and out of his depth. He knew what needed to be done but didn't have the stomach for it. Shadowland had degenerated into borderline anarchy. There was a real possibility of war with both the Jaru and Rymor. Now wasn't the time to take the moral high ground.

"Jon?" I asked. He had been silent tonight, but I wanted all opinions on the table.

"Someone has gotten to Marcus, you know it, Adam," Jon said. "Maybe even before he left Rymor. You said he was acting odd the whole trip. And then for him to bail out on you at Julant? Doesn't matter how or why they targeted him; we need to decide what to do about it."

"That doesn't mean he will follow through. He's back with us now." Adam's sigh held weight. "I don't know why I'm defending him. I agree with everything you've said. I just can't approve killing him, and while only Javid has openly suggested it, I know that's what you all think."

"I think he's going to try and take Hannah," Garren said. "He's always following her or talking to her. My fingers itch to beat the little shit. Maybe I should, then we'd find out why he's here."

Jon snorted. "Let Garren at him, at least then we'll know."

Adam nodded, his face drawn. "I can't think of an alternative. And I agree, we need answers."

"Good," Javid said decisively. "About time."

"Garren can handle it," I said. "Marcus may not be the same

when he's done, but we'll all be a little wiser. Several groups are following us, and they may be part of whatever Marcus is here for. Someone ordered your deaths, and while I cannot see Marcus doing it alone, continuing to watch him, rather than taking action, maintains the risk."

"Unfortunately, he's done nothing to raise suspicion—apart from talking to people. He was a miserable bastard before." Adam seemed resigned at last. "How will we do this?"

"First, we'll talk to him. What happens next will depend on his response," I said. "He may be more forthcoming than you think."

"You don't believe that, though?" Adam asked.

I shook my head. "He would have to provide compelling information for us to stop. Our actions may not be justified. He may be nothing more than a fool who fled and subsequently happened upon our path."

Adam stared at the forgotten drink in his hand. "If we get this wrong, someone is going to die."

"The thirty-fourth rule of Rymorian warfare. If you cannot implicitly trust, then the subject is a threat. You always eliminate the threat... I've found it a very useful rule during my time in Shadowland. It has saved my life more than once. Other people, not so much."

"I only remember the first five," Jon said. "How many rules are there?"

"Fifteen thousand and ninety-two," I replied.

"That's a lot of rules." Javid raised an eyebrow. "You tower dwellers have a strange fascination with rules. How many do you know?"

"All of them."

"Bullshit." Jon gave me a flat look.

I shrugged, fighting a smile.

"There are fifty-seven rules," Adam said. "Seriously, Jon, did you not study military history? And I don't think any of us can claim to

The Warrior in the Shadows

trust Marcus, implicitly or otherwise. It's getting late. When will we do this?"

"Now," was Garren's immediate response.

"A trying night then," Javid said. "I've nothing to offer here that you don't have ample skills for, and I've some issues to deal with. Your younger brother has gotten himself into trouble again. Almost glad for the distraction of that little Jaru skirmish."

Garren laughed as Javid rose. "I think Tanis already sorted it out."

"Excellent." Javid grinned. "I'll leave you to your fun."

"Jon, Adam, it would be better if you're present, but you don't need to be," I said as my father pushed out the tent flap.

Adam wore the haggard bearing of a man delivered into his own personal hell. "I need to hear what he says. There's no way back from this, is there?"

"No, Adam, I'm afraid not."

At a commotion outside, all faces turned toward the tent flap. I felt the kick of adrenaline. Garren, perhaps heightened to alertness by the conflicts surrounding Marcus, was the first out of the tent. We followed on his heels.

Alid, Garren's second, pushed his way through the gathering crowd, along with five of his men, dragging a much smaller beta man whose face was bloody and swollen. He thrust the beaten man to the ground before us.

Marcus?

"Two of the tower dwellers are dead, and another is injured. We've sent Yan to heal the injured one," Alid said.

"Hannah?" Garren asked.

"Missing," Alid said. "No one knows where she is."

Chapter 14

Tanis

Garren's jaw was locked tight, and his eyes were filled with rage.

I never expected Marcus to kill. Two dead and Hannah missing—we had all fucked up.

"I've sent a dozen men to search," Alid said.

Catching my nod, Kein left at a swift jog.

"This one said he knows nothing." Alid gave Marcus a nudge with his boot. "I cannot see how she could have been taken, but if she has been, she cannot be far."

Garren muttered a curse under his breath. "Stay with Marcus." He stabbed a finger in my general direction and took off running. I'd envied him for having Hannah, but now I saw the greater consequences. He was halfway to bonded with her, heat or not, his focus was laser sharp. If she was dead, it would destroy him. I still envied him, but I also pitied him.

Jon's face was a grim mask, but Adam looked broken as he followed after Garren. The deaths and Hannah's disappearance weren't Adam's fault, but I could see that he would blame himself.

The Warrior in the Shadows

It was my fault.
I took a deep breath and focused on the matter before me.
Alid waiting for my order.

I also wanted to search, even knowing Garren could handle it. Instead, I was left dealing with Marcus and fighting a strong desire to beat the shit out of him. That would be of questionable benefit in the short term—Alid had obviously already given that a good go.

Aware that people were waiting for my instructions, I unclenched my fist.

Alid gave me a wary look before handing over a thin cord. "He killed them as they entered the tent. The third tower dweller interrupted the second kill, and he raised the alarm."

We'd searched him for weapons when he first arrived, but the fine cord was effective and easily hidden. "Find us somewhere to question him privately," I said. Alid hauled Marcus to his feet. "Strip him in case he has anything else hidden."

The men about Alid were swift to assist. I turned to Jon. "You better check on your people. I'll see if Marcus knows anything about Hannah. When Yan is done there send him over—I don't want Marcus dying before I decide."

Jon nodded, and he rubbed his brow with shaking fingers. "That's a Rymorian weapon, isn't it? They don't make cord so fine or strong out here."

"Yes." I gave the garrote an experimental tug. "What else have the bastards brought out here?"

"Too much," Jon said before heading after Adam and Garren.

∽

Hannah

"What the fuck are you doing here?"
I jumped, my heart lodging in my throat at Garren's roar.

Snatched from my feet before I could gather my wits, I was crushed against the wall of his chest.

He was holding me too tight, his purr manic. I could barely breathe, yet his palpable fear for me pummeled me far harder.

Setting me away as fast as he'd dragged me close, he checked me with feverish hands for imaginary damage.

My heart was hammering in my chest as I tried to process his reaction.

"I-I needed some air. Some alone time. I'm sorry." Memories resurfaced of Tanis' fury when I'd wandered off at Julant. Only this was a thousand times worse, and Garren wasn't even shouting at me.

"Alone time!" he roared.

Okay, the shouting had begun.

"I ought to spank your fucking ass until you can't sit for a week. Only thank fuck you weren't in that tent."

He picked me up, turned and stalked back to the camp. I clung to him, feeling his hands shaking where they held me, and the wild purr vibrating in his chest.

"Ah, you've found her! Thank god! Hannah are you all right?"

"I-yes?" I turned, wriggling to get down when I saw Adam's ashen face. "What's happened?"

Garren growled at my wriggling, but he set me down only to plant a possessive arm around my waist and haul my back to his chest.

Jon and Red were right behind Adam. Red looked from me to Garren and raked a hand through his short hair.

"I'm sorry, Hannah," Adam said. "Marcus—he—" I shook my head, the malaise crawling over me, making my skin prickle. "Daren and Edward are dead. Marcus killed them both. Had you gone into the tent, he would have killed you too."

My world imploded. My legs lost all ability to hold me, and a terrible sound erupted from my chest. Garren went down with me, hauling me against him and holding me close while my horror delivered tears.

The Warrior in the Shadows

Not Edward, so young and happy, always teasing, barely begun life.

Not Daren, so brilliant, surviving the capture and escaping, only to be taken away forever.

"I need to go," Garren said gruffly.

Clinging to him, I cried harder.

"I need to find out who the fuck he's working for and remove the threat."

I didn't want him to go, had to be pried away so he could hand me over to Red. With a growl and a barked order to his guards to not let me out of their sight, he left.

"I need to go, too," Adam said. "I need to hear what he says. I'll update you as soon as I can." Then he was leaving, along with Jon, disappearing through the trees.

"They captured Marcus," Red said as he sat me down near the base of a tree.

At least twenty heavily armed alphas surrounded us at a discreet distance.

Three things became apparent to me as tears streamed down my cheeks, and I came to terms with what had happened.

One: Tanis hadn't lied when he said nowhere was safe.

Two: I'd never trusted Marcus, but I trusted my instincts less. I'd known something was wrong, but I'd ignored it, and now people were dead.

Three: Garren's feelings toward me and mine toward him had shifted at some point. He was so much more than a passing alpha I was exploring pleasure with. He was important in a way I'd never felt before. And I didn't know what that meant beyond understanding that my heart was already all in.

Only that lives had just been destroyed and nothing would be the same again.

Tanis

I found Marcus waiting in a poorly lit tent, kneeling on the floor with his hands tied behind his back. The tent was empty of anything other than two of Garren's men who stood watching the captive, a few crates to one side, and a single lantern that cast weak light. I grabbed a crate and placed it with a deliberate thud a few feet from where Marcus knelt, then I sat down. I was unmoved by his plight and determined to have my answers.

Marcus shrank back, only to find the two Shadowland soldiers behind him.

I rested my forearms on my thighs, leaned a little closer, and asked, "Where's Hannah?"

Marcus stared at the dirt floor. "I don't know."

"I suggest you start talking before Garren returns." *Or he doesn't, which will be much worse for you.*

Marcus glanced up before snatching his gaze away.

"I need to know where she is."

"I don't know!"

"I don't believe you." I didn't realize my fingers had closed around his throat until he made a choking sound. "Don't piss me off right now."

The rush of the tent flap opening was all the warning I got before Garren barreled in. I blocked him—just. "Don't. Kill him!" *I can do that part all by myself.*

Garren glared at me. "I wasn't going to kill him." He stepped back.

I gave him a—*yes, of course you weren't*—look as the tent flap opened again to admit Jon and Adam.

"I was only going to punch him."

Caught unprepared, I could only watch as Garren's fist smashed into Marcus' face. Marcus landed in a heap on the floor, his weak groan indicating he was still alive.

Garren's shrug was innocent. "Hannah's fine. She had wandered

The Warrior in the Shadows

off for some alone time." He rolled his eyes and muttered, "Fucking alone time."

I raised my eyebrows, and a disbelieving snort escaped me. Someone needed to have another chat with her about safety.

In the background, the two silent members of Garren's section dragged Marcus to his knees. "What happened?"

"Two people, he killed two," Adam said. He stood at the edge of the tent, lost in the shadows. "Daren, one of the technical masters, and Edward." He rubbed his fingers across his face and let out a tired sigh.

My troubled gaze shifted to Marcus. We needed answers, to learn of his plans, and who he worked for. Only he'd already been broken by someone else, and I wasn't convinced he'd survive long enough to be useful.

The tent flap opened once more to admit Yan.

"Better check him before we start," Garren muttered without enthusiasm.

Marcus cringed away from the little healer as if fearing Yan was about to begin the torture himself.

Yan set about prodding and probing his head, neck, and jaw with his usual efficiency before working his way down. He stood with a nod, his expectant glance shifting between Garren and me.

"Make yourself comfortable, Yan," I said.

"I don't know anything." Marcus' voice wavered.

"So, you decided to kill two of your own, for no reason?" Garren demanded. He cuffed Marcus around the side of his head. "You're going to die, Marcus. It's your decision how much pain comes first." Garren leaned down and caught a fist full of his hair.

"They told me I had to. They said they'd kill me—I thought they'd kill me." Blood dripped from Marcus' nose and temple, and his breathing turned choppy.

"We figured that part out." Garren released his hair and cuffed him a little harder. "When and where?"

"After I ran. They found me. They said they'd take me home, but they lied." His words tumbled fast and furious. "I don't want to die. I didn't want to do it!"

The smack of Garren's palm connecting with Marcus' jaw echoed through the otherwise quiet tent. Marcus collapsed. Garren's men dragged him back to his knees, where he coughed and swayed. "They said they'd find me and kill me if I didn't."

He began to sob. It was a pitiful sight, tears, snot, and blood dripping. Unfortunately for Marcus, no one in the tent cared.

"How could they kill you when you're the only one in the camp? Or are there more of you?" Garren hit him again, an open-handed slap across his bloody face.

I winced.

Adam stepped out of the shadows. "I don't believe it happened then. Someone approached you in Rymor, didn't they, Marcus? Maybe even before you joined the field scientists." His face twisted with repulsion. "I know it happened in Rymor. You were never part of our team. We all knew it." He drew another shaky breath, and dark emotions glittered in his eyes.

Then he was on Marcus. The smack of fists meeting flesh and the thud of hard boots filled the tent, interspersed by Marcus' terrorized cries and Adam's snarls of fury.

"Why the hell did you do it? Why, Marcus? Why?"

I shook my head when the two guards looked at me askance, deciding to let this play out. Jon and Garren remained impassive. But this wasn't Adam. Marcus had driven a good man to a sordid place. Not that Marcus was wholly responsible when he was merely another pawn.

Marcus begged and sobbed as he drew himself into a tight fetal position on the floor that offered little protection from Adam's savage attack.

I motioned to the guards, who pulled Adam off. He strained against their hold, chest heaving and tears streaming down his face.

"Enough!" I snapped, relieved when the fight finally left Adam.

Yan stepped over to assess the damage.

The Warrior in the Shadows

Marcus moaned and tried to drag himself further into a ball. "They told me I was helping Rymor!" He flinched away from Yan's hands. Not to be thwarted, Yan motioned the two guards to pull the protesting Marcus up.

He screamed like he was still being beaten.

"What a racket," Garren muttered. "If we didn't need to question him, I'd gag the bastard before I beat him to death."

"The ribs are bruised, the lower two might be broken," Yan said. "Avoid it if you want him to live."

I nodded. Marcus was back on his knees, slumped over.

I picked up the crate, knocked aside by Adam's attack, and hauled up the resisting captive to sit him on it as he screamed and begged for mercy.

"Kill him already," Garren said, losing his patience.

"You're not fucking helping," I said. "Shut up or get out of the fucking tent."

He glared at me, chest heaving before nodding and stepping back.

"Marcus, you need to tell us what you know if you want this to end." I drew Marcus' head up and tapped the side of his face until I had his attention. "This hasn't gone well for you. It will go worse if you don't talk." He was a wreck, and I needed him to focus. "You know Yan as our healer. He helped Adam recover after the Jaru attack when we first met. Yan also knows a great deal about pain without death. Do you need Yan to help you to remember who sent you here?"

"No! God no," Marcus pleaded, bloody face contorted with swelling. One eye had swelled shut, but the other was filled with terror as it turned toward Yan.

Yan was the furthest thing from a torturer in the tent, but Marcus didn't know that. Although some of the things he did to save you felt like torture. Yan blinked back at me. He knew better than to offer an opinion at this point, but would be sure to remind me when I was in a more vulnerable position that he preferred not to be involved with interrogations.

"The man in charge is called Karry," Marcus said around thick, bloody lips. "That's all I know. He said he was working for the intelligence service, and that I'd been selected."

Garren's disparaging snort brought an inward smile. "I don't think Garren believes you're selection material, Marcus. What does Karry look like?"

Marcus tried to pull away, but I tightened my grip on his jaw. "I need you to focus on what's happening, Marcus, on where you are. No one is coming to rescue you. You're here alone because no one else can get into the camp, and you have killed two of your men. Now, what does Karry look like?" I kept my voice calm, which was hard when all I wanted to do was start banging Marcus' head enthusiastically into the ground.

His chest heaved. I was losing his focus again.

"You have seconds to start talking before I hand you over to Garren."

"He's in his fifties, slim, he's a little shorter than me, black hair," the words spilled out. "He's from the eastern province, he has their accent."

"Any other people? Other names?"

"No one used their real names. I'm not even Marcus. My real name is David Renner." He broke down, his final words punctuated by sobs. "Oh God, I'm never going home!"

Releasing him, I leaned back. "No, you're not."

"We're wasting our time," Jon said heatedly. "This gives us nothing. We have nothing."

"We have plenty," Adam said, his tone bleak.

"It would be nice to know the source, but it was always a long shot." I studied the pitiful sight that was Marcus, David, or whoever the fuck he was. "I think I'll leave the rest to you, Garren. Find out how he was to let them know after it was done, and then deal with it."

"My pleasure." Garren's grin had a sadistic edge to it.

The Warrior in the Shadows

Marcus began to babble and beg again.

"Get something to shut him up," Garren said. One of his men disappeared out of the tent as Marcus' pleading took on a hysterical edge.

"Wait, PLEASE! I can be useful! I can tell you about the war!"

I stopped, and silence settled over the tent as I turned slowly back to Marcus. "War?"

Marcus swallowed, and his one open eye was nervous as it landed on me. "That's why they sent me back. Karry's boss was furious. Said Rymor was already mobilizing. Weapons and soldiers to crush Shadowland once and for all. They're going to Thale. Going to reduce it to a pile of rubble and break the Shadowlanders for good."

I offered nothing.

Marcus began to talk into the vacant space, spilling every tiny detail his desperate mind could recall. He didn't know much, guesses and rumors, but there were enough pieces to draw disturbing conclusions. The dialogue continued into the night and early morning. Eventually, it became apparent he had exhausted the useful information, and the tales gained an elaborateness that suggested he had begun to conjure new truths. Perhaps realizing his error, he lapsed into silence.

"I'm going to get some rest," I said at length. Beyond the tent, the sky had lightened. I had a lot to reflect on. We all did.

"Yeah, we're done," Garren said, scrubbing a tired hand down his face. "Gag him." He motioned to the guard, who stuffed a rag in Marcus' mouth to the prisoner's hoarse protests. "What do you want us to do with him?"

"He may offer more after a break, or further embellishment. I don't think he has any more revelations in him." I shrugged. "It's your call. As far as I'm concerned, he's dead."

Chapter 15

Hannah

A ll I kept thinking was I'd known that something was wrong but I'd ignored it.
Daren and Edward were dead, and I felt as responsible as if I'd made the killing blow.

I sat beneath the trees a short distance from the tents where Garren had left me. It was another hot day, the sun sending little splashes of light through gaps in the canopy to dapple me in a warmth that didn't penetrate my soul. Red stood watchfully nearby but made no attempt to engage me in conversation. He had told me a dozen times that this wasn't my fault. I still hated myself.

My mind offered the image of waves crashing, cold and relentless. The waves brought death and sorrow. They brought terrible memories.

Edward was gone. It seemed unreal, more unreal than anything else.

I should be accustomed to this crazy by now—I wasn't.

Garren had returned to me briefly in the early hours of the morning. He had about him that rumpled look of a man who'd taken no

The Warrior in the Shadows

sleep. I'd not done more than doze myself, allowing Red to comfort me at times, only to push him away; because people were dead, and I didn't feel worthy.

Garren had told me that Marcus was still being questioned. I didn't want the details, and he hadn't offered anything more.

I was exhausted, yet sleep was out of the question when I couldn't even sit still for more than a few minutes. Edward's death might not be the first, but it was worse to die at the hands of one of our own people, especially after surviving so much. He had brought lightness to dark moments. He had been a good man, and now he was gone.

I didn't remember the loss of my parents. Thinking about them was like viewing something from a distance, like I was missing something, but didn't understand exactly what. I had hated the sea ever since. This new pain was raw and inescapable. Edward had been part of my life for months, every hour of every day.

Adam came to talk to me. I asked him to leave me alone.

Garren came yet again and told me he was leaving. I couldn't meet his eyes.

"Don't do this now, Hannah. I need to fucking go." I could hear the exasperation in his voice, but I was sinking in on myself. Crouching down in front of me, he caught hold of my chin. "It's not your fucking fault."

I shook my head, stupid tears pooling in my eyes. He kissed me, and for that brief moment, I could almost forget, and then he rose, said something terse to Red, and strode away.

I felt twice as alone.

Red gave me a look of disapproval.

"I have plenty of guards. I don't need another one," I snapped.

"Hannah." There was a warning in his voice.

I was being unkind. I knew it, but I couldn't work out how to stop.

Eyes closed, I rested my head against the tree, determined to wallow in my misery.

Which was working fine until a shadow passed over me, and looking up, I found Tanis looming. A glance past him confirmed Red slipping away; leaving me alone, save for the discreet guards, with someone I wanted to avoid at all costs. Threatening to kill him, and the subsequent kiss, had both left an imprint, albeit in very different ways.

"Garren seems to think I can talk some sense into you. Not sure where his sudden faith in me has come from, but Garren doesn't express such opinions often, so I thought I'd humor him."

I blinked up at him. "I don't want to talk to anyone."

"Yes." He sighed. "I'm aware of that."

"I don't want to talk to Adam, Red, or Garren, and I definitely don't want to talk to you." I winced as the words spilled out. Last time I'd accused him of being a criminal breaking into the station. Later, I learned that Adam had let him in. Not only did I threaten to shoot him, but I'd also insulted him. My brain had no filter around Tanis.

"Thanks. That cleared any misconceptions about why Garren asked me to speak to you," he said dryly. "You know you can't wander off alone, but for once I'm glad you did."

If I hadn't, it would be me lying dead and not Edward, or maybe both of us.

I tried to ignore Tanis, staring at the ground, hoping he would take the hint.

He didn't, and I reluctantly lifted my eyes.

He had a strong, dominating presence. They called it the warrior gene out here, but in Rymor, they were known as alphas. Shadowlanders came in all shapes and sizes, including omegas, and a large beta population. But the alphas were always significantly more powerful and, as might be expected, made up most of the garrison ranks. He was tall, solid, dressed in a combination of plate and leather armor, and carried himself like he was ready for war.

He *was* ready for war, as I'd witnessed during our very first meeting where he'd killed a Jaru poised to strike me down. Afterward, he'd dragged me to a safer location, his pace never faltering

The Warrior in the Shadows

despite my frantic struggle and the stream of Jaru assailants. My understanding of the world changed that day.

Tanis reminded me of the difference between the two parts of Serenity. He belonged here. I did not.

To my frustration, he sat opposite me and propped his back against a nearby tree. "It's lucky for you that Garren's been so preoccupied."

I was sure either Garren and Adam would have dealt with my actions considerably harsher, but Garren had been, as Tanis said, preoccupied, and Adam had been barely conscious of anything except the deaths. Garren had threatened to spank me. I wished that he had. I wished there was a physical outlet for my grief, because any pain was better than this mental entropy that left me delirious, without reason or logical thought. "I don't want to talk about it."

"I know."

"I don't understand why you're still here."

"Me neither."

He stared back at me in that unwavering way of his as my emotions bounced between exasperation, distress, and interest.

The fiasco at the station weeks ago when I pointed a PB gun at him still plagued me at unexpected times. The kiss made me feel slick and urgent.

I wasn't comfortable around him. He was stunningly handsome, had spent significant parts of his life killing people, and had an abrasive personality. The second two generally made me forget about the first, until times like this when it caught me unawares, and I found myself mesmerized.

If he started being nice to me, I would be a lost cause.

"It's not your fault."

"I know that." The urge to cry was sharp and sudden, and I turned away from his scrutiny.

"Do you?"

My head snapped up. "What is this, some kind of psychoanalysis? I get enough of that from my sister. Don't even try that with me."

Only it *was* my fault, my inner critic disputed.

"So, not only does your sister see right through Bill, but also gives you a hard time when you're feeling sorry for yourself."

I wasn't feeling sorry for myself.

"A great pity I'll never meet her," he continued. "I'm sure she could give me some fascinating insights—particularly on your desire to shoot me right before you kissed me." His lips tugged up in a smirk. "Did you tell Garren that we kissed?"

"Yes."

His smirk shifted toward a broad grin. Oh, that amused him, did it?

The emotion pinball slammed about inside me, lighting up different sectors so fast that my head started to swim. A surge of anger gave way to alarm at the idea of him talking to my sister. I could imagine them shaking their heads as my internal fears and quirks were laid bare to their assessment.

I never could hide them from Ella.

He chuckled, and the sound brought a sense of normality. "That must have found a mark. So is your sister opinionated, intuitive, or does she just know you very well?"

"She's a psychologist," I said. "And she knows me." In all my glorious, troubling detail.

There was something in his comments, his tone, as if Tanis also knew me, when he didn't, and he couldn't. Yet as unlikely as it seemed, when we'd barely spoken, I did feel like he knew me.

"What made your sister become a psychologist?"

"Our parents died." I wondered at the merits of telling him the truth, and why I hadn't offered a lie. The door was open now, his earlier playfulness gone, leaving an indefinable expression on his face. "I was seven when it happened. I don't remember much about them, but Ella was ten years older, and the loss was harder on her. Afterward, we stayed with relatives who didn't really want us. I became reserved. I think I'd always been that way, but their deaths made me more so. She worried about me—a lot. Ella always wanted

The Warrior in the Shadows

to understand people and to help them if she could, but I think she chose to become a psychologist, at least partially, because she wanted to help me. I feel lucky to have her. I miss her."

"I can appreciate that."

"She has two boys, who are four and six, and an amazing husband. I miss them all so much. I wish we hadn't argued before I left."

"Last conversations have a way of plaguing us. She sounds like the sort of person who would be able to put an argument into perspective."

I felt hollow suddenly. "Ella told me she didn't want me to stay with Bill. Said she couldn't watch me with him. She asked me to choose between my family and him." Saying it out loud made the wound deeper. I hadn't told anyone about it and felt relieved to let it out.

"A little forceful for a psychologist?" He raised an eyebrow. "I think I would have taken a more subtle approach... like beating the shit out of him."

My laughter startled me. "That's subtle?"

He smiled. "Well, it's subtle for me. She was right. You know that now, don't you?"

My smile faded. I didn't want to talk about Bill—not today. "I don't know what to think."

"You should do." His eyes glittered with anger. "You should be crystal clear by now. He was once my friend, my best friend, to be exact. We came traveling in Shadowland together. I was eighteen at the time. He had reached his majority, barely."

My shock must have shown because he shrugged.

"I was big for my age. We used unorthodox means. Jon Sanders came with us at first."

"What happened between you?" I was drawn into it now. Confused that they had once been friends.

"What happened is a long story, and I think you've had enough trauma for one day. Let's just say he enjoyed the freedom Shadowland offered a little too much. He changed. We both did, I suppose... I'm not a good person, Hannah, don't delude yourself that I am because I can sit here and talk with a measure of concern. I have principles, sure, but of my own making. And I've made mistakes, some of them too deplorable to be forgiven or forgotten. There are degrees to wrongness, though, and in that respect, Bill belongs in a category of his own. I nearly killed him. I still wish that I had. If Jon hadn't been there, if he hadn't reminded me that we'd once been friends, hadn't told me that I shouldn't have this on my conscience, then, I believe, I would have... I let Jon take him back to Rymor. I stayed here. Bill has been sending people to try and kill me ever since. Make no mistake, if I ever meet him again, I won't hesitate to finish the job."

His insights left me confused about the rift between them. It felt like a wall had risen, not just between Bill and me, but between Tanis and me.

"I blame myself—about Marcus, and Edward's death."

"I know you do," he said, and his soft tone brought a stinging weight to the back of my eyes.

"I should have said something yesterday. He was acting odd. I knew it. I don't know why I didn't. I wish I had."

"It's not your fault, Hannah. We all knew there was something wrong. We were watching him and discussing him every night. Garren wanted to skin him the first day. As your leader, Adam couldn't condone the death of one of his team. However much you blame yourself, Adam blames himself more. He's not the only one. I could have ordered Marcus be removed, killed, or questioned. Ultimate accountability lies with me."

Tears pooled in my eyes. We had all been foolish, and I felt instant empathy for Adam in making an impossible choice. As for Tanis, he had no blame here.

"This is Bill's fault. Don't forget that. Marcus is another victim, as are all the Rymorians stuck out here. Bill won't stop until he gets what he wants, and now he's sending people to kill you. Then there's the war."

The Warrior in the Shadows

"War?"

"According to Marcus, Rymor is still very much on the path to war. He could be lying."

"But you don't think he is?" It wasn't really a question. That he had mentioned it meant he believed it.

"Yes, I believe him, and I believe that Bill is behind it."

I was still raw at the loss of Edward and Daren, and for Luke, who had died many weeks ago. But the war was something even worse. I wanted to believe that Marcus was lying, but his earlier comments played back in my mind. "He mentioned the war to us last night. It didn't make sense at the time. He seemed to think the Shadowlanders were about to launch a war against Rymor. Perhaps that's the excuse they're using."

"He told us the same."

Marcus' story was consistent, if nothing else. Rymor had a reason for the war, at least a reason they would be telling the masses about. The deaths I'd witnessed were sad. They didn't deserve that kind of ending. Yet war was death many times over.

I was grateful that Tanis had come to talk to me, and in his unique way, for allowing me to put some of my personal guilt to rest.

"What has happened to Marcus? Is he... Is he dead?" I wasn't sure why I was asking, or whether I wanted to know.

"No, but before we move out, he will be. As much as I feel he deserves to be held accountable to the people of Rymor for his actions, it's too dangerous to keep him alive. He's working with others, and we need to find them so we can question them, given we are about to find ourselves in the middle of a war."

He stood and motioned to someone behind me. I stood to meet, not Red, as I expected, but a slight, sandy-haired man.

"Hannah, meet Kein." He indicated the man whose calm expression immediately put me at ease. Unlike the beards more prevalent in Shadowland, Kein wore a long mustache drooping to either side of his mouth. "Kein is a scout. He will know what to do should any trouble arise. Garren is leaving to look for Marcus' associates, and, in his absence, Kein will remain with you. Never leave him, and do as he says. I trust Kein, so does Garren, and so should you."

I regarded the man, who wasn't much taller than me.

He bowed, brief and formal, but his lips twitched with a smile when he straightened.

"Will the Rymorians stay together?" I asked, worried he might intend to separate us again. I'd been rude to both Adam and Red and wanted a chance to apologize.

"They'll be riding with you and Kein. When Garren leaves he'll take some of his section, and those that remain will report to Kein in his absence."

I passed a critical eye over Kein. He was not an obvious replacement for Garren.

Tanis smirked like he was reading my mind. "Let's say both men command respect, via slightly different means."

Embarrassment flooded my face with heat.

"We'll be leaving later this morning. Try and get some rest before then if you can."

I nodded, and he turned to leave. I felt his dismissal, my shoulders suddenly heavy.

"Do you think Garren will find them? The people Marcus was working with?"

Tanis stopped, and when he turned back, his expression was guarded. "Honestly, I don't think so, but we should still try."

He nodded at Kein and walked away.

I watched him leave. I didn't want the truth today. I wanted lies. I wanted to know that everything would be fine, and everything would work out.

When I dragged my eyes from Tanis' retreating form, I found myself the subject of Kein's watchful gaze.

"It doesn't cross his mind to consider your feelings. He doesn't often consider people as individuals. It is hard to see the few or the one, when you are so focused on the many."

The Warrior in the Shadows

He put his arm out to indicate the way and I fell in step beside him. "Am I that obvious?"

"Yes."

Great! I caught Kein's swift grin. The man was about as diplomatic as Tanis. In other words, he wasn't diplomatic at all. "I know, Kein, and I'm grateful. Tanis has treated the Rymorians well. Given everything that had happened, I would understand if he was less inclined to." It was hard for me to reconcile that he ruled over everything outside. How fortunate for us that he cared for Jon and that their friendship extended to include the field scientists and, therefore, also me. "It was kind of Tanis to talk to me." There was something about Kein's unassuming presence I liked. Tanis thought highly of him. I was grateful that Tanis had considered my well-being to allocate an important scout to watch over me.

"Kind, yes." He still looked amused.

"What?"

He shrugged, which further baffled me.

"Shadowlanders are not often so open a book. It's fortunate that Tanis doesn't notice what you are thinking when you look at him."

Why did I feel like we were having two conversations? And what do I think about when I look at Tanis? I thought frantically.

Mostly anger and a lot of irritation—mostly a lot of things.

Only I knew what I thought about. It was all I ever thought about around him.

"You may be his for now, but you were always mine."

Maybe he'd forgotten he said it. Maybe they were only words intended to mess with me...or Garren. Tanis not noticing my feelings had to be a good thing. "You think Tanis doesn't notice?"

And now Kein was openly grinning. "You're now concluding that I was only trying to make you feel better. The truth is, I was speculating. I'm not speculating anymore."

It appeared that Kein was worse than my sister!

"I'm not sure I want you speculating or concluding, or anything else." I sounded defensive, not that it mattered when Kein was clearly very astute.

As we reached the tent, Kein indicated the flap. "I've been watching you for a while, Hannah Duvaul. You are interesting. Get some rest, and I promise I'll keep future speculation to myself."

I scrubbed my hands over my face and headed inside. I definitely didn't need his conclusions; thankfully, I was exhausted enough to finally sleep.

Chapter 16

Rymor

Richard Dance, personal advisor to William Bremmer

I hadn't seen much of Bill over the last couple of weeks, but I'd been busy with supporting activities related to the war at his behest, and only a chance cancellation left an opportunity for me to accommodate Dan Gilmore's meeting request.

As an advisory member of the Senate, my office was away from the humdrum of State Tower and located in the much more civilized financial quarter. I had several sidelines, including board positions, and it suited my principles to keep myself separate from the rest of the political posturing.

My love of the high life and the impact of four marriages kept greater career aspirations at bay. Yet, events had drawn me into the political spotlight too much of late. While I was sympathetic to the challenges that Bill was facing, I didn't believe a military operation was the answer Rymor was looking for. Especially not with so many other internal conflicts as well as the recent bombing.

As far as I was concerned, sending an army into Shadowland was tantamount to using a hacksaw to take out a splinter. I supposed removing a limb would remove said splinter, but it wasn't the logical first step, or even the second.

Dealing with Bill had become increasingly complex. Even yesterday, Bill had been abrupt and distracted after receiving the approval for war. Perhaps the process had been too drawn out for the chancellor's liking?

I feared this would end poorly for him. Wars were infrequent, and my recent research suggested they could as easily break as make a political career. Much as I enjoyed dabbling in the occasional bout of juicy turmoil that followed Bill Bremmer, this one was becoming too rich for my tastes. There were homeland issues to be dealt with, particularly given the fact that security forces had defused two more devices over the last week. Yet Bill, along with the rest of the world, was far more enamored with the prospect of a Shadowland war.

Either way, it was time for me to extricate myself before the rolling snowball gathered an unstoppable force.

I was also curious about what Dan Gilmore, the last remaining ancient tech specialist, wanted to see me about.

As Dan entered, I was embarrassed to realize that my office offered the bare minimum of requirements for a personal mover. I wasn't alone in judging the financial district as a prime location. Real estate was hard to come by, and expensive, hence the compact nature of my suites. Bill had offered me more grandiose accommodation in State Tower, but I'd been reluctant to more obviously align myself with him more than I already had, despite the profitable nature of that liaison.

"Dan, a pleasure to see you again," I said as my assistant brought through some drinks before withdrawing from the room. Dan Gilmore wasn't a person I considered a friend, but he was more than an acquaintance. We had first met thirty years ago at a celebratory event of a mutual friend who had introduced us, knowing that we

The Warrior in the Shadows

both harbored strong feelings about what was publicly considered the archaic custom of being religious.

As far as I knew, Dan had been religious all his life. Perhaps his scientifically confounding disability was responsible for Dan seeking an alternative philosophy from a very early age, or perhaps his parents were also religious and had passed their beliefs onto him. Whatever had driven Dan to take the unorthodox route, it was well embedded and ensconced into every aspect of his demeanor. I wasn't uncouth enough to pry into the reasons.

A stillborn daughter had been my personal catalyst into connecting with religion, although I had a very different understanding of religion compared to Dan. Katherine, my partner then, had wanted the pregnancy to be natural. What she considered to be invasive pre-natal care had been kept to a minimum. I was in love and foolish, so I'd bowed to her opinion. When the baby had become still, it was already too late. Katherine had blamed herself. If I was honest, I'd blamed her too. The death was avoidable. More rigorous monitoring would have noticed the problem sooner, and the baby, who had been nearly full term, should have lived a long and healthy life.

Katherine sought help from several counseling groups immediately after the death, but found the greatest comfort and resonance for her grief in religion. It created a great divide between us. I had despised her alternative thinking since it had resulted in our daughter's death. It then seemed absurd that a fictitious deity should be deemed a viable alternative to speaking to real people. I considered, with some merit, the possibility that Katherine's grief had sent her mad. It was, ironically, her religious awakening and not the death of our daughter that had driven a rift into our relationship.

We parted ways two years later. Traumatic events, it seemed, were universally fickle in their conclusion, whether political or more domestic in nature.

"Thanks for seeing me at such short notice, Richard." Dan's voice, absent of its natural warmth, shook me from my thoughts and sparked my curiosity.

"A pleasure, Dan. An unexpected cancellation made it easy to fit you in."

Dan's face darkened. "Yes, I'm sorry about that." He gave me a shifty look. "I was desperate. Although I dare say talking to Hannah at the station will make the security breach of your systems insignificant in the grand scheme of things."

A short disbelieving burst of laughter escaped me before I snapped my mouth shut. In the space of a sentence, Dan had confessed to violating confidential information and speaking to a woman who was dead.

"You spoke to Hannah? While she was at the station?" I was sure I'd heard Dan clearly, yet the information refused to sink in.

Dan nodded, his face solemn.

"She was reported to be dead. Was it actually her? The real Hannah, and not her spirit?" My own experiences with grief said that people did strange things. Imagined they could still talk to people who had gone. It was common knowledge that Dan and Hannah were close. Bill had expressed once during a candid conversation that he thought Dan was an interfering religious freak.

"No revelation of a spiritual nature." Dan chuckled, which set me at ease, but it faded as his shoulders sank as though under a great weight. "I'm not saying I wouldn't mind a bit of help or direction, if you know what I mean." His sad eyes met mine. "I'm sorry, Richard, for bringing this to your door. I know we're not friends, but I'm a desperate man. I'm staking my life, and the lives of people dear to me, on you believing me, and on you understanding me, when I beg you to help me stop the war. Hannah contacted me from the station three weeks ago, right after the news had reported her dead. Yes, our conversation was all too grounded in reality."

"But the station is still inoperative?"

Dan's gaze was steady. "It's operational, and has been since I spoke to Hannah. If Homeland Security realized the kind of data I have access to, they would've shut me down by now. The barriers are back, Richard, and there's no reason for the power restrictions... And

The Warrior in the Shadows

it's not the Shadowlanders we should be fighting. Hannah said a garrison helping them was the only reason they made it to the station alive."

The information hit me like a blow. His confident delivery and the underlying convictions were hard to refute. "But that can't be right. Why would such news be kept secret? As for the Shadowlanders helping, there must be some mistake. We have evidence—a significant amount of evidence—to the contrary."

Had Hannah's claimed support from Shadowland garrisons been the cause of Bill's earlier angst? "I spoke to Bill this morning as he finalized the plans for the operation. He made a public announcement—you must have heard it?" My thoughts turned over slowly. "I'm surprised he didn't let the public know that Hannah was safe and well, though."

I noted Dan's stillness. Something in his expression solidified my concerns, and the realization that there was much wrong in this situation covered me like a too-heavy blanket.

"Why didn't he mention Hannah?"

"Because she only spoke to me," he said. "Briefly, twenty days ago. I've heard nothing from her since. And because she asked me not to tell anyone."

I tried to formulate words, but none would pass my lips, and Dan plowed on.

"I thought the military operation would stop once the power was back. She nearly died, Richard. One of her team did during the Jaru attack. Another one fled in the night, not long after, panicked by the situation, she thought."

I felt physically unwell, and my usually astute mind was struggling to play catch-up with the troubling implications.

"Richard, I'm taking a risk coming here. A huge risk. We need to stop the war. The power is restored. I can't understand why no one's been told. My conscience is screaming at me. I wish my reasons were more noble, that I had the greater good of innocent lives in mind, and certainly that is part of it. But I'll be honest with you, Richard, for me this is about Hannah. She's like a daughter to me, Richard. I've known her since she was eight and first showed an interest in technology. She's out there, vulnerable, and we're mere weeks away from war."

"If it's been three weeks, have you considered that she could be nearly home by now?" I asked.

"I don't believe she's coming home."

"Why didn't she talk to Bill?" I asked.

"I don't know," Dan said, which wasn't very forthcoming of him.

I allowed myself to explore the information, wondering what I could or should share, and finally settled on a middle ground. "We had contact from a field scientist from her team. He reported everyone was dead. Perhaps he genuinely thought they were—extreme events can confuse even the most stable of minds. His testimony was one of several strong factors leading to the decision for military intervention."

"Well, the man's an idiot," Dan said vehemently, "and his leaving would've put everyone's lives in danger. Perhaps he said it to save his own skin. People have made up stories for less."

"That's as may be, but we have his recorded interview telling us the Shadowlanders attacked, and he was the lone survivor. The only thing that can refute that is Hannah stating he lied. Even so, it could get unpleasant. You do have her message recorded, I assume?"

Dan shook his head.

I bit back an uncharacteristic curse. "Dan, you do realize that you're coming to me with nothing if you don't have even that?"

Dan nodded again.

"Why would you not record it?"

"She asked me to delete it," he confessed.

"What in God's name for?"

Dan shifted uncomfortably. Perhaps Hannah held bitterness toward Bill for sending her on the mission. Given she had nearly died, it wasn't a wild stretch of the imagination. I had judged her to

The Warrior in the Shadows

be a pleasant young woman with a sensible head on her shoulders, yet I didn't know her well.

And being out in Shadowland was enough to addle anyone's mind.

Dan had no such excuse. He should have recorded it anyway.

"Without a recording, we have no grounds to propose stopping the war, and making any claims without evidence would be political suicide. For all I know you could be a Moiety supporter and extremist, fabricating stories out of a misguided desire to protect indigenous lands."

"You know I'm not," Dan offered softly.

I sighed, my reluctance to get involved overwritten by my instinctive belief in Dan.

"I've no idea what I can do here. Perhaps if you'd approached me sooner—when Hannah was still there and could be contacted, maybe. The military operation is progressing, and troops are mobilizing. I've been canvassing support for months, both behind the scenes and in public. I don't see how I can credibly change my position to support you, without any evidence and after so long. No one would understand my sudden change of opinion without it... Then there's Bill to consider, and how everyone thinks the station is inoperative." I didn't put further thoughts into words, but my buried concerns about the war reared and demanded attention. Bill's most recent actions were dubious, and I'd told him as much. My original notion that the war was, in fact, a poor idea returned to me. I was no longer sure how or why I'd allowed Bill to persuade me otherwise, and, worse, supported it.

"Can you at least prove that the power is back?"

Dan's nod was swift.

If Bill chose not to make that public, what else was he hiding?

It hit me then that I might have already aligned myself too closely with Bill. The money had been easy and bountiful, and, until this most recent event, little had stirred my conscience to prevent me from taking more of the same. It was in my nature to accept facts presented to me at face value, yet I'd had a rising awareness that Bill might be equivocating. Even if this was a simple misunderstanding, there could be other parties at work, unbeknownst to Bill. For what aim, I couldn't say, but there *was* something amiss.

Then there was the underlying conflict between John Tanis and Bill. I'd felt great empathy toward Bill when he had confessed the cause. Yet, I'd watched Bill giving a public speech contrary to his personal beliefs on many occasions. A skill I expected all politicians to deploy to manage voter mood. Talking up policies you knew would have short-term pain because data and advice suggested it was the long-term best approach. Keeping personal opinions out of the public eye was essential in such a role.

Today, and in light of new information, Bill's ability to speak with a genuine passion for something he felt no genuine passion for struck a note of discord. Bill was a master manipulator, but were his motivations good or bad?

My conflict was apparent. Telling Bill would endanger Dan if my most extreme suspicions were true. Yet Hannah was Bill's partner. It would be callous to withhold the information, and, further, would court his wrath.

"I cannot tell you what to do, Richard. I can only tell you what I know. I trust you to do what you can."

I felt the weight of Dan's blind faith in me and perhaps a misguided sense of kinship that religious people should be good. I didn't feel worthy of his faith, or comfortable, when I'd led a frivolous, superficial life.

After my daughter's death, I'd lost myself and nurtured an unhealthy addiction to fast living. Eventually, I'd found myself in a deep hole and no means of escape. I'd cried, crashing waves of delayed grief at the loss of a daughter and the collapse of my marriage. The grief had seemed endless and insurmountable. When exhaustion had won over, I'd put a call through for medical help.

At the time, I'd been seeking the welcoming numbness of more drugs.

The Warrior in the Shadows

I'd gotten that for a while.

My family was wealthy and funded the best rehabilitation money could buy. It had taken several more months before I'd reached the bottom and began a slow journey back to life.

In the vacuum left as I emerged from my grief, I remembered the counseling Katherine had sought. Surprisingly, religion didn't seem so far-fetched anymore. I felt curious and hopeful and so I pursued the understanding and peace that I found in religion.

I'd married three times since Katherine, and had never once been tempted to try for another child.

The two parts of my life sat in conflict. My inability to find contentment in my personal relationships had driven me to live a superficial and flamboyant life. On the other side lay the deeply comforting peace I derived through religion. Two souls within one body—forgiving myself on one level and relentlessly punishing myself on another.

I prayed in an attempt to reconcile the whole, but it had eluded me so far.

Was it time for me to take the hard route? Do more than take the money and delude myself that I was doing good?

"I'll need to consider the best approach," I said. "But if I do talk to Bill, as I believe I must, you'll need to provide a full statement. I make no guarantee that anyone will believe you, but I will support your claim."

"Thank you." Dan's eyes shone with gratitude, and I knew my decision to help him was sound.

With confirmation that I would be in touch when I had news to share, Dan left me to my troubled thoughts and limited options.

Unfortunately for me, none of those options were good.

Chapter 17

Bill

"I hope you know what you're doing, Bill," Councilman Carl Stevens said as he joined me on the veranda of his home on the northern shores of Jade Stone Lake.

The phrase lake house didn't do justice to the pretentious monstrosity; the sprawling mansion incorporating at least four different classical styles. Either the architect had been a madman, or the customer had far more money than taste.

"You can trust me on this one, Carl. My misspent youth has some use."

Carl's laugh was deep and generous. "Yes, I heard some rumors about that. Your late father had a skill for covering your escapades. The details remain a mystery."

"That was probably for the best, Carl. Political careers are based on a man's public image. While my personal history might be viewed as character building to a forward-thinking man like yourself, the more sanctimonious members of the political game are not so liberally inclined."

The Warrior in the Shadows

Carl chuckled. "Let's leave it at that. What I don't know can't hurt me. You got your approval. It's over to you now to see this operation through."

I nodded solemnly, feeling that the moment required such an act. Approval to send troops into Shadowland had come this morning, and there were no more hoops to jump through or barriers in my way. Details, for sure, but I would ensure issues were resolved swiftly.

"I'm happy to take on the responsibility." I nodded my head at the view. "I appreciate the invitation today. It's an amazing place you have here. A unique style." I said diplomatically. Carl's wealth and taste, or lack of it, were less important than his influence as a member of the upper council. My interest in the councilman's daughter was also part of Carl's agenda—I'd seen the cogs turning the first time we'd met after Hannah's death had been announced. Rochelle was intelligent, articulate, and stunning, in the way real money guaranteed. It was clear she also saw the association as an advantage. Whether it was a means of getting noticed, or she shared her father's desire for a stronger relationship, I neither knew nor cared. The association was mutually beneficial, and I intended to stay in Carl's favor.

Rochelle had consoled me on my loss in a platonic way in public, and been far less reserved in private a week later, determined to help me forget about my bereavement in the most comprehensive ways. Rochelle wasn't quite as predatory as Margaret or near as sweet and filthy as Hannah. But she knew her way around the bedroom and wasn't afraid to make the play enjoyable.

I was happy to let her think she was leading the way.

"Glad you like it, Bill!" Carl offered. "My partner designed it. He cleaned up the awards that year."

I shuddered inwardly at the strings he must have pulled to deliver that award. Carl clearly wasn't above using his influence for personal reasons. I filed that information away for later use. Any man who could move such mountains as the architectural elitists to favor such a preposterous design was a man to be reckoned with.

"Why don't we have a drink before dinner?" Carl said. "I hear you have a new man looking after Homeland Security?"

We headed into the house together. The inside was as horrific as the outside, with bold, overused colors better suited to a sweetshop than a home. "Kelard has proven invaluable so far. The right find at the right time. Perhaps I could introduce you when you're next visiting Serenity?" Kelard Wilder was a recent addition to my inner circle and had proven himself invaluable. A man who kept to facts and data and didn't waste energy on emotion, he slipped easily into my team.

"I'd appreciate that," Carl said as he loaded two tumblers liberally with a dark golden liquid. "Here you go."

I accepted the drink with a grateful incline of my head. It warmed my throat and, unlike the decor, was genuine quality.

"Daddy, Bill, I hope you're not still talking about that war." Rochelle's entrance brought an instant and indulgent smile to her father's face.

"Not anymore, Precious, how's your father doing with the dinner preparations? All organized?"

Rochelle was the epitome of wealthy beauty, and graceful in an effortless way. Her dark, glossy hair was coiled into the latest style, and her clothing was expensive and stylish. She kissed her father's cheek before approaching me to do the same.

There was the slightest slip in her father's jovial expression at her greeting me in such a familiar way. Perhaps Carl hadn't wanted us to become close after all?

"Busy overseeing his latest culinary creation as we speak," Rochelle said, either oblivious or unconcerned by her father's reserve. "I did encourage him to leave it to the chef, but you know how much he enjoys cooking."

I inwardly cringed at the prospect of the deranged architect crafting food.

Rochelle winked for my eyes only. "I think I'll join you for a

The Warrior in the Shadows

drink. I mentioned bumping into Bill while visiting friends in Serenity, didn't I, Daddy?"

"You did, Precious, and I did tell you that Bill was a busy man." Carl took a liberal gulp of his drink. "Thanks for making time for my daughter, Bill. As you may have noticed, she can be tenacious when she gets a notion in her head. Like her other father in that respect, I'm afraid."

"It was my pleasure," I said with a smile. "It's been a difficult time for me. Genuine compassion is rare in the political world, and I'm grateful Rochelle took the time. It's nice for someone to inquire about something other than the war."

"Well, I'm glad you two are getting along." Carl managed an amiable tone, but I noticed that Rochelle wore a hint of smugness. Was she out to shock her *Daddy,* or did she have an agenda of her own?

"These are testing times, Bill, and there'll be more tests to come," Carl said, his smile tight. "Unfortunately, I doubt you'll get many opportunities to forget the war in the foreseeable future. Let's make the most of tonight. I'll take you up on that offer of an introduction to your new man Kelard. I've plans to be in Serenity later this week. Heard good reports about him. The upper house members like to be kept in the loop. Keeps them sweet in case you need further concessions."

"Not a problem, Carl," I said. "I'll have my assistant schedule a time."

"Daddy, you promised you would stop talking about the war." Rochelle offered the mild reproach with a sweet smile, and joining me, she looped her arm through mine. "Why don't we head through?"

"Your daughter is a hard woman to refuse, Carl." My rueful smile brought genuine warmth to the older man's face.

"You're quite right, Bill. Better go through before we see the less congenial side."

We left the room together, putting the war aside to enjoy a

surprisingly pleasant meal. Tomorrow I would be back in the thick of it. An urgent message from Richard to meet had been an unwelcome reminder that it was impossible to escape my commitments for long.

I would enjoy the anticipation of seeing the culmination of my plans. Hopefully, in the interim, Rochelle had a plan for tonight.

Chapter 18

Shadowland

Red

The world had gone to hell, good people were dead, and Shadowland was on the brink of war with Rymor, which wasn't going to be a war at all, given Rymor had weapons and was set to unleash them on the innocent people here. I felt a lot of guilt that I should come out of it with something good.

Hannah's seeking comfort from me confused me at first. She was with Garren or possibly Tanis... There was no doubt the appointed leader had interest, too. So when she asked the first night after Edward's death if she could lay beside me, I'd been uncomfortable but all too willing.

Perhaps sensing my conflict, Adam took me aside the next day. "Look, I know this is difficult," he said.

He was our leader out here, but back in Serenity, he'd been the head of the field scientist division, and I presumed why he'd been called up for this operation in the first place. I felt the weight of this 'discussion' in whatever guise it might take.

"I'm sorry," I said. "I overstepped my place. She just looked so—"

He held up a hand. "I'm not angry with you, Red, the opposite. Kein thinks Hannah coming to you for comfort is a good thing. Newly awakened omegas need care. Her hormones will be raging with Garren gone and someone needs to fill the void."

"That someone is me?" My voice sounded a little gruffer than usual.

He shrugged. "Hell if I know what's for the best. We're on our own out here. But I trust Kein. Fuck knows why she wasn't given medical suppressants before we left; I can only assume it was an oversight." His lips pulled into a grimace that said he thought this operation had ventured beyond a fuck-up and into a gangbang with bells on. "She's been sleeping with an alpha for weeks. If they're not bonded, it's not for the want of trying. I thought Tanis might—yeah, that's not my business." He scrubbed his hand over his face. "If she wants to sleep beside you, and assuming you don't have a problem with it, then Kein suggested it would help her."

"I, ah, have no problem."

"Good," he said, patting my shoulder and stalking off to help ready the horses with a speed that suggested he'd found the conversation as awkward as me.

I swallowed.

Not that I was complaining. Hannah was gorgeous, had shown incredible courage, and had enough sweetness and feistiness to soften the hardest hearts. I was halfway in love, my dick full way in lust, and having her pressed up against me as she sought tactile comfort during the night was both heaven and hell.

So, I wanted her, offered a silent prayer of thanks every day that Garren remained away, and she shyly came to me at the end of the day to ask if she could sleep beside me.

For five straight nights.

Five *long* nights.

The Warrior in the Shadows

It would destroy me when her alpha returned and she fell into his arms, not mine.

"Red, do you think I could..."

I turned from where I was unhooking my horse's bridle to find Hannah standing all sweet and unsure, bedroll in her hand.

I should tell her to sleep beside someone else for self-preservation reasons.

"It's fine, Hannah, you don't need to ask. If you need something I can give you, I'm here for you."

Fuck, that sounded like a poorly worded come-on. My damn dick had now hijacked my mouth as well as my brain.

"Thank you!" Her smile was spontaneous, and she rose onto her tiptoes to press a kiss against my cheek before carrying her roll into the tent I shared with five other men.

That smile was like fucking rainbows and unicorns, and I felt like a complete ass because I wanted to bang her into next week.

We ate supper, turned in, and she snuggled beside me like she belonged there.

It took me ages to get to sleep, and when I woke up, it was pitch back and we'd turned in our sleep. We were on our sides, my arm curved around her waist. Her sweet ass was nestled against my crotch, and my dick was fully erect and onboard with getting laid.

Fuck!

How the hell had we ended up so close? It was hot even during the night, so she slept in a t-shirt and panties—I kept my boxer briefs on, but I always made a point of shoving the blanket between us for this reason.

Beyond the tent, owls hooted, while inside resonated with a medley of snores.

Great. I was never going to get back to sleep.

I eased back, creating a little distance, and, careful not to wake her, rolled onto my back. She had lost someone she was close to, we all had, and here I was, a sick asshole thinking like a horny teenager.

She murmured in her sleep, rolling over. Sprawling all over me, she pushed her knee between mine and wedged her pussy against my thigh.

I froze.

Every cell in my brain switched off, and all the ones in my dick switched on.

She murmured again, humping against my thigh.

Was she wet? Yeah, she was wet. I could feel it smearing over my thigh through her panties as she rocked against me.

I needed to get her the hell off me before she woke up and screamed.

Carefully, barely breathing, I closed my hands on her waist, which was a really bad idea because now my hands were against her soft, warm skin where her t-shirt had ridden up.

My palms turned sweaty. My dick spat an enthusiastic gob of pre-cum out like it was show time.

Not that she needed any extra lubrication.

Do not think about that!

She murmured, wriggling.

The hot tent, filled with snores, was suddenly suffocating. My hands tightened on her waist. I should have been shifting her away, but my mind shut down, and my thigh lifted as I palmed a handful of her ass to wedge my thigh more firmly against her wet heat.

She moaned. Her hand slipped down, and her small fingers wrapped around my dick through my boxers.

I coughed.

Fuck! She was going to wake up and scream, then Adam would lambast me, after which, Garren would kill me when he turned up!

She had an alpha. She was just asleep and confused. Only, fear of Garren wasn't enough to persuade my dick, nor even was thinking about Tanis, who would probably beat the shit out of me, stab me, or maybe castrate me... maybe all three. He knew how to handle a knife. I'd seen him work over prisoners without a hint of emotion on his face. The bastard wouldn't lose sleep about ending me.

None of this was helping my wayward dick situation, nor was the

The Warrior in the Shadows

way her small fingers were rubbing up and down my shaft, spreading the flood of pre-cum around.

Sweat popped out across my skin. Her sweet scent was all up in my nose, and I was high. Everyone claimed betas were immune to omega scent. Maybe I didn't start panting when one was near, but this close, with her hand working erratically over my dick, heralded the end of my free will.

"Hannah," I whispered, trying to gently ease her fingers off me without fucking coming.

"God, please," she mumbled. "I need you."

Fuck! Was she still asleep?

Taking advantage of my mental shutdown, she hooked one leg around my waist and somehow got the tip of my cock under the seam of her panties.

All air left my lungs in a hiss as the head of my dick slipped through slick folds.

My labored breathing sounded unnaturally loud against the snoring—enough was enough.

I rolled, taking her onto her back and putting the wall of my body between her and the rest of the tent. Only something went wrong. My body, caught in a primitive pull, was no longer under my command, and my dick slid into her hot silken pussy like a heat-seeking missile dead on target.

She gasped and arched up just before her eyes sprang open.

I was so busted.

Fighting to get my ragged breathing under control, I stared down at her through the dark, wishing I could see her face so I could judge what the fuck was happening. She hadn't screamed. Seemed likely she would soon.

"Fuck, I'm sorry!" I whispered. "I—" What the fuck was I saying? My cock was all up inside her, deep enough to feel her pulsing and quivering around me. Her panties were stretched, wedged inside a small way, and the only thing that was preventing me from being balls deep. As it was, no more than an inch separated me from full penetration. What possible excuse could I give to justify fucking into her?

I went to pull out.

"Um... what!" I huffed out when her slim thighs wrapped around me and held tight, wedging my dick a little deeper into heaven.

"Please don't stop. Please! I need you, Red. I feel so alone, and I want to be close."

Her words undid me. Every part of me softened except *that* part, which turned to stone.

"Hold your panties out the way, Hannah," I whispered, voice deep and rough with need. "I can't get inside you like this."

What the fuck was coming out of my mouth?

She didn't miss a beat, fingers searching between our sweat-damped bodies as I pulled out far enough for her to drag the material aside.

We both groaned as I sank all the way in.

"Keep quiet, baby." I kept my lips against her ear. "We'll need to go slow so we don't wake anyone up."

She wrapped her legs around me and one arm around my neck.

I eased out, grabbing hold of her hip. "Spread for me a little."

She did, opening her thighs wide and emitting a hot little whimper of need as I took the first careful thrust.

"Shhh." I pressed my lips to her ear, feeling her tremble with need. "Nice and quiet for me, or we'll have to stop."

She buried her head in the crook of my throat and nipped.

My dick flexed. Fuck! I needed to get her off before I embarrassed myself and came.

Like she could read my mind, her fingers bumped against my aching shaft as she rubbed her clit.

"Good girl," I said. "I'm going to move slowly."

It was awkward, Hannah trying to pet her clit and hold her panties out of the way, me trying to thrust slow and carefully so as not to wake anyone up. Every sound was amplified in my ears, every tiny moment a thousand times more pleasurable than anything I'd felt

The Warrior in the Shadows

before. And her pussy, wet, pulsing, trying to suck me back as I slowly drew out, clenching lovingly over me when I was all the way in.

I kissed my way down her throat, over her jaw, before claiming her lips in a hot kiss full of tangling tongues and breathy gasps. I wanted to inhale her, draw her under my skin, wanted to rip her panties off, and fuck her hard and fast. Only I couldn't, and somehow this achingly gentle fuck in a tent full of snoring men was off-the-charts hot.

Sweat damped our flesh. Her scent, her slick pussy, and the filthy wet noises all made me buzz with the fear of discovery even as they turned me on.

She was a fucking revelation. If I died after this, I didn't even care.

Then her perfect pussy locked down, and I swallowed her moan just in time. Balls rising and hot cum dumping deep, barely holding my own groan in as she clenched over me in waves, drawing every drop of cum from me until I was drained and utterly spent.

I dragged my mouth from hers, trailing kisses over her cheek until my lips brushed against her ear. "You okay?"

Her answer was to tighten her legs around me to keep me close and press her palm against my cheek. We stayed like that for a long time, letting our breathing even out, allowing the heady glow to peter out.

The intensity of the moment wrapped around us both. I'd had my very first hit of an omega...of Hannah. I was addicted, and I knew I'd take risks for a chance at her again.

Little kisses were peppered along my jawline before she nipped at my ear lobe, bringing a hopeful twitch to my softening cock.

"Tomorrow, I'll slip my panties off once I'm under the covers," she whispered.

I was so fucking gone.

Chapter 19

Rymor

Richard

After a troubled afternoon of deliberation, I made the reluctant decision to discuss Dan's revelation with Bill. A decision that had led me to be waiting, nervous, in Bill's outer reception room.

As a man practiced in offering counsel, it had been unexpectedly hard to provide counsel to myself. Nor was this a decision that could be slept on. The pull of Dan's concerns directly conflicted with my belief that Rymor's appointed leader couldn't possibly be fabricating the war as part of some personal vendetta.

That the war was now halfway in motion exerted pressure on me as if I were personally pivotal to halting the most momentous event in Rymorian history.

I didn't desire such glory and was grateful that my only dilemma was whether to approach Bill immediately or find a more subtle way to inquire and influence. Yet I also felt I had no right to withhold the

The Warrior in the Shadows

information. It was my duty to tell Bill whatever I knew, and Bill's duty to know what to do with it.

Theo was still absent, I noted. Bill was angry about the sudden disappearance of his personal assistant. When I had inquired where Theo was a few weeks ago, his response had been sharp enough to make me pity his former personal assistant if and when he should reappear. Whatever the reason for Theo's absence, his replacement, Nielsen, had been brimming with inappropriate speculation.

As it happened, Bill had been busy when I first asked to see him, which had offered me a few hours to plan what to say. Not that it helped. I couldn't anticipate with any level of confidence how he might react.

I also worried about Dan's part in this, fearing it would end poorly for him. Bill had openly expressed his dislike for the renowned technical master. When Bill disliked a person, they generally suffered. My neck was being stretched out on the same block, but I'd promised Dan I would support him, and I would keep that promise.

"You can go in now," Nielsen said, and I dragged my gaze from the wall of windows of Bill's reception room.

"Thank you, Nielsen."

Shadowland provided a dramatic backdrop for the room that I entered. Bill sat in the informal part of the office where chairs were positioned around a low rosewood table. To his right, with a drink in his hand, was Kelard Wilder.

I smoothed out my expression, sensing my coveted position as his counsel had been displaced. How much influence did I still hold? How much had I ever had? Not much, I suspected. I was a means to an end with Bill. My family's political standing was probably the deciding factor, not me.

Seeing someone step into my place still chafed even as I questioned whether I wanted it anymore.

Kelard gave me a nod of acknowledgment. Bill greeted me with the usual, "Richard." And indicated the empty seat.

I felt clumsy as I took a seat, in a way I'd never done before. I hadn't expected someone else to be there. Bill must have sensed my reserve and turned towards Kelard before directing his attention to me. "Go ahead, Richard."

"I've been informed that the station is operational—and who it was that got it going again." The words I'd practiced earlier today eluded me, and instead, a blunt calamity tumbled out of my mouth.

Bill's expression turned shuttered. He already knew the station was operational, I was sure of it. When Dan had dropped that bombshell revelation, I'd convinced myself there was a system anomaly at fault, that Bill might have similarly been in the dark.

I was no longer in his confidence, Kelard was.

"Who started it?" Bill asked.

"It was Hannah. She made contact while she was there."

Bill's face blanched.

Kelard's gaze shifted toward Bill before returning to me. "I'm assuming you have evidence."

I shook my head and wondered how we'd arrived at this point so swiftly. "Dan Gilmore visited me. Said that Hannah contacted him from the station. They spoke briefly, but in summary, she was well. Her team had come under Jaru attack. A Shadowland garrison came to their rescue, and further assisted them in reaching the station."

"It's been operational for weeks," Bill said flatly, confirming he knew. "Why are you only telling me this now?"

"I found out yesterday," I said. "Asked to speak with you immediately."

"And you believe Dan?" Bill raised both brows. "Is his evidence credible? I'll need my team to go over it. Given his skill level, he could fabricate evidence."

Looking at Bill, I saw all of Dan's fears showcased on a stage that left no room for misinterpretation. Even if Dan provided a recording, it would have been discredited, and Dan would have been accused of falsifying evidence.

"There is no evidence other than Dan's word. The message was

The Warrior in the Shadows

never recorded, a great pity." Hannah's part in this, at least, appeared to be news to Bill.

Kelard issued a contemptuous snort.

Bill's expression was once more closed, yet I got the impression that Bill wasn't happy to learn Hannah was alive.

"You believe him?" Bill asked.

I swallowed down the sickness forming in the pit of my stomach. "I saw no reason to mistrust him. Hence, I came to you. Someone had started it and there are only three choices."

"Dan Gilmore?" Kelard asked Bill.

"Yes, the last remaining technical master," said Bill. "And as the ultimate expert on ancient technology, I find it astounding that he comes to this with nothing but his word."

He was right, of course.

"A reliable source gave evidence that she was dead," Bill said coldly. "I don't believe the Shadowlanders are helping her, but I can believe she's alive, or at least she was twenty days ago. And if she is, then I think it's past time we brought her back."

Relief washed over me. "I was so worried you wouldn't believe me." I smiled. "So, we're no longer going to war?"

Kelard's chuckle snagged my attention. My smile faltered.

"Oh, the war is definitely happening," Bill said. "Dan Gilmore is known to have ties with Gaia. I wouldn't be surprised to find out he has links to Moiety, too. Why else do you think he deleted her message? There's only one plausible explanation, that he wanted to put forward his own narrative. And even supposing Hannah did message and tell him the garrisons were helping her, she's far too trusting. Who knows what Adam might be feeding her, given his ties to Moiety. No, there are only two possible scenarios here, either Hannah was mistaken, or Dan has blatantly lied. Given Dan's personal pursuits and the fact that there's no recorded message suggests he's making this a personal save the indigenous crusade." He barked out a short, demeaning chuckle. "I mean the man's a Heretic, for fuck's sake. A man who converses with an imaginary deity can hardly be considered sound of mind."

A hole opened in my stomach, and my world crashed out. "You have no measurable doubts? You still intend to pursue war?"

"None," replied Bill. "In fact, I'll do everything in my power to expedite our forces leaving as soon as possible."

Kelard nodded. "You have my full support, Bill. We have her location and a time of her being there. It would be dangerous to delay."

"Thank you, Richard," Bill said, "for bringing this to my attention."

I was dismissed.

I rose unsteadily, vision coming through a tunnel. "Don't speak to Dan about this please, Richard. I'll need to bring him in, and better if he's not forewarned. News of Hannah must also remain under wraps. Timing is everything in this. I'm sure you understand."

I mumbled my acknowledgment, my mind tuning blank as I blindly headed out.

Once in the outer office, I hurried past Nielsen straight to the washroom, where I emptied my stomach in a violent, churning rush.

What had I done?

Chapter 20

Nate

"You really need to find a way of doing this that doesn't give me heart failure," Dan grumbled as he entered his apartment and found me waiting for him.

"Sorry," I said, preoccupied with how to broach the subject of Theo heading for Shadowland.

"You're looking tense. Come on, out with it. What have you been up to?" Dan made his way to the printer. "Want a drink? Or have you already helped yourself."

I shook my head. Printers were now synonymous with Theo creating a beanbag while we'd been at Bill's summer residence.

"Finding out a few more details about Bill, and about Richard—who you thought you could trust."

"What about Richard?" Dan's brow furrowed as he paused in the task of getting himself a drink to glance back.

"He spoke to Bill this morning, and whatever he said appears to have escalated the preparations for war."

Dan sighed and, leaving the printer, wheeled over to me.

"Richard's a good man. I don't believe he's done any worse than trying his best."

"What he is is irrelevant," I said. "Bill's more determined than ever to proceed with the military operation in Shadowland—he's going to bring you in for questioning."

Dan's expression turned solemn. "I expected that he would."

"You can't go with them," I said, alarmed by his grim resignation. "Let me get you out. I could take you somewhere safe." My mind turned back to that harrowing scene in Azure when I'd watched, helpless, as Ella had been shoved into the back of a transport.

And how, only a short time later, I'd found out that she'd been killed. Panic gripped me at the thought of that happening to Dan. "If you go in for questioning, I fear you may not return."

"I have to speak up," Dan said. "If there's a chance I can slow that war machine—even for a day—I have to try. You know I do. Besides, how would it look if I disappeared? I'll not spend my life in hiding, and that's what you're asking me to do."

A dull pain radiated from the center of my chest. For reasons that eluded me now, I'd assumed Dan would come with me. Yet, hiding wasn't Dan's way, any more than abandoning Hannah's cause was.

I felt a greater understanding of being human, the elusive concept of love, and how multifaceted it was. Dan loved Hannah with the gentle affection of an adult who had watched a child grow.

"Ella didn't come back," I said quietly.

"I know, Nate, but you can't blame yourself. We can't let fear stop us doing what's right."

"I understand." I respected Dan's decision, even though I hated the potential consequence of it.

"I'm sorry, Nate. I know you've only been with me for a couple of years. I know you're worried—I'm worried too."

"I don't trust Bill," I said. "Less so since we infiltrated his home."

His sharp gaze held mine. "I don't trust him either, but I told them I know the station's operational when no one else in Rymor does, and that I spoke to Hannah—who's reportedly dead. You can't

The Warrior in the Shadows

make that kind of declaration without questions. I'd be more surprised if they ignored me. I'm the last remaining ancient technology expert. A few youngsters are coming through, but it's not a path that many people tread. And I'm not being arrogant when I say it's a path many simply don't have the capacity to comprehend."

"Do you think that will protect you? From what I've discovered, I'd say Bill's insane enough to do anything, including killing you."

"So, what *have* you discovered?" Dan asked.

I forced my shoulders to relax in the hope it would ease my underlying tension. "He's been watching people, a lot of people: Hannah, Theo, politicians, business moguls, and even his friends. He has this secret room at his home where he reviews the information, and a tagging system that trawls the monitoring systems looking for specific words or people. There's a lot of data, and, really, when I say a lot, it's a bit of an understatement."

Dan's face turned slack. "How much does he know about us?"

"He knows Hannah told you she was leaving for Shadowland, and that Coco met with Jon Sanders before he left on the transport. He doesn't know about Theo or me, or anything that happened at your home near Azure. He has people in Shadowland, at least a hundred, maybe more, and has been setting up a base at the old, abandoned Shadowland fortress at Talin. He's got people in his back pocket everywhere, the senate, the upper council—and his influence over the military is comprehensive. I don't think there is a faction that he doesn't have some control over. His greatest weakness is the field scientist division. The man in charge is squeaky clean and detests Bill —he's high on Bill's watch list, as you might expect. Gaia's another weak spot, but he has leverage on two key players there, so it's been keeping them quiet."

Dan let out a shaky breath. "I didn't—I didn't expect it to be so bad."

"I would say that he's already unstoppable, and that's why Theo decided to take a drastic step."

"What step?"

"How much do you know about Coco's son?"

"Not much," Dan said, frowning. "His father is a Shadowland alpha she met while out there. The alphas have a modified gene that made them something more than human. They were designed to be soldiers, killers. They are designed for war. With whom, I don't know. Maybe the Jaru, or some other force or people who are long gone now."

"There's a bit more to him than that. He's the leader out there. All the fortresses work autonomously, but are united under his banner. That's why Theo decided to go into Shadowland—he's going to bring John Tanis back."

"What?! That's a ludicrous idea!"

"Maybe." I shrugged. I wasn't completely convinced by Theo's plan, but admitted it was the best one we had.

"What are you bringing John Tanis back for? To assassinate Bill? To tell everyone how bad Bill is?" Dan snorted in disbelief. "You know what Coco said about the Shadowlanders. John Tanis is a genetically engineered killer, and now you're telling me he's taken over Shadowland by force. Not exactly the paradigm of virtuous behavior. If Bill's been watching Coco, then you can be sure he already knows what John is, and he will certainly be aware of his conquests in Shadowland. No, John Tanis belongs exactly where he is. The pair of you are crazy if you think John Tanis will return to Rymor, or that his coming back will do any good."

"And Bill had Ella killed!" I said, feeling my helplessness bubble up.

"And you're planning on replacing him with someone who could be as bad! Worse maybe!"

"We weren't planning on replacing Bill with John Tanis," I replied.

"No? Just aiding him in assassinating Rymor's chancellor, then. Do you even hear what you're saying? You're about to throw this country into anarchy. What else do you think will happen after Bill's dead?"

The Warrior in the Shadows

"I don't know," I said. "It wasn't exactly death I was anticipating, more someone to overthrow him. We're running out of options, Dan; you know that, right?"

Dan sighed. "I know." He rubbed his hands together restlessly. "Where's Theo now?"

"He left a week ago. He'll be deep within Shadowland by now."

"What about Coco?" he asked.

"Bill has been watching her for years. I believe he'll take her in for questioning soon. I'll keep track. If I need to, I'll get her out."

"She may not go." Dan said, his lips tugging up in a tired smile. "She has a stubborn side. A bit like me."

"I may not give her any choice," I said in all seriousness.

Dan surprised me by chuckling. "She's a good person and worth saving, but don't take risks over me. I don't believe it'll come to that, but please promise me that you won't."

"I can't promise that, Dan." I shook my head. "Don't ask me to promise that."

"Look at me," Dan said. "I'm nothing but a shell. Don't endanger yourself for me. I couldn't bear to think of it."

I wasn't going to give him that promise.

"Damn," I muttered as the devices integrated with my body alerted me to the arrival of Bill's men. "They're here for you. I thought we'd have more time." I wasn't ready to say goodbye to Dan.

"You need to leave," Dan said thickly.

A crushing weight accompanied Dan's words. "I'll find you if you need me. I promise."

"What a pair you and Theo are," Dan said, voice thick with emotion. "Go on. You better get going."

The surveillance feed on my retinal viewer showed the black-suited men entering the elevator. I hugged Dan tight and left, ignoring my screaming conscience.

Chapter 21

Communication with Scott Harding, Head of Global Operations...

> Scott: Why should I trust you?

> Nate: I was right about the monitoring device, wasn't I?

> Scott: You've been right about many things. That's what's making me nervous.

> Nate: You have to trust someone.

> Scott: I trust lots of people. Well, a few less now—thanks for that. Nothing like having your faith in your fellow men destroyed.

> Nate: It had to be done. You were walking into a trap.

> Scott: And this isn't a bigger one? Just one more time—why should I trust you?

> Nate: Because you need to trust someone, and because I'm all you've got. Besides, you already trust me.

The Warrior in the Shadows

> Scott: Okay, I'm in. Let's see how deep this hole goes...

Nate

I had done crazy things in the short time since leaving Dan's summer house. I'd infiltrated the CIA and the home of Rymor's chancellor, watched my generated brother disappear into a door bound for Shadowland, and watched Dan be taken away by those men in black suits.

Oh, and I'd also fallen in love.

Now, as if this wasn't enough, I was about to enlist—or attempt to enlist—the aid of the only man in Rymor who appeared to hate Bill as much as John Tanis did.

Scott Harding was the head of Global Operations, and in my opinion, a scary man in his own right. I'd been watching him ever since I had been at Bill's home, and then I had been in virtual contact for a week. Bill had tried to implicate Scott in the supply of arms to Shadowland. I'd destroyed the fabricated evidence, but the shock of what had almost come to pass had left Scott suspicious of everything and everyone—even me.

Gaining Scott's support wouldn't be easy, but it was necessary to save Shadowland from war.

Scott was having a dinner party at his apartment tonight. His home was in Tranquility, the second largest Rymorian city. As the closest to the wall, it made the obvious choice of base for the Field Operations headquarters.

I waited in a quiet service area of the building for the party to finish. The guests had all left except the final one, who lingered. My new life consisted of a lot of loitering in the shadows. It was the least fun consequence of my skills.

Finally, the remaining guest left and, as she entered the elevator, I slipped out of my hiding place to buzz Scott's door.

His smile greeted me. Perhaps Scott thought his female

companion had returned. His smile fell instantly, and a suspicious frown took its place.

"Who the fuck are you?" Scott barked, checking the corridor as if anticipating a hit squad to descend on him then and there.

"It would be better if I could explain myself inside. I can erase myself from the system, but as yet my skills do not extend to wiping the human mind."

Scott's frown deepened. Damn, the man was scary.

I drew a measured breath. "You wanted to see how deep the hole goes, I believe?"

"Uff!" I was yanked into the apartment and slammed back against the nearby wall. The fingers wrapped around my throat were tight and constricting. Not how I planned our first meeting to go.

Scott didn't say anything for long moments, and I couldn't, due to the chokehold. He was a tall man with a lean build and a crooked nose, which fascinated me. Who wouldn't get that fixed? Given the way he crushed me against the wall, his build was deceptive of his strength.

Released abruptly, I wheezed air into my lungs.

"I don't like surprises," Scott muttered before stalking back into his lounge.

"Yes, I... ah... noticed that." I followed, massaging my throat.

"I'm having a coffee. Want a drink?"

"I—" My body metabolized caffeine instantly, delivering none of the pleasing effects. "Thank you, that would be great!"

Scott pulled an espresso shot out of the printer and passed it to me with a doubtful expression.

When I took it without complaint, he made himself another. Scott sipped his coffee. "How'd you get in the building?"

"I have some unusual skills," I offered. Perhaps I should have spent more time in virtual communication before rushing into a meeting...or given Scott a date and time.

"Special ops?"

"Clearly not," I indicated my bruised throat with a grimace.

The Warrior in the Shadows

Scott grinned. "Don't feel bad. I spent years in Shadowland before they turned me into a desk monkey. I reckon I could give special ops a hard time. May as well get comfortable, since you're here."

I nodded and followed Scott over to the seating area.

"So, you've bypassed the monitoring Bill has on me?" he asked.

"No, not exactly," I took the seat opposite. Scott's apartment was modern and pleasant. The city of Tranquility was located a little way inland on the estuary of a river. The apartment was unremarkable, but it did have a stunning view of the harbor where the more grandiose apartment towers stood watch over the gently swaying boats and cruisers. "I can erase myself from the surveillance. As I mentioned before, the systems don't remember me, people do, but so long as I don't do anything notable, they soon forget as well."

"And how do you do that?"

"It's a little complicated to explain, and—classified."

"Classified by who?" Scott scoffed. "You just said, in not so many words, that you don't work for any government agency, pretty boy."

The man was *abrasive*. "Yes, well, I still saved your ass."

Scott grinned again. "I'll give you that. I'd like a little more detail since I'm sitting in a room that's crawling with monitoring. How do I know our mutual friend isn't listening in?"

"How do you think monitoring works?"

Scott shrugged. "Recordings, people watching, systems watching too, I suppose."

"There's too much data, even for Bill's personal watch-list, and too many locations: Global Monitoring, Field Operations, and the Serenity Technology Center, to name but a few. There are many more, an insane number in fact. Humans could never review so much information, so they use algorithms and data breakdown. They don't even record images unless the system flags an anomaly. They do record people's movements and conversations in the raw format. I'm encouraging the system to decide that nothing interesting is happening here."

"And what *does* the system think is happening here?"

"You're alone and asleep, as you were last night."

"There's definitely no humans involved?"

"Not in the surveillance of this room. That's for Bill's eyes only."

"What if he decided to look in? Sick bastard probably likes to fantasize about slitting my throat while he watches me sleep."

"Bill's occupied—and it's not with watching your apartment."

"Yeah? Who's watching the watcher? Who's watching Bill?"

"Me."

Scott goaded. "Could've fooled me. Looks like you're sitting here talking to me."

"I have exceptional multitasking skills." I grinned. "Bill has a new acquaintance, Senator Stevens' daughter, Rochelle. He's been seeing a lot of her lately. He's currently entertaining her in his Serenity apartment—intimately. I believe he may be occupied for some time."

Scott burst out laughing. "Does Senator Stevens know about that?"

"Ah, yes. And he's not too enthusiastic."

Scott chuckled. "Bill doesn't waste time does he? His pretty little technical master has been dead for only a matter of weeks."

"She's not dead."

Scott's eyes narrowed to slits. "How do you know this? Why the fuck am I talking to you?" He slammed his coffee cup on the table and ran a hand down his face.

"I've already proven myself to you," I said quietly. "Hannah had a sister; her name was Ella. Bill had Ella terminated—killed." Time didn't make this easier to discuss. "I found this out by walking into the CIA headquarters and hooking into their central information hub. I know stuff, and I can do stuff; that's as much as you need to know. The barriers, the sea-shifters, and all the other power-hungry commodities are operational because the power station is operational, and that's because Hannah Duvaul reached the station despite the impossible odds."

Scott let out a hiss.

The Warrior in the Shadows

"I can prove to you about the power. The rest I cannot. Not at this time, anyway."

"Who are you?" Scott asked. His eyes had narrowed again, and he appeared wary.

"I'm a nobody," I answered, and that much was true.

"A nobody, huh?" Scott said slyly. "What do you want from me, nobody?"

"I want you to help me save the Shadowland from war."

He raised a brow. "So, starting with the simple stuff then, nobody?"

I grinned. "Got to start somewhere."

"So, what's the plan? How do you propose we stop a war?"

"Firstly, we need to warn the Shadowlanders. Secondly... Maybe we should focus on one thing at a time. We need to get information to our people out there, to let them know when and from where the strike will occur."

"Secondly?" Scott raised an eyebrow. "Okay, I can park that. Who's out there now apart from Hannah? Adam and his team are still with her?"

"Adam, and Jon Sanders who left an encoded message for you via the waypoint near to Thale. I had to do a little information manipulation to keep it hidden. Bill's watching for waypoint communications."

"Fuck yeah! Jon Sanders, you're kidding me! When did he message? What did he say?"

I held up a hand. "I need to know that you're all in before I show you more."

"Of course, I'm in. You think I can walk away from this now? You think I'll let you walk out that door without telling me?"

I produced what Dan referred to as my winning smile. "Better get yourself another shot of coffee," I said. "This could take a while."

Chapter 22

Shadowland

Red

Somehow, I got through the next day without making an idiot of myself, but all I could think about was the evening, wondering if there was going to be a repeat, or whether she would come to her senses and would tell me to fuck off, because she already had an alpha, thanks.

I was on edge all through the evening meal as we sat outside the tent. It was hot and humid, but a fire had been lit for cooking and provided light, along with a couple of lanterns. Hannah had been riding beside Kein today, and I'd been riding behind them, wondering what they were chatting about.

Had she seemed a little less solemn today? Was I the reason? Or had Kein let her know that Garren was due to return?

"Red, do you think I could sleep beside you again?"

I'd been so lost in thought I hadn't noticed her approach where I

The Warrior in the Shadows

sat staring broodingly at the fire. "Ah, sure." Did my voice sound a little rougher?

Joshua had already turned in, as had my former travel companion, Michael. No one paid us any attention as we headed into the tent. Like she belonged there, she slipped into my prepared bed roll and wriggled about. I bit back a groan, knowing she was slipping her panties off. Trying to get a grip of my wayward thoughts long enough to strip down to my boxer briefs without getting a hard-on was a challenge.

Everyone took to their bed except Adam and Jon, who kicked over the fire and set a lantern on low to continue their conversation on the other side of the tent.

I took longer than necessary folding my clothes, gripped by nerves, and willing Adam and Jon to shut the fuck up and go to sleep.

They were still talking as I slipped in beside her. She was lying on her side facing away from me and my hand connected with her naked ass first.

Fuck!

Her soft giggle accompanied her pushing her ass back against me.

"So impatient," I whispered next to her ear.

She moaned way too loud, and I clamped my hand over her mouth. "Shhh, be a good girl, and I'll play with your tits while we're waiting for them to go to sleep." I'd done my best to move our bedding a little away from the others, but space was limited, and there was only so much I could do.

She all but thrummed with joy as I slipped my hand under her t-shirt to cup her breast. I squeezed it in my hand, testing the weight before giving her nipple a little tug.

She arched against me.

"You like that?"

"Yes."

"Good, now be quiet and still and I'll keep playing. No talking, understood?"

She nodded, only she did a terrible job of keeping still, twitching as I played with her nipple, flicking, and pinching it before playing with the other side.

She was so fucking responsive. I wanted my mouth on her there so badly, but no way I'd get away with that.

Jon and Adam were still talking, so I did a lot of playing. Sliding my hand down once her nipples were nice and swollen to find her pussy hot and drenched.

Eventually, the light went out, and the sounds of snoring ensued.

"Part your thighs a little so I can get my fingers up inside you," I whispered.

She did.

I took my time, using soft strokes all around her clit and pussy entrance before carefully easing my fingers inside, wondering if I could find the slick gland omegas had, which was supposed to be so sensitive.

Ah... just there... As my fingers skimmed over a rough patch of skin, she jerked.

"More or stop?" I whispered against her ear.

"More, but it's sensitive."

I went slowly, sliding only the tips of my fingers lightly over that little puckered patch of skin. She bit down on her fingers.

I smirked and began to slide my fingertip from side to side over it. I got my other hand around so I could play with her nipple at the same time.

She went rigid, and her pussy clamped down over my fingers as she rode through a climax, thighs squeezed around my hand, holding me inside.

"Open up, baby. It's going to feel so good when I slide my dick into you after you've come. Lean forward for me, that way I can make sure I catch your gland while I fuck you from behind."

The bed rustled when she moved too fast.

Faint snores sounded still, and as far as I was concerned, that was a green light. Playing with Hannah and having her come for me had my dick stone hard and my balls aching to empty.

The Warrior in the Shadows

I pushed her further forward, lifted her upper thighs, and slid into her from behind, fighting back a groan.

She panted, her uneven breathing mingling with the snores. *Fuck!* Tightening my fingers on her hip, I took a few shallow thrusts, adjusting the angle slightly until that little jerk of pleasure ripped through her.

There we go. Jackpot.

I made sure to catch her gland with every thrust. Keeping it slow, teasing both of us with anticipation of the completion we craved. I wanted to do her hard. She was an omega made to take an alpha's full lust. I caught Garren fucking her once. I must have been deaf to have walked up on them without hearing what was happening. I'd backed away pretty sharp, but damn if I could ever erase the image of her small body getting fucked roughly by a huge, powerful male.

Only he wasn't here, was he? And my cock was hitting all the right spots.

She came, her nails scoring my arm and pussy crushing my cock, and I was helpless to do anything but come, dumping hot cum deep against her womb, hips jerking and failing to contain a ragged grunt that accompanied the last heady rush of pleasure.

Her sigh was one of contentment. Carefully, she pushed back against me, my cock still inside, both of us covered in sticky cum. Fuck knows how we were going to hide the mess tomorrow.

None of that mattered because she was fast asleep within seconds, and my body and mind relaxed in response. I held her close, letting my cock soften inside her, enjoying the feel of my cum in her pussy. I was an attentive lover and learned what my partners enjoyed, whether it was a one-time or many time thing. But Hannah was made for pleasure and gave so much back with her response.

Yet she was for more than me and belonged with an alpha.

None of this stopped my fool mind from crafting fantasies where she was mine.

I didn't know if it was my imagination, but everyone seemed particularly short-tempered the next day.

As usual, Hannah rode beside Kein, and I rode with Adam. We were closing in on Thale and would arrive in a few days. I didn't want to arrive. I wanted this journey to last forever because, while here, I had a reason to be next to Hannah.

But as we made camp for the evening, my heady glow of anticipation came crashing down when Michael, not best known for diplomacy and universally grouchy, muttered under his breath about needing another tent.

Maybe I was being hyper aware, but I caught Adam's chuckle before he pretended to be busy getting something out of a saddlebag.

I tensed up, sweat popping along the length of my spine. *Fuck!* Had we made too much noise? I tried to remember what exactly had happened, but everything was alarmingly blank except for Hannah's moans.

No point in wallowing in denial. I casually went over to Adam. "Ah, Adam?"

"Yes," he said bluntly. "I heard you, too."

Well, fuck.

"Does... um... Jon know?" I asked. He'd already headed off to speak with Tanis as he often did during the evening.

Adam raised a brow. "Do you know how much noise you made last night?"

I swallowed. "Do you think Tanis knows?"

Adam chuckled again, which didn't make me feel a lot better. "If Jon knows, it would be reasonable to assume that Tanis knows," he said dryly.

I was so very fucked.

The Warrior in the Shadows

Tanis

"He's sleeping with her, you know," Jon said. We had barely sat down to talk, so this statement threw me a bit.

Danel and Han sat beside us at the table and appeared similarly perplexed.

"He?" I lifted my beer to my lips. Someone had found a case at the back of one of the supply wagons, and I was in a happy mood.

"Red."

I choked on my beer. "The actual fuck?" I growled, slamming my beer against the table.

"Been at it like fucking rabbits," Jon said, before puffing out a heavy breath. "I was hoping you might have a spare tent. None of us can fucking sleep a wink."

"I'm going to fucking kill him!"

"No, you're not," Jon said, matter-of-fact, helping himself to a beer as Danel and Han's enrapt gazes swung between us.

"Hannah?" Han asked like there was some confusion about the subject in question.

"She's attached to him now," Danel offered his pearl of wisdom in his signature monotone voice that never changed, whether he was discussing imminent death or the likelihood of rain. "Killing him will destroy any chances you have with her. Thumping him won't be much better. May as well leave it be. Let Garren thump him when he returns and then she can be pissed at him."

A growl bubbled up out of my chest.

"I agree," Han said, ignoring me and plowing straight on with his opinion. "Thumping him won't help. She's an omega. Virtually mated to Garren, and someone needed to step in with him gone."

The tent flap opened before I could say a word, and Kein entered. He stopped and frowned between us.

"Just discussing Hannah and Red," Danel offered.

Kein grinned, took a beer from the crate, and sat down. The scout lived for gossip. This would make his day.

"I thought you might have stepped in," Jon offered, "with Garren out of the way. But, well, it's done now."

Danel opened his mouth.

"Don't," I bit out, "say one more word on the matter." If he told me it was just a phase and she'd get over it, I'd kick his ass. It wasn't a phase with Garren.

He wisely shut his mouth again.

"Some omegas need more," Kein said. He was on the opposite side of the table and out the reach of my fist.

I had a bad feeling he was right.

Chapter 23

Hannah

I rode beside Kein. The Shadowland scout had proven to be a fascinating companion. Thankfully, our conversations had remained in a neutral space, and he'd made no further speculation regarding me, Tanis, Garren, and/or Red.

Kein had known Tanis for many years and Garren longer still. His stories had been enlightening and, I suspected, carefully edited. Nothing was unconsidered with Kein, I discovered. He was a great storyteller with an impressive repertoire of tales, which I'd listened to with avid interest, since it distracted me. My life was already messed up enough from the traumatic events in Shadowland, then there was Garren and Tanis, and my most recent decision to sleep with Red. My speculation about the beta's skills as a lover were well and truly realized. I'd thought after being with an alpha, no beta male could possibly satisfy me.

I was wrong.

He was every bit as addictive as Garren, albeit in a very different way. The things he'd made me feel, under cover of darkness while the tent was filled with snores, defied understanding.

That he was a skilled lover was beyond question.

I squirmed in my saddle, wondering what he might do were we not constrained to be quiet and still.

"I think of Thale as my home now," Kein said as we followed the long column of riders and wagons through the trees. "I've lived in many places, but I believe a person always knows when they have found their true home."

"It's not something I've ever thought about," I replied. "I had an apartment in the city, which was small and practical for my work."

"That's because you've never found your true home." He flashed a smile. "Perhaps Thale will weave its magic upon you too?"

My eyebrows raised a touch.

He shrugged. "Let's see what you think when you behold the greatest fortress in Shadowland."

As he spoke, the trees shifted from dense to scattered before the forest opened, and we emerged onto a gently sloping grassy plain.

As I caught my first glimpse of Thale, I was struck by the startling similarity between the glistening, near-black stonework of Thale and that familiar mirage of Rymor's wall.

My heart skipped a beat at the familiarity, my mind determining for a confused moment that I was nearly home. Had the ancients, in creating the wall, replicated a structure to provide consistency to the indigenous? They must have. Why else would they be so alike?

"I wasn't expecting it to look so much like the wall," I said. Seeing a virtual representation didn't do the fortress justice.

Thale had an imposing presence, and as we drew closer, more details were revealed, with glistening black stonework cut into hard lines. Immense and utilitarian in nature, Thale was devoid of beauty or fey impracticality. It existed for a purpose, and that purpose was apparent in every aspect of its design. There was little in the way of features save for a single row of windows stretched across the highest part of its outer walls and a portcullis that centered the structure and sat like the jaws of a beast.

The Warrior in the Shadows

Thale was foreboding and unwelcoming. How could anyone look at it and think—*home*?

The portcullis began rising, and a curve in the road we followed revealed the extent of the army we'd been traveling with. "I never realized how many we were."

"Such numbers are only seen for war. Who knows, we might be mere days or weeks from traveling again in greater numbers. If all the fortresses join, it will be the greatest army Shadowland has seen."

A cold shiver trickled down my spine. The future filled me with dread and was impossible to ignore. I wondered what was happening in Rymor and what madness might have driven them to consider war.

"Do you believe all the fortresses will support Tanis?"

"He has sent for them—some are already here, I believe."

"Here? As in, inside Thale? Where would they fit?"

He laughed. "Thale is bigger than she looks, she would not be troubled to hold those who come. More likely to be troubled by the arrival of tower dwellers. You're the first of your kind to enter these walls. Your arrival won't be kept secret for long."

The uneasy churning sensation was back. Nowhere was safe. Not here and not Rymor. Would the fortress inhabitants be angry at Tanis for breaking protocol to allow us entry? Would that anger be directed at us?

Last night, Jon mentioned that being allowed into Thale was a highlight in this sorry saga—not a view I shared. Our arrival here felt climactic, like an end and a beginning rolled into one. Our rag-tag group had been traveling for so long that it was hard not to wonder what would become of us once we crossed that threshold.

The inevitability of our arrival at this juncture came sooner than I was ready for. A part of me wanted to linger in an infinite traveling loop. While I traveled, I wasn't committed to this new life. When I arrived, I was forced to accept it.

As I drew my horse through the entrance, I sensed the vastness of the structure close in around me and felt the weight of what was above fold me into its protective embrace.

I couldn't foresee how anyone could penetrate it. I knew the Shadowlanders came to war often, and in their history, these mighty structures frequently changed hands. Yet it still struck me as being an impossible task.

The thought of Rymorian technology coming out here, of powerful destructiveness being unleashed on these lands, or these walls, was horrifying to me. The delicate balance between the Shadowlanders themselves, and between Shadowlanders and the Jaru, would be irrevocably disrupted by that act.

It was interference of the highest order. It was wrong in every sense.

I'd accepted the need to go to Thale. Yet what next? I felt like a helpless leaf floating on a stream, heading toward an unknown destination. My resignation was bitter; it wasn't fair, but life, I'd discovered, wasn't about fairness or right. My idyllic Rymorian assumptions had long since been shattered.

Despite this disquiet, I realized that none of these terrible circumstances had broken me. Rather, I wasn't as afraid anymore. It further instilled a deep-rooted belief that I would cope with whatever should come next, learn from it, and embrace the resulting change.

Today heralded a new chapter in my journey through Shadowland.

Today the weeks and months of travel would end, and tonight we would sleep at Thale.

Chapter 24

Hannah

I'd been given a room, my own room, for me and no one else.
No more snoring—no more hard ground barely softened by a bedroll.

My time within Shadowland had reset my expectations of the basic needs of life. This meager space, barely sufficient to contain a bed with a single high window, was a revelation.

I couldn't see much through the window, just forests stretching out into the distance. Thick black iron bars crisscrossed the outside while the window opened inward and had been drawn wide to allow the warm air. I could fit my head through, and a glance down revealed how the twisting stairs and gently sloping passages had brought me here.

A change of clothes clutched in my arms, I approached the tiny bed and gave it an experimental press with my hand. Not exactly soft, but a million times better than the forest floor. It was a tragedy that Garren had gone in search of Marcus' associates. I hadn't seen him since the day the infamous Rymorian had died, and it would have been nice, for once, to spend time with him in a proper bed.

Only, once Garren came back there would be no more Red.

I hadn't spoken to him all day, and we'd been ushered in different directions on arrival.

A consideration for later...

A woman hovered in the doorway, perhaps a few years younger than me with a mop of curly red hair, a ready smile, and a face covered in freckles. Mari wasn't a servant herself, but she had directed several people to tasks in a way that left me no doubt they *were*. I wasn't comfortable with the idea of servants. I knew such hierarchies had existed in our dim and distant past, but the discovery that it was commonplace on this side of the wall surprised me.

"Are you ready, miss?"

I nodded and was ushered out of the room by Mari and her servant entourage into a vast and confusing maze of corridors. The internal walls were as black as those outside, and few windows could be seen. High stone recesses built into the wall emitted weak illumination. After the warmth and brightness outside, the fortress was cool, dark, and confusing to the senses. As we walked, Mari chatted amiably, distracting me from a blooming attack of claustrophobia. At least my room had a window. I would have ended up going a little crazy if it didn't.

We stopped at a set of wide double doors, and I was urged inside. The room was thick with steam, with curtained-off areas in rows along either side. Mari guided me to one. Behind the curtain, I found a bath, full to the brim, with clean steaming water.

"A servant will wait outside." Mari bobbed her head and smiled prettily. "Take as long as you need."

"Thank you." Those simple words felt inadequate to describe my gratitude.

She left and I closed myself into the humid warmth and placed my clean clothing on the stool beside the bath.

The first dip of my fingers revealed blissful warmth. I stripped out of my clothes with an enthusiasm that bordered on a frenzy and

The Warrior in the Shadows

climbed into the water. I giggled as I sank in. This had to be the closest thing to heaven I'd experienced in many weeks.

With a deep, heartfelt sigh, I sank deeper. The warm water eased my tired muscles and soothed my battered soul.

It was too much and yet too little. Tears sprang from behind my eyes.

My lips trembled as buried emotions surfaced, and all that had been lost came to the fore. The tears fell, dripping onto the soothing water. I missed Edward and his amusing, and at times alarming, conversations.

I missed Molly, the little orphan girl with her funny little forthright ways, and who, at only five, had witnessed the death of her parents and siblings during a Jaru attack. *"The Jaru killed all my family. Tanis promised he would kill them so they couldn't hurt anyone else."* Molly had told me the very first day we met.

Tanis had kept that promise, yet it saddened me to think of Molly at Julant without a family. I wanted to care for Molly, as impractical, or even dangerous, as it might have been. We were both misfits in our own way, lost to our homes and families. It had broken my heart, leaving Molly behind in the village that day.

Most of all, I missed Ella, my sister, and my best friend.

The walls of the fortress were thick and impenetrable, and despite the alienness of the place and the people within it, I felt safe.

I lay in the water, drifting out of time. Wondering about the crazy circumstance that had led to me lying in a bathhouse of a fortress so far from my family and home.

How even more improbable that this bathhouse, and the building housing it, could be turned into a pile of rubble by war.

Despite these troubling thoughts, relaxation seeped in, and the flow of my tears began to ease. The war wasn't happening today. Tomorrow—that was different. My mind refused to stretch past the immediate with any level of cohesion. I felt bad about keeping the servant waiting, yet couldn't be quick.

Being clean was an absent luxury while traveling through Shadowland. I had done my best, wherever possible, but with only the clothes on my back since that fateful first Jaru attack, there was only so much I could do. My hair touched my shoulders, something that had never happened in my life.

I examined the hard soap block—it smelt herby and fresh. I rubbed it into my hair—scrubbed—rinsed—and repeated twice before I started cleaning my body. By the time I'd finished, the water was gray, and I used a bucket of clean water to rinse myself off.

I climbed out of the bath and pulled the strange chain holding a plug to release the dirty water. The clean clothing was coarse against my water-softened skin, but smelt so fresh I didn't care about the rest. My Rymorian boots had survived the journey and were still soft around my feet, if a little scuffed and dusty.

As Mari had indicated, a servant waited outside. A young woman, perhaps late teens, with a cloth hat and woolen dress, gathered the dirty clothes the moment I opened the curtain and directed me out of the room.

"How long until dinner?" I realized I might have spent longer than I should have in the bath. Adam had promised that one of them would collect me for dinner… a meal that didn't involve sitting on the floor. Kein said there would be a more formal gathering in a few days once the other fortress leaders arrived, but tonight the prospect of anything beyond travel crackers was enough to stir my excitement.

"Soon, miss," my servant said, guiding me along passages. I followed no better this time around and after a short while we arrived back at my allocated room.

"Mari sent for tea for you, miss." The servant bobbed a curtsy.

On the tiny table beside the bed was a wooden tray holding an earthen teapot and a cup. There was also a comb and mirror lying next to it.

"Thank you." I smiled at the young woman, who, with another bob, left, closing the door behind her.

I didn't move for the longest time, eyes on the mirror, wondering

The Warrior in the Shadows

if I would look different and if the terrible experiences would be revealed on my face.

My hair had begun to dry, and my attempts to finger-comb it had achieved limited success. Longer than I preferred, the curls had turned wild without the aid of products and my straighteners. The comb was inviting.

Resolute, I picked up the comb, and, sitting on the edge of the bed, began the task of working it through. I made progress with much wincing, tugging, and extraction of clumps of hair. I poured a cup of the strange floral tea. Tried to remember the name of it.

Chamomile?

It made an improvement over water, and it broke up my mission to tame my curls. The comb moved through my hair when I'd finished my tea. The mirror was still resting face up, and I'd yet to decide whether to look. My tangle-free hair was longer than I expected, and I pulled a wispy strand in front of my face to examine it.

I pulled it experimentally—it was very curly.

A knock on the door interrupted me. When I went to open it, I found Red standing there.

We stared at each other for a long time.

He stepped into the room with me, fighting a smile. "That's, um, wow."

"What?" I reached self-conscious fingers toward my hair, before snatching up the mirror as Red snorted a laugh.

Oversized gray eyes, check.

Face exactly the same, check.

Wild corkscrew hair that stuck out in every direction. I guessed cleaning it had unleashed the beast. "God!" I mumbled. "I really need to get it cut."

"It's a little..." Red got his laughter under control with an effort. "Different."

"It's only hair." I shoved the mirror back on the table with a clunk.

Red raised an eyebrow and asked me, deadpan, "How about wearing a hat?"

I shook my head, laughing.

I hadn't laughed, really laughed, in days.

Not since Edward had been killed.

The pain hit me so hard and so sudden that I froze. He'd wanted to see a fortress. Thanks to Marcus, he never would.

"Hey, you, okay? I was only joking about your hair. It's not that bad."

I took an unsteady breath, pushing the sorrow away to roll my eyes at Red.

"Okay, it's pretty bad." He gave me a worried smile.

I felt like I was drowning at times like I couldn't breathe again. Pressing my fingers against my chest, I tried to steady the uneven passage of air. "It's not the hair. I mean—I can see what it looks like. I'm just so sad about Edward. He always wanted to see a fortress or a city. Now he never will."

He gathered me into his arms in a way he'd never been able to. "Yeah, me too, Hannah."

"Sometimes I feel fine," I said, breathing in his clean scent and taking comfort from the steady beat of his heart, "and then I remember, and I'm not. I feel this terrible guilt in being happy, in being alive when he isn't."

He sighed. "It's normal, Hannah. It's called grief."

"I know," I said. "Knowing doesn't make it go away, though."

"It's going to take time, but I understand. I feel guilty too. I wonder what would have happened if I'd gone in the tent next. If I would be dead instead, or if I could have done something different that would have resulted in a better outcome."

He kissed the top of my head.

"Will you stay here with me tonight?"

"Of course, if you want me too."

Was I using him? Was I being unfair, when this couldn't

The Warrior in the Shadows

continue once Garren returned? I thought I might have been, but I couldn't work out how to pull back.

"Come on," he said, setting me at arm's length and winking. "I'm starving and I have it on good authority, the food here is going to be great. After... after I'm looking forward to being with you without a medley of snores." His face softened, and he cupped my cheek before pressing his lips to mine in a brief, chaste kiss. "I don't mean I'm about to jump on you, Hannah. Never think that. If you only want to be held that's fine. Whatever we do, or don't, is always your choice."

"Thank you," I said.

"You never have to thank me." Taking my hand in his, he walked me from the room, out into the fortress, and along the corridors.

Putting aside my sorrow, I resolved to make the best of whatever was to come.

Chapter 25

Rymor

Bill

My transport glided to touch down on the landing pad. My home on the southern coast of Rymor had been procured twelve years ago. While it was a stunning home, its location, so close to a Shadowland access point, had clinched my decision to purchase. According to the records, that access point had been blocked off centuries ago. I'd reinstated it illegally and used it in my younger years when traveling beyond the wall myself.

I was a chancellor, and circumstances meant I hadn't ventured into Shadowland for ten years. I'd considered selling the property, but with hindsight, it had proven an excellent investment that facilitated me sending others out there.

Karry had sent a brief message to say he was back in Rymor, and I was impatient to hear his news. Furthermore, I was surprised he'd returned, given he'd failed to keep the station inoperative.

The Warrior in the Shadows

I'd been furious when Richard had dropped that news about Hannah contacting Dan from the station. The operational status of Station fifty-four was bad enough. Hannah's potential return would be catastrophic, especially if she started proclaiming Shadowlanders as heroes of the day.

The stakes were rising. This wasn't only about revenge now, although that was undoubtedly a large part of the equation. It was also about survival. My hatred toward Tanis was so great that I was willing to sacrifice anyone and anything in my quest for revenge.

Tanis had told me once that I didn't possess a conscience, and I remembered looking up through a haze of pain at him as he stood over me.

"What made you this cold, Bill? You really don't give a fuck what you do or who you do it to," Tanis had said, and nearly unconscious, I'd simply stared back.

"The only thing you understand is pain. Well, I can give you that."

I'd watched Tanis' fist come down like it was happening to someone else. It was the last time the two of us met in person.

Many men had been sent to kill him; all had failed. The station provided the perfect opportunity to change that. Tanis had become too powerful—I still struggled to accept just how powerful—and a Rymorian army was the only way to see the job done.

My lack of control beyond Rymor's wall had become a growing source of frustration. With the satellite coverage restored, I'd gained some access to visual monitoring. But communication outside the wall was via the waypoint system, which remained under the control of the Field Monitoring Services, a subsidiary of Global Operations. Scott Harding, the appointed head of Global Operations, was making waves the size of a tsunami. I couldn't afford for Harding to get wind of a waypoint communication. Hiding activity had been easy when there were thirty active teams, but impossible when there were only two teams officially on active duty, both of which had been declared MIA and presumed dead.

The waypoints remained unavailable to me, and the remaining sixty or so field scientists under Harding continued to abstain from active duty.

I wondered how much Karry knew about the station restart and Adam's team... about Hannah being at the station. It had been operational for a month, and a lot could have happened during that time. I was curious about how Hannah might be faring. Shadowland was a harsh environment under normal times, and these were far from normal times. Hannah's parents dying when she was at such a tender age must have left scars, and would doubtless increase any sense of abandonment out there.

Tanis' former partner, Ava, had been a confident, self-possessed woman, strong enough in her convictions to have walked away from Tanis. Yet, she had broken swiftly once she found herself in Shadowland. I thought Hannah, with her past family tragedy and repressed omega status, would be challenged in far greater ways.

The transport powered down with a diminishing whirr, and the doors opened under laborious, safety-constrained automation. It was a pleasant day, and I left the walkway to my home uncovered—the sharp, salty air hitting me the moment I stepped out. Although cloudless, the sky had a washed-out haze, the sea a shade darker with white-tipped swells.

Hopefully I didn't half-kill Karry this time.

Purposeful strides took me to my home as I considered the fate of those beyond the wall. My own activity there had expanded again this week when Damien Moore left with a group of eight reconnaissance specialists, aiming to meet with Ailey after crossing the Jaru border.

The Jaru Warlord's hatred of Shadowlanders was well-known, and I'd struck a deal with him many years ago. Our initial agreement involved gifts. Later, I'd had his only known weakness, his daughter, taken captive to provide greater leverage. She had been my guest ever since. Ailey would do his part in aiding Damien and the team.

Once inside, I admired the sweeping views across the gardens

The Warrior in the Shadows

and the sea beyond. I enjoyed being here when I needed a little solitude or could afford to dedicate time to my viewing room—a rare indulgence lately. With a few hours until dusk when Karry was due to arrive, I was drawn toward the window where I stared out at the sea.

I'd been slowly removing Richard from my inner circle and bringing Kelard further in. Richard had served his purpose, and I could see him being useful again when this war was over. In the current climate, I needed the new skills held by men like Councilman Carl Stevens and Kelard Wilder.

The last impediment to war had been removed with the upper house's approval. Richard's visit had increased my sense of urgency. Within days, forces would be en route to Thale, the source of Tanis' power. A ground assault wasn't my preference, but an air assault had been dismissed. While accepting the need for force, Gaia had been restrictive on the type and power of weapons that could be used. Indigenous casualties and structural damage should be minimized.

I could work within those constraints. All I needed was Tanis.

There was a time when I'd wanted Thale reduced to a pile of rubble and Tanis' head on a pike outside. But my interest in Shadowland had shifted since that fateful day of the earthquake. This war wasn't only about removing Tanis. Many things had become apparent after I'd established a base at Talin, the old abandoned fortress closest to the wall. It was clear that the ancients who left us their technological legacy had once played in the lands beyond the wall. I wanted to see Thale, the greatest of the fortresses, for myself. I welcomed the war as an opportunity to open that door and bring Tanis to his knees.

Within Rymor, there were still a few people I needed to manage, including Coco Tanis and the ever-meddling Dan Gilmore. The technical master knew more about ancient technology than I'd realized. That made him dangerous, and I didn't keep uncontrollable, dangerous people around.

Removing Dan would be a delicate task, but his frailty could be exploited.

And perhaps, like Ella, his removal might deliver unexpected benefits.

Chapter 26

Bill

It was late by the time Karry arrived, and the gardens beyond my windows were lost in shadows, with only the weaker of the two moons in the night sky.

I'd been drinking, perhaps not the best idea, but the wait had increased my impatience, and the warmth of liquor had seemed the right way to go.

Karry, a tall, slim man who had aged poorly, sat opposite. Before the former convict uttered a word, I could tell that he had nothing good to say. He had been part of my reconnaissance efforts in Shadowland for five years, paid from personal funds, which allowed me complete autonomy on how to use him.

I drank from the crystal tumbler in my hand, feeling the warmth trickle down my throat and into my gut. I hadn't offered anything to Karry, nor did I intend to.

He rubbed his fingers restlessly over his jaw. "Things haven't gone to plan." He barked out a sharp laugh. "You probably guessed that."

"I'm surprised you came back." My rage was building. I rarely gave it an outlet and found the sensation so stimulating that I was inclined to draw this out.

Karry shifted under my aggressive gaze. "I haven't finished the job you gave me. For better or worse, I intend to see this through. I owe you that much. I was in a bad place when you found me. You deserve to know."

I relaxed. He was right. Better I had the news, whether good or bad. Hannah might still be alive—a month ago, she was. "Go on."

"No easy way to say this, so I'm gonna spit it out. We lost them all —the people from the transport that we were holding at the trapper lodge. Never got to Adam Harris' team either. They're still with Tanis' men—maybe with Tanis himself. We tried to stop them reaching the station, but it didn't work. I assume they got someone in; on the last day of the battle we heard it power up. Thought it was another earthquake at first. Could have been Hannah. Could have been one of the others. I mean, I think there was time. The Jaru were already whipped by then. I've no idea how many garrisons came to support Tanis, but it was carnage and the Jaru fled. Ailey took the survivors and regrouped over the border. That was the last time I spoke to him. That's when he told me the trapper lodge had been hit."

I blinked slowly as that disaster settled in.

Karry fidgeted in the seat. "I owe you. I'll make this right."

I put the drink down slowly and stood. "What was Ailey's part in this?"

"Ailey? I don't know exactly. We both screwed up."

"And Jon Sanders?"

"Not sure, either. Could be dead or could have escaped."

I'd lost control last time. I was determined not to do so today. This time I needed to be in control. My hand moved as if in slow motion, fingers closing into a fist before the sharp ripple of pain shot the length of my arm as I smashed it into Karry's face.

Karry collapsed, another satisfying crack as his skull hit the stone floor. The barest groan escaped as he rolled himself onto his knees.

The Warrior in the Shadows

I failed my quest for control, and the sensations melded into a blur. The sharp satisfaction intensified with every blow and every agonized cry Karry made. The sting in my fists echoed the darker pain of my victim and only increased my fervor. The inner voice told me to stop, but it was easier to ignore.

By the time I did stop, my ragged breathing was loud against the sudden quietness, and Karry lay bloody and deathly still on the blood-splattered floor with bruises ringing his neck.

Anger surged at what I'd done. I hadn't gotten all my answers yet.

I pressed his fingers against Karry's neck. "Fuck it!" I kicked the lifeless body to hear the crack of bones snapping. Only it was no longer satisfying because Karry was already dead.

With a tight growl, I stalked from the room and collected a medical scanner. It was a long shot, but the damage might not be irreversible if I worked fast.

I crouched, dragging Karry onto his back, and ripped his shirt apart before sinking the short, sharp probe into his chest.

The health indicator panel lit a row of red, confirming his deathly state. The violent jerk of its defibrillator sent Karry convulsing before he gasped a hoarse breath.

One red light turned green.

"Lie still!" I said tersely, fisting his upper arm and using my weight to pin him against the floor. The last thing I wanted was Karry ripping the scanner out halfway through whatever it was fixing.

Karry coughed in a feeble, watery hack. "What happened?"

"You died," I said coldly.

Karry coughed weakly again. Sweat glistened on his gray face. "Feel like I've been stabbed in the chest."

"Don't touch the scanner. It's still embedded."

Karry's horror-filled eyes stared down at the shiny white scanner embedded in his chest. "You're not supposed to stab people with them, or were you being creative?" He rasped up another wet cough.

"You do if their heart has stopped beating."

"Fuck me," he muttered between pants. "I thought you were messing with me."

The red lights on the health indicator panel were slowly turning off. "I can take it out now."

Karry swore again when I extracted the probe. I placed it on the table beside my chair, sat, and picked up my drink. I downed what was left.

"I don't think it finished. I feel like shit." Karry ran a shaky hand over his chest.

"It's fixed enough. You're still here."

He rolled onto his side, drew his knees into his chest, and lay motionless.

"Is Hannah still alive?"

Karry shifted and then scoffed. "Opening my mouth seems to get me killed. Better explain why I should do that again?"

"Keeping your mouth shut will get you there quicker. Is. She. Alive?"

He muttered another curse. "Yeah, she's alive. She was ten days ago, anyway. She's probably in Thale by now."

"In Thale?" The muscles in my body locked up as this information settled in.

Karry rolled to a sitting position, his legs splayed, and his shoulders slumped. "I need some water." He dragged himself up from the floor and collapsed into the seat.

"Keep talking." I rose and collected a glass of water. I was invested now, and glad I'd thought to bring him back.

"I sent David Renner, aka Marcus, back in to try and kill them. Couldn't think of any other way to get through to them. Figured they knew him, and would welcome him back in. They did. Not sure what happened but we came across his body left where they knew we would find it."

I handed the water to Karry, who proceeded to gulp it down.

"How long was he with them?"

The Warrior in the Shadows

"A week. We were following them—as much as you can follow an army of ten thousand."

I blanched as I returned to my seat. "Ten thousand? Are you exaggerating to save your neck?"

"No, I'm not. Now perhaps you see the issues we had." He fumbled in his jacket pocket and pulled out a crumpled piece of paper.

I believe that I enjoyed Marcus' (David's) company far more than he enjoyed mine. Although he became very eager to please as our short acquaintance progressed.

Do you still dream about that sword coming down?

And do you ever dream of it coming down a little to the left?

I read the note. Then read it twice more.

Tanis was going to die—slowly.

"Do you think it was him? Do you think Tanis wrote it?" There was the tiniest hint of awe in Karry's voice, which really pissed me off.

"No." *Yes, of course, it was Tanis!* "It could have been anyone."

"It's just that bit about the sword, sounds a bit odd. Like a message or something."

"Or something," I said. Screwing the paper in my hand, I tossed it aside. "Let us be clear on this, you sent David Renner back into Tanis' group, and he comes out dead seven days later after squealing every single thing he knows?"

"Probably." Karry eyed me warily.

"Not the best idea you've had. Did you really think Renner was capable of killing the Rymorians? All of them? And then getting himself out? If you even try to think again, I'll leave you dead next time."

I lost it completely the second time. There was nothing afterward beside a gaping hole in my memory and a crumpled lifeless body with one arm snapped at the elbow and bone and cartilage poking out.

I thought about pushing it into place, but the puddle of blood rendered it a secondary concern.

It took many minutes to bring Karry around as the defibrillator jerked his body like a tormented puppet that splattered the floor, furnishings, and me with a grisly, bloody pulp.

Karry remained still for a long time, even after his heart started. His face was a waxy kind of gray. His arm hung limp. Although it was sealed and wasn't life-threatening, it would be useless without professional correction. That delay was going to be frustrating since I'd decided to send Karry into Shadowland again.

"I want Hannah back. I want her out of that fortress and back in my control, and I want you to do it."

"Screw you," Karry said. "Just kill me again and leave me dead."

"Everyone has someone they care about, Karry," I said calmly.

Karry's bitter laugh turned into a wet, hacking cough. "Screw you," he said softly.

"I want her extracted," I repeated.

"Who do you care about, Bill?" Karry demanded. "Who do you give a fuck about?"

I stared back. "Planning to obtain some leverage?"

"Not everyone cares about someone." Karry scoffed as he swung his deformed arm. "May need to fix my arm first." His voice came out over gravel, and he fell into another bout of violent coughing. By the time he'd gotten it under control, he was sweating profusely and slumped back in his chair.

"So, get it fixed and then get back there. Take a team and weapons—whatever the fuck you need."

Karry gave me a flat look. "You're taking the restrictions off?"

I nodded. "You'll need technology to extract someone from a fortress. Once she's out, question her. You may use coercion within reason, but nothing permanent in nature."

The Warrior in the Shadows

Karry laughed, nasty and low. He started to cough but clamped his mouth shut, and it settled into little bubbling rasps. "You just killed me—twice—and now you're telling me I can have a little fun with Hannah Duvaul? You really have a way. If I didn't still feel half dead, I might be able to figure out how fucked up all this is."

"Question her. Frighten her if need be. But no permanent damage. Touch her sexually, and you'll wish I left you dead. Understood?"

Karry nodded. "Sure, but don't ask me to account for what's happened to her before we find her. She's been in Shadowland, probably already acquainted herself with half a dozen of those thickheaded bastards. Maybe Tanis has been dipping into that hole. Are you sure you want her back?"

Somehow, I contained my temper. I thought Karry wouldn't survive another round. For now, I needed him to bring Hannah back.

"I want to know what's happened to her and how much interaction she's had with John Tanis. She still has the tracker in her, so use it. Get me answers, then take her to Talin."

Karry's gray face paled further. "Talin? You're kidding?"

"I don't joke, Karry. I've no intention of returning her to Rymor. She's already exactly where I want her."

Karry's slow chuckle had a harsh, raspy, unhealthy sound. "You're going out there, aren't you? That's been your intention from the start. And you'll keep her out there with you, a little secret all for yourself."

"Don't start thinking again, Karry. You recall what happened last time. Make the preparations. Use my transport, get your arm fixed and get a team back out there."

"Sure." He rose unsteadily and left, without a backward glance.

I stared sightlessly at the bloody floor for a long time before calling the cleaner. The industrious little unit trundled in and began a cleaning frenzy.

I had much to deliberate on, and some adjustments would be

needed. The night had already been long, and I was tired, but I knew what would soothe me.

I hadn't taken the time to go to my secret room in recent weeks; it was more than overdue.

I spent longer than I should have down there and drank far more than was healthy. Then I hit the drugs, a heady cocktail, before staggering to my bed. I stopped dead when I entered my bedroom and swayed, wondering if I was hallucinating. A bright blue beanbag sat on the floor in the middle of the room. I stared at it for a long moment, then approached cautiously, and poked it with a finger to be absolutely sure. An empty Berry Blast bottle was propped in the middle of it.

I let my breath out on a furious hiss.

What the fuck was that doing here?

Chapter 27

Shadowland

Tanis

From the prestigious location of the high table on the dais, I surveyed Thale's hall and the feast taking place. Sometimes I almost forgot that I was a leader with a country, fortresses, cities, and towns under my command. Tonight, I was reminded of all I had achieved as well as all I could lose.

Tonight, nearly seven hundred had been crammed into the space that comfortably seated five hundred, with tables, chairs, and other essentials for the feast having been dragged out of storage. It represented a fraction of the number of those living at Thale, and included the most influential people. The rest would eat in the lower food halls flanking the kitchens and barracks.

A season had elapsed since I'd passed under the portcullis of Thale's entrance, and spring rains had given way to the warmth of early summer. The temperatures would soar soon, making it the worst possible time of year to be contemplating a battle of legendary proportions.

My likelihood of surviving to see another spring wasn't looking good.

I wasn't usually so melancholic. In all my years here, all those near-death encounters, I'd never felt my fate's inescapability as I did now.

There were always options. I could give up, flee Thale, and abandon my lands to whatever Bill was about to unleash. I could hide in a remote location and bide my time for revenge.

The idea held merit.

Yet I was sick of the cloud hanging over me, all the people he sent to assassinate me, and the sense of always looking over my shoulder for the next poisoned blade or attack. One way or another, I was ready for this to be over.

This wasn't all about Bill and his plans for war revealed by Marcus' confession. There was more at work here than my former friend's desire to decimate Shadowland. The Jaru attack on Valoret had been the tipping point for so much more. Their numbers spilling over the border close to the station were equal cause for concern.

There were too many moving parts, and I explored in detail my own desires and motivations for the actions I might take.

The bottom line: I hadn't sought power, but now that it was mine, I liked it. If someone wanted to take it from me, they'd have to pry it from my cold, dead hands.

"Any news on Garren?" Javid sat sprawled in his chair to my right in a pose that reminded me of my absent brother. The similarity between Javid and Garren had always been striking, the same sandy blond hair and blue eyes, the same mannerisms, and the same nonchalant approach to life. Javid embraced the potential arrival of Rymorian troops with the same concern as any other attack, which, in summary, was not at all.

"None," I said.

I should probably send a scout to bring Garren back.

The Warrior in the Shadows

I should have called for his return a week ago.

Tomorrow, I decided, my attention drifting to where the Rymorians sat at a table in my line of sight, a location of my determining because I preferred to have them close. Gatherings such as this were few and far between. It was only a matter of time before the night degenerated into drunken debauchery, violence, or both. I'd given my guards orders to escort the group from Rymor to their quarters at the first sign of trouble. Weapons had been removed from anyone entering the hall, but that left plenty of scope for brawling or fucking. A war was coming, and Shadowlanders embraced any excuse for excess and revelry.

A woman came to refill my cup. There was an easily accessible gap on the other side of the table, but she chose to squeeze between Javid and me and, with seeming nonchalance, positioned her cleavage at perfect eye level.

She took an inordinate amount of time to complete that simple task. "You're not a servant," I observed with narrowed eyes.

"Everyone has been so busy, what with all the guests. It seemed charitable to offer to help."

"Uh huh." I gave her a speculative look.

"I have a friend," she whispered loud enough to elicit a chuckle from Javid. "She is very charitable, too."

I decided I'd missed my home a lot.

Her smile was unashamedly coy, and she squeezed up against me as she left.

"So, shouldn't you have called him back by now?" Javid asked, voicing my earlier thoughts, and distracting me from my perusal of the retreating woman's ass. "You two haven't had a good brawl for a while. Always a pleasure watching you thump one another. I think Garren might be gaining the edge on you, son."

I pushed my plate away and snatched up my full cup of wine. The Thale cooks, enthused by the multitude of high guests, had excelled themselves, and the food had been delicious. "Not in this lifetime," I said.

Javid laughed, delighted to have gotten a rise, and returned his attention to the pretty brunette on his other side.

My gaze shifted to Hannah, whose hair looked particularly wild, an impressive feat given how bad it looked most days. As if aware of my critical study, her hand reached to pat it down—washing it clearly hadn't done it any favors.

My eyes shifted to the sidelines, not far from the Rymorians, where Kein stood, staring back at me, grinning.

I took another hefty gulp of the wine.

For all Kein's intelligence, he was an outrageous gossip and astute at picking up cues. Not that he needed such skills tonight, given I was staring broodingly at Hannah, sitting next to my father, which was always a recipe for a tense night.

Although now I thought about it, I wasn't feeling as tense as I usually did. My father was mainly occupied with his companion, which minimized his propensity to bait me. This particular woman wasn't much older than Garren, and Javid certainly wasn't opposed to her attention. Now that the servants were clearing the plates away, I expected the situation to go downhill fast. Javid had been without a partner since his last wife died during the childbirth of his youngest daughter, Hawley. As a fortress leader, Javid was considered quite a catch—enough to overlook his trying personality.

"Good gathering," Lari offered from my left. Lari was a taciturn man with frizzy red hair. He was a head shorter than me, which didn't make him exactly short, but he made up for this by being twice as wide. While the muscle of his youth had turned toward fat, he still terrified most of the fortress garrison who reported to him. The rest of the fortress inhabitants harbored a healthy sense of respect. As Thale's commander, Lari and the fortress steward had been tested by the arrival of additional people, horses, and supplies. Thankfully the tunnel complex underneath was extensive and had coped with the swell.

I'd often wondered what the fortresses had been like during the early years of their creation. The vast underground complex and stores, which could keep food cold and dry, were sufficient to house and feed a population ten times the current size.

People didn't often build more than they needed.

"Yes, a good gathering," I agreed. Adro, the ruler of Galin, was already here, having aided me at the station. He sat with his section leaders at a table to the left of the dais. Given that Adro and Javid only communicated via verbal threats, keeping them apart as much as possible was for the best. Greve, the ruler of Techin, had arrived earlier today, which left only Falton, the ruler of Tain, to confirm his arrival date. His was the furthest fortress from Thale, though, so his late appearance wasn't yet remiss.

I noticed a scout talking to Kein. Their conversation exuded a tension that picked at my resolve to remain relaxed. They would notify me if the matter was important, yet I still rose from my chair and headed over. As I passed Javid, my father's raucous laughter accompanied his companion climbing onto his lap.

The mood was sliding downhill fast.

"What has happened?" I demanded the moment I reached Kein.

"It seems it was prudent to leave a couple of tower dwellers at the waypoint with Danel," Kein said, voice low so as not to carry. "You have communication from Scott Harding. It was for the attention of Adam Harris, and you."

I raised both eyebrows. Scott Harding was the head of Global Operations, which included Field Operations and field scientists. Scott had taken exception to me back during my brief time as a field scientist. Phrases like 'out of control' and 'troublemaker' had been tossed around long before Bill declared me a terrorist and exiled me from Rymor. Scott wasn't one to mince his words, and I doubted that had changed. Why the fuck would he want to contact me?

A loud *thud* and the sound of a woman's laughter came from behind. Glancing over my shoulder, I found my father reaching for his belt with his companion spread out on the table.

"For fuck's sake," I muttered. "Could he not wait until the tables were cleared?"

Kein chuckled. "Like father, like son."

I narrowed my eyes on Kein. "Garren's not here," I pointed out. And thank fuck for that because if he tossed Hannah on a table and fucked her in front of me, there would be blood on the floor.

Kein's expression was one of feigned innocence. "I was thinking more of you."

I huffed out a curse.

"Would you like me to escort the Rymorians from the room?" Kein offered, still grinning.

"Yes, by all means, escort the Rymorians from the room," I said, irritation dripping from my tone. "At least no one has started a fight yet."

As if on cue, a cry came from the other side of the room, and a brawl broke out. Roused into action, my guards began ushering the Rymorians out. "Bring Jon and Adam to my room," I said to Kein as the hall degenerated further.

"I thought you might already have plans for tonight," Kein said, his face completely straight.

"I might have," I said, lips tugging up. "But given she either blackmailed, bribed, or offered favors so she could serve me a drink, I'm confident that she and her charitable companion can work out how to find me when we're done with our discussion."

Chapter 28

Red

The food was excellent, and the beer was plentiful and strong. Many troubles were brewing on the horizon, but it felt good to put them aside for once. Then, as the feast started to get interesting, we were ushered out of the hall.

Not that I minded, when it would give me more alone time with Hannah.

There had been frequent conversations regarding Rymor's mobilization. I knew it bothered Hannah that she was excluded from this, but that was Adam's decision, not mine. She wasn't alone in being excluded. Joshua, the remaining technical expert, was similarly out of the loop, also at Adam's discretion. I didn't see much of either of them during the day, but the nights were mine and Hannah's, and I took every moment of joy I could get. Soon Garren would return, or war would come, either of which would rip me from the pleasure that was mine when I was with Hannah.

The mood was buoyant as we were escorted back to our rooms. Glancing down, I caught Hannah's gaze and smiled before capturing her hand in mine.

Jon had nabbed a couple of beer flagons, which provoked a rare chuckle from Adam. Only we never made it back to our part of the fortress before a couple of wolf guards came to take Adam and Jon away.

Jon handed the beer over to one of the team. "Save me some," he said, winking, before heading off.

The others dispersed, heading into Adam's room, which was the largest and served as a hub of sorts.

"You want a drink?" I asked Hannah, trying not to show how eager I was to get her alone.

"No," she replied, her cheeks a little flushed. Perhaps an effect of the beer she'd sampled during the feast, or perhaps, like me, something else was on her mind.

"Want me to walk you back to your room?" I didn't need to walk her anywhere when the ever-present guards would ensure that Hannah, an unmated omega, was always safe.

She nodded.

Her room was only two down from Adam's and the smallest of them all. My feet hung off the bottom of the bed by a good foot—it was a tight squeeze—but I'd still take her cramped space to be next to her if she let me.

"Do you want me to—uff." I was dragged over the threshold and pushed up against the closed door.

"Kiss me, Red," she commanded.

Her humble servant in every way, I gathered her close and found heaven when her lips parted for me. She was impatient, already fumbling with my belt buckle, clumsy as we kissed, and I tried with equal enthusiasm to divest her of her clothes. I was hard and ready for whatever the fuck she needed from me.

My buckle clattered as it came undone, and she sank to her knees, directing the head of my cock to her parted lips.

"Ah, fuck!"

She sucked me straight to the back of her throat, swirling her tongue around the head and making me see stars. "Fuck, baby, I'm not going to last." I took her hair gently, drawing it from her face, watching her cheeks hollow in the lamplight. She was so beautiful: wild, and a little broken by circumstances. I should be worshiping her, yet I could deny her nothing. "I'm going to come, Hannah. Fuck, I can't hold it. You feel too fucking good."

Her small hands tightened on my ass, holding me close like I might resist.

"Fuck!" Stars danced behind my eyes, and my legs shook like I was caught in a storm. My balls tightened as I came in hot, heavy jets down her willing throat. Worried I might collapse, I slammed my palm against the door behind me, breathing heavily, trying to lock my knees.

I pulled her off when she was intent on going for round two. Her cute whine made me chuckle. "Baby, I'm a beta, we need a bit of down time, hmm?"

I'd never envied an alpha more than I did at that moment. She'd gotten wilder since we'd arrived at the fortress, was unafraid to say what she wanted, and was so fucking responsive to every touch. Much as my pride didn't want to admit defeat, I knew she could handle a lot more than I could give.

I tightened my fingers a little on her hair. "You want it rough, Hannah?"

She nodded.

"Tell me, then," I demanded. "Say the words."

I was big for a beta. She was so tiny on her knees before me, yet every bit of power sat squarely with her. "Please, Red, I want it rough." Her face flushed. "I want you to do that thing... like you did last time."

My eyes widened. My cock, recently depleted, gave an enthusiastic thump.

"Strip these clothes out the way then, baby. I want you on the bed, spread open and ready for me. But we'll go slowly. If I think you are ready, and can handle my fist all up inside you, then I will. But only if I'm sure you really need it and are thoroughly aroused."

She scrambled up and tore out of her clothes. I watched her undress, lost in a daze over what she wanted me to do *again*, undressing myself, although my entire focus was on Hannah, as, gloriously naked, she lay down on the bed.

Her chest rose and fell unsteadily as I came down over her, kissing her gently, nibbling the corner of her lips, feeling her impatience in the way her fingers curled at my shoulders, petting, making tiny fists, then petting again. I took my time, kissing up her mumbled nonsense, trailing my lips along the delicate column of her throat, sucking on her earlobe before kissing over her collar bone and teasing her breasts. Her legs fell open, her wet pussy smearing over any part of me she could rub on.

I ignored it. Pinched and twisted her nipples until she gasped and twitched, making her tell me she wanted it harder at every stage, making her beg for it. Then sucking on them alternately while she fisted my hair and humped my thigh.

Only when she was good and desperate did my kisses trail lower, over her trim waist, until I found her hot, wet core, parting her, and taking a long lick.

"God, please, Red. I'm ready. God, it feels so good when you do it. I need it so bad."

I slipped two fingers inside her, curling them upward, finding that little puckered entrance to her slick gland and tracing circles around it.

She came, gasping and scalping me as I lapped at her clit, gushing all over my fingers, squeezing and releasing me in little waves.

I thrust a third finger inside, and she arched up off the bed.

"God yes!"

My dick was stone hard and smearing pre-cum all over the rough blankets. "Relax for me, baby. You're tensing up, and I can't get inside you if you do."

She dropped back against the bed, fingers tangled in my hair as I went back to circling her clit with my tongue and working her open on my fingers. This was so fucking depraved, opening her up, forcing

The Warrior in the Shadows

my fingers, knuckles, and hand inside her, working her up to taking my whole fist. My cock was thumping with her every twitch and groan.

Omegas were meant to take this. I reminded myself that Hannah could accept a fat alpha cock and his knot all the way in her pussy. She could take my fist. She had taken it before. Yet it was a fucking revelation when I got right up inside and slowly, carefully, mindful of her every hitched breath, folded my fingers and thumb into a fist.

She came hard, neck arched, making those little oh-oh-oh sounds, clenching over my fist as I slowly worked it a little way in and out. I was out of my head and in another sphere of existence. I hadn't know this level of debauchery existed, but I was a fucking junkie and was getting my fix.

When she came the third time, I carefully withdrew, knowing I couldn't last. If I didn't get inside her in the next thirty seconds, I was going to come all over the bed. I flipped her onto her hands and knees and fucked her hard and fast, pounding into her hot, gaping cunt as she begged me for more, harder.

And it was filthy, fucking good, the lewd wet sounds as our flesh slapped together, and the sweet clenching as she kept on coming triggering my climax.

I came, fingers strumming her clit, setting her convulsing around my length as I dumped cum deep inside.

We both panted after, collapsing against the bed where she turned and clung to me, both of us sticky and sweaty and not caring a bit.

Tonight, and now were the only certainty, for tomorrow, time or events would rip her from me.

Chapter 29

Tanis

I spent the night talking.

I'd rather have spent it fucking. Only it wasn't the two servers who were not servers, nor any of the other women who had offered to welcome me back privately I was thinking about, but a certain Rymorian omega who had no business being out here or anywhere near me. Garren would be back soon. She was sleeping with Red, which infuriated me despite him being a beta, and no real threat.

When I explored my reasoning by not simply taking what I wanted, I found the answers to be complex. I genuinely didn't give a shit that she was with Garren. It had never stopped me before...it had never stopped *him* before...yet something about this scenario was different. I couldn't entirely dismiss the instincts that demanded I challenge, for only by a challenge could I claim her as mine.

I wanted to claim her, as stupid as that was on a thousand different levels. It was only hormones, I told myself. Yet, I'd been around unmated omegas before, had been offered plenty, and hadn't lost my damn head. I was about to embark on war and might soon be

The Warrior in the Shadows

dead. Challenging Garren, claiming her in any way or form, would drive a rift between us, perhaps an irreparable one.

As the saying went, my dick wanted what he wanted, and be damned with the consequence.

Yet circumstances had thwarted me, the discussions occupying my evening had been difficult ones, and I'd drunk liberally of excellent wine.

Hungover and bad-tempered as morning approached. I called a meeting with the fortress leaders first thing.

The fortress stateroom was windowless with cold, stone walls that kept much of the warmth at bay. In summer, it was pleasant. In winter, it was more like a tomb. Fortress life had taken some getting used to.

"So, it's true the tower dwellers are coming?" Javid asked, sprawled in the seat to my right with a tankard of beer close at hand. If he was hungover from last night, it didn't show. "How long until they get here?"

"Worst case, a few days. Best case, a few weeks. It depends on the route they decide to take," Jon Sanders said. He sat opposite Javid and me on the other side of the long, fully occupied state table. He was here to provide us with insider knowledge and, by doing so, prove his loyalty to Shadowland—essential if he wanted to be accepted, which he did. This was the first time Jon or any Rymorian had set foot inside a fortress. There had been a few censorious looks around the table when Jon arrived. The fortress was similarly rife with tales of the tower dweller visitors and the war.

Shadowlanders were notorious gossips, so I was sure they were also talking about me, a former outsider who had risen to rule them all. My position was ever in a delicate balance. If dissension came from just one fortress leader and I would be well and truly fucked.

I'd made it clear I would deal harshly with any insubordination. For some of those present, my overthrow was a fresh memory, while for others, enough time might have passed for them to smell an opportunity.

Falton was the only lord yet to arrive at Thale. He was reported to be en route, but the Lord of Tain had been edging the line of respect for a while, and I regretted not dealing with him sooner.

"That doesn't tell us much. Which way do you think they'll come?" Adro ruled Galin fortress. He was the only beta fortress leader, and most people assumed there was Jaru in his bloodline, given he was shorter than Kein. Sensitive to the slight, Adro loathed the Jaru and had been swift to mobilize his forces to help at Station fifty-four.

"I believe they will come by land, but none of you fucking trust me, so I'm nervous about committing," Jon said evenly, holding up well in a stateroom full of hostile Shadowland leaders.

Javid chuckled.

Finding out a few of those inside Rymor were sympathetic to the Shadowlanders was a boon. Yet my faith in Rymor was tainted. Scott Harding had once called me an out-of-control delinquent, which was a fair assessment at the time. There was no loyalty between Scott and me, save I believed Jon when he said Scott hated Bill... the enemy of my enemy and all that.

Even with Harding's intelligence, the odds were not in Shadowland's favor, which was why I had a couple of backup plans I'd kept to myself.

"I'd sooner not trust a tower dweller," Adro said.

"You're halfway to Jaru, Adro," Javid grumbled. "I'd sooner not trust you to stick a knife in everyone's back."

Adro jumped out of his seat, his hand grasping the empty dagger sheath at his waist.

"Sit down," I ordered. Thank fuck I'd ordered weapons removed.

Adro sat with a sneer for my father. "I promise you'll see me coming when I kill you, Javid."

"Whenever you're ready, little man."

I shot my father a glare, which he pretended not to see.

Jon was doing an impressive job of keeping a stony face, but I could tell he was fighting a smile. Jon had helped my mother to

The Warrior in the Shadows

escape Javid, yet begrudging respect existed between the two men who cared for my mother in very different ways.

The fortress leaders barely tolerated each other, at best, and bringing the four of them together was precarious. The impending war, and then my breaking a taboo by letting Rymorians into a fortress, only added to the volatile mix.

Kein, my head scout, was here to offer an opinion on logistics, while Lari, the taciturn commander of Thale, was abreast of the fortress's readiness in case of attack. That left Greve, the Lord of Techin yet to voice an opinion. Greve was often the last to speak and was usually painfully blunt when he did.

"We still have the Jaru to deal with. They're massing at the border again in even greater numbers," Lari said, scratching at his ginger beard.

"I can't afford to sit and wait," I said. "For the first time in their history, the Jaru are working together. If they continue to burn great swathes of our farming region to the ground, Rymor won't need to do anything."

"The fortresses have enough food to manage years without trouble," Adro said. "We don't need to rush into battle with the Jaru if the tower dwellers are about to attack."

"You think we should let the Jaru decimate our farming region?" I asked.

Adro shrugged. "Bring them into the fortress."

"For how long?" Greve demanded. He was the eldest of the fortress leaders but by no means old. His straight dark hair formed a widow's peak, and a touch of gray at his temples lent a distinguished air to his strong alpha features. "May as well hand our lands over to the Jaru. And what about the cities? Will you abandon them, too?"

"I'm not going to abandon my homelands to the Jaru." Javid grinned suddenly. "Not like you to turn down a chance to slaughter your cousins, Adro."

Adro snarled although he remained in his seat this time.

"The rumor is that Rymor wants your head, Tanis," Greve said, his words bringing a hush around the table. "Why don't we give them what they want?" His dark eyes held mine boldly.

The silence stretched and was eventually broken only by Javid chuckling to himself.

"If taking my head was easy, someone would have already done the job," I said at length.

"You know me, Tanis," Greve said with a wry smile. "Only voicing what certain circles already think."

"Falton's an idiot," Adro said.

Had Falton been bending the other fortress leader's ears, seeking their support in a coup or independence? I thought it likely he had.

The weight of my earlier suspicions came to bear. Managing the respective fortress leaders was complex in normal times, and these were far from normal times.

"Let's see what Falton has to say when he arrives," I said. "Troubled times can leave people confused about where their loyalties lay. I hope, for the sake of his family, that he finds clarity of thought."

No one questioned me, and the conversation returned to the Jaru, although I felt my father's troubled gaze more than once. I didn't make idle threats. I needed everyone behind me if we were to keep the country safe. A legacy was lost or held by the decisions its ruler made. Falton would make his own decisions and live or die by them.

Now, more than ever, I would need to watch my back.

Chapter 30

Rymor

Bill

After months of delays, meetings, and persuading and influencing, both behind the scenes and in front, the war on Shadowland had begun. I'd finished a meeting with the Gaia representatives, and an agreement had been reached on the final details.

I stared down from the window of my reception room in State Tower at the dense forests of Shadowland, feeling in better humor despite a recent bombing in a coffee shop in one of Serenity's upmarket districts. Moiety had already claimed responsibility for the attack. Those internal troubles could be parked for now as I anticipated gaining control of Shadowland under the guise of national security.

To me, those lands were already mine to conquer, subjugate, and own. I wanted that freedom back, freedom to explore that forbidden world.

Perhaps I would choose to live in that vibrant world, far from the sterile restrictions of Rymor.

My childhood and its harsh inconsistencies were being disconnected from my daily life with every step. My lack of control at that time drove me ever onward to gain more and more power now. The humiliation of my beatings and fierce determination to rise above them made me unwavering in this resolve.

The abandoned fortress at Talin had begun as an unofficial base. Now it progressed under official funding to support Damien Moore's search for the lost colonist ship, news of which had flown under the radar with so much focus on the war.

Then there was the news that Hannah was alive. I wondered how her time in Shadowland had changed her. As was inevitable, I again drew comparisons between Hannah and Ava. Both Rymorian women were thrust into the savage lands beyond the wall through very different circumstances. It was more than ten years since I'd taken Ava out of a misplaced desire to please Tanis. It hadn't gone to plan. She had nearly died, and, although Tanis had rescued her, she had despised him after.

I frowned. Would Hannah be grateful to me for saving her from that terrible place, or would she despise me the way Ava despised Tanis?

It was all too late now.

Rather than linger on past mistakes, I looked forward to a new era of the planet's history with the six great fortresses under Rymor's control. I would go down in history as the man who made it happen.

A message from Nielsen informing me that Kelard Wilder was here brought a familiar surge of irritation. Theo was still missing. I needed him found, even more so after discovering my coastal home had been violated.

A fucking beanbag? What kind of moronic criminal even liked that retro-shit? I was still incensed by its appearance.

"I'm about to head over to the operations room and thought I would bring you my update in person."

The Warrior in the Shadows

Kelard wore his signature black suit that was as sharp as the man within. He'd replaced Andrew Jordan, the former head of Homeland Security, to oversee the Shadowland operation. I appreciated his candid style, and he'd increasingly replaced Richard in providing counsel.

I thought Richard was more relieved than put out by his sudden exclusion. He'd been rattled since learning about my negotiations with the Jaru. Our conversation about Dan and Hannah was the first we'd shared in several weeks.

Dan had been brought in for questioning in a public, above-board way to assist us with inquiries. While he wasn't under arrest, he also couldn't leave.

"I appreciate your diligent efforts in this. Have there been any further issues with Jordan?"

"No, he's on board with this now." Kelard's smile was cool. His new position effectively demoted Jordan. No one, including Jordan, was confused about this being a permanent change. Kelard had managed the transition faultlessly. "Four teams are leaving in the first pass for reconnaissance. Two further teams are being deployed to search for our missing people. The rest are on standby pending reconnaissance, but all going well, they will be leaving within forty-eight hours."

I nodded, wondering who remained alive. Karry had a head start on the official teams. Given he'd taken weapons and other technology to assist him, my expectation was higher that he would succeed. Ailey should be occupied with Damien Moore's journey into Jaru territory, although he couldn't be left unattended for long. If nothing else, Karry had been useful for keeping contact with Ailey.

"The order of attack?" I asked.

"Thale is first as their leader's home base. Once that falls, we anticipate the rest to fold swiftly. We know they have our technology, so we're not taking any chances... It would be beneficial for you to be at the final briefing. Your personal address will heighten that motivation. We're about to strike a mighty blow for Rymor, one that will resonate through our histories for lifetimes to come."

I nodded. "There's something else?" I asked, feeling a silent question in his look.

"I know you wished John Tanis dead, although you have only suggested as much privately. I understand the depth of your feelings given his crimes, but if he were returned to Rymor, and brought to justice, that would be far more fitting. In light of the recent bombing, which Moiety claimed responsibility for, it would be an excellent time to make an example of one of their own."

I did want Tanis dead, but forcing him to witness his own downfall was even better. To look him in the eye, to have him kneel, broken before me... to see his hope crushed.

"Agreed. I've allowed my personal feelings to go unchecked."

Kelard's appeal was immediate. "You're human, Bill, nothing more."

"I'm grateful to have your counsel. You've become invaluable to both Rymor and me. I ask you to make every effort to bring John Tanis in alive to face charges for his crimes. For me, for that woman he wronged ten years ago, and for the Rymorian people he killed in that terrorist attack."

"It will be my pleasure, Bill," Kelard replied.

I got the impression that Kelard, like me, enjoyed wielding power. That he would genuinely enjoy bringing Tanis down, I had no doubt. I clapped the other man on the shoulder. "Looks like I have a final briefing to attend."

Chapter 31

Shadowland

Garren

I arrived at Thale half a day early, deep in the night. I should have gone straight to Tanis, but after weeks of trailing all over Shadowland and achieving fuck all, there was only one thing on my mind.

Dismissing my men to get some rest and food, I took the stairs two at a time to the highest section of the fortress where the Rymorians were quartered.

It was late, and I should have waited until morning like a reasonable male might do, go to my room where I could clean up, eat, and rest. Yet none of that mattered when a willing omega was waiting for me.

There were guards at the end of the corridor, which pleased me. She was safe.

She also wasn't with Tanis.

"You don't want to go in there," the guard said, moving to block my path.

Leveling a scowl at the ballsy fucker, I slammed him against the wall. "Interfere and I'll end you."

His companion shuffled about, getting twitchy. The one I had by the throat lifted both hands. "Don't say I didn't warn you."

Warn me about what? I released him, my frown deepening and a sick feeling blooming in my gut. Was she in her room? Was she with Tanis, after all?

"Where is she?"

He nodded toward the far end of the corridor. "Last door on the right."

I stalked over and threw open the door.

It was a tiny space with a small barred window casting moonlight over the startled occupants of the bed. My entire body coiled into a tight ball of rage so potent I could barely see. The position of her sprawled naked over *him*, the rich smell of slick and his cum, along with pheromones, hers and his, weak because he was a beta, yet his sweat was still all over what was mine.

I roared and charged, tearing her from him, slapping him aside when he dared to try and ward me off. He crumpled back into the bed as I snatched her up and, stalking for the corner of her tiny room, put my back to him with my body between them.

"Garren, Garren, Garren," she whispered, her tiny hands skittering all over my shoulders, throat, and face, urgent kisses and nips that didn't have a hope of soothing my feral beast. "I need you, Garren, please."

I understood she was only seeking to calm me to save her other fucking mate.

Mate.

Everything inside me roared. Worried about what had happened, I'd ridden like the devil was on my tail after receiving the order to return. I was expecting to find my half-brother balls deep in the

The Warrior in the Shadows

omega, and my claim shut off. Only it wasn't Tanis, but Red I found in her fucking bed.

"Garren, please."

Betrayal burned like acid in my stomach, ignoring the instincts that said she needed me, her alpha, after all.

"How long?" I demanded, grasping her chin to hold still when she kept nipping and kissing the column of my throat.

"Since you left." Her pretty gray eyes searched mine in the moonlit room. "I needed—"

"Shut the fuck up," I growled. My lips were on hers, hungry, the kiss brutal as our tongues tangled, my mind lost to a dark, barely human compulsion demanding I reestablish my claim. I wrenched my lips from hers so my teeth could find her throat, and was only satisfied when I tasted blood.

"Please, Garren, I need you. Please, knot me. I can't bear it if you don't."

I rose and pinned her against the wall, her arms and legs wrapping around me. Ripping my belt open, I shucked my pants past my hips and fumbled between us to grasp my hot, aching shaft and line it with her wet heat.

I thrust deep.

Her squeal was one of savage pleasure. My knot was already half-formed.

"Take it," I growled, mindless to everything but her welcoming heat. "You're going to take it fucking all."

"Yes, yes, yes!"

I rutted her hard and fast, slamming into her, feeling her slick and his cum, determined to push every drop of his weak seed from her cunt and fill her with mine and only mine.

I came with a roar, blind, dumping cum deep, knotting her, feeling her nails rake the flesh at the back of my neck and her teeth tearing at my throat, bloodying me as she began crushing my cock and knot in hot, heavenly contractions and coaxed another gush of boiling seed... to further stake my claim.

The faint creak and shuffling sound on the other side of the room indicated that I hadn't killed Red. My growl was low and steeped with aggression, knowing he'd been fucking her and enjoying what was mine while I'd been far away.

Only, his raspy, aroused breathing didn't piss me off as I thought it might. No, I wanted the fucker to see how well Hannah came like a good little omega for her alpha.

She continued to soothe me, petting and kissing me, although I resisted her now, keeping my head up and my mouth out of reach as I came to terms with what she had done.

My purr was halfway to a growl as I tempered my fury, and all the while, I kept coming into her in hot, heavy gushes.

I sank to my knees, taking her down onto the ground, knowing I'd need to fuck her again soon.

∽

Hannah

I didn't recognize Garren.

Oh, he looked the same, and his delicious scent that I sometimes convinced myself I could smell on my clothing was also familiar, but not the wildness, not the beastly male who took me with barely tempered aggression.

The wooden floor was rough and cold beneath my naked skin, while the male crowding over me was a hot wall of muscle, still mostly dressed.

I had done this to him. I was no fool, knew we were bonding in all ways, save heat and the final connection which that would make, yet I'd gone willingly into the arms of another man. My stomach churned sickly with a terrible fear that I'd damaged him in some way, fearing the playful version of Garren, so ready to smile, might be erased forever by my callous act.

I was an omega. People had assured me that this was normal, that we sometimes needed more than one male. Yet I'd grown up in a country where basic sensuality was frowned upon, a polyamorous relationship unheard of, and so guilt had me in its hold.

He still wouldn't kiss me, and I needed him to as I was desperate for reassurance through intimacy.

I could hear Red moving but didn't dare turn to acknowledge him or even check that he was well. Garren had backhanded him as he snatched me away. I reasoned that Red was tough and had handled a punch from Tanis, but I still wanted to see for myself.

"Please," Red said. He was still naked, holding out a blanket on my periphery.

Garren growled a low warning at the other male not to approach.

"I know she's yours," Red continued, not backing down nor away. "That you're her alpha, that you can read her and give her all the things that I can't. But please, the floor is cold and hard, put this blanket beneath her. Omegas may be tough, but she doesn't need to feel the cold floor."

I kept my touch light and focused on Garren, kissing his throat, feeling him pulsing inside me where we were locked intimately together. His chest vibrated under my fingers like a wild animal on the brink of attack. I'd never seen this side of him, never understood an alpha in the fullest sense.

Today, I did.

I petted him, ran my hands over his shoulders and chest, his handsome face, and along his jaw, feeling the fury seep out of him while Red waited patiently with the blanket in his hand.

Finally, he took the offered blanket with a growl and, lifting me, put it underneath me.

Then he fucked me again, tearing the swollen knot out, and pounded into me with his arm braced under my ass.

And I loved it, came so hard over and over, knowing Red was close, watching me. I arched into it, a primitive and inexplicable need to show the beta how much I could take my alpha and why he didn't need to worry about using me roughly. Nothing Red did could come close to the savagery of my enraged alpha.

When the knot softened for the second time, I sensed the man in Garren returning.

He pulled out roughly, sending slick and cum spewing all over the blanket.

I hissed at him. He growled in my face. My stupid body responded, pussy clenching and pushing out another gush, my legs falling open and face turning to the side, giving him my throat to bite.

Instinctively, I was submitting, offering myself to him.

"At last, you remember your place," Garren said. My heart rate picked up, and I turned slowly to face him hearing the humor in his voice.

"Fuck!" Red muttered. "Shit, sorry. I mean, fuck! That's so fucking hot the way she submits to you."

Garren's face swung right, and he bared his teeth at Red's interruption. Only it wasn't aggressive, unlike before, more a ticked-off alpha than one about to rip his adversary limb from limb.

"Uff!"

Garren yanked up his pants and staggered to his feet before tossing me over his shoulder. Yanking the door open, he stormed out.

"Where are you taking her?" Red called.

I caught a glimpse of the two guards staring after us through my wild hair. Peering back, I found a naked, puffy-nosed Red following after us.

"To my fucking room where there's a bed big enough to rut my woman in peace."

Okay then...

He stopped abruptly, spinning around so I could no longer see Red, and my breath caught as I worried he was about to punch the beta for following.

"You may join us," Garren said magnanimously, the offer making my pussy squeeze with interest. "You may watch me fuck her, or you can fuck off. I don't care either way. Interfere and I will break you."

The Warrior in the Shadows

"Don't interfere," Red said. "Got it. No problem. Watch? I... ah, yeah, I'm probably going to regret this, but I definitely want to watch."

"Don't talk, either," Garren growled. Oh, he definitely sounded amused.

Red huffed out a breath.

When he didn't speak, Garren grunted and, pivoting, strode off down the corridor.

I peered back at Red as I bounced about on Garren's shoulder, tired and a little grouchy at the unpleasant mode of carrying, but also buzzing with interest at this development.

Red's beautiful lean body glistened in the weak light as he followed, grinning broadly.

My eyes lowered to his cock, hard and ruddy, pointing straight up. I swallowed as my belly took a slow tumble, and when I glanced up again, Red winked at me.

"You're about to get fucked," he mouthed at me.

Wasn't I just?!

∽

Red

The bastard had popped my nose good when he backhanded me, and it throbbed like a bastard.

But so did my dick; I didn't think I'd ever been this hard in my life, which might have embarrassed me given I was walking naked down a corridor, only it really didn't because this was Shadowland, where sex wasn't viewed as dirty or taboo.

The Shadowlanders' liberal approach to intimacy had definitely been a draw when I'd first considered field science as a career. I'd always been physically active, and I topped out all my areas of study. What many people forgot was that field scientists really were scientists in the field. I had a Ph.D. in botany, and in between dodging Jaru and recording Shadowland activity, I also studied the plants.

It was understood we indulged in more than strictly scientific study. Further, there were classes dedicated to culture, so we didn't fuck up and end up on the wrong side of an irate alpha. So, it was well documented that Shadowlanders had a different approach to sex. I'd been invited to share betas and even a couple of omegas with their mate or husband. Every single experience had blown my mind.

But none of them were like Hannah.

I held no delusions as to my feelings being involved. I loved everything about her, from her sensual wildness to her intelligence and strength of character.

I thought Garren liked fucking her in front of me and the power it afforded him. I'd been around alphas enough and understood that their animal side enjoyed dominating in all kinds of ways.

I also thought he might be inclined to let me do more than watch once he'd fucked her a couple more times.

He shoved open a big wooden door. "Shut the door," he growled at me. "One nosey beta with his cock out is more than enough."

I shut the door, still grinning, as he stalked over and tossed her onto the enormous four-poster bed.

The room was spacious and well appointed, as befitted his status as the brother of Shadowland's leader. No windows and the fireplace was empty, but the luminous rocks that ringed the walls where they met the ceiling provided enough light to see.

As I clicked the door shut, Garren was already stripping from his clothes. His huge cock was hard, and his knot semi-formed. I swallowed, eyes shifting to Hannah, sprawled out on the bed, legs shamelessly open, with eyes only for her mate.

I threw a look heavenward and mentally prepared myself for the agony to come. I was pretty sure I was going to spontaneously ejaculate at some point without even touching my dick, throbbing nose notwithstanding.

The Warrior in the Shadows

I took the chair, shifted it to a good position for viewing, and sat my ass down.

Boots and clothing were tossed aside before he crawled over her on the bed. Garren was big even for an alpha, his musculature extreme and ripped, although he had a mat of hair on his chest, abs, and groin that softened the edges.

He palmed her throat and pinned her to the bed before lowering his mouth over her.

Her sweet purr, the way her arms and legs wrapped around him, found a direct line to my balls. She was so fucking enthusiastic, so sensual—did he even realize how lucky he was?

Yeah, of course, he did.

He moved down, closing his mouth over her tit. She moaned and arched up. My dick jerked, and I swallowed hard.

Fuck! I bit my lower lip, squeezed my dick hard, and convinced myself that coming already would be embarrassing. Damn, I was leaking pre-cum everywhere.

Garren's lips popped off, and he threw a look my way.

"Hands off!" he barked. "Come before I say, and you'll regret it."

I snatched my hand away, and nearly fucking came at what he said.

He smirked and went back to Hannah's tits. Only she was staring at me now, watching my face as I watched her, and I swear, seeing her pretty face scrunch, her mouth hanging open as Garren tormented her, was off the fucking charts hot.

Fuck, his hand was definitely between her legs, and her twitching said he was petting her slick gland.

"Don't come," he growled against her tit. I had no idea if he was talking to her or me, but I was sure, consequence be damned, I was about to erupt.

He stilled and lifted his head to Hannah's cry of frustration and, pinning me with a look, grunted. "No fucking restraint," he muttered.

"You want to suck him off while I rut and knot you, Hannah?" he demanded, turning back to the panting omega on the bed.

"Please. Yes, please."

His hand started to move inside her again, slowly, as his mouth lowered to her breast where he sucked hard—making her arch up—before letting his lips pop off.

"Are you going to swallow it all down like a good little omega?"

"Yes! God, yes."

Another tease to her breast, another slow slide of his fingers in her cunt.

"I don't want to hear you choking around his small dick. You can take that all the way to the back of your throat, and when he comes, you're not going to spill a drop."

"God, please! I won't."

I should be insulted at him calling my dick small because I wasn't short in that department. Only I was confident he could bat any insult my way, and it wouldn't matter. Their rich pheromones saturated the air. I was fucking high on the two of them, the image of them together, and the possibility of getting my dick anywhere near her.

"Get your ass over here. You don't get to come unless it's in or on her. She clearly likes the idea of being shared; I've never seen her gushing slick like this."

He didn't need to ask me twice.

I stumbled, half fucking blind, for the bed. She reached for me as my knee hit the mattress, her fingers wrapping around my aching shaft and pulling it toward her parted lips.

"Ah, fuck!"

"Good girl. Suck him nice and deep."

"Fuck! Fuck! Fuck!"

He leaned up, closing his big palm over her throat.

"I want to feel him here. Relax your throat for him, Hannah, right fucking now."

She swallowed around me, and I began to deep throat her with every thrust, feeling her hum around me.

"Fuck, that's so obscene the way she can take you so deep,"

The Warrior in the Shadows

Garren muttered gruffly. "I can't get half my dick in there without her tapping out. Does it feel good?"

"Fucking amazing," I grunted, desperately trying not to come because this was fucking insane, and I wanted more.

"I bet it does," he rumbled. "Hot, wet, tight mouth, dick all the way down her throat. She hasn't had more than my fingers in her ass yet. I bet she can take you there like the filthy, needy little omega she is."

I came. Hot jets spewed down her throat, and my body disconnected from my mind for long seconds as I dumped cum down her throat. And she sucked it all down, small nails biting into my ass when I tried to ease out, swallowing around me until I saw stars.

"Hannah, baby. Shit! Damn, I'm sensitive, please ease up."

I managed to extract my dick to her whine of displeasure just as Garren plowed her cunt.

She came instantly, her whole body contorting. I didn't think, just collapsed next to her and leaned down to take her lips, to kiss her and swallow up her cries, and Garren slam-fucked her through another wild climax.

Needing breath, my lips slipped away from hers, and my gaze slid the length of her body to where Garren was plowing her with his thick cock. The ruddy knot was already swelling, glistening with her slick as it squeezed in and out.

"Fuck! Look what he's doing to you, Hannah." I lifted her head up for her to see, torn between watching for myself and looking at the rapture contorting her face. "He's going to knot you."

My hand lowered to her belly, feeling it ripple with every thrust. My brain went into a kind of shutdown as I realized how deep he was, all up inside her, filling her. She was stretched obscenely around his knot, his thrust slowing until he bulged outside and finally slipped in one last time.

A ripple passed through her, and she groaned.

He growled back, low and satisfied.

I'd just come down her throat, but the image of them coming

together had my dick jerking and balls tightening in a dry climax that was strangely different, yet intensely pleasurable all the same. My hand moved of its own volition, finding her clit, slipping fingertips back and forth over the swollen nub, petting her, and coaxing another climax from the spent omega.

Hannah

I couldn't tell you what was up or down. I was spinning and coming, over and over.

Red's fingers were playing with my clit. My pussy was stuffed to capacity, squeezing lovingly over Garren's knot.

God, could a person die from too many climaxes?

I never expected Garren to let Red touch me, not like this, so openly before him, nor for him to encourage Red to use me roughly.

My throat ached where he'd thrust his cock in there.

I wanted him to do it again.

The knot softened a little, and Garren, who was in a particularly savage alpha mode tonight, tugged free to my hiss of displeasure.

I gasped as he grabbed Red by the throat, terrified that violence would ensue. Though he was big for a beta, Garren handled him like a child.

Red grunted in surprise.

It turned to a groan as Garren shoved the other man's head between my spread thighs. "Clean her up, and I'll think about letting you fuck her ass. Don't think it escaped my notice that both of you went off like a poorly disciplined bowman at the mention of it."

I was sensitive down there and was sure I didn't want or need further attention of any kind, but, from the first lick of Red's tongue, pleasure began to coil up again. He groaned against my pussy, probably half high on alpha and omega pheromones, and ate me out like he was starving for the taste.

The Warrior in the Shadows

My hooded eyes found Garren watching with a smirk, the playful side I loved so well once more in place.

I moaned, squirming as Red got his fingers inside, searching with unerring accuracy for my slick gland. He didn't pet it with the ruthless disregard for sensitivity that Garren did, but carefully circled it. All the while, he kissed, sucked, and licked my pussy everywhere but my swollen clit.

Garren lay down, propped on one elbow beside me, his cock thick, long, and proudly erect as he caught my chin and kissed me. Our tongues tangled, fueling the desire running rampant through me.

"I'm so pissed at you," he growled against my ear, tugging my nipple with an edge of cruelty before he nipped my throat. "Letting him fuck what was mine. You're supposed to come to me first if you want another male. Ask me." He nipped harder. "Beg me." He licked along my jaw before hovering his lips over me. "Do anything and everything your needy omega mind can think of to convince me to let another male into your bed." He kissed me far too briefly before holding his lips out of reach. "Inside *my* cunt. But you skipped all of that." He kissed me again. "I don't blame you entirely. You're new to Shadowland. Don't know our customs. But you'll have to forgive me if I'm a little"—he sucked my breast hard just below my nipple, making me arch up as sweet achy pleasure shot directly to my clit—" rough with you as I come to terms with this."

I came, squealing, one hand in Red's hair and the other in Garren's, holding both of them to me as I rode Red's face and come in hot, heavy waves.

"Glad we got that discussion out the way," Garren said, smirking. "Red, there's a bottle of oil in my bedside drawer. Better work her up to her taking you in the ass, fast, because I'm feeling particularly alpha bastard and impatient."

My pussy performed a slow, deep clench. Red groaned and surged up the bed, wiping his mouth with the back of his hand before fumbling in the bedside table.

"Over you go," Garren said, tapping my thigh as he rolled onto his back. "Sit over me and feed me your tits while Red tries not to blow his load while he's fingering your ass."

"Fuck!" Red muttered.

I giggled as I tumbled over Garren, slick and sated but also fiercely aroused by the prospect of having them both.

∼

Red

Garren was right to call me out. I'd never come so many times in one night. I was close to coming again. The sounds of her moans and giggles as Garren played with her tits made my fingers clumsy around the stoppered bottle.

I got the lid off, slipped, and poured too much out. Fuck it! I put the stopper back and dropped the bottle on the bed, then slathered some over my dick before letting the rest trickle from my fingertips down her ass toward the little puckered entrance.

She glanced back as my finger sank a small way in before Garren did something, and she let out a loud, lusty groan.

"God, please, Red, hurry! I want to come with you both inside me."

She clenched down tightly, moaning as I thrust my finger all the way in. When I slipped all the way out, I pressed two fingers carefully into her entrance. Her only response was to push her ass out, canting her hips back.

"I'm feeling fucking impatient, and she's very needy, Red," Garren growled.

Fuck, she was so tight, but the oil made her super slick, and my fingers slipped easily into her tightness. She groaned and pushed back. Fuck! She really liked this.

I finger fucked her ass, mesmerized by her tightness, how she stretched open, and imagined how it would feel once I got my dick in her. The squelchy sounds were filthy and fucking hot.

The Warrior in the Shadows

"She's going to fucking come if you don't get your dick in there!"

Garren's growl snapped me out of my daze long enough to line up my cock. Sweat popped along the length of my spine as I watched the head of my dick slip into her ass.

We both groaned.

"Fuck, I'm close," I grunted.

Garren muttered something I couldn't catch, but she was slick, my dick was slick, and it had a mind of its own as I sank balls deep with alarming ease.

She clenched around me like a silken vise.

"You okay?"

"God, yes, please move!"

I watched her tight, puckered hole take my cock, her ass fluttering over me as I began to pump my hips. Fuck, she was really doing this, taking me here and fucking loving it.

"Hold still," Garren growled. Big hands clamped over my hips.

I heaved a breath.

"Feed my dick into your hungry cunt, Hannah."

I swallowed. It was tight, insanely tight, as he began to sink in.

The cry that left her lips didn't sound human, and I couldn't judge if it was pleasure or pain.

"You can take it," Garren said, voice strained but determined. "Sink all the way down like a good girl for me. Then we're going to fuck you so good, fill you all up like you need."

A sob burst from her lips. "Please, Garren. Oh, I'm going to come."

Then Garren drew all the way out and slammed up into her while I was still balls deep inside from behind.

We began to move, taking turns to fuck her, filling her front and then back, and all the while, Garren ordered both of us not to fucking come. It was so hard to obey when every stroke was slick, rippling heaven. But we were all falling down the dark abyss, pleasure rising with every thrust, opening her, using her rougher, and she was loving all of it until finally, we began to fuck her together, filling her over and over.

She came first, clenching over my dick in tight waves that demanded I come.

I followed her straight over, dumping cum into her clenching ass as Garren's slippery fingers and knuckles brushed up against my balls as he massaged his knot.

He came with a roar, holding both of us still, filling her to her limit.

We breathed heavily, Garren offering his purr, open-mouthed against her throat even as my lips moved over the back of her neck. Touches turned gentle; the urgency now passed.

If this was life with an alpha and omega, I was all fucking in.

～

There was no night or day this deep within the fortress, but as I lay behind Hannah, listening to her soft snores as she snuggled against Garren, my body clock said that dawn was close.

Her small hand curled against my thigh like she needed to be connected to us both, her ass nestled sweetly against my raw dick which had finally given out and didn't so much as twitch.

As for Garren, I was surprised by his acceptance in some ways though not in others. For an alpha, he was easygoing and dominant, and I'd loved every one of his filthy commands. From the perspective of enlightenment, I could see how he adored Hannah, how he would embrace whatever his omega wanted or needed, even if that something was another man.

I loved her so deeply, had done for a while, and the thought of being forced from her life by a possessive alpha had been eating at me. Only, Garren wasn't that kind of alpha. In fact, in all my years here, I'd found that few alphas were. My fears had manifested because I had been seeing the situation through the lens of my rigid Rymorian upbringing.

The Warrior in the Shadows

I'd worried, too, that she might reject me when he returned, that I was merely a poor stand-in for the main event.

It was early in the relationship, and we were all new to one another, but the connection between us held all the joy of permanence.

Into the peace of understanding, regret rose its ugly head. Tomorrow I was leaving, along with the other Rymorians, the many garrisons, and the fortress soldiers. A war against the Jaru was terrible enough, but this one involved impossible odds, as primitive weapons would be going up against powerful technology.

Adam had asked me to wait until the plans had been formalized and he could tell her in person. I'd wanted to tell her anyway; had intended to last night. But she had needed me, and, after, she'd looked so peaceful that I couldn't find the words. Then Garren had arrived and thrown our lives into a debauched kind of chaos. The time had never been quite right.

Selfishly, I knew that if I'd told her, none of what we'd shared would have happened; that a different mood would have taken hold.

I traced my fingers across her shoulders before brushing my lips over the soft skin there, sad that we were being ripped apart when we had only just begun.

Chapter 32

Tanis

What a pity you gave them back their wall—Garren's words played back in my mind as they had done many times since I'd discovered Rymor's plans for war. I was seated in my private rooms with the select company of Kein and Jon. I wasn't one to keep such a close circle, but the less people involved in today's discussion, the better, given the sensitive nature of the subject.

My rooms were located in the southern wing of the fortress and looked out from a lofty sixth story onto the inner courtyard. It was one of the few rooms with windows, which lay open to let in the early morning light. The sun didn't do much to brighten the room and the dark wooden floors and glistening black stone walls could be oppressive. The fortress did have a way of getting under your skin. At first, I'd loathed it, but over time my response to it had transitioned through acceptance and into an odd sort of comfort. It was my home now, and I had embraced it.

I wasn't about to give it up.

The Warrior in the Shadows

The route I contemplated taking was problematic in its own way. Endless repetitions of Garren's now infamous words had slowly chipped away at the previously unthinkable.

"Can you really take this war to Rymor?" It wasn't the first time Jon had asked this.

Over the past weeks, I'd discussed with these two the possibility of launching an attack on Rymor. In the earlier iterations, the threat of war had been less tangible.

Now it was real.

Two members of Adam's extended team had been left at the nearest waypoint under Danel's watch. They had sent the news by carrier bird today of Rymorian troops entering Shadowland.

The fires had been lit. We *were* going to war.

"It's about survival," I said. "And yes, if necessary, I will take the war to Rymor." Sending an army of eighty thousand into Rymor was, admittedly, extreme. Yet what choice did we have?

Jon's sigh was heavy and filled with his frustration. "Can you really do it? I-I don't know if you can."

"I'm not the same man I once was, Jon. Bill saw to that. You think I should play nice? Let them take what's mine?" My face twisted as I met Jon's troubled gaze. "I gave them their wall, with my blood, and my men, hundreds of them slaughtered. I gave them protection. I gave them their wall back, and I can also take it away."

"This is not their fault," Jon bit out. "You know who's to blame here, and you can't condemn a whole people because of the sins of one man."

"But it's okay for Bill to do that?" I snapped back.

Jon lifted his hand in silent surrender.

The first part of my life seemed far away now, and the events leading to my exile felt like they had happened to someone else. I'd often wondered what I would do if the barrier were gone—not so long ago it had been. I'd had that opportunity for revenge, but I'd forgone it out of a misguided sense of duty; instead, by helping Rymor, I'd set up the perfect storm for them to destroy me.

I wouldn't make that same mistake again.

"I can and I will," I continued. Jon's resistance only sharpened my resolve. I didn't often dwell on the reason I hated Bill Bremmer, the event leading to my exile, and how I became the man I was today. My conviction remained constant. In the still of the night, I dreamed of killing Bremmer, could almost feel my blade slipping through his ribs, feel the satisfaction of seeing his life drain away.

Ten years ago, Jon Sanders had stopped me—another mistake I wouldn't repeat. "Just as I will eradicate every member of Falton's family after I finish with Rymor. I meant what I said in the council chamber."

Kein's fingers smoothed down the length of his mustache. "It's no more than they deserve," was all he offered, but whether he was talking about Falton, the Rymorians, or both wasn't clear.

Scraping back his chair, Jon paced over to the open window, where he stared out with a brooding expression. "The Rymorians are your people as much as the Shadowlanders. Your own blood—can you slaughter your own blood?"

"They lost that right, Jon. Lost it when they brought weapons outside the wall. They're coming for me—coming for you. Did you forget how they left you to rot on the edge of the Jaru plains? I can't do this anymore, and I won't. It's time Rymor learned the hard lessons of life. They put their trust in the wrong man. Now they pay the price."

"Your mother still lives there." Jon's face was crumbling.

"I'm not going to slaughter the people of Rymor, just anyone who gets in my way." My mother may have failed her parental duty, but I wished her no ill. I missed her, even as I saw her influence in the man I'd become.

Not all of those influences were positive. Only after I left, and the changes began, did I discover my mother had been drugging me. Her misguided attempt to suppress the genetic traits I'd inherited from my alpha father. An act I still found hard to believe. I may have been the by-product of an illegal liaison, but her actions broke fundamental trusts. While I understand her motives, that didn't make them right.

"What about afterward? You think you can control eighty-thousand men on a blood-march?"

"I control them now," I pointed out.

"It won't be the same once you're in there," Jon said, returning to his seat with an air of defeat.

"What would you have me do, Jon?" I asked. "Turn myself over? Let them destroy my home and the innocent people here? Are they any less worthy because Rymor labels them savages? It's time for change. I bring change. It's what I've always done."

Jon said no more, and his face remained blank as if his emotions had been wrung out.

"We do what we must to survive," Kein said softly.

The circumstance that had brought such an intelligent mind into my life was as obscure as mine in coming to rule Shadowland. He often cut to the heart of a matter, just as he did now.

Garren wasn't here to offer his opinion, but he was predictable, and besides, it was Garren who had brought this idea to light. Garren understood about doing whatever was needed.

"I'll need a technology expert," I said slowly. "I could get through the station door, but I'm not confident I could disable or damage the station sufficiently for my needs. Skills aside, I am better placed with the main force."

Jon shrugged reluctantly. "Joshua," he said. "Not that you have much choice since Marcus killed one of them. He's half-way lost it already. He'll do as he's told to."

"And if he develops a conscience?"

Jon's laugh was bitter. "Yeah, he'll break if that's what you're asking. He's been like a zombie since Daren was killed. It won't come to that, I guarantee it. Hannah's a different story. Don't ask her to do it."

There was a warning in his voice, one I heeded, not that I would have asked Hannah anyway.

Yes, my reasons were selfish and personal, and making decisions for either reason was foolish, given my back was against the wall.

I nodded. "After I've updated Lari, I'll speak to Joshua. I'd like you to be there, Jon. For now, we'll keep the Shadowland leaders out of the loop. I'll tell Garren later, assuming he gets back before we leave—he should be back today. The rest of my leaders will be told when I need them to be. I want them focusing on the Jaru and Rymorian threat."

I worried about how Javid would handle the news of an incapacitated wall. I liked to believe he wouldn't indulge in a scheme regarding Coco, but my father had been reckless over her once, and I didn't trust him entirely with the knowledge.

"We still need to discourage the Jaru," Kein said.

"I know," I replied. "But if they don't cross that border in masses, then I'm not going to chase after them."

Kein nodded. "Do you want me to check on their movements?"

"No," I said. "I'd prefer you to accompany Joshua. The station is key. Whatever else happens, I know I can trust you to get him there and ensure he follows through with the destruction. Once I've spoken to Josh and assessed his mental state, I want you to take a dozen from Danel's team here and meet up with him at the waypoint. Small and fast will work best."

"I will ensure it is done," Kein said.

I trusted that he would.

A knock sounded at the door, and at my command, it opened to admit Lari, the taciturn commander of Thale. "Garren's back," Lari said. "He's in the armory, and from the state of his weapons, he's been busy." Lari grinned. For such a brutish man, Lari had a soft spot for Garren. He had trained Garren and Javid's younger sons at Luka before I brought him to oversee Thale.

Javid still grumbled about losing the man, but Lari had been a loyal and capable commander and took my rise to power as the natural order of things.

Lari's loyalty to the Luka family was unwavering; he had

accepted me as the eldest son as simply taking my rightful place. He adapted to the shifts in power, and Javid's edgy deference to me solidified Lari's sense of duty.

"Good," I said, glad Garren wouldn't need to catch up and eager to find out what his searching had revealed. "Did he find anything of note?"

"No," Lari said. "More's the pity."

"It was always a long shot," I said. "He's in a bad mood, then?"

"Testy and bound to end up in a fight with someone before the day's out."

I laughed. "Duly noted. I'll leave speaking to Garren until the end."

It was time to deal with the mundane issues, then Joshua and Garren. My last day in my fortress was going to be long.

Chapter 33

Hannah

Last night had been a wild experience, and I slept in late after Garren and Red left.

Garren's room was unadorned and windowless, although a perpetual glow seemed to be emitted from the stones skirting the ceiling. Like all the rooms in the fortress, two ventilation shafts brought a fresh breeze in and out.

The bed was enormous, as was needed for an alpha, and smelled of him. I wished someone had brought me here, even without the windows, instead of my little room.

I was dressing when a knock came on the door, and Mari breezed in.

"Morning, miss!"

There was nothing to indicate she thought it anything out of the ordinary that I was in Garren's room, sitting in a heavy-set wooden chair before the fireplace, fastening up my boots.

"I brought you some tea and breakfast!"

A tray was deposited on the table beside my chair. My nose twitched as she lifted the cover off to reveal bacon, eggs, two sausages,

The Warrior in the Shadows

and a thickly cut slice of crusty bread. My stomach rumbled. I reached for a rasher of crispy bacon and shoved it in my mouth before finishing my boots.

God, the food here was freaking amazing, definitely unhealthy, and tasty enough that I didn't care.

Mari busied herself straightening the bed, chatting about the feast a few days ago and how her brother had gotten a black eye during a tussle with another alpha. There was admiration in her voice, like her brother's brawling was a source of family pride.

I shook my head and stuffed another slice of bacon into my mouth, crunching it happily as I made a sandwich with the sausages and an egg. I wouldn't normally eat this much, but between Garren and Red, I had expended a lot of energy last night.

My stomach did that little dip thing. Yes, I definitely wanted to do that again, all of it, even the parts that had terrified me until they didn't.

I sighed, and my buoyant, post-lust high seeped out of me as I ate, and Mari chatted about this and that.

It had been a strange time within the fortress, and the excitement of arrival had shifted toward melancholy. I no longer had a purpose. There was no technology, no challenges here to occupy my mind. I had been a misfit in Rymor. I was more so out here. The field scientists were absent during the day, doing goodness knows what, goodness knows where. Only my nights with Red had offered some relief from the depression I was sinking into.

Joshua was little more than a shell, and being with him only reminded me of everything that was wrong. I knew I should make more effort with him, and I'd tried without success. Yet how could I help Joshua when I suffered the same confusion about my worth?

The initial comfort of being safe, and the delight in being clean, had evaporated within days. The fortress was hollow and alien, and after forced companionship for so many months, alone time had morphed into deep, depressive grief. There was just too much of everything, too much time for reflection, too much that had been lost.

"You're very quiet, miss," Mari said, coming to join me. Her lips thinned as she noted my half-eaten sausage and egg sandwich. "I saw Red and Garren come out of the room. You're going to need to eat more after that."

I snorted a laugh.

Her lips tugged up, telling me she was pleased with herself at getting that reaction from me.

"You're an omega, miss. It's quite normal for you to take men of your liking to your bed." She giggled prettily. "Or their bed. I know several omegas who have more than one life mate. For most though, it's more common during heat. Omegas with a single alpha often instruct him on suitable males as their heat draws near so that arrangements can be made."

I flushed. It was all still very alien to me, both the polyamorous relationships and the mystical event known as heat. There were omegas within the fortress, but I hadn't been introduced to any, being as I was unmated and so would be seen as a threat.

"There," she said, "best finish it off. Going to be quiet around here once they've all gone."

"Gone?" I'd picked up my greasy sandwich but at her words I put it back down with a frown.

"For the war, miss," she said as though this were obvious. "First light tomorrow, all the garrisons will be leaving to head off attacks from the Jaru and tower dwellers. Largest army in all of history, so my father said."

I blanched, the food I'd eaten making me feel queasy.

I rose from my chair and stalked out the door, Mari following hot on my heels. There were no guards outside, but they often disappeared when Mari was with me during the day.

"Where're you going, miss?" Mari asked, following in my wake.

"To get some answers," I replied. I'd learned my way around the fortress, at least enough to find the key locations of the bathrooms, kitchens, and grand hall. Following the corridor and stairs, I descended into the depths of the fortress.

The Warrior in the Shadows

Ahead the double doors of the grand hall lay open, and I stalked in—then stopped dead.

It was empty of everyone other than a servant sweeping the floor and two small clusters of Shadowland soldiers.

My mind decided to throw up memories of the feast where I'd been treated to a procession of women presenting themselves to Tanis, and his father—yes, that part had been worse. I was certain Javid had been about to fuck his companion on the high table in front of the whole room. Then someone started a brawl—an actual brawl—indoors. It was bad enough that they could barely restrain themselves from that kind of thing outside.

"You may be his for now, but you were always mine." Did Tanis really say those words, or had I conjured them up out of my imagination. Did he really kiss me, or did I imagine that as well?

All the time Garren had been gone, his seeming compassion in coming to talk to me after Edward's death, not once had he followed through on that promise. Maybe he was toying with me. Maybe he wanted me to tell Garren about it so as to piss his brother off. Who even knew how the mind of a ruler worked? Bill had far less autonomy than Tanis and was a complete nut.

"Where is everyone?" I asked, frowning.

"They're in the armory," Mari said. "They're leaving tomorrow for the war. Where else would they be?"

"I'll need to go into the armory, then."

Mari's face fell, and she wrung her hands together. "You know only members of the garrison are allowed to enter. I wish I'd never mentioned it. It's made you all tense and angry, and it's all my fault. Oh, I'll be in such trouble!"

I drew a deep, resigned breath, then let it out slowly. "It's okay, Mari, I'm not going to do anything rash,"—although I definitely wanted to—"I'm glad you told me. I just wanted to ask someone about it."

"What about a bath?" Mari suggested, smiling.

Yes, a bath where no one could see me fall apart behind the curtain.

I hadn't seen Adam since the feast. Did he know about this?

Did Red?

Did Garren?

Yeah, I thought, all of them did. And the realization that they'd kept it from me burned, each for a different reason. I slept with Red every damn night. Why would he keep this from me? Garren had only just returned, and to be fair, last night had been a little wild.

Red had no such excuse.

The sudden absence of the field scientists during the day made a lot of sense.

Why wouldn't he talk to me about something so important?

Maybe they were waiting until they had the complete picture?

Maybe they still didn't trust me?

Yeah, that one burned the most. "Do you know where Joshua is?"

"In the library, last I saw," Mari said cheerily.

"And what about Tanis? Where does he hide away?"

"He was in his council room earlier, miss," she said in a hushed whisper, "but you can't go in there."

I wasn't usually one for breaking the rules, but I thought it might be fun to barge into the council room and demand answers. From my short time here, I'd learned that omegas were much indulged in Shadowland and could get away with pretty much anything. "And where does he go when he is not in the council room?"

"Well, he could go to the armory, or he could be in his rooms, but you can't go there, either."

"And where are his rooms?" I asked, because I was a dog with a bone, and I needed a backup plan.

Mari's gaze darted to the corridor that disappeared off the far side of the hall. Two guards stood on either side of the opening... one of them was Tay, a member of Tanis' wolf guard. I wasn't convinced Tay would know how the war might impact the Rymorians, but if I was desperate enough later, I might try her.

The Warrior in the Shadows

"In the southern part of the fortress where all the lords and high guests stay." Mari's face turned pink as she realized the implications of what she'd said with regards to where my room was.

I chuckled, suffering no delusion about my status. Some residents tolerated us as outsiders, while others were more openly curious, especially about me being an unmated omega at the grand age of twenty-five. But with the large influx of people, we had gone largely unnoticed.

"Well, you'd be there too, excepting Lord Tanis specifically said as you and the tower dwellers should be placed in rooms with windows. Can't understand why anyone would want to be in a room with a window, myself. I just know I couldn't sleep at night worrying about someone getting in." She shuddered as though horrified by the mere thought.

My room was six stories high above a featureless solid stone wall. As if that wasn't sufficient protection, iron bars as thick as my arm crisscrossed the window.

Yet Mari's concerns were valid from her viewpoint. They also brought home to me that this wasn't my world, and I didn't fit in. "Let's go to see if Joshua is in the library."

I trailed behind Mari along the gloomy corridors to the library, yet another windowless room, of which the fortress possessed far too many examples. A single lamp cast questionable light, wooden shelving filled every wall, and thick leather-bound books spilled from every shelf. The vast, cavernous room had a strange smell reminiscent of dry leaves and was empty save for Joshua, who sat at the sturdy wooden table in the center of the room.

He glanced up and a brief smile crossed his face on seeing me enter. "Hannah, you won't believe what book I found when I was—"

"They're leaving tomorrow, for the war," I interrupted.

Joshua dropped the book. It hit the floor with a thud, but he barely glanced down. "Leaving? Who?" He fumbled for the book.

"Has anyone been here?"

"No, I've—No." He grasped the book, dragged the heavy thing back up, and placed it on the table. "Who's leaving?"

"Tell him what you know, Mari."

"I don't know if I should say any more." Mari fidgeted at the doorway.

"It's okay, Mari," I said gently. "Joshua won't be angry, and you're not telling him anything the whole fortress doesn't already know."

Mari wrung her hands as she regarded Joshua. "The news came late last night. Lord Tanis will be leaving with his armies at first light."

Joshua turned back to the table and opened his book.

"Did you hear what Mari said?" I asked, frowning.

He opened it with trembling fingers. "We knew it was coming and there's nothing we can do," he said quietly.

"Nothing?" I shook my head. "Don't you care that this is happening? Don't you want to know the details, what it means for us?"

"Of course, I care!" He lifted his nose from the book to glare at me. "What do you think we can do? It has nothing to do with us anymore. We're not Rymorians anymore, not here, we can't be, unless we want to end up dead."

His morose reaction baffled me. "You can't stay in this room forever." I swallowed. "What if the field scientists are leaving with them?"

He went back to the book and started flipping through the pages. "At least the field scientists have a possible place. There's work here that I may be able to do—ways I can be useful. We need to be useful, Hannah. You think they'll keep feeding and protecting us if we're not?"

This wasn't depression talking. This was something far worse. He was right. I had no value here. What was I to Garren or even Red? Just an opportunity for hot sex, or something more? I'd thought I was more, yet neither of them could be bothered to talk to me. I felt both vulnerable and used. "You think they'll kick us out?"

Joshua's mouth twisted into a sneer. "I'm neither young, nor a pretty omega, and I'm not sleeping with one of them." His sudden laugh made my stomach churn. "How long do you think you'll be safe here once they've gone—once your alpha has gone?"

"What are you saying?" A dull thud began pounding at the base of my skull.

"I'm saying they're going, all the people who have protected us thus far, and for how long? Maybe they'll return, or maybe they won't come back at all." He shook his head. "This isn't Rymor, Hannah. If they don't return, what do you think will happen to us?"

"We have to know. Maybe you could go to the armory where they are." I wasn't convinced Joshua would be granted entry, but he had a better chance than me.

"I don't want to know, Hannah. I can't get involved."

He looked down again, his jaw set, his expression blank.

I couldn't stay a moment longer in a room thick with angry, desperate words. "I'm going to my room, Mari. I think I'll stay there for the rest of the day."

I forced a smile when her face fell. "It's okay, Mari. I'm going to read for a bit." I turned back to Joshua. "If anyone wants me, tell them where I am."

He nodded stiffly, still staring at the book I was sure he wasn't reading.

Tonight, Red would come to me, or Garren, or maybe both. Until then, I would have to play the waiting game.

Chapter 34

Tanis

I found Joshua in the library. According to the servants, he'd been in here all day, every day, since arriving at Thale.

Joshua's gaze snapped toward the door as Jon and I entered, and his posture turned so rigid I got the impression he was about to barge past me and make a run for it.

"No need to leave," I said, trying to put him at ease. "I was looking for you, Joshua,"

"Of course." Joshua placed the leather-bound book on the table, hands shaking.

I pulled out a chair and sat down opposite him. Jon took a seat to his right. "You may already have heard that the Shadowland army is leaving Thale tomorrow." He nodded, hanging on my every word. "Certain things have come to light, and I'm going to need your skills to help."

"My skills? Yes, anything." Joshua glanced toward Jon before returning his wary eyes to me. "I want to help, if I can."

"I'm glad to hear that. However, this is an unusual request, and

The Warrior in the Shadows

delicate in nature. I need someone to deactivate the wall again. Do you think you could do that? For me?"

He opened and closed his mouth, eyes darting once more to Jon, who offered a nod. Joshua frowned. "The wall? You want me to make it inoperative again?"

"I do."

"I-I don't think it would be possible...or even if I could." He stared down at his hands. "It's not a simple request. Most likely, I would need to return to the station, then break it irrevocably. There are fail safes in place to protect it from sabotage...so it would need something extreme." His voice began to waver. "You're asking me to destroy the wall, permanently: forever?"

"If that's what it takes, then that's what it takes," I said. "I need it inoperative; how that happens is less important." It hadn't been my original intention to destroy the wall permanently, but the idea held merit. The path before me was shifting, and the impact of words in this room would be amplified through the histories for generations to come. I would be infamous. Would take on, in reality, the terrorist label Bill had long ago adhered to my name.

My resolve hardened, even in taking this drastic step. The Shadowlanders were my people, and I would neither give them up nor abandon them.

The silence stretched, and Joshua still hadn't answered. "A war is happening, Joshua, I suggest you pick a side."

My words were blunt, but the matter was too crucial for half-measures, and I needed Joshua to be all in. He was an asset and it would be far better if the asset recognized its one and only use.

The acceleration in Joshua's breathing didn't bother me, nor did Jon's sudden and absolute stillness.

"What about the people of Rymor?"

"You have a family back there?" I asked.

"I... yes," Joshua said. "My partner, and a son. He's twelve." He paused, his face creasing. "He'll be thirteen by now."

I nodded in understanding. "My mother still lives there. I don't intend to slaughter the people of Rymor, just those who get in my way. You can't go back there now, none of you can. That door closed the moment Rymorians chose to keep you prisoner. I'm sorry for that, genuinely sorry. If there's a way I can reunite you with your family once this is over, I will do it. You also need to recognize your lack of choice in this. I need the wall inoperative. I help those who help me."

"I think he gets it, Tanis," Jon said quietly.

"It's okay, Jon," Joshua said. "I do want to help. I will. I've spent a great deal of time thinking since Marcus, or whoever he was, killed my friend. My life has changed. I've accepted it. I had no expectations of seeing my family again. I'd do anything for a chance of changing that. I lost everything the day I got on that transport."

Jon sighed and raked his right hand over his short dark hair. "I know. Don't I know."

"What about the rest of the Rymorians who are here? Will they be staying at Thale?" Joshua asked

"The field scientists will be coming with us," I said. "Most will accompany you to the station. The remainder will accompany me."

Joshua nodded, his hands moving restlessly against each other. "What about Hannah?"

"Hannah will be staying here." A necessary decision for her safety, although I had lingering regrets in regard to the omega I had largely ignored. The truth was, I didn't trust myself to talk to her, never mind touch her. If I touched her, I was going to force her damn heat, and that would be disastrous for me, and the people of Shadowland, should my focus be split. I didn't delude myself that I was a good man, but I wouldn't subject Hannah to a life bond just because I was incapable of controlling the brain in my dick.

Joshua bobbed his head again. "That is for the best. I think it may have been too much for her if you wanted her to travel. She was very upset when she learned about the war, and returned to her room a few hours ago saying she didn't want to be disturbed."

The Warrior in the Shadows

I nodded. "I have matters I need to attend to, but Jon will go over the details with you now."

"I'll speak to you later," Jon said as I stood.

I gave Jon a meaningful look before regarding Joshua again. "I keep my word, Joshua. Make sure you do the same."

With that, I turned and left the room.

Chapter 35

Kein, Shadowland Scout

The armory was heaving, which was to be expected given that eighty thousand soldiers were about to pack up and leave tomorrow. Everyone was busy checking weapons, collecting weapons, and making last repairs to weapons. A corridor-like room, it was housed in the underground complex with exits leading to the various barracks off to the left. On the right, an open accessway provided a thoroughfare to both the above-ground courtyard and smiths' halls.

My armor was lightweight leather. I wore a short sword, carried a bow, and a knife, and that was it. I traveled light, even when I was part of an army.

I had never been part of an army of this size, though; none of us had and it was clear that Tanis was once again making history.

Years ago, I'd recognized the importance of Tanis to Shadowland; how he was different, and not only because of his heritage. Gaining the approval of such a man, and being considered part of his inner circle, gave me great satisfaction. Yes, I'd done well for a child from the northern borders, forced from my home at nine when the Jaru

The Warrior in the Shadows

raided my family farm and left everyone dead. My hatred of the Jaru was fierce, and I was grateful such attacks had dwindled under Tanis' rule.

Until last year when the Jaru began to unite.

Now the Jaru were not the only challenge we faced, but I had little doubt we would face them better under Tanis' rule.

Han sat to my left, engaged in a detailed study of his great sword. His ax rested on the top of the table, while he made sure his sword was in perfect order.

Tanis entered from our left and paused, a dozen paces from where I sat, to speak to one of his wolf guards. Most occupants noted his arrival—he had a way of drawing attention no matter where he was. His rise to power over the last ten years had been brutal, and the tales that lingered were dark and destructive. I'd played a part in those events and knew the stories were pale echoes of what had transpired.

"He doesn't look happy. There's still no word on Falton then?" Han asked, lifting his head briefly before resuming the examination of his sword in the flickering lamplight.

"Nothing that I know of," I said. "And Garren's heard nothing either while he's been out."

Garren stood with his section, deep in discussion with one of his men fifty paces to my right. Seeing Tanis enter, Garren dropped the conversation and stared at his half-brother.

I watched the interplay with interest. Watching people was one of my vices, and Tanis provided a bounty of fascinating insights. If Tanis was unhappy, then Garren's scowl suggested he wasn't happy either. The two brothers hadn't engaged in anything more significant than a mild verbal set-to in months, and while they had been occupied with more important matters, a confrontation was overdue.

Reports of the tower dweller army had caused Tanis to recall the last of his soldiers. Garren and his soldiers had returned to Thale last night. Their task, to find the group who had been with Marcus, had yielded nothing of worth. That failure would doubtless have been a source of frustration to Garren, along with his separation from Hannah for so many days. Like everyone else, he would be leaving again at first light tomorrow. Such was the way of life here; there wasn't always time to rest.

I felt that Garren saw what was coming with Hannah, but was also in denial about what that would mean. If I were a betting man, I would be betting on Garren being very pissed at some point.

"I think we're about to have our long overdue confrontation," I said, nudging my head in Tanis' direction.

Han lifted his chin, and his attention was snagged as Garren pushed through the crowded room, stalking toward Tanis.

"What's bothering Garren?" Han said, his sword forgotten. "He's been away for weeks, and they haven't had a chance to wind each other up since his return."

I grinned. Han narrowed his eyes at me.

Over the last few years, Garren had grown into a strong leader and led a well-disciplined team. He fought hard and fearlessly and instilled the same values in his men. There was no doubt he respected Tanis, but at times he was apt to explore the boundary between leader and subordinate more than was healthy. Tanis took this dissension in his stride. Perhaps Tanis could see Garren's value and felt the rest could be managed. Tanis wasn't the kind of leader who surrounded himself with opinionless people. Still, Garren was young, and his opinions were strong and vocal. They had come to physical conflict on many occasions.

I could see them becoming great friends, assuming Tanis didn't kill Garren first.

"You think I don't know what this has been about?" Garren's cutting tone carried through the sudden quiet, capturing the interest of the room, and many made subtle moves to find better positions.

"I don't give a shit what you think," Tanis said.

An underlying conflict had existed between Tanis and Garren from the day they'd first met. Perhaps some legacy of Tanis killing Garren's older brothers, or perhaps a case of personalities too similar.

The Warrior in the Shadows

For some reason, Tanis took a certain sadistic pleasure in these conflicts.

"Harsh," Han said, then cast a suspicious glance at me. "What do you know about this?"

"I have an idea," I said with a knowing smile.

Han's attention returned to the proceedings. "Are you going to share?" he grumbled. "I thought they'd been getting on better lately?"

"Yes, they were," I agreed. "Until a certain Rymorian came along."

"Ah," Han said before turning back to his sword. Ten paces away, Tanis and Garren stood nose to nose. "Danel did mention something a while back. No point in me trying to stop them, then."

"None," I agreed. Garren clearly wasn't about to back down. Given that he'd been caught in more than one incident with the Jaru and had subsequently been riding hard for days, his current determination to push Tanis was foolhardy. Still, he certainly had balls.

"What's so important about this one? Is it because she's from Rymor?"

Garren's tone was sufficient even without the subject matter. I smirked as Tanis returned the kind of unrelenting stare that historically had precluded him ripping Garren apart.

"You don't need to look so smug," Han mumbled as silence settled over the nearby section of the room. "I'm the one who'll have to stop the idiots killing each other. Where the fuck is Danel when I need him?"

"I've no idea why you care. Her being Bill's cast-off and all," Garren bit out.

Tanis punched him—hard. I winced. Garren soaked it up, then, a heartbeat later, they were at each other like they meant business.

Han did an impressive job of ignoring them and maintained his attention on his sword as if it were the only thing in the world. "I'm going to let them slug it out. They need to wear each other out, or it'll flare up again."

"Ah, the voice of experience," I said, enjoying myself immensely.

The room became notably busier as the fight continued. It added a bit of interest to everyday life and would likely soon be retold with embellishments for those who missed out on front-row seats.

A rack of weapons went crashing to the ground. Neither man noticed. Neither man cared. The resounding smacks of fists connecting with flesh filled the room, interspersed with the occasional grunt after a well-placed blow.

Garren ducked, and Tanis punched the unfortunate spectator behind him. The poor man went down, out cold.

Han put his sword aside and scratched his beard as he stared at the two men setting at one another with abandon.

"Do you think they're tiring?" I asked as they continued another enthusiastic round of trading blows.

"No," Han said. "But they'll never be fit to travel tomorrow unless I stop them." He shrugged. "I'll try."

Han pushed through the crowd surrounding the fight, positioned himself behind Tanis, and motioned to the men standing behind Garren. Between them, they dragged the two men apart. It took three men to hold Garren, and for a long nervous moment, I feared they weren't enough.

Then the fight left Garren suddenly, and the men restraining him relinquished their hold.

"Let go!" Tanis snapped the words out so hard it was a wonder his teeth didn't crack. Han held him for a second longer before slowly releasing his grip.

Garren was bleeding from his nose and temple, and his right eye was starting to swell shut. Tanis looked no better, and they were both breathing hard. Han maintained his position, watchful, like he expected them to go at it again.

"Stay away from her, Garren," Tanis said. "If I find out you've been anywhere near her before we leave tomorrow, I *will* have you flogged."

Order delivered, he turned and stalked from the room.

As the door banged shut behind him, Garren swore, and the

The Warrior in the Shadows

armory dissolved into an uproar. I pushed through the mass to reach Han and Garren as people began to disperse.

"You asked for that, my friend," Han said to Garren, his expression grave.

"I know," Garren said. He winced as he probed his right cheek. "I need a drink."

A rare smile found Han's face. "A far better idea than trying to slug it out with Tanis," he said.

Chapter 36

Hannah

I had spent many hours alone in my room waiting for the elusive visit from Garren or Red. Mari brought my dinner and took it away uneaten. Still, I remained none the wiser about the preparations for war.

I stared at the book before me and tried to remember when I'd last turned a page. The confronting conversation with Joshua played over in my mind. The more time went on, the sicker I felt.

The sun set, and darkness descended. Time was escaping me. At first light, Garren would be gone, possibly Red too.

For war.

Resolving that I needed to do something, I set my book aside and left the room.

The corridor was quiet, with no sign of Mari or even the guards. When I checked the rooms of my fellow Rymorians, I found all of them empty.

Even Joshua was gone.

The pitfalls of wandering around without Mari or guards as chaperones were not lost on me, but I couldn't wait another minute in

The Warrior in the Shadows

this state of not knowing. I doubted Garren would be in his room, even assuming I could find it, so I headed for the great hall, which I was confused to find empty. Neither Tay nor any other wolf guards were stationed in the corridor leading off from the back.

The ones that led to Tanis' rooms.

Yes, I was going there...

The corridor meandered, doorless, for several minutes before I reached a set of curving steps that carried me upward for several floors. At the top, it came to an abrupt end, and it was there I found myself, out of breath, face-to-face with two wolf guards.

I'd been hoping to find Tay, who I thought might at least answer my questions, but neither of them was female, neither of them was known to me, and neither of them spoke.

They were posted beside an imposing wooden door and regarding me with interest. I was here now, and turning around would only make me look as stupid as I felt.

It was late, though, maybe too late. Tanis could be asleep or busy. He might not even be here.

Think like an omega, I told myself. According to Mari, omegas could brazen through anything and not get into trouble. I squared my shoulders. "I want to speak to Tanis."

The guards looked at one another without any discernible change in their expressions. Then, without a word, the man on the left reached to open the door.

This wordless response unsettled me, but I stepped inside, bracing myself for something far worse than I got.

His rich pheromones hit me the moment the door closed. All the little hairs on the surface of my skin rose to attention, and heat kicked off in my womb. Tanis sat at a table facing the doorway in a spacious room with familiar glistening black walls. There was a single large window on one side, darkened with the turn toward night. Several lamps provided a soft glow that left much of the room in shadows. The heavy oak table was sufficient to seat a dozen people with ease. On the tabletop sat a thick pile of canvas maps, which he appeared to be studying. A tall-necked green bottle rested there as well, close at hand.

He glanced up and frowned on seeing me before picking the bottle up, lifting to his lips and swallowing a mouthful down. His right brow-line bore a cut, as did the cheek below it, which was shiny, swollen, and purple. The knuckles of the hand that was wrapped around the bottle were red and raw looking.

"What... ah... happened to you?"

He set the bottle back against the table. "What are you doing here, Hannah?" His familiar clipped tone and condescending air instantly grated on me.

When I didn't answer, he returned to his map like I wasn't there.

"I heard you were leaving tomorrow. That Shadowland was at war with Rymor."

Long, agonizing moments ticked by. He drank once more from the bottle before pushing the top map out of the way so he could study the one beneath. This was all very awkward. I began to wonder if Mari had been mistaken and if there wasn't a war at all.

"This is not a good time," he said as I was about to beat my retreat. "I feel like shit and have been drinking"—he paused his map study to check the tilted bottle—"a lot."

"You didn't answer my question," I said.

"I believe you made a statement." He picked up the top map and drew it closer to his eyes.

"It was phrased as a question," I said, feeling defensive and confused. Why was Tanis acting so weird? "Why are you ignoring me?"

He sighed, dropped the map back to the table, and leaned back in his chair, making me the object of his undivided attention; something which, now I had it, I regretted seeking.

"Ignoring? No, not really, it was simply more of a priority that you leave the room."

I blinked several times as he took yet another drink, torn between leaving, since he had made it clear that I should, and staying to demand answers.

"I'm not in the mood for company," he said dryly.

Company! My eyes narrowed. Why had the guards let me into the room when he was—as he so eloquently stated—not in the mood for guests? "I just wanted to know what's happening."

He continued to fix me with a level stare.

"Perhaps I should leave, then," I said a little mulishly.

"Perhaps you should," he agreed with a magnanimous incline of his head.

Oh, that ticked me right off. I didn't leave, but couldn't work out why a streak of stubbornness should choose to grip me now. The silence stretched, and Tanis continued to regard me. Then, without apparent cause, he chuckled, a rich, raucous sound that made me jump.

His amusement subsided to a smile. He drank once more before pointing the bottle tip at me. "You're still here. Why are you still here? Why for once in your life can you not do as you're asked?" His eyes narrowed suddenly as his smile faded. "Wait. Did you wander over here on your own?"

I swallowed, realizing I'd fucked up, forgetting he was such a stickler for my safety, although he was also an asshole who kissed me, made wild declarations about claiming me, and then never followed through. Oh, how my fantasies of alphas had taken a hit. None of them had ravished me, although I supposed Garren had come close last night.

I folded my arms. "No."

He gave me a flat look. "I don't believe you."

"I just wanted some answers," I muttered, wanting to take the bottle from his hands and smash it over his arrogant head.

He raised an eyebrow.

"I'll go then," I said, only I didn't move. It seemed as if my body was divorced from my mind, mesmerized by the play of strong muscles in his throat as he took another drink.

He put the bottle back down with a *thunk* that snapped me out of the daze. Why was he rising? The scrape of his chair across the wooden floor seemed exceptionally loud.

Why did the sight of him rounding the table, and the steady cadence of his boots drawing nearer, make me want to run? What should my response be?

I turned and ran.

With both hands on the handle, I yanked the heavy door open an inch, but that was as far as I got before he slammed it shut.

My chest heaved as his scent filled my nose. My traitorous pussy clenched and pushed out a flood of slick. His palm pressed flat against the door to my right, holding it closed. "Okay, I'll leave now," I whispered, fingers still locked around the metal door handle. All the while thinking about him tossing me over the shoulder, taking me to his bed and ravishing me.

Why had I come here?

"You needed to leave some time ago," he said. "I may have mentioned it once or twice."

His hand slid down with a deliberate slowness that my eyes tracked until he closed it around my wrist. The ease with which he plucked my fingers from their death grip on the handle was embarrassing. He turned me around before backing me against the door.

Why was it only now that I realized how freakishly big an alpha was?

"Do you know what Red Alrin is?"

"Red Alrin? No?"

"Green bottle on my table." He gestured over his shoulder.

He was acting odd, but he didn't look or sound drunk. I shook my head, puzzled.

"It's medicinal, with some interesting conscience-blocking side-effects. Red Alrin and company never mix well. Sometimes you end up killing someone. Sometimes you end up fucking them. It can be hard to predict."

I swallowed hard, everything inside me revving up. "There are

The Warrior in the Shadows

two guards right outside the door," I said, like this might bring reason to the moment. Despite how much I wanted him to put his hands on me, I also thought it might be the mother of all bad ideas.

He leaned in close, drawing his head down so that his lips were close to my ear. "They're not standing out there for *your* protection, Hannah."

No, they were there for his, which was laughable, given he was the last person to need help. "You don't want to... ah... kill me."

He leaned back enough for our eyes to meet and grinned. "No, I don't want to kill you."

"Can I leave now?"

"No."

"Why did your guards even let me in?!"

"They were probably curious."

"Curious?" What kind of sick guards were they?

"Garren returned, and we had a rather public discussion about you. So, yes, they were probably curious."

He placed his hands against the door to either side of my shoulders in a slow, measured movement.

"What sort of discussion?" The verbal conversation happened on one level while our bodies engaged in a different dialogue.

"Garren was unhappy at being away for so long, and unhappy to be leaving again so soon. He seemed to think I'd planned it, that I wanted to keep him from you." He smirked. "If I'd wanted to stop him from fucking you, I would have told him not to fuck you. In the heat of the moment, when our discussion got out of hand and we finished pummeling each other in the crowded armory, I told him to stay away from you."

I swallowed and tried without success to process that. "Why would you say that? No one would say something like that. It's so—" Rude? Barbaric? Fucked up?

"If I'm blunt—and it's hard to be anything else when you've been drinking Red Alrin—I like holding complete domination over people," he said. "I like the power, and, yes, at times, I even like being an asshole. It certainly gave me immense satisfaction to tell Garren he couldn't have you, and even greater satisfaction to know he would obey."

"You really are obnoxious," I said inadequately. Would Garren really abandon me because Tanis had told him to?

He shrugged, smirked again, and stepped back, nodding his head at the door. "Get out."

I sucked in air, shocked by the sudden coldness of his tone. "No."

"Was that in some way confusing? Get out of my room." He stabbed a finger at the door.

"No!" A little voice in my head questioned my defiance, but I was also enraged that he dared to order Garren away from me. Really, he had a lot of nerve thinking he could tell everyone what to do.

He reached to grab me, to throw me out, I presumed, but once he had his hands on my waist, he froze. Heat flared in his gaze as he stared down at my open collar, at my throat. The heat blazed hotter still as his eyes rose to meet mine.

How had I ever thought him cold and indifferent? He was a burning maelstrom sucking me in.

"I thought you wanted to leave," he said.

"I don't know what I want," I answered honestly.

"Don't think I'm going to fucking share you," he growled. "I'm not that kind of alpha."

My nostrils flared, and my mind went into free fall as my scrambled thoughts tried to gather his words to make them somehow coherent. Was he saying this would be a one-time thing, or that I must give up Garren and Red? His scent was in my nose, rich and potent, his warm hands at my waist setting my body to riot. I wanted him. I'd always wanted him, right from the very start.

"Those are my terms, Hannah. It's always an omega's choice. Anything but yes, and I'm putting you outside the door."

"Yes."

He growled, lifting me, shoving me roughly against the door, and pinning me with his big, powerful body. He swallowed my moan, lips

The Warrior in the Shadows

crashing over mine with an ownership that made a mockery of any denial. I wrapped my arms and legs around him, opening to the kiss, reveling in the feel of his body caging me, his scent, and the heated delight as he ground his hard cock against the sensitive place between my legs.

He was the leader of Shadowland, an alpha, *the* alpha, and the one who ruled them all.

My body and mind were all in. I'd wanted Tanis, and this, for so long, that I felt a little mindless with the desperation ripping through me.

He badly wanted me, too, evidenced in the tremble of his hands and the low, growly purr emanating from his chest.

Tomorrow, I already sensed, would bring regrets.

Tomorrow, he was leaving for war and for danger.

Tonight, I wanted only to feel him inside me.

Tonight, I wanted to forget.

Chapter 37

Tanis

One moment I was about to drag open the door and throw her out, and the next, I sank my fingers into her ass and slammed her back against the door. Her legs wrapped around me, and I kissed her like I wanted to consume her soul. Hanging on to my control by a thread, I faced my self-destruction.

Hannah. Me. Inevitable.

And naked.

I needed her out of these clothes and in my bed, where she belonged.

I staggered toward my bedroom with her in my arms and my mouth locked on hers. I missed the bedroom door, crushing her into the nearby wall, where I continued to devour her before finally making it through the elusive gap.

I collapsed on top of her on the bed.

"God, please, hurry."

Yes, hurry. Except my brain-to-hand coordination was shot, my hands shaking so badly I couldn't get a single button undone.

What the fuck is wrong with my hands?

The Warrior in the Shadows

"Strip." The word came as a barely discernible growl. Maybe it was close enough to human language to understand, or she was simply on board with getting naked. Either way, she removed her clothes with a sob of raw need.

Rising from the bed, I tore my clothes off too, only everything was coming out of sequence... shirt... pants... I still had my boots on and nearly landed on my ass. "Fuck!"

Undo boots... kick them off along with pants.

I heaved a breath, relieved to be free of the restrictive clothing, head swinging back to the bed and the source of the delicious scent I'd never fully cleared from my nose since that day we first met.

She was kneeling there naked in the middle of my bed.

My throat worked, my hands clenched and unclenched as I took her in, from all that wild silver-blonde hair, her beautiful face with those unusual gray eyes, her pert tits, and trim waist, onto her hips and open thighs smeared with slick. Her pussy was lost in the shadows of the room, and I felt disproportionately pissed that any of her was hidden from me.

I needed to touch her. Didn't trust myself to. Thought I might be on the brink of madness.

"Lay down."

She did.

And never had there been a more perfect image than Hannah lying naked on my bed with her hair tangled about her face. She looked tiny, delicate, and everything I was not as she stared back at me with those solemn eyes, her lips puffy and pink from my kisses. Either I'd died and gone to heaven, or someone had left an angel in my bed.

Slow, I needed to go slow.

Somehow, I did, coming down over her, resisting the call of her cunt and how my mouth watered for a taste, brushing her hair back from her hot cheek, cupping her face in my hand, and pressing my trembling lips to hers.

Slow, I'd go fucking slow, even if it killed me.

It did. Each feather-like brush of my lips to hers was like a searing brand. Her soft skin, her sweet fuck-me scent rising, her restless and stuttered sobs as she tried to take more; all of her conspired to overwhelm.

"Hush," I whispered. "Let me worship you."

She settled, opened to my deeper kisses, and submitted to the stroke of my rough hands over her shoulders and down her arms. Both of her small hands were reverently kissed before I gave myself permission to take her mouth again.

My blood pounded through my veins. My dick was hot and heavy and leaking pre-cum against the bedding.

I ignored the burning fire within me and kissed down her throat like I had all the time in the world. Then, the fire inside me stoked higher as I saw the marks on her. Subtle smudges against her soft skin telling me someone had been there first.

Someone else had a claim.

A claim on what was mine.

I banked the fire, let it do what it needed to inside me, kissed her pretty tits, squeezed them together, and sucked her nipples gently until they were stiff and dark rose pink.

But those fucking marks were like a beacon on a dark night, calling to my primal side and my clamoring instincts to eradicate them.

My lips found each and every mark, sucking gently over them, thinking about what I wanted to do, and telling myself I shouldn't. Her trembling body, her hands in my hair, holding me closer, and her open thighs and slick pussy rubbing against me could only soothe the beast within me so much.

She wanted this, wanted me, and had come to *my* room.

My fingers found her hot core, and she arched up.

"Hush, Hannah," I said, lips against her tit. "We go at my pace or we stop."

I wasn't going to stop. A fucking army couldn't make me stop, but she didn't know that, nor how I held myself in tight check, of how delicate her situation was, how the slightest trigger might tip me over the edge.

She settled again, pussy soft and open, all slick and hot around my fingers as I explored her at my leisure. My fingertips brushed over the stiff bud of her clit before slipping inside and curling to find the entrance to her gland.

"Are you going to come for me?"

"God, please, I need more."

"Not yet. I want you soft and relaxed. I want a sweet, gentle climax first. If you're good for me, I'll think about giving you more."

I played. Careful of my roiling emotional state, keeping touches and kisses light, coaxing her toward that place of no return, watching the rapture contort her face as she gently tipped over, her chest heaving and pussy spasming over my fingers, mouth opening on a breathy gasp as her body shuddered through her release.

"Good girl," I said. "Now, I need a fucking taste before I lose my mind."

Hannah

His head was between my thighs: mouth, tongue, and fingers moving over slick flesh that was still tingling from my climax. I was going to come again, and could feel it building faster, like the deep, intense orgasm was merely a prelude for the main event. His light touches maddened me.

On the surface he seemed like still water, yet underneath he was a boiling sea.

I'd noted how his lips lingered over the marks left by Garren and Red, sensed his tempered rage as evidenced in the tremble of his lips when they passed over them. He wanted to obliterate them. To replace them with him.

And I wanted him to, wanted him to rip his self-imposed restraints away and give me my dues.

Only this was sublime, and I didn't want him to stop.

The magic of his tongue and his calloused fingers penetrated me, stretching me.

My next climax side-swiped me out of nowhere.

A flood of slick gushed out.

He growled, tightened his grip, and continued to feast.

I was sensitive, chest heaving, and empty inside. Fingers clenching around his hair, I gripped and tugged.

His head popped up, he growled at me, then something caught his eye, and his head turned to the left.

A bruise, a deep purple mark on my inner thigh that Garren had left.

My stomach took a slow dip at his stillness and the way his entire focus was locked upon it. My pussy throbbed, and a pricking awareness washed over my skin, my breath barely moving in and out of my lungs.

Then, slowly, oh-so-slowly, he lowered his lips to it.

He sucked hard.

A gasp escaped my lips, but he growled, pinned me so that I couldn't move, and sucked harder still.

I squirmed, gripped his hair and tugged, even knowing it would only drive him on. Slick flooded in response to his possessive display. God, yes! I wanted all of this, wanted him unleashed and as desperate as I felt. I ached, a deep, pervasive ache that lit up my core, and I knew when he eventually lifted his head, Garren's mark would be well and truly gone.

His lips popped off, and chest heaving, he examined what he had done.

"Fuck me," I begged. "I want you to. I need it."

The Warrior in the Shadows

Tanis

My mind seemed to fog over, hearing the desperation in her command. Like a sleepwalker lost to the thrall of a dream, I was doomed to answer the call. Crawling over her, I closed my mouth over hers, kissing up all those sweet, needy sounds, trying to consume her, imprint myself upon her, and own her through a kiss.

It wasn't enough.

Nothing was.

"Please, please, please."

As I sucked hard over a particularly vivid mark on her throat left by her other lover, her mumbled words finally penetrated the stupor.

Rising to my knees, I fisted her hair and dragged her lips to cock. "Suck!"

I didn't need the words. Hannah fell on me like she was starving for the taste, her hot, wet mouth sucking me deep.

"Good girl, use your tongue."

Her eager whimpers followed as I used her hair to direct her on and off. Her nails scored my thighs, and her tongue lavished my cock with every deep stroke.

When was the last time I'd been with an omega?

Many months.

When was the last time I'd had one all to myself, and when had one unhinged me like this?

Never.

I was sinking into a feral state, all too aware of the dangers of my mental condition, that I craved the roughness that might well trigger her heat. Worse, I could smell Garren on her, and since I knew he hadn't visited her after my orders—trusting Han to keep a watch over him—that meant Garren had been with her before that.

Either that or their pheromones were mixing.

I should have done this long ago, separated them, told Garren to fuck off when it first began, claimed her, put my mark on her, and forced her heat.

I had created this situation and now I had to live with the consequence.

The sounds of her gagging didn't ease the savagery of my use, pre-cum and saliva coating her chin and chest. But her small hands were gripping my ass like she was afraid I might deny her her toy, and her even more delectably aroused scent thickened the air.

Omegas were made for everything an alpha craved. Was it some twist of nature or the result of a mad scientist? A little of both might be behind the push and pull, the animalistic dichotomy between two human extremes.

"I'm going to come."

She swallowed around my every thrust, snuffled breaths snatched where she could.

Here, with Hannah on her knees before me, as I looked down upon her, god-like, I experienced a sensual epiphany. A deeper understanding of the power of lust and how it entwined with love, how the two strong emotions delivered something even more potent when combined.

Love? What the fuck did I know of love?

I didn't trust women, never had, and never would.

Yet this omega on her knees, praying to my cock, who I had worshiped earlier with a reverence I'd experienced to the depths of my soul, was destined to be mine. Not in the mystical sense, nor the spiritual, but the cold, hard fact that I had determined it would be so.

Extremes that fit perfectly together should not be squandered or lost.

Maybe it wasn't love but a fancy taking my lust-clouded mind.

Maybe I could pretend I didn't see sufficient strength of character in this fragile woman, enough to set empires to war.

Maybe I could delude myself that she was nothing but a passing interest, a hot fuck, an itch that would be relieved by a good scratch.

Only I prided myself on my intelligence, and while I had many failings, being delusional wasn't one of them.

The Warrior in the Shadows

Worse, I knew that Garren, and even Red, understood the value of the omega who accepted them into her bed.

I came, a hot gush spewing from my cock, choking her, trickling down her chin, and onto the bed. My mind blanked to nothing as I came over and over, filling her mouth as she tried to keep up.

She gulped it down like a greedy little omega, lapping me clean as I found myself among the pieces of the shattering climax.

It was only then that I noticed her fingers busy in her cunt, touching what was mine without permission, chasing pleasure of her own.

I shook her. "Fingers out!"

She hissed at me and defiantly carried on.

Brat!

I had her face down in the bedding, my hand collaring her throat and her wrist pinned to the small of her back.

"Ass up," I barked. "The only thing going in your pussy for the rest of the night is my cock. Present, show me where you want and need me, and I'll think about giving it to you."

Her knees drew under her, and she popped her ass up and out, arching up, tossing a look over her shoulder that was all challenge. "I want it rough," she said without missing a damn beat. "If you can't give me that, then I'm leaving to find a willing alpha who can."

My nostrils flared, and I bared my teeth and growled.

She was baiting me.

Only I was too far gone to care. My cock was hard and ready, and my knot halfway formed. I needed inside her more than I cared about being led.

And besides, I might teach her a thing or two about making demands of an alpha.

I smirked. Hannah's eyes widened.

Ah, Hannah, you might have just bitten off more than you can chew.

Flipping her onto her back, I hauled her to where leather cuffs were chained to the sturdy bedhead for just such a purpose.

She struggled the moment she realized what was coming.

Not that it mattered. And, really, the way her eyes lit up when she realized she was restrained was a delight.

"You just keep these here?!" She twisted this way and that, then I caught her ankle and spread her open, filling her in a single, deep thrust.

We both groaned. The chain jangled. I drew out and slam-fucked her again.

Her pussy clamped over my dick.

"You like that?"

"God, yes."

I huffed out a chuckle that turned into a groan as I fucked into her again. Opening her thighs wider, I dropped her knees over the crook of my arms and pounded her into the bed. Mouth hanging open, she stared up at me, face contorted with pleasure, pussy quivering around me. It took not even a minute before she was squealing and coming all over me.

I didn't stop. The darkness took me over, my awareness centering on the omega beneath me, the vessel for my cock, knot, and seed; her breathy pants, her hot milking cunt, her glazed eyes when I hit the entrance to her womb, and the ecstasy rippled through her face and body as my fat knot locked us together.

I roared as I came, dumping cum deep, grinding against her softness.

The time for gentleness was over.

A need so great it transcended understanding had me a willing prisoner.

Those marks called to me, and I obliterated them one at a time, fucking her over and over, knotting her, not even caring about the risks I'd counseled Garren to avoid.

Her other mates and war were for tomorrow.

Now and here, I could pretend there were only the two of us.

Chapter 38

Tanis

I had a great deal on my mind as I prepared for the coming journey, none of which involved the journey.

Soldiers, horses, and supplies congested Thale's central courtyard. Dawn had yet to lighten the sky, but some sections had begun moving out to provide enough space for the subsequent groups to assemble.

My fingers shook. I clenched and unclenched them, without notable improvement, then adjusted and readjusted the saddle and packs in a vain attempt to distract myself from the raw, chaotic jumble of images rolling through my mind from last night.

I'm never drinking Red Alrin again.

Unfortunately, the damage was done. After my fight with Garren in the armory I'd sought solace in the miraculous healing properties of Red Alrin. I hadn't been expecting company and had a hellish journey ahead of me.

I thought about killing the two guards at my door who had let her in, who knew she was going to get fucked when she refused to leave the room.

Like anyone under the influence of a potent drug, I'd remained cognizant of what I should do, in a distant way that had little to no impact on my actions. Despite everything that she had been through, she trusted everyone—including me. I'd started out wanting to shock her into thinking about her safety. Women didn't usually wander into my room for an evening chat.

If I was honest, it was delusional to think last night's events could be categorized under 'good intentions', nor could I rationalize it—when, as Garren had pointed out—she had once been with Bill.

I still couldn't figure out what had happened. One moment I'd been about to drag open the door and throw her out, and the next I'd sunk my fingers into her ass and slammed her back against the door. Her legs had wrapped around me, and I'd kissed her, and she had kissed me back. I'd been hanging on to my control by a thread, and it had all gone downhill from there. The word *inevitable* sprung to mind.

After that, my only coherent thought was getting her naked and in bed. I had stumbled toward my bedroom with her in my arms, a zigzag path across the room with my mouth locked on hers.

Somehow we'd made it to the bedroom where I collapsed on top of her on the bed, and attempted to undress her with a lack of prowess that hadn't registered as embarrassing at the time, but now certainly did. Frustrated by the clothing, I had given up and ordered her to strip.

I'd torn my clothes off in a random order, almost fallen over when I got my trousers stuck on my boots, and cursing up a storm, I'd grappled to get the damn things off.

And then I'd stopped since she was kneeling there naked in the middle of the bed. I'd stared at her for a long time, before ordering her to lay down. *Yes, my bedroom charisma knows no bounds.*

Hannah lying naked on my bed. Allowing myself to embrace the delusion that she was mine, when she was only ever mine for now. She looked tiny and delicate, and everything I was not.

The Warrior in the Shadows

I'd gone slow at first, but it hadn't stayed like that for long.

The first part didn't seem so bad, on reflection. But the gentle knock of the guard at the door, to tell me it was time to prepare for the day, had woken me to the consequence of my fevered mind the night before. The results manifested in claiming marks and bruises where I'd been too rough. They littered her body. I'd known what I was doing, marking her as mine, obliterating any trace of another male from her memory or flesh—*and then I'd walked out.*

I ran a tired hand over my face. Yes, and I was praying she didn't wake up.

Worse, I'd have killed another man for doing half of what I'd done. I hated myself with an intensity that surpassed any past regrets I'd had. I'd rarely treated Tay that roughly. It was inconceivable to my now sober mind that I had been so with Hannah.

When I opened my eyes, the horse was still there, and my trembling hands were poised against the saddle, the knuckles still raw from yesterday's fight with Garren.

Still gripped by my self-disgust, I registered the presence of someone beside me, so glanced up from adjusting the girth—again—and copped a fist to my jaw.

I staggered back, dazed. My sword was in my hand before I registered it was Garren. Once I *did* register that it was Garren, I elected to leave it there.

Garren's eyes widened, and then he half-drew his sword, too.

Neither of us moved.

"Garren! What are you doing?"

Han's gruff demand didn't penetrate the red haze in my mind. Garren's punch had tipped me over an edge, now only his full submission could pull me back.

The crowd and Han melted away. If today was the day that Garren would die, then so be it. It had been hanging over us for years. I'd become numb to such events, and, like my behavior last night, it reinforced the belief I had that I was beyond redemption. I considered the impact Garren's death would have on Hannah, then dismissed it. It wasn't as if I could sink any lower in her opinion. She hadn't thought favorably of me before last night and doubtless thought a lot less of me since.

"Garren, lower your fucking sword!" Han stood a couple of paces away. The deathly stillness of the crowd finally penetrated—*could I have found a more public place?*

"He drew first."

Garren sounded pissed. He had every right to be.

"And he will lower it last." Han's voice held weary resignation, and that stirred at some buried remnant of my conscience. "You know this, Garren. You know that he *will* kill you. Are you really ready to die today?"

The tension washed over me without finding any purchase.

Garren growled in furious capitulation, withdrawing his sword a little further in a swift, angry motion before slamming it back into the safer home of its sheath.

Turning on his heel, he pushed past the men who had gathered to watch our conflict. Red, I noticed, stood slack-jawed for a moment before pushing through the crowd in pursuit of him.

Fucking great! Now the two of them were in alliance.

I lowered my sword, noting that my hands no longer shook, and turned to find myself the singular focus of Han's penetrating stare. Despite his gruff appearance, he wasn't stupid.

"That has been a long time coming," he said at length. "I don't think he ever realized there was a boundary. He does now, and that will change him. He may decide to leave."

I gave Han a flat look.

He returned a hint of a smile. "Being stubborn is a family trait, I fear he will decide to stay."

I grunted noncommittally and shoved my sword back into its own sheath. It was long past time we were away, and worries about what Garren would or wouldn't do were lost under a deluge of more urgent ones. At the forefront were Bill and a war I couldn't possibly win.

The Warrior in the Shadows

No, that wasn't entirely true. If we destroyed the station, and through it, the wall, victory remained a slim possibility.

And if that didn't work, I had another half-formed idea that might just save Shadowland.

Chapter 39

Hannah

I woke up in Tanis' bed, alone.

Yesterday it had been Garren's.

A cold weight settled over me as I moved my head on the pillow, and acknowledged the significance of the sunlight streaming through the open door that led to his day room.

Dawn had long ago broken.

Everyone was gone.

I lay there and wept.

I'd cried far too much in the days since Edward's death. These tears weren't about Edward but a collective lump of misery for the events that ran roughshod through my life.

I didn't regret sleeping with Tanis. He was abrasive and arrogant, and the power he wielded had definitely gone to his head. But he was also fierce, dominant, insightful, and even compassionate. I'd wanted him from the moment I'd met him, and he rescued me from a Jaru warrior who'd been set to carve me up.

He'd tried really hard to get me to leave his room.

The Warrior in the Shadows

I'd ignored him because, deep down, I just wanted him, the biggest, strongest, and at times, most ruthless alpha.

Tiredness overcame my tears, and I slept for a while before waking restless and needy for attention.

My fingers skimmed over my tender breasts and belly to the sticky place between my thighs that ached from his rough rutting. The exact circumstances leading to me waking up in Tanis' bed were muddled in my mind. I tried not to dwell on it, but scenes and memories bombarded me regardless.

My pussy clenched over my fingers kicking off a sweet, needy ache. Only I didn't want my fingers. I wanted Tanis, Garren, and Red.

"Don't think I'm going to fucking share you," Tanis had growled at one point. *"I'm not that kind of alpha."*

At the time, his possessive declaration had been wildly arousing. On reflection, it made me feel torn and sad. How could I even be upset with him being possessive, when a kind of demented fever gripped me at the mere thought of him with another woman?

How could I reasonably expect three men to dedicate themselves to me and only me?

It wasn't common for omegas to be with multiple men outside of heat, although Mari assured me a few did.

My fingers slipped from the sticky mess he'd left, and I sighed.

Why had I gone to his room? I could have waited for Red to return, which he would have done eventually, I realized now.

I was furious with Red for keeping this from me, for not telling me he was leaving imminently and that I must stay.

I was also angry at Garren for being away so long and then leaving me again.

My mood was justified with regard to Red, not so much with regard to Garren.

I rose, got cleaned up, and dressed.

As always, Mari had a sixth sense. The outer door opened, and she swept in carrying food.

"I'm not hungry, thanks, Mari," I said. Her pretty face fell. "They've gone, haven't they?"

She nodded and put the tray down, coming over to hug me.

I hugged her back.

I also cried. Again.

"There, miss," she said, patting my back. "Don't cry. Why don't you have a nice bath?"

I hiccupped. "Okay." I figured I didn't have much else to do.

The day stretched out before me, empty and odd. The fortress was quiet now that so many soldiers were gone. Mari accompanied me as usual, but I was restless, confused, and completely at a loss. Nothing could distract me or occupy me for long.

Joshua was nowhere to be found, although his absence was as much a blessing as a curse. Words had been spoken, the kind that hurt, yet I craved the connection he still provided to Rymor, and I missed that he wasn't there.

At midday, Mari took me to a great barrel of a man with frizzy red hair named Lari. He was Mari's father, and the overseer of the fortress whenever Tanis wasn't there.

If not for the red hair and the questionable nature of the family naming convention, a parental connection would have suffered a complete lack of credibility. But I took comfort in his daughter being my companion.

He explained the situation to me, how the garrisons had gone, leaving a skeleton force behind.

The other Rymorians, including Joshua, had also left.

Everyone except me.

And that hurt so sharply.

My sentiments toward Tanis shifted, and the sensation of being used without care demanded my attention. I wanted to rant at him, ask why he hadn't told me, and why I wasn't taken. Only he wasn't here, and I couldn't.

I ate a little supper and went to bed early. Sleep was hard won,

The Warrior in the Shadows

but I eventually dropped off, only to be roused by a strange grinding sound.

My dreams remained fresh, a disjointed set of scenes involving Tanis, Garren, and Red that left me feeling hollow when I remembered all three of them were gone and Tanis didn't share.

And then all of them had left me.

A whole day had already passed, and the people I'd come to care about would be far away by now, along with that vast army the likes of which Shadowland had never seen. I didn't understand why they were leaving or how they hoped to stop a Rymorian army.

I would have gone with them too, had they let me, which was ridiculous since I was utterly sick of horse travel and would make a terrible soldier.

Why were none of them trying to find a peaceful solution? Why wouldn't they let me talk to someone? Rymor couldn't wage war on Shadowland!

Only they could, and they were going to.

And here I am, left behind, a prisoner trapped for my own good.

The faint grinding noise was louder and closer. I frowned, coming to full wakefulness.

My heart rate kicked up.

Someone was here.

My eyes strained to find the source of the sound in the dark, but there was no one, and the room was far too tiny to hide a person.

A shadow passed my window, blocking the moonlight.

A cloud? A bat or bird?

The shadow returned, solidified into the shape of a person... Who was...outside?

How could they...

A sharp pain pricked my shoulder, blackness descended, and my last fading vision was of the thick metal bars protecting my window being pulled away.

I roused in increments, my mind groggy and gray. Underlying the fog was a deep restless sense of unease that dragged me toward consciousness.

I lay on my side with my hands bound before me. My head hurt; a pounding so intense that my skull felt like it might crack open. My mouth was dry and pressed against soft gritty earth. I was dribbling, which disproportionately distressed me compared to my other more pressing woes.

The loose shirt I had slept in covered me, but not well, leaving me exposed. The air around me was warm and cloying against the dull thudding in my temples.

Then it hit me—I was outside, and panic pushed past my lethargy. Weak and woozy, it took all my effort to rise to my hands and knees.

"She's awake," a voice called.

Outside and not alone.

I staggered to my feet, shapes and shadows coming for me. A scream ripped its way from my parched throat, ringing loud and shrill against the still night air.

A person loomed before me, and a blow silenced my scream, ripping the air from my lungs and sending me tumbling like a discarded rag. I landed in a crumple of limbs against the gritty ground. My cheek became a source of sharp pain that robbed me of thought. I tasted dirt again, along with the bitter metallic flavour of blood.

"Get up," the man said, standing over me. His accent held the lilting drawl of the far eastern provinces and confirmed he was Rymorian.

I did as he bid, mind numb with terror. His grin, a stark flash of white teeth in a thin, angular face, had an edge of madness. A dozen more men filled the area behind him, along with horses and supplies, suggesting a journey of length.

"Don't pretend you don't like it. Looks like someone's been

The Warrior in the Shadows

having fun with you before we came along," the man said with a sneer, his pale eyes luminous in the moonlight.

A chill enveloped me despite the warmth of the air. "What do you want with me?" My tongue felt thick in my mouth, and my speech was slurred. He was obviously from Rymor. But I wasn't dead yet, and that had been Marcus' aim. Was he part of the same group? Something different? Something worse?

"Want?" He sounded amused now. "It's not me who wants anything. Friend of yours." He leaned in close, his voice low enough for my ears alone, and whispered. "By the name of Bill."

I shuddered. "Bill wouldn't want you to hurt me," I said, although I sounded uncertain.

He laughed, a baying sound that slid rapidly into a ferocious hacking cough. A part of me died then, taking my last delusions, all hope, and a piece of my soul. It was like I was breaking into pieces, ground down until nothing was left but dust.

He got the fierce hacking under control. "Think you've forgotten Bill. Sick son of a bitch beat me to death. Some days I wonder if he brought me back. From the look of you, his replacement's the same way inclined." As he stepped closer, I fought an urge to draw back. Something kept me still and told me not to show fear. His fingers bit into my jaw, and he turned my face into what poor light there was. "You been fucking one of them?"

I yanked out of his hold. "No, I hate them. Why would I let them touch me?"

"Shadowlanders aren't known for making it a choice."

"They're not interested in me. I'm Rymorian," I said.

"Not sure I believe you. I can't imagine it putting them off." He gave me a thorough appraisal that made bile rise in my throat.

"He wouldn't want you to hurt me," I repeated, but I sounded even less sure this time.

The man before me flashed his teeth again in a jeering smile. "He told me I could do what I want with you, with one exception. Pity about the last bit. I've learned the hard way not to piss Bill off, so I'll be sure to keep that in mind." He winked. "He'd be disappointed if I didn't push right up to that limit, though."

I was dead in every way that mattered. This was worse than everything, worse than the path, worse than losing Edward, worse than any of my nightmares of the Jaru.

It was the still of the night. We were deep in the forests, far from the fortress and from the false sense of safety it had offered. No one would know I was gone for hours yet, and even then, who was left to help? Everyone who knew me or cared for me had abandoned me. Supposing word could get to them, how could they possibly find me?

My sense of isolation hit me as hard as the blow that had left my cheek still throbbing, and it broke me up a little bit more.

No one was coming.

No one would save me.

I was utterly alone, and the man in front of me was taking me to Bill.

Chapter 40

Rymor

Bill

"What have you got for me?" I asked the man standing on the other side of my State Tower desk.

The private investigator, Bernie Justice, had been on my books for years. His hairless head and smooth, full cheeks lent his features an angelic aspect. Bernie's unassuming exterior and easy-going way served him well. People often talked to Bernie.

His professional suit was immaculate, yet his usual direct and confident façade was missing its edge today.

"He's gone," Bernie said, his coarse accent thick. He shifted where he stood. "Vanished, literally. Not a trace."

"Yes, I know he's gone, vanished, et cetera. That's why I'm paying you to find out where he is."

"No, you don't understand," Bernie continued. "Look, I'm not trying to piss you off here. The guy has gone—poof." He made a little upward motion with both hands. "Like he never existed."

"Bernie, you're not making any sense," I said, losing my limited grasp on patience. It was now imperative that Theo be located. That scene in my home with that preposterous blue beanbag and the bottle had left my skin crawling. I was determined to resolve both Theo's disappearance and the break-in swiftly. The conundrum of Theo, in particular, had been left unanswered for too many weeks. I wanted Theo back under my control so I could squeeze him until he broke and willingly offered up every tiny shred of information his machine-like brain contained.

"I know it doesn't make any sense," Bernie said, running a nervous hand over his shiny, naked skull. "But all traces of him have gone, and I don't have any idea where to start. Even his apartment has been gutted."

I straightened in my chair. "I had the apartment placed under federal protection. How is that even possible?"

"It's an empty shell. Someone must have fucked up. But really, that's the least worrying part of this case. When I say everything has gone, I mean every system record, every notice, every recording, wiped—like he never existed."

"You can't wipe an entire person!"

Bernie shrugged. "Yeah, I always thought so, but somebody did. I've never seen anything like it. I mean—shit, I agree, people don't just disappear."

"Absolutely everything? He worked in my office for five goddamned years. There must be something?"

Bernie huffed. "Bill, I know my job. When I say everything, I *mean* everything. As far as Rymor is concerned, you never had a personal assistant called Theo. He was never born. He never lived in his apartment. No images. No records. He wasn't a sociable guy. Apart from you and a few of your frequent visitors, no one remembers him—and I don't even have an image to show them to jog their memory." Bernie suddenly grinned, reminding me of a cheeky cherub. "Unless you have a sweetheart retro-print on hand."

"Of course, I don't have a fucking retro-print! Only simple people use retro-printing."

"My nan loves retro-printing," Bernie said in defense.

"Exactly!"

Bernie smoothed his fingers over his bald head once more. "Look, I hate to admit it, but I'm at a loss," he said. "Never had to track a puff of smoke, and that's pretty much all we've got. So, unless you have something tucked away, a private recording that's not on the grid, we've got nothing. Whoever did this knows their stuff. You know I pride myself on providing a service, but I got nothing to offer you here. Maybe look up a technical master—oh, yeah, that's right, you don't have any of those, do you?"

I raised both brows. "You know I do. Are you implying our last technical grand master had something to do with this?"

"Not unless the guy can work magic from behind a technology barrier. You brought Dan Gilmore in for questioning a week ago. I'd already started collating information when it suddenly disappeared three days ago."

"Are you saying only a technical master could do this wipe?"

"I'm saying I don't know shit. Whoever did this has got skills. Can't be Dan Gilmore, which means you've got someone else to worry about. Who knows what they may erase next. Maybe you?"

A sense of malaise rose its ugly head. Was this Theo himself? Was Dan's connection to the systems still working despite my secure location? I hated being in the dark. Someone had been in my home, had disabled my state-of-the-art security, and placed an empty Berry Blast bottle and a beanbag on the floor! They wanted me to know.

They wanted to scare me.

"I can get you a recording."

Bernie grinned slyly. "Now, how did I know you were going to say that?"

"I want this as your highest priority. You work exclusively for me until this is resolved."

Bernie nodded. "Understood. When will I get it?"

"Later today. I'll have it delivered."

"I'll clear my other workload. Anything else?"

"Yes, what happened with that bottle I gave you. The one I wanted DNA sampling on?"

"Yeah," Bernie gave me a shifty look. "Had a bit of a problem. There was a miscalibration or sample contamination at the laboratory. Someone got fired—but still, not much help. The company has an impeccable reputation. That's why I use them."

I frowned. "Contaminated?"

"No match was found."

My vision tunneled. The silence stretched.

"Where did you get the bottle anyway?" Bernie's pale brows puckered, giving his child-like face an angry cast.

"It was in my home," I said slowly.

Bernie's brows reached for his invisible hairline. "Your home? Not the same home where you keep those recordings?"

Fuck.

"They didn't miscalibrate the sample, did they?" Bernie asked slowly.

"I suspect not."

"Well, well. Looks like your man is a bit of a surprise. A bit too coincidental. And in my line of business, coincidence rings a bell."

"It's ringing a fucking symphony right now," I said.

"Want me to check out your house?"

My coastal home was a private escape. I was reluctant to grant Bernie access. "I need to check something first. I'll call you later with the details."

"Sure," Bernie said. "I'll get the company to send me a record of the sample, so we have something to compare it with. May need your official request for confidentiality on the unregistered DNA."

The Warrior in the Shadows

"I'll have it arranged. Leave the organization details with Nielsen...and get them to retro-print the damn record."

Bernie chuckled. "Retro-print it is." His laughter followed him out of the room.

Chapter 41

Bill

Lush lawns stretched out before me, with neatly manicured shrubs and flowerbeds beyond. Further still lay the rolling hills of the Soane region of Rymor. Neat rows of grapevines were visible in the distance beyond the tall trees that bound my family estate. Soane's vineyards were renowned for quality wine. My father had run a boutique family brand on our estate, now under the care of a manager, which produced a few hundred bottles a year that were kept for private use and gifts.

The winery had been my father's passion, a façade of class for a man who arguably had none. My father had seen it as a sign of status. Few people could afford such a sprawling estate in the area, and fewer still could let such fertile land be used for landscaped gardens with only a hobby interest in wine.

"You must bring your parents," my mother said to Rochelle. The two women had been chatting amiably for the last hour. My mother was graciously charming, and Rochelle easily fit into the setting.

A lot more easily than Hannah, who was more readily engaged by complex technical puzzles, and, even without their gaping social

The Warrior in the Shadows

divide, had often struggled to maintain interest in my mother's endless talk of charity functions and high-society gatherings.

"That would be delightful! I will be sure to extend your invitation to them. Thank you." Rochelle sipped her tea. A delicate china plate rested on the table before her and held one of their chef's sweet creations. The veranda offered a spectacular view, and Rochelle's gaze drifted a little wistfully to regard it, perhaps reflecting on the difference between taste and money. I might have despised my father, but the man had taste—the Stevens' family estate revealed only their money.

Still, it was important to keep Councilman Carl Stevens engaged, and my mother's invitation would further cement our relationship.

"Would Sasha like a treat?" In a silly singsong voice, my mother addressed the fat pug that waited expectantly at her feet. The ugly beast's tongue lolled out the side of its mouth and its excited panting increased. Its big brown eyes stared back at its mother with witless affection. "Good girl, Sasha." My mother selected a culinary delight from the table and fed the dog from her fingers.

There were surely more elegant pigs, I thought wryly, as the dog gulped and slobbered the treat down.

I forced my attention away from the awful scene to find Rochelle watching me. She was biting her lip in an attempt to hide her amusement. I raised an eyebrow and found myself grinning. She was surely a miracle for making a typically trying day bearable.

"Does Charlie want one too?" my mother inquired of the other fat pug that was only sufficiently motivated to raise its head, from where it lounged on the warm flagstones, at the offer of food.

"Come on, Charlie, good boy." Not to be thwarted by the lazy mutt, my mother selected another tiny, delicate cake and took it to the beast. Charlie leaned over to eat it. Not even bothered enough to get up.

"I think Charlie needs to go on a diet," I couldn't resist baiting.

My mother's eyes narrowed. "Oh, you mean man," she said, as she always did whenever I mentioned putting her fat dogs on a diet.

She gave Charlie a gentle, consoling pat before rising and returning to her chair. "He's getting old. Poor darling can't walk so well anymore."

Rochelle had found a sudden avid interest in her tea.

It made a nice change to come here and feel relaxed when usually I couldn't wait for the visit to be over.

I decided then that I wanted Rochelle to stay exactly how she was. The prospect of compartmentalizing my life and Rochelle's part in it interested me. I'd no intention of forgoing any of my less civilized pursuits, but there was no reason for Rochelle to know. I had resumed relations with Margaret Pascal semi-regularly and was convinced losing access to that kind of sexual outlet would be a dangerous idea. Besides, manipulating people was a game that I enjoyed, and the possibility of Rochelle discovering the real me was more of a thrill than any genuine fear.

"Why don't you show Rochelle the rose gardens?" my mother said, leaning back in her chair with a fresh cup of tea.

"An excellent idea." I rose and extended my hand formally to Rochelle. She smiled warmly back before placing her tea on the table and accepting my hand.

We wandered a short distance in amiable silence before Rochelle spoke. "I get the impression you find visiting your dear mother a challenge." She smiled knowingly at me.

I waved a dismissive hand. "Yes, my dear mother, who let my father beat the shit out of me."

Her gasp made me regret that uncensored slip. "Oh, how terrible," Her tone was instantly contrite. "Was it very awful?"

"Nothing that couldn't be fixed by a medical scanner," I said dryly.

"Perhaps she didn't have a choice?" she offered as we arrived at the rose gardens that bloomed in a rich medley of colors with a fountain, complete with a plump cherub, forming the centerpiece. "Or was simply too fearful to know what to do?"

"She had a choice," I said bitterly, while wishing I could change

The Warrior in the Shadows

the mood back. I guided her over to the stone bench and sat with a sigh. "It didn't matter how he abused us. She still worshiped him. He was a monster who didn't deserve her adoration."

Her fingers reached to squeeze mine. "Love sometimes confuses people about right and wrong. Whatever happened to you then, you have risen above it. You should be proud of that."

"You don't know me, Rochelle," I said bitterly. "Perhaps I'm a monster just the same."

"I don't believe that," she said softly.

She was sincere, I realized. Should I pity or revere her?

"It is terminal," I said. "I'm beyond salvation."

"No one is beyond salvation."

On days like today, my life exhausted me. Sitting here, I could almost forget that the man I'd loved like a brother had tried to kill me. All because a woman he was better off without had blown an event out of all credible proportions. Forget that my father was a monster that needed putting down. Only, forgetting the past would make me someone different. No matter how enticing it might be at weak moments like this, to forgo the pain that had birthed me, I had no desire to change.

I lifted her hand to my lips and gently kissed her smooth skin. "I think we should agree to disagree."

Chapter 42

Coco

It had been a full day at the conference, and darkness had fallen when I arrived home to my apartment. The busy day had taken my mind off my worries, but now I was tired and preoccupied by the prospect of a cup of tea and a nice long soak in the bath.

Consumed by these simple needs, I didn't notice a man sitting on my old blue couch, but then I did, and a short, sharp scream escaped before my brain could process who it was.

"Nate?" That stupid question popped out, and, of course, that made him grin.

"Coco." He appeared the epitome of relaxed.

I knew that I was frowning at him and that I ought to be happier. It *was* nice to see a friendly face, but I'd not heard from Dan or Nate for over a month, and his sudden reappearance concerned me.

"What are you doing here, Nate?" His rich auburn hair was a touch too long to be neat, and as a broad smile split his handsome face, I mentally rolled my eyes. It was like I was back walking through the quaint town of Azure, as if the subsequent madness hadn't happened. He was exactly the same; still quintessentially Nate.

The Warrior in the Shadows

He raised an eyebrow. "I thought you might be pleased to see me?"

My face softened. "I am, Nate. Of course, I am. It's just a shock seeing you sitting there—seeing anyone sitting there, actually. I'm not a socialite under normal circumstances, and I haven't encouraged visitors of late."

I dumped my bag on the table and headed to the printer. "I need tea. Do you want anything?"

"Coffee would be great."

"Coffee?" I asked. "I thought you didn't drink coffee. It's not about to render you comatose, is it?" He *did* have some unusual quirks.

He laughed, and I thought it had a pleasant timbre.

"No, I'm not going to pass out or come out in a rash." He came over to join me. "Or swell in any unexpected places."

He was standing beside me now. "More's the pity," he said, and I nearly dropped his drink.

I dumped it into his waiting hand and busied myself, making the tea while trying to ignore my strange reaction. *What is wrong with me?* I berated myself.

My internal dialog helped to restore calm until Nate placed a hand on my shoulder and said, "Coco, I'd like you to leave with me—today—it's not safe for you here," and I dropped my tea.

The cup and saucer shattered against the floor, and eighty-eight degree Celsius water and blue and white china chips scattered everywhere. The water burnt my legs, tipping me over an invisible edge, and I fell apart. He gently coaxed me out of the slippery, broken china as the cleaning unit made its way to deal with the decimation and pulled me into his arms as if this were a natural transition, and I went, tears falling helplessly.

"I can't simply leave, Nate," I said through my emotional onslaught. "That's a ridiculous thing to suggest."

"More ridiculous than you telling a waitress that I come out in a rash if I eat anchovies?"

I could hear the smile in his voice. *It was cream,* I thought, surprised I could recall the details. He was still holding me and appeared about as willing to release me as he had my hand in that ill-fated coffee shop. *I don't do hugs,* I admonished myself. But it was comforting and pleasant in a way I didn't allow myself to experience often. Rarely, now that I considered it.

I leaned back, determined to face the news.

"What's happened, Nate? Why do I need to leave?"

"Happened? More like what hasn't happened." He released me slowly, and stepping back, he kneaded the back of his neck. His attention settled on the cleaning unit, which continued its diligent work.

"I tried to speak to Dan. He's not answering," I said when he offered nothing more.

"That's because they took him in a week ago."

My face blanched.

"He's okay," Nate said quickly. "Helping them with the emergency, *officially.*"

"Have you spoken to him since?"

"Yeah, a couple of times until they took him out of his chair yesterday. They must have suspected it had more than the basic set-up," he said. "He is a technical grand master."

"What kind of masters would remove him from his chair?" My brows drew together, and a sense of disquiet rose. "I don't like that they have him. He's not exactly well. The troops have left, haven't they? The army? They've gone into Shadowland?"

"Yeah, they've gone."

Something in me crumbled. No, this couldn't be happening. They couldn't be about to kill thousands of innocent people, could they? Dan's best efforts had achieved nothing.

Nate's wary expression instantly put me on edge. "What is it?"

He remained silent for a while, increasing my anxious state.

"Do you know what your son does out there?"

"Does? No, I don't know." I sighed. "My son has been the master of his own destiny from the moment he could articulate for himself."

The Warrior in the Shadows

The very nature of his areas of interest from early childhood had tarred him with his father's proverbial brush. Still, he didn't deserve to be convicted as a terrorist in a closed trial, supposedly responsible for the death of over twenty individuals in a bombing ten years ago—the reason for his exile. He was now supposedly behind the station disruption and reputedly planning a war against Rymor. The first part I knew in my heart wasn't true. But the war? He had reasons to hate Bill, but I didn't believe he hated Rymor, nor wished its people harm.

"There are gaping holes in my knowledge of my son's life since his exile," I admitted. At first, it had hurt to talk about him. It had been easier to deny that it had happened. I knew Jon Sanders still met with him occasionally, but it was too painful to ask for details. Perhaps I should have done. I sensed I was about to be blindsided by whatever Nate knew. Had he changed so much? Was he really planning a war? No, I couldn't believe that. "What does he do?"

"You really don't know, do you?" Nate said, his eyes searching mine. "He's the leader of Shadowland—all of it."

I shook my head and took a step back. "That's impossible."

"Ten busy years," Nate said with a humorless smile. "Five fortresses, all under the command of a single man. It's a formidable army. A hundred thousand—most of them are waiting at Thale, the nearest fortress to the wall, bar Talin."

I started to hyperventilate.

"Perhaps you better sit down." He guided me over to the couch just as my legs gave out.

"I need to work on my 'how to give shocking news' skills," he mumbled to himself and dragged a hand through his hair. "You would think I would know better after the fiasco with Scott Harding."

"Scott Harding? As in the head of Global Operations?"

"Yeah, that's the one."

"Why were you talking to him?!"

"I needed to get information to the field scientists in Shadowland, and the waypoint seemed the best way. I can control what's coming through and stop Bill's minions seeing the communications. Scott hates Bill—a lot—and he's on board now. The army is out in Shadowland and heading for Thale armed with weapons. It will be a slaughter without our help."

I put a hand up to stop him. He had offloaded far too much for my shocked mind to take in. Pride surged at what John had achieved, only to be doused in frigid water as the terror of technology beyond the wall sank in. "You're communicating with the field scientists in Shadowland?"

"Yes."

I rubbed at my temples and then shot Nate a *get on with it* look.

"All right, but no more turning gray."

"For goodness' sake, Nate!"

"It was Jon Sanders at the waypoint. He's with your son at Thale again now, probably."

"Oh!" I put my trembling hands over my eyes. The seat beside me dipped, signifying the arrival of Nate's body.

"You okay?" He sounded worried.

As he bloody should!

"Yes—No—I've no idea."

He poorly stifled a snicker.

I took my hands down and glared at him. He appeared contrite and amused in equal parts. "They were both well, Coco," he offered earnestly.

I nodded, my relief overwritten by spikes of tension. How had my son managed to unite the five fortresses? The fortress leaders were not the kind of men to bow down.

My heart lodged in my throat. Had my son inadvertently killed his father?

It was then that I suffered an epiphany. John hadn't killed his father, but I was suddenly convinced they had met. Suddenly many of Jon Sanders' half-conversations made sense. *They have met.* A wild flock of emotions took to flight in my chest, ushing from abject terror to loving warmth and back again so rapidly that I felt faint.

The Warrior in the Shadows

I'd last seen my son ten years ago, and the pain of loss never got any easier. I'd made mistakes with John that I would regret for the rest of my life. And now he was with his father, Javid, the man I'd tried to keep him from. I asked myself how I felt about this, missing time with my son but knowing he had gained a father, in whatever capacity that might be. The truth was that it comforted me. As much as I wanted to hate Javid for his high-handed, barbaric ways, I'd never been able to. The man did nothing by halves. If he was in John's life, it would be with all his considerable heart.

"Ah, Coco, you're doing that gray thing again."

"I'm fine. It's a lot to take in, but I'm fine. This is good," I said. "But I don't understand why I need to leave."

"Bill's going to make the announcement about the war, tomorrow. He'll name your son as a public enemy, along with a number of field scientists who are reputedly acting in collusion with him. After, he'll bring you in for questioning. He has an extensive list of charges, and, under the war act, you'll be given no access to counsel. He can keep you imprisoned indefinitely."

"He can't do that." As the words left my lips, I knew he could and would. Bill had been illegally sending teams into Shadowland for five years. He had instigated trouble between the Jaru and the Shadowlanders. Both Dan and Jonathan had told me as much. Now, he was going to war. I knew too much about his past. I was a loose end he couldn't afford to ignore.

"He can, and he will," Nate said, reaching to take my hand.

I stared at the connection and wondered if I should demand he give it back. There was so much more to Bill's plans than just my son; certainly, John's demise was a large part of them. My research trip there thirty-one years ago had brought a bounty of revelations...and a son. As a geneticist I had dedicated my life to studying the different races on our planet. Most scientists acknowledged that the Rymorians were not indigenous to the planet. I firmly believed that the Shadowlanders were also not indigenous—even though they lived outside the wall.

"Bill had Scott Harding stitched up and ready to take the fall for the technology that's allegedly in the hands of your son," Nate said. "He fabricated evidence against Jon Sanders too, but, unlike Scott, who I could help, there was nothing I could do for Jon. Bill is crushing anyone who opposes him. You're easy leverage, Coco, in case something goes wrong. He'll use you against your son, and we can't afford to give Bill that kind of power."

"No. No, we can't," I whispered. After all this time, it had finally come to this. My dear friend Jon was still alive, but now he was being framed. "I still don't know where I'm supposed to go. Won't running only confirm my guilt?"

"It's too late. You're already guilty. Bill wasn't planning on putting you on trial," Nate said. "He killed Hannah's sister, Ella. Don't think he won't kill you, too, once you're no longer of use?"

My heart broke for the tragedy of it all. How could one man break the world and everyone in it for what? A vendetta?

The first pieces had been played long ago. My son and William Bremmer had become enemies where they had once been friends. Subsequent events compounded matters, and now, one way or another, it would end. I knew what Bill was capable of, both the charismatic chancellor and the monster he hid underneath. I still grieved for what had happened to Ava, the unwitting catalyst in this. "How will I get out of here? Where do you think I should go? Won't he be watching me, if he plans to bring me in tomorrow?"

Nate grinned. "Coco, you're about to experience my prowess in the art of stealth. Prepare a bag of essentials. We're leaving, and you shouldn't ever expect to come back."

Chapter 43

Bill

After visiting my mother, I parted ways with Rochelle at Serenity and took my skycar south.

It was here, in my home on the southern coast of Rymor, that I discovered what I'd already suspected.

The recordings were gone, all of them, every single one. As far as the official, and now my unofficial, records were concerned, my personal assistant of the last five years had never existed.

For better or worse, I knew Theo was a fraud. No one would go to such lengths to wipe their DNA and presence unless they had secrets.

This knowledge didn't bring the closure I had once thought it would.

I sipped from the tumbler in my hand, but the usually mellow liquor left only bitterness in my mouth, like everything in this place. Perhaps it was time I sold, or at the very least closed it down and sealed it up.

I put the crystal tumbler aside, and it struck the tabletop with a jarring *clunk*.

Bernie paused his work at the viewer plate of an arm-length silver cylinder he had unpacked theatrically. I'd regarded it with dubious interest. Surely small was better where technology was concerned?

"This is cutting edge," Bernie said as if sensing my skepticism. His finger depressed a section of the seamless surface, and an identical but smaller cylinder emerged. It floated in the air. A tiny hiss indicated hover propulsion was at work.

"What does it do?"

"It's a DNA detector," Bernie said, grinning. "It can sweep an entire house within a few minutes. If you can set the home hub to open all the internal doors, we can begin the sweep."

I appraised the cylinder again as the implications settled in. "DNA?"

"The DNA of every person who's ever been in this house, along with the age of the sample. It'll tell us if we get a match for your unknown DNA, and for any known ones, too. We'll know who's been here. If they are off the DNA register, then we'll know that, too."

"How long will it take to do the analysis?"

"It's pretty much instantaneous," Bernie said. "A few minutes and you'll have a full report."

"Excellent." At the home hub, I opened all the internal doors except *that* door. "Everything is done. If you'll excuse me, I need to make a few calls."

I smiled but suspected it wasn't reaching my eyes when Bernie frowned. "Sure," he said. Perhaps he'd expected me to wait excitedly at his side while the DNA scanner worked.

I slipped out onto the veranda at the back of my home, where I regarded the gray sea with its foamy, white-tipped swell. I sighed. It was a shame, but still, I needed the answers. Unfortunately, I wouldn't get those answers without Bernie.

I put the call through with the briefest twinge of regret. I would see how the situation played out, but life had taught me to prepare for the worst. Once done, I returned to see what Bernie's impressive device had discovered.

The Warrior in the Shadows

Bernie's cherub face hung in slack-jawed surprise. His open gaze shifted to me before whipping back to the screen.

"Bernie, I'm going to need your discretion."

He nodded. "Sure thing. You already had it, you know that, right?"

I approached him with measured steps. "Margaret is a professional, and a member of the senate. Our relationship cannot be made public."

Bernie nodded, still not meeting my eyes.

There was a timeline on one side of the viewer, with the DNA name matches in the center and the sample tissue source on the right. I hadn't been expecting a chronological timeline nor an indication that the sample source was blood.

Thank fuck I made that call.

"He must have broken in while you were... ah... occupied," Bernie offered.

"But he didn't," I replied slowly. It was too late for pretense since I was documented in the home at the same time as Karry, an escaped convict, far too many times. Karry wasn't the only person that would be piquing Bernie's interest. Then there was the sample source of blood matched against an impressive cast of names.

My, I have been busy.

"Did you find the unknown DNA here?"

"Yeah," Bernie said, posture stiff as he focused on the viewer. "Two of them, one the same as the bottle, no surprise there."

"Two?" I asked, frowning, feeling that prickling of unease.

"Yeah, two," Bernie replied, relaxing visibly as we moved to a safer topic. "One matches the bottle we had analyzed, as we suspected, given you found it here."

Theo wasn't working alone. "What else can your device do with the DNA? Any details of physical characteristics?"

"It can do better than that," Bernie said. He tapped the viewer, and two images popped up.

As I blinked at the screen, cold washed the length of my spine.

The hair was a generic male cut that didn't match Theo, but otherwise, it was obvious who it was. The man on the left was the one who surprised me. Other than some subtle differences, he could have been Theo's twin.

"Well, that's a surprise," I said, and Bernie grinned in an amicable agreement. "I'll need this evidence erased from your records...and my home."

"You don't want to keep a copy of this?" Bernie asked, blond eyebrows pinching together.

"I know it's Theo. I know he's working with a related individual who is also off the DNA grid. Keeping a record won't help me, and retaining the information is an unnecessary complication. As for my home, I can't afford for anyone else to bring one of these amazing devices around. I'm sure you understand."

"I can do a clean sweep of your home," Bernie said. "It will erase all traces. Are you sure you want the records wiped, as well?"

"Yes," I said.

Bernie tapped a series of commands into the device, and the screen turned clear. The small silver cylinder floated off along the passage and disappeared out of sight.

The floating cylinder returned a few minutes later, flashing light beams into every corner of the room before it returned to its home in the master device.

The updated report held two entries, one for Bernie and one for me.

"Bernie, your assistance has been invaluable," I said. "Please ask Neilson to schedule some time later in the week so we can discuss the next steps."

"Sure," Bernie said. He pressed his palm against the cylinder, and the viewer retracted seamlessly inside, and a carry handle simultaneously emerged. He picked up the device.

I walked Bernie out of my home.

"You have some visitors?" Bernie said, frowning at the skycar park where a transport had landed while we'd talked inside.

The Warrior in the Shadows

Two black-suited men emerged and began to walk toward me. "They're expected." I nodded at the newcomers. "Thanks again for your assistance, Bernie. I'll speak to you later in the week."

"Sure thing," Bernie said, his troubled gaze on the two approaching men.

It was unfortunate this needed to happen, a real shame. Bernie had been so useful, but anything else was a risk, given the damning nature of what he'd seen. Bernie covered half of the distance to the parking area before his instincts kicked in, and he reached for his weapon.

He dropped to the ground before his hand even made it to his jacket. The silver cylinder clattered against the walkway stone and rolled a little distance before stopping.

The black-suited man on the right holstered his weapon before following his companion toward Bernie, who lay face down on the ground, dead. They rolled the body over and took positions at his head and feet.

I watched them leave, Bernie's limp body swinging with their steps.

Yes, it was a real shame.

I opened my communicator and put a call through as the black-suited men continued their task. "Did he try to send a communication from my house?"

"Yes, sir," said the man on the other end.

"Did you successfully block it?"

"Yes, sir," came the reply.

"Excellent," I said, and closed the call.

Chapter 44

Shadowland

Tanis

We had trekked through Shadowland in an ungainly procession for over a week. Despite the now infamous confrontation at Thale, Garren had elected to stay in my company and had been surly, grouchy, and barely civil ever since. In other words, he was behaving like his usual self.

"He's coping well." Han nudged his head in Garren's direction.

It wasn't the first time Han had made this observation to me—he did repeat himself if the matter was of particular interest. "He's making my life a misery. I thought you said he would be better after what happened at Thale?" We stood beside our horses, taking a brief rest from being in the saddle. It was midday and swelteringly hot. A short distance away, Garren was berating a scout for some perceived tardiness. At least I wasn't the only one suffering the consequences of Garren's foul mood.

The Warrior in the Shadows

"I was only repeating what Kein said," Han said as if Kein was the ultimate wisdom on all things and his opinion shouldn't be questioned. "At least Garren didn't leave."

"Yes," I agreed, as a little tiredness crept into my voice. Garren leaving would have exacerbated an already tricky situation, especially if key members of his section followed. And then, underpinning all of this, was the reason we'd been so at odds in the first place.

Only, consequences be damned, I'd still fuck Hannah again, given a choice.

Garren approached with the scout in tow, dragging me from a well-scripted fantasy where I was balls deep in Hannah's cunt, and she begged me, and only me, to claim her.

"We've news from the waypoint," Garren said. "This idiot has taken three days to bring it."

"The tower dwellers," the scout stammered, casting a worried glance between Garren and me. "Are already in Shadowland, a week's ride from Thale." He held a scroll out to me.

"A week away now, or a week away three days ago?" Garren demanded.

I raised a hand to shut him up as I skimmed through the information. They were here, close, and bearing a comprehensive arsenal of weapons. I'd assumed a ground-based assault would give me more time, that Joshua and the team would reach the station and shut it down before our sides even met.

A tunnel leading from Rymor deep inside Shadowland. How could that have existed for so long without anyone knowing? No way could Joshua hope to reach the station before Rymor's army was on us.

"Fetch Javid." I said to the scout. "Tell him it's urgent."

The scout vaulted into his saddle and wheeled the horse around.

I motioned Tay over and handed her the scroll. "Give this to Jon and ask him to join me."

"What are you going to do?" Garren asked.

"Split the army," I said, my mind scrambling to process what I'd read. Where else might they surface? Where else might they be even now?

"Is that wise?" Han asked. "What are their numbers?"

"Five different groups, nearly ten thousand altogether, but the Rymorian weapons they're bringing worry me more than their numbers, especially so given their proximity to Thale. We need a distraction and only something as momentous as the wall's destruction might turn Rymor around. But the timeline is tight given they're five days from our present location."

"Too tight," Han said. "Even riding hard, Danel won't reach the station with Joshua in time."

"We need to occupy them. Splitting the army is a risk, but we need to slow them down to give Danel more time. The majority will remain on a course to the wall, and we'll block the Rymorians' path with a smaller group."

"I'm staying with you," Han said, making it clear this was a fact.

I smiled. I'd known Han and his younger brother Danel for many years. They had been part of Thale's garrison, and I'd been riding with them the day I received word Bill had brought Ava into Shadowland. They had also been with me four days later when I confronted Bill.

I'd turned my back on Rymor that day, and Danel and Han had taken me with them back to Thale. Although I hadn't realized it at the time, the decision to go with them, to become part of the garrison, had been a defining point in my life.

"Well, I'm staying too," Garren said, his jaw set in a belligerent line. "I've spent the last week dreaming about killing you slowly. I'm not about to let some other bastard do it for me."

"Good to know where I stand," I said. I caught Garren's fleeting grin, and it settled me to know that I hadn't broken things between us. I felt humbled to have the unwavering support of Han, Garren, and every man and woman who had followed me. Most Shadowlanders were curious about Rymorians, perhaps thought them weak.

The Warrior in the Shadows

This war was already heralded as the war to end all wars, yet they still supported me, even knowing their uncertain fate.

It wasn't the Jaru but a new enemy that we faced today; because of me. I'd brought this to Shadowland. The unwavering sense of the right thing to do had abandoned me in painful increments since we left Thale. The responsibility I felt for the Rymorian invasion was a new demon to deal with. My belief that my presence benefited the people of Shadowland was slipping away, and every step we took brought a sharper sense of my impending failure.

We couldn't win against Rymor. Our numbers would be useless against their weapons, and I was leading them to their death.

While the wall remained operational, I had no means to threaten or leverage to even up the odds. "Danel needs at least another week to get Joshua to the station. Let's see if we can buy him that much," I said. There were too many variables, and most of them were not in my favor. I knew too much about tactical warfare for optimistic delusions to prevail.

"We're probably all going to die," Han said, without any evidence of emotional concern. It was usually Danel delivering the depressing news.

"Yes, I know," I said wearily. I shrugged. "I have a backup plan."

"What backup plan?" Jon said, approaching from my left, his eyes narrowing on me. "I just heard." He waved the scroll in indication. "You got some Rymorian weapons tucked away you're not telling me about? Otherwise, we're about to be fried."

"I wish I had," I said. Jon wasn't going to like my backup plan. No one was. Even I didn't like it. "Miracles sometimes happen." History had taught me that luck, on occasion, was the winner and that sometimes, despite the odds, the underdog prevailed.

"Not very bloody often," Jon muttered.

I grinned. Unfortunately, history had also taught me that it didn't often happen, as Jon had so eloquently stated.

My smile faded as Javid and his guards arrived. "Gather all the scouts and ready them to ride out with the news to the rest of the army," I said to Han. "Garren, round up my wolf guards, as well."

"What's the backup plan?" Jon asked again the moment we were alone.

I regarded the man who'd been there for me my whole life. "I'm hoping I don't need it," I said noncommittally. "Once Javid and the main body of the army are underway, we can talk about it."

My options were running out. I was grasping at a wisp of smoke and calling it hope.

I knew I wasn't going to defer Jon's questions for long, and when I did tell him, the man who was as much a father to me as Javid would be hurt and angry.

Chapter 45

Hannah

There was a numb simplicity to my days since I'd left the mighty fortress of Thale.

It was clear Karry did indeed have a boundary, which his tormenting never passed, and there was some small comfort in that. I'd come to love my time in the saddle because nothing bad happened while I rode.

Perhaps it made it worse, that condensed timeframe during which Karry could dole out his abuse. His men found it amusing. At least most of them did. Either that or they were experts at hiding their human side.

The horse I followed pulled up at the edge of a clearing. The sky had darkened with the turn to dusk. There was a sense of inevitability to the routine. There was no evening where I didn't suffer abuse; therefore, there would be abuse. Only the form it took might vary, along with the residual degree of pain.

As the party came to a stop and dismounted, I did likewise. Drawing attention to myself brought the suffering sooner, and so it was better if I remained unnoticed as long as possible.

I was fooling myself. It didn't make a damn bit of a difference. Whatever I did, Karry would hurt me. My fate was inescapable.

That notion settled in.

There was nothing I could do. I had no power here, and the hopelessness of my situation ate voraciously at my soul, battering my resolve and the belief I'd had that I was changed and stronger now. I didn't want to be fearful. It no longer fit with my mantra, and I didn't want to give Karry the satisfaction of any kind of victory.

Soon enough, it would be Bill, and I knew that time would be worse.

An inner determination snapped firm within me with such force that I physically jerked.

He was going to hurt me anyway. I could no more avoid it than I could avoid breathing. Bill was next, and I needed to be stronger than I'd ever been to survive that.

"Get that saddle off the horse!"

I should have started removing the saddle. On any other day, I would've, but today my stubbornness dictated I refuse Karry's request.

Anticipating the blow did nothing to diminish the sharp shock that trapped the air in my lungs and sent me staggering.

Now nothing would make me obey.

His fist gripped my hair. I hated my hair, hated that it was long enough for him to hold. As soon as I was left alone with a knife, I would enjoy hacking every bit of it off.

My scalp ached from the pressure as he thrust my face against the saddle and demanded answers that I ignored. When a bitter laugh escaped my lips, I knew that he would beat me. I basked in my temporary victory, but it soon turned to despair, and then I would have done anything to make him stop.

It was too late. No amount of hopeless begging halted the blows that tossed me about until I finally slumped to the ground, where I heaved up bile.

The Warrior in the Shadows

"Take that saddle off if you don't want more," Karry said, before stalking off.

Burning pain suffused my body, and I dragged ragged breaths in until the pain lost its overwhelming edge.

The others had moved off, preparing tents and food. My horse stamped beside me nervously, the saddle still in place waiting to be removed.

Eventually, the pain became manageable, and I rose sluggishly.

We had been playing this sick game for weeks. Despite my daily fix from the scanner, I knew you couldn't keep damaging and repairing a body without consequence, whether that consequence was mental or physical.

The pain made my fingers clumsy, and I fumbled to drag the heavy saddle off. A thick splat of blood dripped from my throbbing lip to land on the worn leather surface.

I wiped the blood away, my eyes unfocused as another drop followed. Blinking, I brought the blood back into focus. My rebellion had been short-lived. The reality of my situation remained bleak, yet my act of defiance left a sense of empowerment in a place where I'd had none.

With a deep sigh, I stood taller and went to join his party. Usually, Karry would throw some food my way and use the scanner on the worst of my injuries before sleep, but tonight he'd finished eating by the time I joined them. Tossing the remnants aside, he fisted my arm in a bruising grip and hauled me toward his tent. "I think it's time for another chat."

Panic bloomed. He hadn't questioned me for days, and now my foolish act had brought the questions back.

He thrust me roughly to my knees inside, then came over me, his weight forcing me down onto the gritty ground. I tried to push him away, but his fingers closed around my throat, pressing relentlessly into my flesh. Black dots swam before my eyes, and I fought furiously to his cackle of laughter.

Just when I thought I would black out, he loosened his grip, and the dancing blackness receded. Dazed, I didn't struggle.

"What did you talk to him about?"

"Who?" My voice was little more than a croak. I knew who he was talking about, who he always talked about.

His elbow dug into my ribs as he shifted position, bringing his face up close to mine, squeezing my sore throat again to get my attention.

"You know who."

"I never spoke to him."

"That's not what Marcus said."

"That lying, worthless, shit that killed—"

My words ceased as the pressure on my throat increased, and he lapsed into manic laughter at my pitiful attempts to break free.

"Marcus said Tanis saved you from the Jaru. I agree the little shit lied when it suited him. He kept going on about Tanis saving you so many times that I nearly broke the prick's neck to shut him up."

"You know Marcus lied," I whispered when he relaxed the stranglehold. "Tanis never spoke to me. He ignored the Rymorians except for Adam."

"He was friendly with Adam, wasn't he?" He squeezed my throat again in warning.

"I wasn't with them when they spoke."

He shifted position, digging painfully into new places. "I don't believe that he ignored someone who looks like you."

I knew keeping to my story was important, that mentioning Tanis in any capacity would lead to more, or worse, abuse. Marcus had never seen us talk; besides, most of what I'd said was true.

"Tanis never spoke to me, if Marcus said so he was only telling you what you wanted to hear. Marcus was never part of the team. Nobody liked him. He wasn't even around half the time."

Karry released me abruptly and knelt up. I rose weakly onto my elbows, seeking to get away, but he slapped me back down so hard that my head smacked against the ground. My ears rang, and I thought I might be sick.

"Don't expect the scanner tonight. Tomorrow, maybe you'll start talking."

He stood and left the tent, the flap closing behind him to leave me blessedly alone. I rolled onto my side, swamped by misery so great it felt like it could never have an end. Silent tears fell, and shivers wracked me so violently that it felt like they might shake my body apart. It achieved less than nothing and drained what little of my energy remained.

Stupid defiance. What had I done?

Chapter 46

Rymor

Richard

A man was following me. I was convinced of it, and so I hurried the short distance from the transport hub to the anticipated safety of my financial district office.

Perhaps he was more *casually* observing than following. Not that observing felt any better when it had been going on for so long. The man kept appearing at various locations during the day, standing here, sitting there, waiting, and watching, confirming that my paranoia wasn't paranoia anymore.

A week had passed since my meeting with Bill, which was a relief given the uncomfortable nature of that conversation. I didn't know Bill anymore, or, more realistically, perhaps I never had.

Rymorian soldiers would be in Shadowland now. I felt terrible guilt at my involvement, trapped and desperate from the unrelenting pressure of knowing I'd played a hand in this and from a genuine fear for myself.

The Warrior in the Shadows

Entering the bright, bustling office complex lobby was a relief. So far, the man had never appeared anywhere inside, and I hoped it stayed that way.

Why was someone watching me? Had Bill sent them? Was I about to be dragged off to help with inquiries like Dan Gilmore had been?

I'd been to visit him a week ago, both aware that every nuance of the conversation was being recorded and analyzed. He'd seemed well enough despite the mental strain of the situation. We'd spoken of mundane matters, the weather, the latest technology awards, and a senseless barrage of other nonsense. Another conversation had taken place through our eyes, filled with compassion and unvoiced concerns.

Ever since that day, I'd been watched.

Worse than that, whoever it was, wanted me to *know* I was under surveillance.

The elevator was slow to arrive, and I waited impatiently as a small crowd gathered. Perhaps it was part of some ploy to support the fake power restrictions, as no one usually waited more than a few minutes for an elevator. It arrived just as the people began to express disquiet.

The muttered complaints around me soon turned positively and unerringly toward the war, how the power restrictions would be lifted once the Shadowland was defeated.

It was so tragic as to be closer to a joke.

Finally, it stopped on my floor, and I could escape the negative chatter and close the door to my sanctuary and office.

The first thing I noticed was the absence of my assistant.

The second thing I noticed threw my head into a spin, since waiting with relaxed aplomb in a chair in the reception area was my watcher!

My mouth opened, but nothing came out. How had he gotten here so fast? And past the security? What in the name of God did this mean?

"Relax," the man said with a brief smile as he rose from his seat. "I'm a friend of Dan's."

I let out a long shaky breath, relieved that it wasn't someone sent by Bill.

"I must be getting better at this," my strange visitor quipped.

"At what?" I asked, baffled.

"At giving people shocking news," Dan's friend replied, grinning broadly. "Don't worry. I've killed the surveillance. Bill won't hear about any of this."

I gasped.

"Killed, as in disabled," the man said with a worried smile. "No one died." He grimaced as I felt all the blood drain from my face. "I disabled the surveillance *systems*."

I was in shock, so catching up with his words took a while. My eyebrows reached for the heavens. "This room is a private location! It doesn't have any surveillance!"

"Yeah, that one didn't go so well," the young man muttered to himself, raking fingers through his glossy chestnut hair. "You should probably assume, as a close acquaintance of Bill's, that every aspect of your life has been under constant and diligent watch."

"It has?" I asked, blinking, and wondering why this should surprise me.

The young man nodded solemnly.

"What happened to my assistant?" I was distracted from my concerns about Bill's surveillance to worries about my assistant's continuing absence. I conducted a nervous study of the room, half expecting to find the missing man gagged and bound in a corner. I really wasn't one for this cloak-and-dagger stuff.

"Won't be here for an hour," the young man continued in an amiable tone. "Gone to deliver a parcel for you—in person. You know, those power restrictions can play havoc with the day-to-day running of things, and you insisted it was urgent in the message you sent." He winked at me. "I'm Nate by the way."

He thrust out his hand.

The Warrior in the Shadows

Message? I took his hand cautiously. Nate was a very odd fellow.

"Why don't we head into your office? I have an appointment in your calendar and your assistant won't be surprised if we go ahead."

Nate proceeded to open my inner office door and waved his hand in a highly theatrical way to indicate I should precede him.

I sat at my desk as Nate made himself comfortable opposite, and I braced myself for what was about to come.

"Do you care about Dan? About what happens to him?"

"Yes, of course," I said. Although, given Nate had said he was Dan's friend and, further, admitted to tampering with the surveillance, it stood to reason I would play along.

"What about the war? What are your thoughts on that?"

Yes, it would always come back to the war. "How well do you know Dan?" I hedged.

"Very well."

"That doesn't tell me much."

"You can trust me."

"Excuse me, but I don't know you, and you just broke into my office!"

"I'm Dan's... um... offspring," Nate shrugged. "Sort of."

"Offspring? As in son? A secret child?"

Nate shrugged again. "It's complex, but, in short, I've lived with Dan all my life, and he has taken care of me. I would give my life for him, but I'm stuck, and there's only so much I can do. Hence, I'm here talking to you."

"He didn't mention you?" I said, my eyes narrowing on the young man.

"No, he won't. Dan's protective of his... ah... offspring."

My face must have betrayed some of my mounting concerns because Nate leaned forward in his chair. "I understand your reservations, and that this is all very sudden. I can do what Dan does with technology. I put myself in your calendar, granted myself access to the building, sent a message on your behalf to your assistant, and delayed your elevator. I can do an amazing number of things. Unfortunately, the only thing I can't do is get past real people, and it's real people guarding Dan night and day."

"He was doing okay," I said, my eyes softening. Either the man was an accredited actor, or he genuinely cared for Dan. "As well as can be expected. Dan knew what would happen when he approached me about the war."

"Yes, about the war. You never offered your opinion?"

"I don't agree with the war, if that's what you're asking. Things were said, after my meeting with Dan. No, I don't approve of such drastic action. I haven't for a while."

Nate nodded. "I'm here because Dan trusted you. I'm staking his life on that trust not being misplaced. I need to show you something now, something that will change you, I'm afraid. I need you to be in on this completely. Are you ready for that, Richard? Are you ready to help me save the world?"

Nate smiled. It was an encouraging smile that didn't fit the magnitude of his words.

I scoffed. "Ready? No, I seriously doubt I'm ready, but something tells me you're not about to give me any choice."

Nate raised both hands in mock surrender. "Yeah, you got me. Why don't we both get comfortable, and I'll skip to the exciting bit?"

∼

Show me, he did. A sample recording of me taken from my home, another from a high profile senator's office, and yet more from businesspeople of all kinds. Extremely sanitized versions, I was sure.

Then there was a recorded meeting between Bill and a criminal where they discussed the incarceration of the missing transport team, including the two technical experts, over the Jaru border.

The list went on, and none of it was good.

Nate's face was solemn. "You see why we need to get Dan out of there?"

"Yes. Yes, I do." I felt old and worn, drained by the strain of the

The Warrior in the Shadows

past weeks and months and by the unrelenting nature of the continuing pressure. "How do you do this?" I gestured with my hand in the general direction of the viewer. "How do you access it?"

"Non-medical implants, illegal, but useful," Nate said. "I know it's a lot to take in. A few weeks ago, I was where you are now."

A deep sense of sadness enveloped me. Discovering that the power was back, and that Bill had kept it secret left me physically ill. I'd put my career, reputation, and countless people's lives into the hands of a man who had lied, and I had been living on a knife edge ever since.

"The war concerned me from the start," I said. "I ignored those concerns. I think that's what bothers me most, that I knew it was wrong, yet carried on blindly anyway. When I approached Bill after Dan asked me for help, I realized my earlier concerns were valid. I believe he kept news of the operational nature of the station from the public so that he could continue with his Shadowland plans. Bill is a dangerous man, and more so given what you've shown me."

"His influence is far-reaching," Nate said. "But that doesn't mean we should stop. We have to carry on, Richard. We have Scott Harding on board, now, and communication with the people outside. They'll be slaughtered without our help. We need to issue a stop code for the weapons, but only Dan has the skills to do that."

"Well, what you've done so far sounds amazing to me."

"I'm more of your dumb hacker," Nate said, grinning. "I can access and read stuff, but I wouldn't have the first idea how to do something so complex. Dan is the one with all the finesse."

I found myself smiling. Nate was entertaining, if nothing else.

"That's why I need your help, Richard," Nate said.

"I'll help in any way I can."

"I need you to get something to Dan."

"Something?"

His eyes did a shifty thing that immediately put me on edge. "There's an injection I need you to give him."

"Are you insane?" I had anticipated providing a far more subtle form of aid. Now I was expected to smuggle an injection to Dan. "Have you any idea how comprehensive the security is around Dan!"

Nate held up a hand. "That's what makes it so easy. I can take care of the system. I just can't get past the people. Which is where you come in."

"Ha! So says the man who's not on the front line."

"Yeah, the CIA headquarters was a breeze. Trust me, I'd do this myself, but Bill has real people verifying who goes in. They won't realize you have anything with you since the scanning is controlled by the monitoring systems, and I can handle that."

I let out a shaky breath. "You're expecting me to offer you a great deal of trust."

"We're running out of time for Dan. I can't contact him anymore. How long before they revoke access to someone like you? Bill has an army out there. He's building a base at Talin. He sent people to kill the teams left out there. He had Hannah's sister killed. Where will he stop? He's *never* going to stop."

He was right. Bill wouldn't stop, and it horrified me to have played any part in this. I recognized the fervor inflicting Rymor's chancellor, from the perspective of hindsight. Nate's frustration was as genuine as his caring for Dan. Yet he was asking me to go against Bill, to get my hands dirty, and join in the fight.

I preferred to sit on the fence in life, and I hadn't embraced any cause of worth since my daughter's tragic death. I considered how I might feel about this situation were my daughter at risk. Was this my time? Was I about to rise from the shadows, stop watching life through a frivolous lens, and finally get involved?

I returned my distant gaze back to the intense young man sitting opposite. "What is the injection?"

"Great, you'll help?" Nate's grin faded as swiftly as it arrived. "It's... ah... complicated."

"Yes, I'm getting the idea most things are with you," I stated dryly. "But I'm not prepared to give him an injection without asking what it does."

The Warrior in the Shadows

"It's not exactly an injection, more of a device that needs inserting." Nate said, eyes sparkling with excitement. "What if I told you it could fix him? What if I said I could make him whole again, could make him walk? The device will do all that and more. He'll be able to infiltrate systems and communicate with me again. It won't be instant, though. The implants will host themselves within twenty-four hours, but it may take weeks before the changes are complete."

"That's incredible," I said inadequately, "but why has he never done this before?"

"In the simplest terms, because it would draw attention to work he would rather keep private. He only gave me access to this when they took him in for questioning. Maybe he didn't realize how fast I could analyze information." He smiled. "I'm hoping he'll forgive me."

My laugh was spontaneous. The thought of Dan living as he did when a cure was available was crazy. "How exactly do we proceed?"

Nate rubbed his hands together. "Right, it's time for the master plan."

Chapter 47

Shadowland

Tanis

It had come around sooner than I expected, this juncture where I would rather not be. The Rymorian army was close, and the two sides sat in an uneasy truce, separated by a narrow river and the cover of trees.

Would they come tomorrow? In the middle of the night? Or were they awaiting a final command? All my plans to take the war to them were over, at least for me.

I sat in my tent. It was late, and everyone but Jon had been dismissed. My decision was made. No one was happy about this. They had voiced their opinions without reservation.

"I don't want to be here, but I am," I said. "We cannot change this. I cannot let them destroy Thale."

Jon's face was haggard, lined with his worry, and his expression was made harsher by the poor lamplight. "Don't do this, Tanis," he begged in a whisper. "Please—you can't—not like this."

The Warrior in the Shadows

My decision to hand myself over to Rymor was met with ridicule at first. Later that had morphed into anger and confusion. Han had physically dragged Tay out after someone had let my decision slip. She was a subordinate member of my wolf guard, and the intimacy we'd once shared led her to deliver an inappropriate and furious tirade. Had I not been resigned to the more significant problem, I would have dealt with response more harshly. With hindsight, I could see our relationship lingered where it had no place. She slept with other men, and I'd let that persuade me that her feelings were not involved. An oversight, it would seem. She hadn't been angry about Hannah initially, more amused at Garren's expense.

The anger had only come later, when I'd told her to sleep elsewhere.

It seemed insignificant now, like many things, and my decision had shifted a weight within me from one place to another. It couldn't be shifted back.

"I'm going to stall them, nothing more, to give the others a chance. We need a few days. Once the station is destroyed, Bill will recall his forces; he'll have to."

I'd received news today that the bulk of my army was still maintaining a slow, well-hidden course for the wall under Javid's command. Once close, they would wait for news on the wall's status. If Danel got Joshua to the station, Javid would know what to do.

"I don't have any choice," I said. "Whether we run or make a stand, it will result in a slaughter. This is the only way to avoid that."

In the honesty of these last moments, I knew I acted from more than a desire to stall. My last night in Thale was the closing chapter of a life that had been a wild ride. I didn't take the righteous path often and I thought it was long overdue.

Jon turned away. "No one is buying the stalling them story," he said. "Even Garren isn't buying it, and the bastard would as soon run you through himself after you drew your sword on him. No one wants to see you dead like this."

"I'm not going to my death," I said.

Only I probably was.

In the dark recesses of my mind, I hoped that my sacrifice might be enough to stop the war. By surrendering, I gave Bill what he wanted and removed his reason for war. If the Rymorians withdrew, then Javid would make no move toward the wall. Numbers counted for nothing when one side had the technology, and it would be better if Rymor withdrew so we could focus on the Jaru threat.

"Don't bullshit me, Tanis," Jon spat out furiously. "Don't bullshit me. Not now. Not on this."

The words didn't reach me; I was resigned. I was no longer helping Shadowland. I had brought this to them. I needed to take it away.

If I was lucky, once they heard that the wall was inoperative they would promptly slit my throat. If I was unlucky, they would want to learn everything I'd planned before they arrived at the throat-slitting part.

Yeah, I'd never been particularly lucky.

I'd been a prisoner before and had been tortured more than once. I knew I would break, but hopefully, I could mix enough bullshit with the truth to confuse them. The Rymorians had insidious means of extracting information, but it was likely they wouldn't have such technology with them out here. I was counting on it.

Jon let out a shaky breath and, with it, his anger drained. "You know it won't stop this," he said. "They'll kill you or worse. Fuck knows what worse is, but it won't end well, and they'll slaughter us anyway. Don't do this. I'm begging you to stay. If you stay, we have a chance."

"It's too late, Jon, too late for everything. He has me cornered. You were the one telling me not to go to the bloody wall, to find an alternative. Here it is—here's my alternative. I'm handing myself over. It's what Bill wants, but the wall being inoperative again will shake him. Given he has me, he won't go on a killing spree. You should be happy. For once you should be happy that I'm doing something right!"

The Warrior in the Shadows

I had never said those words before, but final moments had a way of freeing the tongue.

Jon's face shone in the lamplight, a tic thumping in his jaw as his bloodshot eyes met mine. "Is that what you think? That I think nothing you do is right? I love you. I couldn't love you more if you were my own son. You've done wrong things. More than a few. And crazy things, too." His smile was sad. "Don't think me sometimes giving you a hard time means I don't support you, because I do."

"It's okay, Jon. I'm okay with this," I said softly. "Perhaps it's time for me to pay my dues."

"Well, I'm not fucking okay with this, and nothing you did is bad enough to warrant giving yourself to Bill."

"No? I think there are people who would dispute that; on both sides of the wall."

He shrugged. "You've done more good than bad. If Kein were here, he would talk some sense into you. And I don't agree with you not telling Javid, either. He deserves to know what an idiot you are. Perhaps he could knock some sense into you."

Javid had tried enough times to know it would be pointless, but I didn't say that to Jon.

An unexpected calmness invaded me. It was late. If I was going, it would need to be soon. "It's time I went."

I stood, and Jon did too. "I'll come with you."

"No, Jon."

"To the river, then."

"And if they have guards posted, you'll end up a prisoner, too. Bill kept you at that trapper lodge for a reason, and he doesn't need both of us to be satisfied—just me."

"I'm coming part of the way." Jon's jaw set.

I raised my hands in defeat. "Part of the way or I'll never get out of this bloody camp. What I wouldn't give for copious amounts of Red Alrin right now." I pushed the tent flap out of my way. Jon followed close behind.

"You outlawed it," Jon said. "Which was pointless, given that the damage was done."

Garren stood in conversation with two of my wolf guards, but seeing me, he stopped what he had been doing and hurried over. "You've not come to your senses, then?" he demanded.

"If you're asking if I'm leaving, then the answer is yes, I am."

Garren glared at me, face tightly drawn. We hadn't spoken much since we'd left Thale. Tonight had been our first conversation of length. It was easy to forget that my brother was only twenty-five and barely an adult from the Rymorian point of view. A deeper understanding sat between us now. A better person might have told Garren to look out for Hannah, but I was a selfish bastard and wasn't about to hand out concessions.

"What about Hannah?" Garren asked, as if reading my mind.

"Don't go there," I growled.

"Fuck you. I hope they take weeks to kill you," Garren muttered. "I'm coming with you to make sure you fucking go!"

"I don't need a fucking parade. I'm supposed to be going quietly."

"This putting you off?" Jon asked Garren.

"No," Garren said, folding his arms.

"Fine." I motioned one of my guards over and reached to unbuckle my sword.

"Leave it." Garren pressed his hand against my arm. "You don't know what you will find there, or on the way."

"Against Rymorian weapons?"

"Just leave it," Garren insisted.

I re-tightened the buckle. "Fetch my horse, and let Han know I'm leaving," I said to my guard. "Han is in command until I return." The man gave his acknowledgement and hurried off.

"Right, let's get this done," Garren said brusquely. "In case you need any incentive when it's getting rough—"

"I don't," I cut him off.

Garren smirked. It was the kind that usually pissed me off, but today, for once, it didn't.

Chapter 48

Rymor

Richard

I'm going to get myself killed! *A sixty-year-old senate member has no business having adventures or playing a hero!*

My new best friend, Nate, was disarmingly direct and far too persuasive. As a political advisor, I felt that should be my forte and that I should have been more resistant. Despite my reservations, I was still here, in possession of a tiny silver cylinder that might as well have been an elephant for how heavy it felt.

The entrance to the facility where Dan languished loomed before me, an architectural creation whose light and bright aesthetic appeal hid a suspicious truth. It was a beautiful prison, but still a prison.

The dark-suited guards at the entrance gave some indication of its sinister intent. My arrival was scheduled and approved via my new best friend, Nate. A part of me fretted that this was a ruse, that the authorities were onto me and were merely playing me to further aid my entrapment.

Nate had been indifferent to these concerns, and his nonchalant smile said he was either amused by them or found them endearing. He patted my shoulder, winked, and said, "Controlling systems is like child's play to me, Richard. Relax."

So much easier said than done. I'd not slept more than a fitful hour last night, leaving me exhausted and edgy.

Gaining entrance proved to be uneventful. The security personnel checked me off a list and waved me to the scanning booth, where I placed my hand on the plate...and walked in.

That should have calmed my nerves.

It didn't.

The silent, black-suited escort at my side guided me to my destination, where he nodded to another black-suited guard at the door.

Did they not buy clothing in any other colors?

The doorkeeper opened the door...and followed me in.

I gaped at him, confused.

"I'm to remain," the man said, taking up a position inside the door.

No! This hadn't happened last time. This wasn't in the plan.

Dan's beaming face distracted me from my internal panic. The smile I plastered on must have come across as deranged. If Dan noticed something was amiss, he hid it well.

"Richard! So good to see a familiar face."

This is a complete disaster!

I hurried over, my mind churning through options. A quick glance at our guard revealed his clinical interest.

"Dan, so nice to see you, too. I'm sorry I've not had a chance to visit sooner. The war has had me engaged with senate commitments every day and long into the night," I rambled as I took the seat opposite.

"Oh, I understand, Richard. Thank you so much for coming today." He reached out to grasp my hand tightly.

The Warrior in the Shadows

It was then that I looked at Dan, really looked at him, and the strain of what the technical master was going through became apparent. From the tight lines around his eyes to the clothes now fitting looser on his frame, it was obvious that he had been affected by his incarceration.

"How have you been keeping, Dan?" I felt calmer as the realization of Dan's dire predicament centered my resolve.

"Oh, a little bored." Dan rolled his eyes, but the hidden words—*It's been hell*—floated silently between us.

My nervous glance back found the guard still watching us.

I returned my attention to Dan, letting him do most of the talking while I quietly had a meltdown.

I could possibly get the pen tip, which would dispense the device surreptitiously against his skin, but I hated to do so without telling Dan first. Nate's confidence in controlling the monitoring so we could talk freely was of little help while a guard was in the room. Dan might call out in surprise or, worse, suspect something nefarious. Maybe he might think I was working for Bill and was trying to kill him.

That this tiny device could fix Dan still felt far-fetched and fantastical, although Nate was convincing in his belief. It was experimental, and something might go wrong. I needed Dan's approval.

"Who?" The guard's sudden comment snagged our attention. "To where?" His face became distant as he listened to whatever communication was taking place before he grunted, and his expression compressed into a grimace. "You better send backup." His eyes shifted to Dan and me. "Your visit is over."

"Over?"

My thoughts flopped about like a fish on land. This must be Nate. It must be.

The door opened, and more black suits crowded in.

This was my only chance. I fumbled into my pocket and extracted the tiny, pen-like cylinder. It was configured for Dan, and I needed only to brush it against his skin for the device to activate and host.

"Goodbye, Dan. I'll arrange another visit as soon as I can," I reached to take his hand. As we touched, his eyes widened. "I think you will notice a pleasant change before we meet again."

I attempted a reassuring smile as the black suits charged in to separate us and ushered me to the door. Dan's haunted eyes followed me, his hand curled protectively against his chest.

Then everyone was hustled into the corridor, and I headed one way, while Dan was herded the other. I hoped that Nate knew what he was doing because my visit wouldn't be flying under the radar now that an incident, whatever that incident might be, had occurred.

I allowed the men to guide me out and passed through the checkout scan in a numb daze.

Outside, I hurried to the parking garage, where I climbed into my personal skycar... And nearly had a heart attack.

"Nate, what are you doing here?!" Eyes wild, I scanned in every direction. The skycar had privacy glass, but it was in a public parking garage, and Nate must have gotten in somehow.

"Did you do it?" Nate's eyes searched mine.

"Yes, I did it. Pressed it against his hand as I left. Was that you? I assumed it was you, whatever prompted them to suddenly cancel the meeting."

"No," Nate said. "It wasn't me. Something has happened. I don't know what yet, but security forces across Rymor have been placed on high alert."

Chapter 49

Shadowland

Tanis

I had experienced better days, but now that I thought about it, I couldn't remember experiencing worse. Everywhere hurt, layers upon layers of pain that merged without end. They had been comprehensive, but I'd expected nothing less.

I was naked, on my knees, with my hands bound behind my back and secured against the thick metallic spike driven into the ground in the center of the tent. I shifted, my thighs and shoulders protesting at the constrained position.

Ignoring the pain as best I could, I forced myself to relax.

I had been here for four long days. They hadn't started properly yet, which made me nervous. Ridiculous, given I was bound and naked in the middle of a Rymorian camp and feeling like death.

They came every morning to beat the shit out of me, only it was never the irreversible kind of damage that let you know the end was coming. I'd tried provoking them, but they remained steadfast.

I was certain now, had been for a while, that they were saving me for Bill.

And that really pissed me off.

Seeing Bill wasn't part of my plans. I'd expected the Rymorians to act. It made no sense for them to sit here waiting. For what? Attack or retreat, they ought to be doing something.

All my hopes had been riding on that station shutting down, and the Rymorians withdrawing now I was within their grasp. Perhaps Joshua's conscience had kicked in, or he's been killed by a stray Jaru arrow in a random attack.

Perhaps giving myself up had been a stupid idea after all.

I worried about what the Shadowlanders were doing, whether they would commit to war anyway or if they were under attack from another Rymorian group.

So many possibilities and none of them were hopeful, yet there was no way out of this now. I'd arrived here resolved to my fate. I could try to escape, but to what end? I hadn't discovered anything of value, and for the people of Shadowland, my best place was still here when leaving could provoke the attack I sought to avoid.

The bottom line was that I didn't trust Bill.

On top of this restless worry for the people who had accepted me as their own was a catalog of regrets that stretched back to that day when Bill had brought Ava out here ten years ago. I'd lost track of the people I'd killed in my quest to unite Shadowland or the countless others I'd left with invisible scars.

My litany of lamentations ended with my treatment of Hannah, and then that moment where I'd drawn my sword on Garren. All she'd wanted was some answers, and instead, I fucked her, then walked away. As for Garren, he'd punched me plenty of times under considerably less provocation. Garren's action didn't justify my response.

While I rationalized that the confrontation with Garren was destined to happen, and while Hannah hadn't objected to at least some of what had transpired in my room, both those memories still

The Warrior in the Shadows

added to the weight that I carried, so that I felt I deserved to be here, and that in some twisted way, every blow was me getting my dues.

The tent flap opened abruptly, and five men entered, which included the usual four guards. The final man, with a lean face and an air of importance, wore sleek black civilian clothes the style of which I hadn't seen since I was in Rymor.

"Who are you?" I asked

The newcomer's smile was cool. "My name is Kelard Wilder, but you can think of me as the man who will be reporting to Bill."

"Really, I'm disappointed." I feigned bored.

"Disappointed?" Kelard asked.

"Are you supposed to be the one that scares me?"

"For a man who is bound and naked, you have a fascinating lack of concern. Perhaps removing your cock will change that."

"As threats go, it's not very original." I shrugged. "Effective—you can assume I'm suitably cowed."

"He mentioned you were arrogant."

"Bill? Coming from a psychopath that's interesting. Did he tell you how I nearly killed him? Letting him live was only the second stupidest thing I have ever done."

"Indeed, I'm sure you're going to enlighten me as to the first."

I jangled my bound wrists. "Turning myself in hoping I'd get a chance to meet him again so I can finish the job."

Kelard ghosted a smile. "Finishing the job? I don't think so. But I'm sure we can arrange that meeting when the time is right."

So, they were taking me to Bill. "And when will that be?"

"All in good time. First, I'm hoping you may have interesting information to tell me first."

"I'm happy to talk. A man doesn't hand himself over unless he's got something to say."

"And what would you like to say?"

"Fuck all to you."

Kelard's smile disappeared. "Perhaps we should progress straight on to the persuasion part. I can see you will need a little help."

"You know I can snap these flimsy cuffs any time I want to, right?" I jangled my cuffs again, chuckling when Kelard jumped back.

A blow from the nearest guard was hard enough to make my ears ring, but not enough to stop my laughter.

Kelard looked on. "I had no idea you'd be so entertaining."

"I haven't even started yet," I grinned. I could feel blood trickling down my chin. I hoped it presented a gruesome sight. "I'm surprised he's allowing me to speak to sharp-suited ex-field scientists like yourself, given what I know."

"I doubt you could tell me anything new. You weren't blameless."

I studied the man before me, wondering exactly what Bill had said and whether I could fuck up his unwavering support of Bill. I doubted Bill would have let him loose questioning me if that were at risk and had probably prepared the man to anticipate my lies? "I doubt he told you the truth."

Kelard smiled without warmth. "Oh, I'm certain he didn't, and I'm certain you won't either, but I will enjoy the enlightenment all the same."

It wasn't often that I felt at a disadvantage, but today I did. I remembered Kelard Wilder's name being bandied about back in my brief time as a field scientist. He was renowned for his aggressive pursuit of results. I had a bad feeling time had allowed him to hone his skills. The man before me wasn't much better than Bill. Nothing I said would shake him or dissuade him from his self-righteous path. I was a traitor. What possible credibility could my words hold? Kelard had been sent here to get answers, and sooner or later, I would talk.

I knew then that it was *that* time. The time when I would be beaten into a familiar, hopeless place from which there would be no going back.

Chapter 50

Rymor

Peter

I hadn't had a single day's vacation since the transport crash, and the daily check-off on my fishing calendar was making me increasingly depressed. If I could have gotten away with it, I'd have developed one of those exotic strains of bug that could lay a person off work for a couple of weeks.

Unfortunately, illness wasn't easily faked, and I was notoriously poor at lying. Even those white lies were a challenge for me—as my ex-partner had been keen to point out.

"I can't believe no one knows still," Tom muttered despondently. Yes, four months without a sniff of vacation had crushed Tom's exuberance, and that was sad even to my jaded view of life.

Tom voiced this opinion daily, on bad days more. I didn't bother trying to distract Tom or keep him quiet—not when I agreed with him.

The most exciting event of note was when the Shadowland army left Thale. We replayed the recording often—studying it for work, of course. While the soldiers had arrived at Thale piecemeal and therefore had not warranted special attention, a mind-numbing eighty-two thousand, one hundred and six soldiers had spilled out of the fortress. It triggered a frenzy of new theories, since previous structural modeling had suggested Thale could house a third of that number at most. New proposals suggested underground chambers, but the exact composition would remain a mystery.

That tiny glimpse into the workings of a civilization we still barely knew had haunted me ever since. Shadowlanders had never traveled in such numbers before, ever.

Sleep had been fitful ever since. The fragility of Rymor and its reliance on a single station was glaringly obvious. What if there were another earthquake? What if Station fifty-four broke down again? However unlikely, it might. We weren't safe anymore, hadn't ever been.

There had been no further sighting and nothing else to indicate where those soldiers may now be. The official news reported the Shadowlanders were heading toward the wall. The information was apparently supplied to the media from a government source. I would love to know how the heck that was possible if even Global Monitoring didn't know.

It smelt like propaganda, adding further burden to my sleepless nights.

"The sensors are picking up movement near the station," Tom said. The minutest hint of interest crept into his voice. "It's not a large group, maybe fifty, less than a hundred anyway."

"Let's have a look then," I felt my own interest rise from a long slumber. The station had never used to be a popular indigenous location. After the earthquake, it had been significantly busier, and Global Monitoring hadn't recorded a damn thing. "I'm surprised anyone would go back there. All those bodies must be ripe by now."

The vast wall viewer transitioned into the satellite view before the cameras zoomed in and panned over the surrounding area. "I

The Warrior in the Shadows

think they've gone through ripe and beyond," Tom said. He was right. Nature had reclaimed its own, leaving blackened jumbles of picked-bare bones. "They're skirting the edges here, see."

He pointed out the area, and I could just make out the movement at the tree line.

"For once the weather is fine, and we're not getting any interference," I said. "If they poke their heads out, I want to know who it is. It's about time we got some decent identification."

The indigenous party continued to work their way around the tree line.

"They seem—cautious," Tom said. "I wonder what they're doing here. Scavenging maybe? Must be plenty of loot lying around."

"I dare say," I said, delighted to see some of Tom's enthusiasm return even if the subject was macabre.

"They're emerging! Let's see if we can get an ID." Tom began reviewing the data predictions. The longer the people remained visible, the higher the accuracy of their identification. If they disappeared back too soon, no match would be found.

"Are they heading for the station again?" Tom's troubled gaze returned to the wall viewer.

"Yes," I said, frowning, "It looks like they are."

And they were, heading directly for the station on foot, giving the ground-based cameras a perfect image for identification. The cameras lost them when they closed in on the station wall. The one over the entrance had been out of commission since the earthquake. "Did you get them?"

"Yes! Shadowlanders 99.998%. Doesn't get much more accurate than that," Tom said, jubilant. Then an access alarm started beeping, and Tom hit the override to reset the sensor. "The station door just opened!"

"What the heck is going on down there?! Look, more are coming!" Another group burst from the forest edge. "Can we get an identification on the new group? We need identification, Tom! How the heck did they open the door? Is it the missing Rymorians, do you think? It must be the missing Rymorians."

Tom's fingers flashed over his interactive desk as I pulled up the sensor data from inside the station.

"Shit!" Tom said.

My fingers froze mid-task. "Are they… going to fight?!"

The sudden and distinctive flash of PB fire preceded the two sides clashing.

Whoever the new group was, they had Rymorian technology.

I flushed cold, then hot. The Shadowlander group charged down the steep slope to meet their attackers. Their numbers dwindled, their people falling under the flash of weapon fire until, finally, the two groups collided in a jumble of chaos and carnage. The weapon's fire ceased abruptly. Some people scattered while others pursued.

It was over quickly. Only half the original numbers remained.

"Oh no, oh no, oh no," Tom muttered. "No, it can't be."

"What?" I demanded. "What is it?"

"No," Tom started shaking his head.

"What the hell is it!"

"The second group, the ones with the PB weapon, I've got an ID." He turned toward me. "They are Jaru 99.998%."

The world shifted around me, and I feared I might be sick. Then the sudden, harsh drone of the master alarm gave me something new to worry about. A barrage of system shutdown messages filled the great wall viewer, scrolling on and on until they became nothing but a blur. The satellites were down. Everything was down.

I swallowed hard.

"Heaven help us," I said. "It's happening all over again."

Chapter 51

Shadowland

Tanis

The tent flap opened, and a soldier stepped in, bringing a temporary respite to the proceedings. Lost under a fog of pain, I squinted at the newcomer, blinking blood from my eyes.

I closed my eyes but opened them again when a wave of nausea hit me. They hadn't asked me anything yet, but Kelard had watched with impassive interest as the natural light faded, and they had switched on the stark artificial lighting. Soon the questions would come.

I couldn't believe they'd brought lighting out here. They must have assassinated every member of Gaia to get away with that.

An animated and whispered conversation continued between the new man and Kelard.

Not that I cared. My head was hammering, and complex thoughts were beyond my grasp. They had been comprehensive. Self-sacrifice wasn't playing out the way I'd expected. I was no longer convinced a noble death was the right way to go when crushing Kelard Wilder's skull with my bare hands was far too appealing—and more so if it would piss Bremmer off.

Kelard swore.

I bit back a laugh. The bastard sounded pissed. At least I wasn't the only person in the tent having a bad day.

"I need to deal with this," Kelard said, his voice a tight snarl. He gestured in my direction. "He can wait."

With that, he motioned everyone outside, leaving me alone.

The intensity of the pain was slow to fade. I hoped something exceptionally bad had happened. Maybe the station?

The tent flap opened again to admit another soldier... a particularly fresh-faced one. Yeah, and why did I care?

I realized belatedly that the man had come to an abrupt halt and was staring at me.

There was staring at someone, and then there was *staring* at someone. "Do you like what you see?"

The man's focus snapped back to my face. I didn't want to linger on exactly where he had been staring while I was in this vulnerable state.

"I-I'm here to rescue you," the man stammered.

"Really?" I raised an eyebrow. It cracked a semi-sealed cut and hurt like hell. "What makes you think I need rescuing?" My voice came out slurred—great, I probably had a concussion!

My rescuer gestured to me, kneeling naked and bound, as if my state of capture was sufficient reason on its own. He couldn't be much past his majority in age, good-looking in an unassuming way, and nothing like the usual military grunt. His attention continued to dart up and down between my face and cock like an erratic ping-pong.

"You have a name?"

"Theo, my name is Theo."

The Warrior in the Shadows

"I handed myself over for a reason Theo," I said. "Being rescued wasn't part of my plans."

Theo's jaw went slack before he began to splutter. "You surrendered? Are you insane? Why would you do something so stupid when Hannah needs help!" He glanced down again, but this time in an unfocused way. "This doesn't fit the profile," he muttered.

Profile? "How do you know Hannah?" Who the hell was this man, another of Hannah's crazy ex-partners? No, he definitely *wasn't* her ex. "My face is up here."

"We don't have time for a discussion," Theo said, blushing furiously, finally meeting my eyes. "Either you will swear to help me save Hannah or I'll leave you here for Bill's men to kill!"

The man had no problem with being serious when he needed it. It was a pity he lacked anything physical to back it up. "That's not much of a threat. If you had any idea who I was, you wouldn't be offering to rescue me under the misguided protection of my word." Given I was questioning the merits of surrender, I wasn't sure why I was pointing this out—*must be the concussion.*

Crestfallen, Theo visibly slumped. Clearly, he'd believed the act of rescue to be the catalyst for my complete and unquestioning loyalty.

It was endearingly Rymorian, and the ridiculous kind of thing Hannah would have assumed when she'd first entered Shadowland—probably still would.

"What exactly do you think Hannah needs saving from? She was in Thale last I saw, which is as safe a place as any else given all the shit that's happening out here." Either my brain wasn't processing properly, or this was the weirdest conversation I'd ever had.

"She's not at Thale, hasn't been for weeks. A team of twenty men are taking her to Talin, and if we don't do something about it, she's going to end up back with Bill!"

"The fuck she is." Rage, the likes of which was recently rare to grip me, surfaced and demanded attention. The guilt that I was somehow responsible for this war released me from its stranglehold.

Dying here today wasn't the right answer, not if Hannah was in danger.

Questions clamored in my sluggish mind, but all of them could wait. "You have a plan to get me out of here?"

"Are you going to help?"

"Are you going to trust me if I say I will?"

There was a pause—I could almost sense Theo's cogs turning.

He sighed. "I wouldn't be here if I wasn't desperate." He gave me a look full of disdain, which was an improvement on his blatant perusal of my junk, and disappeared out of the tent, returning with a bundle, which he shook onto the floor.

Out dropped a familiar sword, clothes, and boots.

"That's my sword?"

"Yes, I know."

"And this was your master plan? To escape soldiers armed with Rymorian weapons?"

Theo shrugged. "I've been told you're very skilled with a sword."

"Given how long you spent staring at my cock, I don't want to know where this is going."

"Sorry," he had the decency to blush. "You're not what I expected, and you don't exactly look normal."

Normal?

"I'm not at my best—people have been beating me and stabbing me—repeatedly—and I'm sure I have a concussion since nothing you say is making any sense."

"That wasn't what I meant," Theo's attention shifted, resting on anything but me.

"How about you undo these cuffs," I said, my brain churning slowly. "Are you working for Wilder? Is this some sort of twisted mind game?"

"No, of course not." Theo hurried over to where my hands remained bound to the post, and then he paused. "You didn't promise to help?"

"You have seconds to undo these cuffs before I rip this pole out

The Warrior in the Shadows

and beat you with it." I was confident I couldn't rip the pole out since I'd tested it a time or two when they left me alone... It helped to pass the time. Still, I probably looked like someone who could rip a pole out.

There was a great deal of uncomplimentary muttering before the cuffs popped open.

Theo put as much distance between himself and me as possible within the tent's confines. "You are going to help?"

I didn't bother to answer, just cursed with frustration as I waited for the agony in my shoulders to pass. I slowly rolled them.

Fuck me. Was he staring at me again?

"I'm not interested in you."

I raised my eyebrows.

"I don't think I am, anyway." Theo said as though confused. "I was sure I was in love with Hannah."

"I feel both flattered and uncomfortable about possibly being the catalyst for you coming out. Perhaps we could skip the part where you analyze your sexual orientation, and get to the escaping part." I steeled myself against more pain and lurched to my feet. My head swam, and my vision turned to sparkling dots. "Got any water?"

"Yes!" Theo searched his backpack like he was happy to be looking away.

I pulled on my clothes with slow, unhurried movements. My armor was missing. Some bastard had probably taken it as a souvenir. How the fuck was I going to get us out of the camp full of armed soldiers with only a sword in my hand and a bad case of concussion?

Teeth gritted, I dragged my shirt on before taking the offered bottle and gulping the contents down. "Don't suppose you have a medical scanner tucked in there as well?"

"No, unfortunately not... How do you feel?"

"Imagine the worst you've ever felt. Times it by ten, and you still won't be close." I picked up my sword, reassured by its weight in my hand. My head was still foggy, and I would be deluding myself if I thought I had a chance of getting out alive. At least I wouldn't die naked. "The Shadowland camp still on the other side of the river?"

He nodded.

Okay, that was one positive.

"So, how do we get past their weapons?"

"Can you walk?"

I scowled at him. "Yes, of course I can walk." I gestured at myself. "My legs are still attached."

"I was only checking," Theo said frostily. "Assuming they don't have Rymorian weapons, do you think you could deal with anyone who tried to stop us?"

"Why would I assume they don't have Rymorian weapons?"

"Because they don't." Theo smirked. "Technology is a family forte. I've had a little assistance from inside the wall. The soldiers have weapons. None of them are going to work."

"Theo, you're a man of hidden talents." I grinned back. "Horses?"

"Yes." He nodded. "Corralled a small distance away."

"How many men are between us and them?"

"Two beside the tent, and at the edge of the camp another five. The rest should be in tents... We don't need to kill them, do we? I mean, it's not their fault."

"Need to?" I shrugged. "Probably not. Want to? Definitely yes." Theo's eyes widened, making me grin. "A few less for me to kill later."

Chapter 52

Rymor

Bill

Peter Packman delivered his report to me in person, waiting in a rigid stance before my desk in my State Tower office.
"Who knows?"
"You do, sir," Peter said. The events surrounding the station had aged him. He'd lost weight, leaving his skin saggy and hollow.
"Who else?"
"Only myself, and Tom, of course."
"Jaru with Rymorian technology," I said.
"They were firing on the Shadowlanders, sir." Peter offered helpfully, a nervous tremor in his voice. "We thought it was the Shadowlanders with the technology, but perhaps we've been wrong all along."
"Indeed, or perhaps they stole it from Shadowlanders," I said. "This changes nothing when it was Shadowlanders who entered the

station and shut it down. They're working with Moiety. I'm sure of it."

Peter nodded, but I couldn't be sure whether it was in genuine agreement or an attempt to pacify me.

"It's hard to say what's going on out there, sir. We lost the satellite feed again, so we don't have contact with our soldiers either. Unless they can reach the waypoint to the north of Julant, we're likely to stay in the dark. The tunnels aren't safe anymore now the access points are exposed. If they flee that way, they could bring the Shadowland army into Rymor. We could be at risk anyway, since, if the Shadowlanders know how to access the station, they could know how to use the access points, with or without our troops leading them there."

The man really didn't know when to shut up. The abrupt wariness in Peter's expression suggested he regretted his rambling mouth.

"What do you want us to do?"

"Your job," I snapped. "Keep monitoring the access points. If one opens, I want to know. If anything else happens at the station, I want to know. That will be all."

Peter nodded stiffly and left the room.

I let my breath out with a hiss of frustration. I would need to call up that gloating cretin Andrew Jordan until I got word from Kelard. I still trusted Kelard to see this through, but needed a security advisor until communication was reestablished with the forces in Shadowland.

I couldn't believe the satellites were down again. Losing access to Kelard was frustrating enough, but without the satellites, I'd lost access to Karry, too. I was cast into the dark just as I'd taken custody of Tanis and Hannah.

Discovering Karry had successfully extracted Hannah had put me on a euphoric high for days. Then, only this week, Kelard had taken Tanis into custody. It hardly seemed possible that plans could fall into place so well. Tanis handing himself over to the Rymorians had surprised me and left me deeply suspicious. Kelard had assured me that whatever Tanis' intentions, the infamous man would be returned to Rymor to stand trial for his crimes.

Tanis had asked only that the people of Shadowland not suffer for his crimes. Very noble and very unlike the Tanis that I knew. I was going to end everyone he ever loved, and if I didn't find that satisfying enough, I would raze his fortress to the ground while he watched. Should he have had any hand in the station, I would show him how creative I could be with the aid of a medical scanner.

While Tanis' capture brought anticipated closure to my personal vendetta, Hannah's kidnapping pleased me for completely different reasons. She was currently on her way to Talin, where I intended to keep her. Even if Karry failed to find anything useful about her relationship with Tanis, I was confident I would.

I turned my seat to look out at Shadowland. The unfortunate business at my coastal home bothered me less now Tanis had been captured. Eliminating Bernie had forced me to call on other resources in my quest to track Theo, who I now knew had visited my home. The image of Theo and his look-alike twin still plagued my mind. There was something oddly familiar about the two men. Something I couldn't quite put my finger on.

A call came through from Neilson. "Rochelle Stevens is here, sir."

I acknowledged him and headed out to find Rochelle waiting in the reception room, projecting elegance in a cream dress that contrasted beautifully against her dark skin and fitted her perfect figure in a way that enhanced every curve. I kissed her cheek, and she tucked her hand under my arm as we headed for a late lunch.

We took my personal skycar, and Rochelle's engaging conversation provided a pleasant distraction to my earlier conversation with Peter. The skycar dropped us off at our venue, a chic restaurant in Majestic Tower with spectacular views of the city and the distant mountains that enclosed Rymor's northern boundary.

We were promptly shown to a seat, where we ordered, and, soon after, our drinks arrived.

"Daddy was asking about the situation in Shadowland. It must be nearly a month since the Rymorian forces left?" Rochelle sipped her wine and glanced at me.

I wondered how long before Senator Stevens started using Rochelle to discover what was happening. Rochelle was only doing what Daddy number one asked her, but it still left me equal parts furious, disappointed, and resigned.

"Three weeks."

"Oh," Rochelle said, perhaps regretting being her father's go-between.

"He could have just asked me, Rochelle."

"Yes, of course." She found riveting interest in her glass of wine.

"I'm disappointed that he didn't," I added with a sigh.

Her eyes shone bright, but it wasn't my intention to hurt her, more to remind her and her father that I was no one's fool.

"I have John Tanis in custody. We captured him a few days ago, but that's not for the public. You may tell your father and no one else," I said. "Now, why don't we talk about something else?"

"Yes, of course." She smiled a little too brightly.

As the meal arrived, so did a communication from Neilson. "Sir, a gentleman by the name of Wyatt has left you a priority-coded update."

I smiled at Rochelle, mollified in the wake of the message, one I'd been waiting for.

After ten years of absence, it was time for me to enter Shadowland.

Chapter 53

Shadowland

Tanis

I'd killed at least two guards, and the others would die soon unless someone had a medical scanner in the camp. Given the many other infringements I'd witnessed, it was likely that they did. Our exit was colorful, and most of that color was red.

It was one thing to talk about getting past guards, and another to witness the violence that led to their crumpled remains lying on the ground. I acknowledged Theo's shock for what it was as we reached the horses to make our escape. "Don't waste your energy worrying about the things you can't control. I've never tried *not* to kill someone before. This was always going to be bloody." Theo nodded wary acceptance, but it was like the first day I met Hannah all over again.

"Can you ride a horse?" I asked when he only gaped at me as I made quick work of saddling the horse.

Cries and shouts came from the direction of the camp. We had moments to get out undetected.

"Ah, no," he replied, shaking, and staring at me, wide-eyed and fearful.

Well, fuck!

"Get up," I said, motioning to the horse.

"What about you? Where are we going? Are we going to rescue Hannah? My scanner shows her fifty imperial miles south of here. That's too close to Thale for my liking."

"You said twenty men were holding her? In case it escaped your notice, I'm a lone man with concussion who has recently been beaten and tortured. I'm going to need some help. We can cover that distance in three days, two at a push. Besides, Bill's an asshole and a megalomaniac, but I can't believe he would hurt her. More likely he wants to use her as propaganda for the war."

"Okay, but I don't like her with Bill's men."

"I don't like her with Bill's men. It will be my pleasure to gut each and every one of them, just as soon as I'm not seeing two of everything. Now, mount the fuck up!" I shoved him into the saddle, hearing the sounds of approaching soldiers. Fuck, he was going to fall off! "Hold onto the pommel, lean down if you need to, and squeeze with your thighs." I mounted my own horse, took his reins, and together we took off.

Once we had cleared the immediate area, I set as fast a pace as I dared between my pounding head and Theo's dubious horse-riding skills.

We arrived at the Shadowlander camp late afternoon to hails and cheers. I felt like death, so I commandeered the nearest tent of size and ordered my key leaders to be rounded up.

Han and Jon were the first to arrive. Jon crushing me in a hug I appreciated even if my battered body didn't.

Han shoved a water bottle into my hand as Jon wiped his eyes. I swayed a little as I drank—at least the double vision had gone.

Garren arrived next, pushing his way into my tent. "Back from the dead I see," he said, fixing me with a disparaging look. "Not that

The Warrior in the Shadows

far back." His attention shifted toward Theo. "What's with the tower dweller kid? Hostage?"

"No," I replied. "Theo is my rescuer."

"Welcome to the other side of the war, Theo," Jon said before directing a broad grin at me. "I can't believe you got out of it alive."

"As Garren pointed out, the alive part is debatable," Han offered in his usual flat tone.

"The station's down," I said around another long drink, which distracted them from berating me. "Danel and his team must have succeeded."

"Are you sure?" Jon asked.

I nodded toward Theo.

"They lost the satellites," Theo said. "I can't tell you if it was related to the station."

"It's the station," I said.

"Let's hope so," Garren muttered. "The scouts picked up another enemy camp north-east of here. A couple of thousand strong."

"Lucky for us we have a way to disable their weapons, then," I said.

Garren grinned. "Do we, now?"

The tent flap burst open as I took another drink, and Tay shoved her way inside. I pulled the bottle down and eyed her cautiously.

"You look worse than they said." Her scowl raked the length of me. "And you only returned because of *her?*" I knew a blow was coming, but I was too tired to try and evade it. She punched me hard enough that my head snapped around from the force.

"For fuck's sake," Jon said.

I held up a hand when he looked like he might wade in.

Chest heaving, Tay's fist remained clenched at her side.

I spat out the blood pooling in my mouth and fixed her with a look. "There's a bit more to it than that, and none of it's your business. If you're staying, I suggest you make yourself useful. Otherwise, pack your stuff and get out of my fucking way."

333

She flinched. But I wasn't in the mood for emotional wrangling, and she needed to get over what had happened. She glared at me. I stared back in a way that made it clear further discussion would end poorly. Finally, she growled and stalked out of the tent.

"We're out of here as soon as I've eaten, and Yan has done his best."

"Out for where?" Garren asked, eyes narrowing on me in a way that said he thought I was an idiot again.

"First, to take out the camp where I was held hostage. Next, to find Hannah."

"Hannah?" Garren asked, frowning. "When did we lose Hannah?"

"Someone snatched her from Thale. How I don't know, but I presume technology was implemented. She's on her way to Talin."

"Fuck!" Garren said. "We've had no word from Thale."

"Which is why we need to eliminate their camp first."

"Can we trust him?" Garren nudged his head in Theo's direction. "What's to say he's not working for Bill?"

"I've been working for Bill for five years and know far more about him than I would like to," Theo said, a little steel entering his voice. Much to my amusement, he'd used that tone on me a time or two since we'd met. The man had courage, and harbored a genuine commitment to rescuing Hannah. "Bill had Hannah taken by a man who goes by the name of Karry. He's a criminal of the worst kind, and he's taking her to Bill. We can't let that happen. If I need to search for Hannah by myself, I will."

"The Rymorians we captured at the trapper station spoke of a Karry," Jon said. "And so did Marcus."

Garren's lips pulled into a grimace. "He scared the shit out of Marcus. Not the kind of man I want Hannah with."

"You didn't mention Karry before?" I said, narrowing my eyes at Theo.

"You didn't ask—and I was busy worrying about staying on the

The Warrior in the Shadows

horse." He gave me a shifty look. "It wasn't only me staying on the horse I was worried about."

"Damn it, Tanis, you're not well enough to ride or to start taking out a camp full of Rymorians, whatever may or may not have happened to their weapons," Jon said bluntly. "I know Wilder, he's got a reputation. Not the kind of man you want to face without your full wits about you. You can barely stand up"—he gestured toward Theo—"or ride a horse."

"It's personal," I said. "And my injuries are superficial. I've suffered worse plenty of times." I felt like I was about to throw up, pass out, or both, and I didn't recall ever feeling this bad, but if Jon figured that out, I'd be going nowhere without a fight—one I'd probably lose.

Jon stared back, a tic thumping in his jaw. "Well, I suppose compared to you handing yourself over to be tortured, this escapade is fairly tame."

Yan entered, followed by Tay, who carried in food. I took the opportunity to sit down.

"Jon, can you take Theo to get some food, drink, and find him some Shadowlander clothes. He will accompany me to the camp, and I don't want anyone to accidentally stab him."

Theo blanched.

"He has a poor sense of humor, Theo," Jon said. "Come on."

Jon and Theo left. Yan gave me a look that suggested he didn't know where to start.

I gestured toward my bloodstained trouser leg.

"How large is their camp?" Garren asked. "How many do we need to take?"

"Two hundred should be plenty. Their camp is small, fifty at most and they have no weapons. You and Han with me. The rest can wait here while we're gone. It shouldn't take long—I won't let it take long."

I took the food from Tay as Yan began hacking my clothing away.

"Better get me some clothes." I stuffed some food into my mouth as Tay left.

"I'll get things organized," Garren said, following Tay and Han out of the tent to leave me with Yan.

I gulped more water. I hadn't eaten properly in days, and the sudden bounty hit my stomach in a welcome but nauseating lump.

"You know you should not be riding with this," Yan said, attention focused as he stitched my leg.

"My back is worse." I felt along my ribs as I worked through the food my body wanted to reject. "I have a concussion and cracked ribs, but I didn't want to say in front of the others. You know I wouldn't go unless I had to."

As Yan had finished with my leg, I carefully drew my shirt off. "Don't suppose you have any Red Alrin?"

Yan huffed. "You will kill someone, probably Garren if I'm foolish enough to give that to you. Assuming you don't keel over and die anyway. You cannot keep doing this to yourself."

"I need something to kill the pain, and I don't have time to rest."

Yan's lips thinned, but he nodded. "I have known Garren since he was a boy, and you for five years. Try to remember that he needs you despite the words that sometimes come out of his mouth." He reached into his bag and pulled out one of the infamous little bottles. "I'll give the rest to Han. I trust *him* at least."

Yan began to apply salve to the stitched cuts and worst bruised areas. Cool, tingling, numbness spread from the salve. I pulled the cork out of the bottle and gulped a mouthful. It burned my throat but settled further numbness over the roiling cocktail in my gut. Sitting had been a bad idea. Getting back up was going to be challenging, so I indulged in another liberal slug. Red Alrin had a distinctive bitter flavor but a pleasant aftertaste.

Tay entered, arms laden with clean clothes and light armor, which was considerate, and more than I deserved given what I'd just said.

The Warrior in the Shadows

She scrutinized me, then sighed. "Do you need help putting it on?"

I finished the Red Alrin as Yan finished packing his supplies.

"Yes, probably."

Yan patted my shoulder. "Garren isn't the only one," he said before leaving me alone with Tay's sad eyes and the painful task of getting dressed.

Chapter 54

Talin

Bill

It had been ten years since I'd stepped into Shadowland. Ten long years of absence that would end today.

The station was still inoperative. Scott Harding was still kicking up a proverbial shitstorm. There remained no insight into Theo or his twin, and Coco Tanis, who I'd been inclined to bring in for questioning, had disappeared. However, as far as I was concerned, the rest of the circus could go to hell, and it wouldn't dim the pleasure of anticipating Tanis on his knees.

Those frustrations took a back seat today because it was time for me to return to Shadowland, knowing Tanis had been captured.

The fortress at Talin had been steadily building its presence. There were now several thousand people, with more on the way. Last week the communications had come online, and over the last few days, my living accommodations were being prepared. Now, it was

The Warrior in the Shadows

time to see in person what my money, initially, and later the government's, had paid for.

And probably time to recruit some less dubious people.

The access tunnel into Talin was buried far below the central courtyard. It was ancient and had been collapsed purposefully, or so long ago that no record of it existed. Only a detailed survey revealed the buried structures. Reinstating it hadn't been an easy undertaking.

That there *was* a tunnel connecting Rymor to a Shadowland fortress was curious, and further supporting evidence that the two people were once closely integrated. This new, direct access would be useful for bringing supplies out here.

I'd taken the precaution of putting a rapid collapse mechanism in place. You never knew when you might need to defend the site from either direction, and I was a man who always covered my back.

When I exited the transport carriage into the tunnels below Talin, the military grunt on duty greeted my arrival with slack-jawed surprise.

I smiled. "I believe you have some rooms set aside for me here?"

The grunt nodded. "Yes, sir! Follow me!"

I did, up several floors, through a cavernous storage bay stacked with haphazard boxes and crates, and out into the fortress proper. Sections of the building had become derelict over time, but there were still areas sufficiently intact to be habitable, and further repairs could be made over time.

"Do you want me to send for Wyatt?" The grunt inquired as we exited the tunnels of the lower fortress and emerged into the great hall.

I paused to turn a circle, the grunt momentarily forgotten as I took everything in. The magnitude of what I'd achieved hit me with full force. I was standing in the hall of a once-abandoned fortress. I felt an immediate connection to my younger self—through many years and much wasted time. The hall was stacked with open crates and rustic furniture placed randomly about. Clusters of people were busy at work. A few of those present noticed me—perhaps my clothing contrasted with the typical fatigues or indigenous attire everyone else wore. One by one, conversations drifted to a stop.

I was master here in a way I could never be in Rymor. No wonder Tanis had thrived here, where he could embrace autonomy free from societal constraints.

"Sir?" The grunt's question brought me back to the moment. "Do you want me to send for Wyatt?"

"No, I'll speak to Moore first."

"Yes, sir. He's been in a debriefing with his team most of the morning. I'll take you there. Wyatt is—Wyatt is out on patrol, but he should return soon."

"That's okay. Moore is my priority."

The grunt's obsessive need to send for Wyatt wore on my patience. Like many of the people first brought out here, Wyatt was a thug. He probably ran the place with greater terror than genuine respect. Still, terror worked well at times.

We exited the far side of the hall into a stone corridor that led us to another smaller hall. Here I found Damien and the team. A viewer leaned against the farthest black stone wall, with other equipment stacked about and a tangle of cables, which led to a micro-generator unit in the right corner.

Damien was pointing at something on the viewer, and an animated conversation was going on. It came to an abrupt stop as Damien noticed me. "Sir!" he said, and everyone turned around.

"Damien," I replied, offering a professional smile. "I thought I would check on progress in person."

On my periphery, I noticed the grunt about to slip out, doubtless to search for Wyatt. "Stay there." I pointed to a spot beside the entrance. The grunt shuffled over to wait.

"How was the trip?" I said, turning back to Damien.

Damien's face split into an excited grin. "You won't believe what we found. We hoped, but we never expected it to be so well preserved." He motioned to one of his team, and a moment later, the footage was displayed on the wall viewer.

The Warrior in the Shadows

Ancient technology appeared on the viewer. The image panned to show a debris-strewn surface that extended on into the distance.

"Did you get inside?" I asked, riveted by the image.

"We did, sir," Damien said. "But the ship is in stasis, and we're going to need equipment—the rare and expensive kind—to study further."

"That won't be a problem." My attention remained fixed on the viewer as the ship's vastness became apparent. I wondered if he'd found the Armageddon switch, but perhaps that was a conversation better done in private.

"Will we be able to go back out there again?" a team member asked, making me realize I had the room's undivided attention.

"Certainly," I replied. "Now that you've found it, we'll want to learn more. Prepare a list of what you need, and I'll arrange for its provision. I have some other business to attend to, but I'll be back to discuss it with you."

I turned from their excited babble of conversation to find the shifty grunt waiting for me.

"Do you want me to send for Wyatt now?" The grunt asked, his voice, for once, uncertain.

"Yes." I paused as I reached the grunt. "No, I want to see her first."

"Her?" The grunt looked confused. "Oh, you mean the Rymorian prisoner?"

"Yes, exactly. Take me to her."

The grunt blanched. "I think I should get Wyatt first," he stammered. "We aren't allowed to see her. No one is."

"But you know where she is?" I said, fixing him with a baleful stare.

He blinked, started to speak, then snapped his mouth shut as he sensibly thought better of it, before responding more appropriately. "Yes, sir."

"Good, then let us go."

"Yes, sir! I'll take you directly there!"

341

He escorted me along twisting corridors and up stairways that took us higher until we came out into a long hallway with stout wooden doors leading off to either side. He paused at the door, swallowing nervously and not meeting my eyes. "I—we're not allowed in there—Wyatt threatened—Wyatt said there would be disciplinary action if anyone entered without his permission."

"I don't think Wyatt meant to include me in that order, do you?" I asked mildly.

The grunt shifted from foot to foot. "No, sir."

"Is it locked?"

"No, I don't believe so, sir. None of the doors lock."

"Wait here," I said.

He nodded and stepped aside, his attention fixed on the opposite wall.

The door creaked as I pushed it open. My brows drew in tightly together as I took in the scene. Rage didn't do justice to all I felt.

Someone is going to die.

"I think you better send for Wyatt now. Tell him to wait for me out here."

The grunt returned a swift nod and left, the rapid beat of his footsteps echoing against the stone floor.

I watched him until he disappeared from sight, then I walked into the room and shut the door behind me.

Chapter 55

Shadowland

Tanis

It had been an exhausting ride back to the Rymorian camp, and I remained impatient to deal with Wilder. It was late, and night had fallen by the time we finally neared their camp. We took a few hours of rest, where I distracted myself from the various aches and pains by imagining creative ways to bring about Kelard Wilder's death.

By morning's arrival, I was more than ready to do it.

"How are we going to do this, then?" Garren asked. He was lying in the cover of the thick forest ferns to my right. Less than two hundred feet ahead of us, tucked into a dip of the rolling tree-filled landscape, the Rymorian camp sprawled out, unaware of our silent watch.

"I'm going to walk in, punch Kelard Wilder in the face, and then give him a personal demonstration on the art of effective interrogation."

"A little rash, even for you," Han muttered. He lay out on the ground to my left and, likewise, peered at the Rymorian camp with interest. "No point in trying to dissuade you, then?"

"That bastard deserves it," Agregor said enthusiastically. He was lying on Han's left and had become the unofficial thirteenth member of the wolf guard, much to Tay's disgust since I'd tasked her with keeping him out of trouble.

My grin had an edge to it. "I've been looking forward to this. Besides, their weapons are disabled, and they're arrogant enough to have brought nothing else to defend themselves. Not that they have a hope in hell, even fully armed with Shadowland weapons."

"They could have acquired some," Garren pointed out. "You caught them by surprise when you left, but there are plenty of places to trade for swords, even bows. They might be better prepared now."

"Yes," I said with a feral grin. "I'm hoping that they are." I rose to my feet, placing myself in plain sight of the Rymorian camp. "Move out."

Garren muttered a colorful curse and surged to his feet. "We're not going for the element of surprise, then."

Behind us, half a dozen of my personal guards, waiting at a discreet distance, also leaped to their feet. "Tay, make sure Agregor doesn't accidentally kill anyone," I called over my shoulder.

She glared at me.

Han scowled at me as he rose and drew his sword. "Are we at least going to mount up?"

"Not much point in bothering," I said as a cry came from the camp below. "On second thought, get fifty or so mounted and have them circle to cut off any retreat. I believe they may start running." Distracted by my quarry, I started walking down the slope toward the camp.

Garren let loose a few more choice curses as he fell in step alongside me.

Han cursed to himself, stalked back into our camp, and began bellowing orders.

The Warrior in the Shadows

"This is all very familiar," Garren said, squaring his shoulders and drawing his sword.

Behind us came the clank and stomp of armed men and women as my personal guards and soldiers hastened to catch up. Ahead, as I'd predicted, the Rymorian camp descended into chaotic panic as men began to run and rush every which way amidst desperate orders and frantic cries.

I proceeded to stalk into the center of the Rymorian camp as men either fled or fumbled with their weapons in the misguided hope that they would miraculously work. There, as if by divine deliverance, stood my personal destination.

Kelard Wilder stared back at me with bitter hatred.

Around us, men collided in pockets as my soldiers overpowered the enemy, snatching useless weapons from nerveless fingers and subduing them with barked orders or fists. A few began to run, but my mounted soldiers cut them off and herded them back into the midst of the camp.

Wilder was too much in bed with Bill to be of use as anything but an example.

As I neared, my pace didn't falter. Kelard stumbled a single step backward before my fist connected with his jaw.

He went down, cold.

Around us, defeated Rymorians were crowded back into the center with my soldiers surrounding them, blocking off their escape and crushing their hope. A pile of deactivated technology began to assemble.

I flexed my fingers and stared down at Kelard's prone body as Garren approached from one side and Han from the other. Several of the members of my wolf guard hovered close by. They had become attentive in shadowing me since my surrender and subsequent return.

"You broke his jaw," Han said, his brows bumping together as he studied the unconscious man before turning to me. "Did you mean to break his jaw?"

345

Kelard twitched on the ground, and blood and drool seeped from his slack mouth.

"Theo!" I shouted, looking about; relieved when I spotted him.

Theo picked his way through the decimated camp, already rapidly transitioning into a new kind of order.

"They must have medical personnel here somewhere," I said. "Find them and see what they can do."

"Oh, God," Theo said faintly. His face had turned pale and waxy, and he gawked at Kelard with horrified eyes.

"Do your best, Theo." Turning back to Han, I said, "Take him somewhere I can question him, and see if Theo can find someone to fix his jaw. Then strip him and remove his cock."

Theo muttered to himself as he stumbled off in search of a medic.

Garren raised an eyebrow. "Never took you for a trophy man, and definitely not that kind of trophy."

"No trophy, just retribution," I elaborated for Garren and then turned back to Han. "Leave it on the floor in front of him where he can see it."

I turned then to regard the cluster of terrified Rymorians.

Time to see who else we have here.

∼

Han hoisted Kelard's limp body over his shoulder, barking orders at the nearby soldiers that sent them hurrying to the task of finding a suitable tent.

I surveyed the now orderly camp and the white-faced Rymorians who had been hustled together in the center.

Military uniforms were so helpful for identifying rank.

Spotting the second-in-command, I walked over. "Anyone found in possession of Rymorian technology will be executed. Tell your people to hand over anything they have hidden."

He nodded, swallowed, and turned to repeat my instructions. A

The Warrior in the Shadows

few more weapons emerged, which were collected efficiently by waiting Shadowlanders.

"Keep an eye on things out here while I'm gone," I said to Garren before turning to Kelard's second. "Come with me." I motioned the man to follow me to where Han had taken Kelard, my ever-present guards following close on my heels.

Two of my personal guards stood outside the tent, and the four that were shadowing me went to follow me in.

"Two is plenty inside," I said. A glaring battle took place among the four guards as they decided who was coming in and who was staying out.

Pushing the tent flap open, I found Kelard secured to a familiar-looking pole in the center of the tent. Once more conscious, he stared back at me with bloodshot eyes. His jaw was bruised but now sat at a natural angle. As requested, he had been stripped, and blood dripped sluggishly from where his cock had once been. The missing appendage lay on the floor in front of him.

"Oh god!" Kelard's second muttered weakly. One of my guards jerked him to the right, and the other positioned himself on the left, between the prisoner and me as though he might pose a threat.

Han stood to one side, waiting with his signature air of detachment.

Theo stood near the tent entrance staring at the viewer in his hands with vacant, hooded eyes. "We fixed his jaw... was dislocated... Han... I couldn't find the medic." Theo fidgeted with a viewer in his hand.

I turned to Han. "Organize a small team to accompany Theo searching the tents. I want a tally of any technology found. Stack it with the weapons. Dismantle the camp and collect anything useful. Burn the rest."

Theo had left the tent before I'd finished talking. Han followed him out.

I returned my attention to Kelard. "Wilder, glad to see you're conscious again. It will be my pleasure to demonstrate to you the art of effective interrogation since you failed so miserably at it yourself. As you can see, I move promptly from the statement of intent to the act." I indicated the floor. "You should bear that in mind during our discussion."

"You're going to kill me," Kelard said, his voice subdued. "Get it over with."

"You came out here to kill me and to destroy an entire people based on one man's unsubstantiated claims." I raised a brow. "Were you expecting my compassion? A bit of a chat about where you went wrong before I let you go in peace?"

"You had to be stopped," Kelard spat back, his former vehemence returning. "You had technology. You destroyed the wall and the transport we sent to repair it!"

"I had fuck all," I roared, my fury spilling over. "I. Had. Nothing. Not one piece of your precious technology when you invaded my lands."

"I don't believe you," Kelard whispered, his eyes glazed.

"And I don't give a damn what you believe," I snapped back. "You're still going to tell me everything you know about Bremmer's plans. As for the wall, yes, I did destroy the wall a week ago, once I knew you were coming for me, coming for the people of Shadowland. You probably wondered why you lost satellite communication—now you know."

"I'll see you in hell before I'll tell you anything," Kelard said, his face twisting into a sneer.

I smiled, one that failed to reach my eyes. "Today must be my lucky day, looks like we're already there." As I approached, I drew my knife.

"This is barbaric—" The second-in-command's words faltered on a choked gasp as my guard wrapped his fingers around his throat and gave the man a vigorous shake.

"Silence," the guard rumbled before releasing him.

Kelard watched the interruption with wide eyes. He knew he wasn't getting out of this tent alive. I supposed I ought to have felt

The Warrior in the Shadows

something—regret, or remorse—for what was about to happen, but there was nothing. I only had to consider what they intended to do to this country to steady my fingers around the handle of the blade.

I met Kelard eyes before lowering mine to watch the tip of my blade slice through the fleshy part of his pectoral, dipping it into the skin far enough for blood to spring to the surface. It trickled down his chest and onto his abdomen in little gory rivers. "Tell me about Bremmer's plans."

The only sounds in the tent were the gasps of pain that escaped Kelard's clenched teeth as he jerked against the bindings, seeking distance from the blade. "Did you realize when you set out on this mission to destroy me and countless innocent people, that it was me that helped the Rymorians reach the station so they could repair it?"

"I don't believe a word you say, you son of a bitch," Kelard rasped out between panted breaths.

I began working on the other side of his chest. "And me that rescued the Rymorian transport survivors held hostage by Bremmer's covert operations out here."

Kelard's second-in-command began retching noisily in the corner.

"You're a monster!" Kelard hissed, spit flying from his mouth.

"And what you did to me was so much more humane?" I demanded. "Perhaps it's time I introduced you to the wondrous pain those little probes produce when they find the internal organs. I'm sure Theo has found the equipment by now."

"He's a traitor."

"He's in good company," I said as I gestured at myself. "Now, you can start talking about Bremmer, or I'm going to enjoy finding out how much of your skin I can remove before you go into shock and die."

The tent flap opening had both guards on instant alert. Theo entered and then froze as he noticed the state that Kelard was in. He swallowed, shifted his focus to me, and nudged his head toward the tent flap.

"I guess you can wait," I said regretfully before following Theo out of the tent. "What is it?"

"There are three men with Rymorian weapons," Theo whispered to me as if there were people nearby who gave a fuck. He jerked his thumb in the direction of the prisoners before indicating his data tablet.

"Okay," I said. The neat row of Rymorian weapons on the floor, according to type, caught my eye. "Come with me."

"Where are we going?" Theo hurried after me.

I selected a PB rifle. "Can you re-energize one?"

"One? Er, no." Theo eyed the rifle nervously.

"Okay, that makes it a little more interesting—activate them all."

"But—" Theo stammered, wide eyes shifting between my weapon, the viewer in his hand, and the cluster of dejected Rymorians.

"Don't overthink it, Theo."

Theo swore—I thought it was the first time he had done so—and tapped some commands into the data tablet.

The weapon energizing in my hands felt strangely comforting. It had been years since I'd fired one, and the targets I'd practiced on had never been human.

"What are you going to do?" Theo's voice was high and anxious.

"Exactly what I said I would," I stated grimly. "Point one of the men out for me." I started walking over to the Rymorian prisoners with Theo in tow.

"Oh, God," Theo muttered, positioning himself half behind me as he hurried to keep pace.

"No, Theo, you're about to find I am considerably worse." On reaching the Rymorians, I stopped and looked back at Theo expectantly.

"Second from the left. No! Third."

I scowled at him.

"It's definitely the third!"

I marched up to the man whose gaze grew increasingly fearful,

The Warrior in the Shadows

and then frantic as he realized he was my destination, before settling on the PB rifle in my hand. His eyes bugged as he noted the telltale blue glow of power.

He reached for his hidden weapon too late, and I shoved my PB rifle into the base of his throat and depressed the trigger.

His head exploded clean off, and blood, bone, and brains sprayed in a sudden, violent fountain. The body slumped to the ground amidst the cries of the surrounding Rymorians, who scrambled to escape. The Shadowlanders looked impressed. There was a certain drama to be gained from a close-range max-power PB rifle.

"I believe I mentioned I would kill anyone found harboring a weapon?" I said casually, and as the catalyst I'd intended it to be, my reminder caused two men to attempt to flee. I aimed the rifle at the center of the nearest man's back and fired. The blast exploded his body, lifting him from his feet before tossing his empty carcass to the ground amidst a shower of liquefied remains.

The last one drew his weapons half out before a Shadowlander cut him down. He searched the body and retrieved the weapon.

"You can disable them again," I said, turning and depositing my PB rifle against Theo's chest.

Theo blinked back at me, fumbling to grab it around the data tablet in his hands.

I gave Theo a couple of encouraging taps on the cheek. "You're doing great, Theo. Make sure the missing items are retrieved. Let me know if you have any more trouble."

I reentered the tent where Kelard hung limp. Blood seeped from his wounds, and he lifted haunted eyes toward me.

"Now, where were we?" I said.

Chapter 56

Talin

Nameless

My life was a cold, bleak, living hell from which there was no escape. The cell, which had been my first home for an indeterminate time, had been my deepest nightmare. My new room wasn't much better, but a single high window offered me a glimpse of the sky. I stared at it often because I needed to be reminded of the light.

Today, I was chained, as I often was, to the wall. The sharp metal cuffs and the sturdy links of chain didn't allow me enough freedom to do more than move a pace. I could sit, but it kept my arms at an uncomfortable angle, so I would stand until I could stand no more, then I would sit until I could sit no more.

Sleep was fitful; I existed in a perpetual exhausted, terrorized daze. The only escape from the chains was when they came to abuse me. There was no fight in me: sometimes that pleased them, and sometimes it did not. There were no words adequate to describe the

The Warrior in the Shadows

horror I'd undergone. I no longer thought of my body as my own. It belonged to a broken person who had once had hope.

My hope had been crushed long ago, and I didn't hope anymore. I prayed for an end, even if that end was death. I wasn't a coward, nor the kind to take an easy way out, but I'd concluded somewhere in the darkness that my mental state couldn't be fixed. My body was a different matter, and no matter how much they hurt me, it kept fighting on. On the few occasions when they'd left me unconscious, waking had been a bitter disappointment.

I wept when I awakened, consumed by the physical and mental disease of my suffering, of its unrelenting nature, and the endless fear of what would come next.

The creak of the door opening stirred me from my rumination. I shrank back against the wall, watching the opening and yet not watching who was entering. Some were worse than others, and every time I fought a battle with myself as to whether I needed to know.

I stared at the floor today as the steady footsteps approached.

The hand that intruded on my vision to cup my chin wasn't the rough kind that typically entered my room. The wrongness of the hand and the quality of clothing on its owner's arm startled me.

I didn't want to look, but he pulled my face around firmly.

"What a fucking mess," he hissed.

The culture of that voice and the sound of it had my head snapping up.

Bill? I shrank back when he went to touch me, but the wall was behind me. His fingers brushing gently across my cheek made me jerk like a current had been forced through me.

"They had a little too much fun." His lips formed a flat line.

I was so confused. What was he doing here?

Was Bill going to hurt me, too? My wild eyes searched the room for an escape, and my breathing shifted toward choppy. He wasn't hurting me yet, but everyone hurt me in this place.

"Shhhh." He ran his fingertips over my cheek, and I flinched when even that gentle touch worried at a bruise. "I'm here now, and you won't suffer anymore." He smiled sadly. "Better get this dealt with first, hmm?"

Turning, he stalked over to the door and flung it open before marching out.

The door remained open—they never left it open, and this new development freaked me out. His heels rang against the flagstone, and there were the sounds of a scuffle before he re-entered, dragging one of the tormentors by the neck. The man fought, but Bill jerked him to a stop in front of me.

I cowered back. Wondering what was next. Whether he would order the man to rape me while he watched.

"This is not what I expected. Not what I expected at all." Bill shook the man as if to emphasize the point. "Was I too early? Is that it?" He shook the man once more before smashing his face into the wall at my side.

Then continued to slam it repeatedly.

I screamed a single shrill scream as the head kept bashing over and over against the wall. The blood spattered everywhere and over me. I turned my face, chains clattering as I strained to get away from the horror.

There was no face, just a bloody, pulverized lump attached to a limp, lifeless body. Still, Bill kept slamming it against the wall, spittle flying from his lips, face contorted with rage and inhuman in his strength.

He dropped it with a final thud.

My chest heaved, and air rushed in and out of my lungs so fast that black dots swam before my eyes.

"Stop it."

I gasped as the sharp slap rang against my cheek. Yet it drove the sparkling dots away and I stared at Bill with eyes stretched so wide they ached.

"I won't let them hurt you again," he said softly.

Why? How?

A body was on the floor beside my feet, and I tried my hardest

The Warrior in the Shadows

not to let it drag my focus down. I kept my eyes on Bill who watched me, assessing me, until my breathing returned to an only slightly elevated rate. He crouched and fumbled about the body. I screwed my eyes shut, terrified I might accidentally look.

My eyes snapped open, feeling his fingers against my wrists. The faint clack of the key against the lock brought a surge of panic. Bad things happened when the cuffs came off.

They rattled as he released them, and the chain dropped, leaving my arm free and heavy.

"Let's get you cleaned up." Fingers closing over my arms, he drew me to my feet. "Can you walk?"

I nodded. Swallowed thickly. And allowed him to guide me toward the door.

A crowd had gathered at the entrance. "Clean up in there," Bill snapped as he directed me along maze-like corridors until we reached another room. Inside, it was clean and furnished, with a bed, a table, and a few chairs. Stacks of cases sat against one wall, and the large window was low enough for me to see out, offering views of the Shadowland forests.

Only this wasn't Rymor, and the forest was too close. I knew I was in Shadowland and had known it for a long time, yet it was still a shock. He drew me over, where I sat trembling, confused, and frightened.

What is he doing here?

What am I doing here?

He rummaged in a case, returning with a medical scanner.

It was only a scanner. I'd seen one many times, and it shouldn't have frightened me. Yet it did. I knocked the chair over as I scrambled to my feet, naked feet slapping against the floor as I fled to the nearest corner. Here I huddled, making myself into a small ball, shaking so hard my teeth chattered.

His footsteps followed me. He sighed before grasping my arm and dragging me to my feet. Holding my jaw firmly in his hand, he pressed the scanner against my cheek. The shock of healing warmth made me tremble anew. He worked it over my forehead, temple, and lips.

"Your nose is a mess," he said. "This will hurt."

His fingers on the bruised, badly broken mess ejected the cry of a wounded animal from my lips. I heard the crack; pain assaulted me, and I blacked out.

∼

I woke up on the floor, the cold seeping through the flimsy and filthy rags that covered me in some mockery of clothing.

Bill loomed over me. "Welcome back. It's not perfect, but it certainly looks better, and I'm sure it will be easier to breathe." The hot healing against the tenderness of my nose brought such intense relief that I sobbed in earnest, so overwhelmed as the layers of pain that had buried me began to peel away. He worked down my arms, wrists, and hands before tearing away the dirty rags and running the magical healing over my bruised and battered body. I cried hard, great wracking sobs that had been denied an outlet for too long.

When he finished, I rolled onto my side and tried to pull myself into nothingness. I used to hate Bill, but I could no longer remember why as overwhelming gratitude rushed through me.

He rose, and panic gripped me that he might leave me and let the tormentors in. I scrambled to my knees, torn between following him and finding somewhere to hide.

He held out his hand. I looked at it, shocked, yet was drawn to slowly place my hand within his, allowing him to help me to my feet. I was naked. Shouldn't that bother me? My mind remained empty, and the concerns drifted away.

"I will send someone to prepare a bath for you." He must have seen me flinch. "They won't hurt you again. You have my word."

I nodded mutely as gratitude sent tears pooling out of my eyes and down my cheeks.

The Warrior in the Shadows

He ran his thumb across my cheek. It no longer hurt, and that made me cry harder still.

"Sometimes you look so much like Hannah. I miss her." He stroked my cheek in a gentle, comforting way. "Not quite as beautiful, but still beautiful. You were always okay with that though, weren't you, Ella? Okay with taking second place." He smiled then, the charming one I'd once thought was fake. "A fair trade since you have the bold personality and fire. I always admired your tenacity, even though it vexed me at times. I admire you more now—admire your will to survive. Hannah would never have survived what you have, I fear."

His hand lowered, and I missed the safety of his touch. "Don't try to leave, Ella, don't even consider it. I will deal harshly with any such attempt," he said. "You're safe now, Ella, safe from everyone. Everyone that is, except me."

Chapter 57

Shadowland

Tanis

I returned to the Shadowlander camp late in the afternoon, accompanied by the Rymorian prisoners and all their useful supplies. Kelard's body had been left to burn, along with the less useful remnants of their camp, in full view of his men.

As messages went, it did the job I'd intended, and there had been no further trouble from my Rymorian guests. There were other Rymorian groups out here that I would later need to locate before we were done, but that was for after and once Hannah was safe.

"So, now we find Hannah?" Garren said. He was full of energy, eager to track down Hannah. While it wasn't Garren's fault that I'd been tortured, my brother's glowing health still pissed me off.

We were gathered with Han and Jon outside my tent in the center of the camp. I didn't bother to do more than climb down from the saddle as we prepared to leave again. "Yes," I replied. "Now we find Hannah."

The Warrior in the Shadows

"Kelard?" Jon asked, watching the subdued ranks of Rymorian prisoners shuffle past.

"Dead," I said. "He didn't have much new to offer. Knew nothing about the base at Talin, or Bill's other questionable pursuits. He maintained Bill's innocence until the bitter end."

Jon shook his head sadly. "How's Theo doing?"

"More terrorized than before," I said. Theo stood a dozen paces away with Red, who was deep in conversation with the smaller man. He was part of this now, I was forced to acknowledge. "I'll leave Theo here with you. He said something about needing to talk to Hannah in person, but it can wait. They're several days' ride from here, and I don't think he'll cope with either the pace or the killing."

Jon rolled his eyes. "Normal people generally don't."

From my left, Tay approached. "And now you're leaving again to search for her?"

"Do not start again."

"I was just checking so I can prepare."

I was confident there was more to it than that. "I'll take Garren and a dozen of his men, Red, and that's it."

Her eyes narrowed dangerously. "None of the wolf guard? They won't be happy about our exclusion."

"They will get over it, Tay," I said, although I was talking in a broader sense. "And I need someone I trust to oversee the prisoners. I'd like you to take responsibility. Once Hannah is safe, I intend to collect a few more."

She nodded, mollified. "I'll make sure they give no trouble," she said before inclining her head and leaving.

I thought the prisoners might be in for a rough time.

"Glad she didn't thump you again," Han said, all matter-of-fact.

"You don't look fit to ride for days," Jon said. "Garren can handle this as well as you. You're no use to anyone, least of all Hannah, if you kill yourself on the way."

"I'm going," I said, holding his gaze to ensure he realized this was final. "I'll need Theo to show Red how to work the stop code in case they have Rymorian weapons."

"Don't worry, Jon. I'll make sure he doesn't die or fall off his horse, even though I could handle this. We both know he doesn't trust me with her." Garren's grin was all teeth. "He's worried she might decide I'm enough."

I grinned back. "There's a first time for everything."

Garren's face transitioned through a kaleidoscope of emotions as my words sank in and his fists clenched.

Han stepped in between.

"Tay tapping him, he can handle," Han said. "You're not going to take a swing. Why do you let him bait you? I thought we were past this?"

Garren grunted, but his fists loosened. "How are we supposed to find her?"

"Bill had Hannah fitted with a tracking device when she left Rymor," I said. "It's how they located her. They're taking her to Talin. If we ride hard, we can reach them in a few days."

"How come you're not taking your guard?" Garren asked.

"They're a little overprotective at the moment," I said.

"So, it's got nothing to do with keeping Tay away from Hannah? She knows better than to do something stupid."

"It's more about one problem at a time," I said.

There was an amused gleam in Garren's eyes as he nodded. "We can get a few hours of riding in before night," he said. "'I'll sort out the supplies."

As he left, I turned to Han. "I want you to track the other Rymorian groups. Their communications are out, but we only have one technology disabler, which I'm taking with me. Don't engage them until I return."

Han nodded. "I'll have the camp move out at first light. What about Javid? The Jaru army is near our border. Perhaps a bigger threat than Rymor now. And there has been no word from Danel and those who left for the station."

The Warrior in the Shadows

Although Han rarely said so directly, he still worried about his younger brother, a legacy of Han taking the role of protector when the Jaru destroyed their village and left them orphans. Their size would have seen them picked up by a fortress scouting party sooner or later, but the death of their family had expedited that turn of events. Han, ever fierce even then, had determined that, where he went, so would his three-year-old brother.

"I need Javid to hold where he is. Holding the Jaru back is more pressing than attacking Rymor at present. If the Jaru retreat, a different matter."

"I'll see to it," Han said.

"Take care, Tanis," Jon said quietly. "And bring Hannah back safe."

Chapter 58

Rymor

Nate

Dealing with Scott Harding was a complex endeavor. He was a suspicious man, made more so by circumstances. He possessed a mule-like stance on everything and couldn't be swayed without a debate of epic proportions. I was coming to the rapid conclusion that Scott wasn't very bright.

"What's the problem with the plan?" I asked. We were seated in my temporary accommodation—a beautiful apartment in the same building Scott lived in on the outskirts of Tranquility. The owners were away on an extended trip leaving it conveniently empty, and I'd been making use of their luxurious home for five weeks.

It made a sensible base. I needed regular contact with Scott and this way I could do so without needing to leave the building. I had the security rigged to my satisfaction. No one, including Bill, was aware of the constant discussions.

"You said the station is now inoperative. That was never part of this plan," Scott said, his tone closer to a growl. The plush, gray, retro-leather couch he sat on was top-end quality and shifted Scott's street-fighter look toward rich, underground criminal... I'd obviously spent far too much time watching the entertainment viewer. Either way, he looked nothing like the head of a prominent government department.

"Would anyone like a cup of tea?"

Coco's interruption couldn't have come at a worse time. We'd finally got down to the discussion after a significant amount of wasted time while Scott had ranted about Kelard Wilder's minions putting their noses in where they weren't wanted. Phrases such as, *Who does that asshole think he is?* and *I would like to knock that smug bastard's teeth down his arrogant throat,* had ensued. His rage gained greater degrees of elaborateness until I called a timeout by asking if we could please get back to the bigger picture of saving the fucking planet.

During the last five weeks, I discovered that effective cursing was the only way to gain Scott's limited attention. I now boasted an impressive cursing repertoire, and my creativity with insults and obscenities was a source of personal pride.

Coco had spent most of the evening in an adjoining room, reviewing the previous day's communications in detail and ignoring the animated and, at times, heated conversation between Scott and me. Perhaps the lack of cursing had persuaded her that it was safe to return. Whatever the reason, her timing sucked.

Catching her eye, I gave a meaningful glance at Scott. When I rolled my eyes, her lips tugged up the tiniest amount.

"Coffee please." Scott's smile was all teeth.

"Nate?" she asked.

"Same, thanks," I said. When I turned back, I found Scott watching Coco leave through hooded, lustful eyes.

"Tea?" he muttered once she was out of earshot. "Pointless drink. Especially that grim chamomile stuff she prefers. I've been coming here for weeks, and not once have I said yes to a cup of tea. Still, she's hot. I can overlook the tea fixation."

Scott had made numerous confidential comments to me about

Coco's 'hotness' since the two of them had first met. There were now a hundred such statements lodged in my faultless memory, and every one of them pissed me off. Coco *was* an attractive woman and ageless in the way that those wealthy enough often were. I didn't like the ugly territorial instincts clamoring in me. I had no right to be territorial. She might even like Scott and reciprocate his interest.

"Isn't she too old for you?" I asked. It came out with a grunt, and I was definitely scowling. Thankfully, Scott lacked the most basic emotional awareness, and it passed him right by.

"Old? You're kidding me, right? I mean, who wouldn't want to tap that? Are you telling me you haven't thought about it?" Scott raised his eyebrows before his face split into a grin. "Ah, pretty boy, you have thought about it!" Leaning forward in his seat, he slapped my shoulder and chortled to himself as Coco returned with two coffees.

Scott took the drink with a broad grin. "Thanks, Coco."

She passed me my cup. "Thanks," I mumbled, praying she hadn't overheard.

"I don't know what happened at the station," I continued, determined to get back to business. "I'm not aware of everything happening out there. It could be anything. Maybe the fix was a temporary solution."

"I think Hannah would have mentioned it to Dan if that were the case," Coco said. She returned carrying a cup and saucer. Even before the floral scent wafted into the room, I knew it would be chamomile tea.

"Yeah, you're probably right. There could be many reasons it failed. Other parts could be broken, or it could be another precautionary failsafe. I can't get access to all the monitoring information, and even if I could, I don't have the skills to interpret it."

"Ancient technology was never an easy subject," Coco said reasonably. "The information you're able to provide is amazing. But I agree that a station such as fifty-four is vast and complex. Global Monitoring might be similarly in the dark about what's wrong. It's going to need Dan to make sense of this." Her earnest eyes searched mine. "When do you think we may hear from him?"

"I wish I knew," I said. "It takes at least twenty-four hours for the implants to host themselves, and Dan might not realize what's happening. I was expecting it, and it still took me a while to interpret the information. Unfortunately, Richard was interrupted, and he never got to tell Dan what he'd done. It's been over a week, so, soon, I hope." I didn't voice my inner concerns. I wasn't Dan and didn't possess his finesse with ancient technology. Had I replicated the ones he gave me correctly? Would they work? Or worse, would they hurt him?

"And Theo?" Coco asked.

"I spoke to him the day before the station went down. He was poised to infiltrate Kelard Wilder's camp and see what he could find out about the operation. He said he would update me once he got in—but then the satellites went down." I knew Theo would find it challenging to communicate once he entered the camp, but I was starting to panic and was worried that something terrible had happened.

"Without Dan, we're flying blind," Scott said before he stilled and sent me a speculative look. "The station's down, and we have no satellites, right?"

I nodded.

"Then it's about time I got some of my people out there and evened up the score. Wilder's got men and weapons out there. A shit-load of other technology. I've done my stint beyond the wall. They're just people, and they don't deserve this bullshit war. I've got my own people out there, vulnerable and isolated. You can hide people. Keep them off the radar. How about we send a few field scientists out there—unofficially."

"It would be wonderful to have a presence out there," Coco agreed. "The waypoint communication has helped, despite being sporadic. But how will you get your people out there when Bill controls all the exits?"

"Actually, not all of them," I said. Both faces turned my way. "They could use the tunnel Theo took."

"Now, we're talking." Scott rubbed his hands together and bestowed us a crooked grin. "Time to roll out the show. Send me the details, Nate. I'm going to make some calls!" He clapped me on the shoulder as he stood. "Better get some rest. Tomorrow's going to be a busy day."

I thought about pointing out that I didn't need rest.

But, yeah, he already thought I was weird enough, so maybe not. It felt quiet in his absence. Coco picked up her personal viewer and began reviewing the data. "Well, I'm delighted by the prospect of getting support for our people out in Shadowland," she said as I sat beside her and reached for my half-finished coffee.

"Me too," I agreed. "Do you think the field scientists will agree? It's a big ask."

"If they're anything like Scott, we'll have more trouble holding them back," she said dryly. "I'm still worried that no one has checked in via a waypoint recently. But I'm glad that we may have a way to help them. I don't think I have ever seen Scott quite that focused!"

"Trust me, he can get focused," I said. "You should hear some of the things he says when you're not in the room." I hadn't meant to say the last part out loud, and I sent a surreptitious glance Coco's way to determine her reaction.

"You mean the swearing?" Her focus remained on her viewer.

"Er, not specifically." I sipped my coffee.

She put the viewer down and turned to study me. "After the look you gave me when I came to offer you both a drink, you're lucky I didn't throw your coffee at you. And after I'm sure I heard him laughing. What were the two of you talking about?"

A bombardment of inappropriate Scott conversations filled my mind as I blinked at Coco. This close, her dark eyes and thick lashes consumed my thoughts. I swallowed. "Nothing, he was being a dick."

Her eyebrows crawled up into her head. "Your language has become atrocious since you met that man."

The Warrior in the Shadows

I chuckled as I put my empty cup on the table. "Despite my lack of personal experience, I'm sure you sound like a mother."

"Well, I suppose I *am* a mother so it can't be helped. And now I'm sure I couldn't have overheard you both talking about having sex with someone you think of as a mother because that would be extremely awkward."

My eyes bugged. I'd never heard Coco mention sex before in any context, and in Scott's terminology, it was hot.

She smiled and raised a single eyebrow.

"Ah, yeah, about that conversation."

"It's okay, Nate. When you have been around as long as I have there's not a lot that surprises you. Scott propositions me every time he visits, so there are no surprises there."

Fuck!

"Ah, and have you?" The question jumped out of my mouth without any interaction on the part of my brain. In the wake of those words came the realization that they could have been engaging in sex daily, for weeks. I was out of the apartment for extended periods. There had been plenty of opportunities.

I was convinced that they had.

I felt sick.

Her hand resting on my arm snapped me out of this painful rumination. "No, Nate, we haven't. I don't jump into bed with every person who asks me—only the ones that I care about."

My entire focus centered on the hand that rested lightly on my arm. "What if I asked you, Coco?"

"Are you asking, Nate, or testing a theory?" I couldn't look at her, but I could hear the smile in her voice.

"I'm asking."

"Then my answer would be yes."

Chapter 59

Shadowland

Hannah

Our tents had been pitched on the outskirts of a village, away from the wary villagers. A light, warm breeze buffeted the walls of the tent where I sat.

It was early morning, when we would usually be readying for travel. But today, Karry was in no hurry to move on, and bound my wrists in a way that brought a familiar sickly panic.

There was no longer any logic to Karry's routine. My wrists were bound and, coupled with the lack of travel preparations, I thought he was about to question me again.

My helplessness and suffering beat down on my wounded soul. I was still hurting from last night and thought he might finally break me if he began his cruelty again.

"I don't understand what you want." My stomach was full of a familiar sickening flutter, and my heart rate elevated with fear. The intensity of the questioning increased with each passing day. I was

The Warrior in the Shadows

disorientated half the time, sleep-deprived through fear, and never healed enough.

"I want the truth." Karry's face twisted in a perpetual sneer. He sat opposite me, sprawled against a supply pack, playing restlessly with a knife.

I had come to hate his face as much as I hated the man it belonged to.

"I'm going to be sorry when we reach Bill. I enjoy our little chats. Look forward to them. Of course, nothing I do will be right by Bill. He's probably going to be pissed. Perhaps I've been too hard on you, or not hard enough."

Cold blossomed in my chest. Fear of Bill was the only thing keeping Karry in line. If Karry believed he'd already failed Bill, what more might he do.

I wasn't ready to die, yet in that deranged man's mind there were worse things than dying.

He started tumbling the knife handle against his palm. "It doesn't matter what I do. I can fix it if I want to." Tucking his knife into its sheath, he stood.

I recoiled, but there was nowhere to go.

He fisted a handful of my hair. "You're probably going to make shit up. Women do stuff like that. Take their revenge. If I'm getting blamed anyway, may as well enjoy it."

I fought to break free, but he slowly tightened his hold until my eyes watered, and I felt chunks of hair ripping out.

He pushed me backward, forcing his knees between mine, and crushing me under his weight. He gently pushed a damp strand of hair from my face with his free hand. The unexpected tenderness of the action brought bile to my throat.

"No!" Fury and failure sank me as he began undoing the buttons at my throat. My breathing turned choppy as I fought to free my hands trapped between us.

He shifted to get a better hold, ripping out more hair and a scream from my throat.

The binding on my wrists snagged the handle of his knife, and my fingers instinctively wrapped around it. The knife jerked free in a sudden rush when he moved to the next button.

Warm liquid bathed my hands. Karry hissed, and his hold on my hair suddenly relaxed.

We stared at each other, both wide-eyed. The knife had sunk into someone, and that someone wasn't me.

He gritted his teeth, tightened his fist in my hair, and slammed my head against the ground.

My vision swam with lights and dots, and my teeth cut my lip, but I gripped the knife like a lifeline, determined, whatever the cost, not to yield it. A desperate struggle ensued, but he had lost much of his strength.

Dragging my knees up, I got them under his crushing weight. I strained to push him off, finally getting enough leverage to roll him to the side, where he collapsed, panting, covered in blood.

Disorientated, I staggered to my feet. I blinked at him, realizing what I'd done before my gaze lowered to the knife in my hands. It dropped to the ground and I took an unsteady step back.

"I'm going to kill you, bitch" he croaked weakly. He tried to rise only to slump back with a whimper that turned my stomach over despite my abhorrence for the man.

I needed to get out of there right now!

Crouching, I retrieved the knife, sawing awkwardly through the bindings on my wrists. The blade was sharp, and I cursed as I cut my flesh along with the rope. I watched Karry as I worked, but he remained slumped on the floor, panting, face damp and gray.

My wrists were as bloody as the rest of me by the time the rope finally snapped.

"Where's the scanner?" I pointed the knife at him, unwilling to step any closer in case he was able to make a grab. When he didn't answer, I searched the tent quickly.

"It's not in here, you dumb bitch," he grunted from the floor.

Was he lying? I didn't think so. It was in his saddlebag, then. I

The Warrior in the Shadows

was reluctant to leave the knife, yet carrying it outside would draw attention. Yeah, and the blood wouldn't? I tugged at my clothing to hide the stain as best as possible and dropped the knife to the floor. Then, with what I prayed was my last ever look at Karry, I turned and fled the tent.

It was stark and bright outside after the dull, hateful interior of the tent. None of Karry's men stood nearby, but several tended to the horses—horses I had hoped to use.

One man noticed me. His gaze shifted to the crimson stain before returning to meet my eyes.

I ran, and his cry followed me into the trees.

They would follow in pursuit, but fear had me in its hold and I was set upon flight.

Running along the path became an endless race through a tangle of trees and scrubby bush. Where the path forked, I took the narrower way. When it forked again, I took the wider track and followed it, but then it narrowed again to an animal trail.

A cry from behind said they were gaining on me fast.

The trail offered no opportunity to hide or evade the pursuit. The thud of footsteps and the crack of snapping branches followed me, but I kept running, my breath ragged.

A second man skirted through the trees to my right, seeking to cut off my escape. With each step, the gap closed, bringing the pounding sound of pursuit closer. Then he lunged for me.

I cut left into the thick undergrowth and rounded a sturdy tree before sprinting back toward the village.

He cursed, skidded, and took up pursuit again.

My legs and chest burned. The men were gaining again, their breath and heavy footfall chasing me.

A scream tore from my lips as I was tackled to the ground. We sprawled in a heap. I kicked and scrambled before an arm clamped around my waist. I fought, made wild with desperation.

I couldn't go back. Whatever Karry had done before would be nothing compared to what he would do now.

Fingers circled my throat, and I clawed at them as my vision faded to black.

"Don't fucking kill her!"

Released abruptly, I landed in a dazed heap. Pushing to my hands and knees, I swayed, wheezing in air until my head began to clear.

They were arguing about what to do with me but suddenly fell silent.

The silence wasn't all pervasive; now I could hear distant screams.

My head lifted, turning toward the village, heart hammering with new dread as heavy footfalls approached.

"...too late," one of the men said, "whatever's happening, we need to get her back."

I shook my head and stumbled forward, but fingers closed around my neck, yanking me tightly against him.

He fisted my throat, dragging me against a hard male body. He squeezed. Choking, I kicked out uselessly against the ground, fighting to pry him free. My ears rang, and the world slowed to the steady thud of blood pumping through my veins as I fought a desperate battle against the blackness.

Chapter 60

Rymor

Nate

I decided that my life was complete as I sat beside Coco on the couch with unfettered access to her hand—among other things.

"Nate, you know last night wasn't typical, don't you?" Coco asked. She extracted her hand from mine and collected her cup of coffee from where it had been sitting on the table. It was probably significant that she was starting her day with coffee.

"Not typical how?" I decided that my life might be a few notches off complete as a sudden and acute sense of fear gripped me.

I caught her smiling around her coffee, and my fear turned to bafflement. I skimmed through a detailed assessment of last night in my head. I was reasonably confident she had enjoyed it multiple times, and even after she had asked for a rest, she had definitely enjoyed that.

I should probably stop thinking about it because it had a noticeable impact, and I was confident I was alone in this desire at this point in time.

"Don't worry, Nate. Not typical in a good kind of way," she said, still smiling, and then glanced down at my lap. "I would offer to help you with that, but I'm not sure I have the stamina or time for another eight-hour marathon."

Wait? Did that sound like my stamina was a bad thing? "It was four hours and thirty-six minutes," I pointed out with a frown.

"Yes, exactly, most men can't do a four and half hour stretch without rest breaks, nor can they remember the duration to the nearest minute. I certainly don't want you to enlighten me as to which one of your enhancements produced that particular side effect."

"I think it's just me."

"Really?"

"Ah, well, it can happen quicker, um, if I want it to, that is."

"Well, thank goodness for that." She chuckled. Once having started, she couldn't seem to stop. She put her coffee down as if fearing she would spill it.

I wasn't sure as to whether her amusement should make me feel hopeful, but a particular part of me was hopeful enough for both of us. "Maybe we could try quicker?"

"How quick?"

"An hour?"

"That's not exactly quick."

"Thirty minutes?"

"Five," she countered

"Five?" My eyes widened, and my voice came out in a squeak. She was definitely amused again.

"Five minutes," she repeated, eyes narrowing like she wasn't prepared to negotiate.

I decided that this was a new but worthy challenge. "I could work with that."

The Warrior in the Shadows

The door buzzed. I groaned. Damn Scott and his enthusiasm! It was barely morning.

Muttering under my breath as Coco reached for her coffee with a smirk, I pulled up the surveillance of the hall on my retinal viewer.

"What the hell?"

I leaped up to open the door.

"Theo?" I said, frowning, yet even as the words left my lips, I knew it wasn't Theo.

"No, of course not, you fool."

"Dan?" Coco's arrival at my side confirmed what my sluggish brain was struggling to accept.

"Why didn't you let yourself in? Why didn't you tell me you'd escaped?" I stepped back, allowing him to enter.

Dan avoided eye contact as he shuffled in with ungainly steps. "Going to have to be honest, I don't think you got some of the implants right. They were a little sporadic to start with, and now some have stopped working altogether. I might need to fix a couple of them when I get the time."

Oh, what have I done to him?

"And you were, ah, busy," Dan added, looking everywhere but at me.

Great!

"It's so good to have you back." Coco enfolded Dan in a hug that spoke of their many years of friendship. When they parted, tears glistened in her eyes. "I was so worried about you, Dan."

"You and me both," Dan said with feeling before turning to me with a smile. "Get over here, you great idiot." He enfolded me in a hug, and how wonderful and strange it was to have him hold me so tight. "Can't bloody trust you to leave things alone, can I? And thank God. I don't think I'd have survived there much longer. At first, I thought Richard had given me a lethal injection out of misplaced kindness. Nearly had heart failure when the changes started. Thought it was the beginning of the end."

"Dan, I'm so sorry," I said. "They cut the meeting short, and Richard had to act."

"Well, John Tanis being taken into custody sent the CIA into a spin. It's lucky you acted when you did since they rescinded all access after."

"Tanis is in custody?" My eyes shot toward Coco, who had gone deathly pale. My relief in seeing Dan, the new Dan, who was younger and standing, safe after so long, was abruptly eclipsed by broader concerns.

"Not anymore, though, I believe." Dan took hold of Coco's hand. "Theo was already in the camp. I sent him the weapon stop code once I realized I could infiltrate the operational systems. The Rymorians outside the wall no longer have functioning weapons. Then an hour later, the station was destroyed... Got to be honest here, I would never have given Theo the stop code if I thought we were about to lose the wall. Unfortunately, without the station, we have no satellites, so I don't know what has happened since."

Without a wall or weapons, Rymor was vulnerable in every sense. "That's terrifying," I said, inadequately. "Do you know what's happened at the station? Why it failed?"

Dan's lips compressed into a tired line. "It was the Shadowlanders and my fellow technical grand master. They've destroyed the station. I think it's fair to say that John Tanis has shifted the balance of power."

"That complicates things," I said, frowning.

"Yes, it does," Coco said, soberly, before taking a deep breath. "I've had many shocks in regard to my son, but, whatever is or isn't happening out there, there's nothing we can do, short term. I can only assume the station destruction was done out of defense with a Rymorian army in their lands. I don't know my son anymore, but I don't believe he intends to attack Rymor, not when he helped protect our people who were out there with him. You made the best call you could, Dan." Her eyes softened as they settled on her friend. "I can't

The Warrior in the Shadows

imagine how terrible it was. You have done amazingly well to get here."

"It's been a testing time," Dan said, with a sad smile. "But with the station down again I don't know what any of us can do. I've been worried about Hannah ever since she left, and now I've got Theo to worry about, too."

"Well, it's probably a good thing we've been working on a backup plan." I said with a small smile. "Dan, I think you're going to like my new friend, Scott Harding. Why don't we all grab a seat, and I can tell you all about his plans."

Chapter 61

Shadowland

Hannah

There was a crashing sound from out of the trees, and my eyes struggled to process a blurred shape that emerged. The echo of metal meeting metal rang through the air, followed by a sickening animalistic squeal.

A sword whistled over my head so close that I felt its passage through the air. The force of the blow flung my captor back, blood splattered, and, still caught within his grasp, I crashed back with him.

A short, sharp scream escaped my lips as I sought freedom from the sticky horror and sickly, bloody odor.

"Hold still!" The harsh command delivered by an unexpectedly familiar voice brought a wave of giddy relief. The weight pinning me disappeared and the lifeless body that trapped me landed several feet away with a wet thud. "Are you hurt?"

"I—" Was I hurt? I didn't think I was hurt, but perhaps my terror-

The Warrior in the Shadows

ized mind was blocking it out. My eyes struggled to focus on the face that leaned close to mine. I wasn't dead. How was that even possible?

Tanis' brows were drawn together as his rough hands wiped the blood from my face and neck. "Why aren't you moving? Is something broken?"

"No." I grimaced as I sat up, pressing my fingers to my sore throat, and then gasped as he caught my arm in a bruising grip.

"What the hell is this?" He examined the lacerations on my wrist and then scrutinized my face when I didn't respond quickly enough.

"I was tied up," I said by way of explanation. The cuts weren't deep, and barely registered in light of everything else.

"What happened?" He remained crouched beside me and relinquished my arm so he could grasp my chin to review the bruising on my neck.

Yes, I was hurt, everywhere. I murmured a protest and tried to prize his hand away.

"Answer me!"

"A man tried to choke me."

"I think there's a little more to it than that." He ignored my attempts to remove his hand until he was ready and proceeded to poke and prod the rest of me.

"What do you want from me? I thought I was about to die!"

"You're still here," he said in a cutting tone. "And unless there's something that I'm missing, you're not about to die." He tugged at my clothing, intent upon a much more thorough search.

"There's nothing else!" I slapped the nearest roaming hand with more energy and vehemence than I credited myself capable of.

He stopped. "Okay, I guess you're fine," he said, and a hint of amusement entered his tone before he asked in seriousness. "Tell me what happened."

I dragged in a ragged breath and straightened my clothes with shaky fingers. "They took me from Thale the day after everyone left. They were taking me to Bill. They asked about you—a lot. They seemed to think that I knew your plans." I stared down at my grubby fingers, unable to meet his eyes.

"Hannah?"

I shook my head. "I've had weeks of questions." A watery pressure settled behind my eyes, but I blinked it away. "Please, I don't want to talk about it now." I swallowed as I remembered what had happened in Karry's tent. This could have ended much worse—for me, at least.

"I need to know what happened," he said softly.

I looked into his eyes and found a face covered in bruises and cuts. "The leader's name was Karry. It was the same man Marcus was working for and who held the other Rymorians hostage. He said Bill told him not to—leave permanent damage. That he couldn't—" I closed my eyes and swallowed, then winced in pain as my sore throat rebelled. As Tanis hissed, I paused to regain my composure. "Today he changed his mind—he didn't care." *And that's when I stabbed him.* "That's when I ran."

His face shuttered as he said, "I'm very glad you did."

"He wasn't well. He said Bill had done something to him—tortured him, I think. He kept asking about you. He seemed obsessed with my relationship with you." Not that we had a relationship. "I told him I didn't know you."

Tanis raised an eyebrow and stood, sheathing the sword I hadn't noticed lying on the ground. "I am both impressed and worried by your newly acquired lying skills."

The pound of approaching footsteps drew my attention toward the forest path in time to see Garren and another man burst out. I caught sight of the fleeting concern that Garren directed my way before he turned back to Tanis.

My heart did that little squeeze thing when Garren didn't immediately come to me. Did he know what had happened between Tanis and me? Did he hold it against me?

"You racked up an impressive tally of ten dead in less than five minutes, minus the two I managed to restrain you from killing."

The Warrior in the Shadows

Garren's focus shifted back to me. "Oh, and it was Hannah who took Karry's knife to him." He grinned. "Gutted like a pig." His gaze swept over the two half-dismembered bodies that lay a small distance away. "A skill you appear to have in common."

Tanis cursed under his breath.

Was I really thinking I could keep that a secret? Had I really gutted him like a pig? I tried to calm my pounding heart and choppy breathing as I looked between Tanis and Garren, trying to decipher their feelings on this matter. Garren was amused, perhaps impressed—the man was half savage so there were no surprises there. Tanis was harder to read. I swallowed. "Did I kill Karry?" A year ago, the thought of killing someone would have been the highest order of trauma, but now I felt nothing, at least not toward Karry.

"No, you just made a mess." Tanis' response was terse and made little sense given he had learned from Garren that I'd stabbed Karry.

"We need to get back to Han, but that's no place for her," Garren said. "Not if the news about the station is true."

"What news about the station?"

"Like hell." Tanis shot me a furious look. "How badly are you hurt? Can you ride?"

That he ignored my question added to the discord. "I can ride." I tried to put weight on my legs, but they gave out, and I gritted my teeth as I rolled inelegantly to my knees. What did Garrett mean? Was he suggesting Tanis abandon me somewhere? I would rather be with Tanis, no matter how dangerous. It was safer than this village, safer than Thale even. I'd thought the great fortress was safe, but now nowhere seemed impervious to danger. Nowhere except with Tanis.

That realization found a place deep within me that had felt lost for a long time. It was self-preservation, I told myself, nothing more. Tanis knew how to kill and that met the entirety of my needs.

"She looks worse than you did three days ago, and that's saying something. There's no way she's up to this journey." Garren gestured at me. "Look at her. She can't even stand up."

Had someone put a knife in my hand, I might have stabbed Garren for that uncensored opinion, made worse because it was true.

"You think I'm going to leave her here with you?" Tanis said, rounding on Garren when I continued to fight against exhaustion and gain my feet.

"I'm only stating the facts," Garren said.

I was definitely going to stab him.

The two men stared each other down until Tanis directed his glare my way. "She was supposed to be safe at Thale," he said, tone disparaging. "I worry that she will break her neck walking about on level ground. I'm sure as hell not leaving her in the middle of Shadowland, with or without someone watching her."

His assessment of my competence hurt and reminded me that I would be dead now had he not arrived. I hadn't given up, even when it seemed hopeless. That had to count for something, right? I wasn't a complete burden.

I hadn't intended to kill Karry or even to wound him; I'd only wanted the terror to stop. And yet now that I knew I might have, I couldn't summon any level of remorse.

"I get a say in this, and I want to go!" Despite the injustice of Tanis' words and how unfair it was to measure me against a world I wasn't born to be part of, I still wanted him to take me with him. I would swallow every bit of my damaged pride as long as he didn't leave me here.

I fought to stand, determined to prove that I wasn't a burden, but my shaky legs lifted me no more than an inch before I fell back to my knees with a frustrated grunt—it turned into a yelp as Tanis grabbed a handful of my collar and yanked me to my feet.

My legs refused to hold my weight, and I teetered, grasping blindly at him to stop myself from collapsing back to the ground.

His hand came around my waist, dragging me against him. "Of all the times," he muttered before hoisting me into his arms.

Garren barked out a laugh—he still had the worst sense of humor. "I'd offer to help, but I'm going to enjoy watching you struggle."

The Warrior in the Shadows

"So glad I'm here to make your day," Tanis said sarcastically as he started walking toward the village.

Garren, still chuckling, fell in step behind.

After so many days of constant fear for my life, of wondering what would happen next, and of nights with only snatches of sleep, my newfound safety drained the last of my energy away.

Was he limping? "Did you hurt your leg?"

"Someone stabbed me in it," he said tersely.

I thought about offering to walk but sensed he would reject it. And besides, I doubted my legs would work any better now than they had a minute ago.

When we came out into the village clearing, I noticed a cluster of his men. Every single face turned my way. I buried my nose against Tanis and closed my eyes in an attempt to block it out.

Questions clamored in my mind, but the tension rippling through Tanis told me that now wasn't the time. How had he come to be here? Had he stumbled upon me by accident?

"You can take a nap later. I need you to concentrate on staying upright in the saddle," he said, and my eyes flew open as he dumped me onto the saddle of a horse.

My fingers closed instinctively over the reins at the pommel. Stay upright in the saddle; that was hilarious. The man must have been taking humor lessons from Garren.

Tanis went to talk to a couple of the nearby men, but I couldn't focus on the conversation once I noticed two of Karry's soldiers bound upon horses. From the looks of it, they'd resisted, and I was obviously turning into a monster because I found that I liked their suffering.

I took the reins in my hands. It was a large horse—with a single grubby white ear.

Oh no, I wasn't riding with Tanis. My glance down told me the ground was an alarming drop, but, determined, I slid out of the saddle.

"What the hell are you doing?" Tanis demanded. He shoved me

up as I fought to get back down. An inelegant battle between his grip and gravity ensued.

He won the fight.

Mounting swiftly behind me, he crowded my body with his and took the reins from me.

It was too much, and my breath hitched with the choppy onset of tears.

The sudden sting of his hand landing on my thigh shocked them away. "You don't have the energy to waste on self-pity. Not unless you really do want me to leave you here?" He nudged his horse into a trot.

I shut all thoughts down and dragged several deep, steadying breaths into my lungs as the group pulled out at a brisk canter that consumed my concentration.

The nightmare was over, and once more, I was setting off into the unknown. Only, now, Shadowland wasn't so unknown anymore, and the tall forest trees and the dirt path we followed offered both familiarity and comfort.

It had become my home.

For the first time since leaving Rymor months ago, I felt a new identity unravel inside. I was an alien born of a race that had invaded a planet, and somehow, against all probability, I was now a part of that indigenous world.

I had picked myself up many times from situations and circumstances beyond my control, but I was still alive, still physically whole, if not mentally quite the same. There was comfort in this breaking and mending cycle of self. I was broken, remade, broken again, and remade again.

I was something new. I was reborn. I had survived so many things.

I thought I liked my new self considerably more than the old one.

Chapter 62

Talin

Ella Duvaul

Standing before the window, as I often did, I watched dusk fall. My fingers trailed down the transparent barrier and I studied the streaks they left with interest—fingers never left a streak in Rymor. The glass fascinated me; I dedicated many days to wondering if something was wrong with my eyes.

A few clouds dotted the sky today, I noted. One resembled a fish, except the tail was too long. An odd fish, then, to match this odd window.

Despite its oddness and alienness, it was a nice room, much better than the last one—and infinitely better than the one before that.

Memories of the first room haunted me. It had been dark, cold, and damp, and cruel acts had happened there. They had also happened in the second room, but at least that one had had a window.

I'd lost something precious in those two rooms that I could no longer remember. The nightmare had ended, though, the day that Bill arrived.

When Bill was here, everything was well.

I was no longer worried about my life in this strange prison. The days of my existence merged into an eternity that stretched from now to an unknown future and back to an unknown past. There had been another life with other people before. It seemed little more than a fantasy now, but I recalled it had once bothered me like I'd misplaced a part of my soul.

I often dreamed of a young woman with sad, gray eyes. The image troubled me and comforted me in equal parts, yet I couldn't determine why.

Then there were the children, two little boys with mischievous grins, copper hair, and eyes the same unnatural shade of gray, and a little girl with a riot of the lightest, frizziest hair and those signature gray eyes in a far too solemn face.

The cloud changed as it drifted and now resembled a bird poised for flight. My fingers pressed into the glass as I caught sight of smoke rising from the trees. I froze, riveted by its presence. Growing in density, it billowed toward the skyline and dissipated until it had totally disappeared. Then another plume rose up and did the same. Amazing, I hadn't seen any smoke since—I blinked to make sure I wasn't dreaming. People were down there, real people, free people.

I began to laugh, and it sounded so strange to my ears that I laughed even harder, so hard that tears welled in my eyes and my side hurt from the strain. A sob escaped my lips, and I collapsed to my knees, caught in the grip of grief so great that I wondered how I didn't simply die.

Memories flooded back.

I had a husband and sons somewhere far from this wretched place.

My body trembled. *Why did I need to remember?* Forgetting was far less painful.

The Warrior in the Shadows

The tremors subsided, and my sorrow became a dull ache. I rose to my feet and stared out the window through tear-weary eyes at the smoke that had brought those buried memories back. I laughed again, only this time there were no more tears to follow it, and I stared resolutely out at the forests of Shadowland. Only I wasn't merely looking at Shadowland; I was *in* Shadowland.

Hannah was out in Shadowland; I could feel her, sense her, and knew it to be true.

I watched more rising smoke as it drifted across the sky until darkness hid it from view. Forgetfulness would not overcome me again; I must be ready.

Turning from the window, I went to bed, my legs cramped from standing still so long.

When I closed my eyes, the dreams came, but tonight they didn't bring me sorrow, for tonight, my dreams held hope.

Chapter 63

The Jaru Plains

The Master

I sat at the entrance to my cave, which presented a stunning vista of snow-capped mountains to the right, and the endless plains of the Jaru to the front and left. To the far north of the plains, on the foothills of the mountain range, the Outlier tribes lived isolated from the rest of the Jaru, out of necessity.

Unlike the plains-dwelling Jaru, who lived a violent, brutish existence, our philosophy was peace. Although this seeming mindset disparity from a single people might have confused an outsider, internally, we knew better—at least, Outliers did.

It saddened me that the plains-dwelling Jaru didn't possess the cognitive capability for self-awareness, nor to escape their basic existence, to become more, or to change. They possessed little in the way of empathy. Their needs were basal and brutish, viewing weakness as a burden better cut from the whole.

Like all Outliers, I carried the weight of knowledge of who they

The Warrior in the Shadows

had once been, and our demise was an open wound that had never healed throughout the eons of our existence. We were an ancient people; nobody remembered how old, not even I, who was their elder. Time had stretched and contracted; it was infinite. We retained only what was important, and our enduring purpose was to hope.

"It is a risk leaving here; a grave risk," Sirius said, his lips curling as he reached to smooth his already pristine tunic.

"Indeed, but we must try," I replied. "This is our one chance. The one we have prepared and waited so patiently for."

I would miss this cave and the tranquility it afforded, but still, we couldn't complete the greater task without a level of discomfort. My gaze roamed the dwelling I would soon remember with nostalgia. The term cave didn't do justice to a home that consolidated the practicality of technology into structural artwork hewn from the marble cliffs. It was sympathetic to nature, with smooth, curving lines dissected by meandering internal streams and pools that then all spilled out onto the terrace to the left of the cave entrance, where they gave birth to a spectacular waterfall.

"You have no doubts?" Sirius persisted.

"None," I replied. "The wall is gone, and this time I believe for good. The signature is completely different. It would be foolish to let such an opportunity slip by through fear, and besides, the gifts are ready for the one who has united us."

Sirius sneered. "He is a killer with the warrior gene who will slaughter us all," he said. "We cannot give him the gifts if we are already dead. What then of hope? We are *children* to him and therefore expendable." The Outliers had termed the plains-dwelling Jaru *children* soon after the rift since the Jaru masses *were* children, angry children with adult bodies but no comprehension beyond a child's greed and need.

"There are many risks, but the *children* revere us, and that must inspire some curiosity from the one who unites us," I said, my lips pursed in thought. "At least then we can protect the *children*."

"It is not the *children* I worry for," Sirius said, impassioned. "It is for myself, and for you, and for the other Outliers I worry. We are the shadows, the remnants—if we lose ourselves, we lose everything."

"He has united us. We will pay homage to him, and in doing so seek redemption."

Sirius shrugged, his face solemn. "Redemption? Is that possible for us? We are broken. We are regressed."

I paused, thoughtful again, and my attention cast out toward the vista below us. "There is a chance."

"Not much of a chance," Sirius said, his sad face turned down.

"Not much of a chance," I agreed. "And if not, then knowing that we have tried must be enough."

"What about the one at Talin?" Sirius asked, turning his gaze once more to me.

"He is searching for the switch in the belief that it will give him power, but he won't find it without our help." I smiled. It was a warm, contented smile.

"The switch could destroy everything," Sirius said, his cool, gray eyes troubled.

"It is part of the cycle," I said. "Since you cannot mend something unless it is broken."

"Broken?" Sirius asked, his lips forming a thin line. "We are already broken. This whole planet was broken the day they came."

"Well then," I said with an indulgent smile. "We must do what we can to change that. What was divided has been broken, but now it seems we must shatter it absolutely, and perhaps only then can we rebuild. It is time we left our comfort and our past behind. It is time to reach out for a new future, whatever that future may be. It is time to leave."

"As you wish, Master," Sirius said, rising gracefully and offering a respectful bow. "I will call the gathering so that all might prepare."

My gaze lingered on Sirius's retreating form, and then searched the idyllic vista. It would be hard for us to leave the safety of our homes and enter the world once again. We had withdrawn during a

The Warrior in the Shadows

time of desperation to survive the ravaging that had left us so irrevocably changed, but it was time to hope for a better future.

It was time for the Outliers to rise.

About the Author

Thanks for reading *The Warrior in the Shadows*. Want to read more? Book Three, The Master of the Switch is available on pre-order!
Amazon: https://www.amazon.com/author/lvlane

Where to find me...
Website: https://authorlvlane.com
Blog: https://authorlvlane.wixsite.com/controllers/blog
Facebook: https://www.facebook.com/LVLaneAuthor/
Facebook Page: https://www.facebook.com/LVLaneAuthor/
Facebook reader group: https://www.facebook.com/groups/LVLane/
Twitter: https://twitter.com/AuthorLVLane
Goodreads: https://www.goodreads.com/LVLane

Also by L.V. Lane

The Master of the Switch

The final installment is coming soon…

Made in the USA
Monee, IL
21 March 2024